Patricia Cornwell is one of the world's major international best-selling authors, translated into thirty-six languages across more than fifty countries. She is a founder of the Virginia Institute of Forensic Science and Medicine, a founding member of the National Forensic Academy, a member of the New York OCME Forensic Sciences Training Program's Advisory Board, and a member of the Harvard-affiliated McLean Hospital's National Council, where she is an advocate for psychiatric research.

In 2008 Cornwell won the Galaxy British Book Awards' Books Direct Crime Thriller of the Year – the first American ever to win this prestigious award. Her most recent best-sellers include *Scarpetta*, *Book of the Dead* and *The Front*. Her earlier works include *Postmortem* – the only novel to win five major crime awards in a single year – and *Cruel and Unusual*, which won the coveted Gold Dagger award in 1993. Dr. Kay Scarpetta herself won the 1999 Sherlock Award for the best detective created by an American writer.

Patricia Cornwell
Blow Fly

sphere

SPHERE

First published in the United States in 2003 by G.P. Putnam's Sons,
a member of Penguin Group (USA), Inc.
First published in Great Britain in 2003 by Little, Brown
Paperback edition published in 2001 by Time Warner Paperbacks
Reprinted by Time Warner Paperbacks in 2003
This reissue published in 2010 by Sphere

3 5 7 9 10 8 6 4 2

A CIP catalogue record for this book
is available from the British Library.

ISBN 978-0-7515-4493-0

Typeset in Garamond by M Rules
Printed and bound in Great Britain by
Clays Ltd, St Ives plc

Papers used by Piatkus are from well-managed forests
and other responsible sources.

MIX
Paper from
responsible sources
FSC® C104740

Sphere
An imprint of
Little, Brown Book Group
Carmelite House
50 Victoria Embankment
London EC4Y 0DZ

An Hachette UK Company
www.hachette.co.uk

www.littlebrown.co.uk

They shall lie down alike in the dust,
and the worms shall cover them.

Job 21:26

1

Dr. Kay Scarpetta moves the tiny glass vial close to candlelight, illuminating a maggot drifting in a poisonous bath of ethanol.

At a glance, she knows the exact stage of metamorphosis before the creamy carcass, no larger than a grain of rice, was preserved in a specimen vessel fitted with a black screw cap. Had the larva lived, it would have matured into a bluebottle *Calliphora vicina*, a blow fly. It might have laid its eggs in a dead human body's mouth or eyes, or in a living person's malodorous wounds.

"Thank you very much," Scarpetta says, looking around the table at the fourteen cops and crime-scene technicians of the National Forensic Academy's class of 2003. Her eyes linger on Nic Robillard's innocent face. "I don't know who collected this from a location best not to contemplate at the dinner table, and preserved it with me in mind . . . but . . ."

Blank looks and shrugs.

"I have to say that this is the first time I've been given a maggot as a gift."

No one claims responsibility, but if there is a fact Scarpetta has never doubted, it is a cop's ability to bluff and, when necessary, outright lie. Having noticed a tug at the corner of Nic Robillard's mouth before anyone else realized that a maggot had joined them at the dinner table, Scarpetta has a suspect in mind.

The light of the flame moves over the vial in Scarpetta's fingertips, her nails neatly filed short and square, her hand steady and elegant but strong from years of manipulating the unwilling dead and cutting through their stubborn tissue and bone.

Unfortunately for Nic, her classmates aren't laughing, and humiliation finds her like a frigid draft. After ten weeks with cops she should now count as comrades and friends, she is still Nic the Hick from Zachary, Louisiana, a town of twelve thousand, where, until recently, murder was an almost unheard-of atrocity. It was not unusual for Zachary to go for years without one.

Most of Nic's classmates are so jaded by working homicides that they have come up with their own categories for them: real murders, misdemeanor murders, even urban renewal. Nic doesn't have her own pet categories. Murder is murder. So far in her eight-year career, she has worked only two, both of them domestic shootings. It was awful the first day of class when an instructor went from one cop to another, asking how many homicides each of their departments averaged a year. *None*, Nic said. Then he asked the size of each cop's department. *Thirty-five*, Nic said. Or *smaller than my eighth-grade class*, as one of her new classmates put it. From the beginning of what was supposed to be the greatest opportunity of her life, Nic quit trying to fit in, accepting that in the police way of defining the universe, she was a *them*, not an *us*.

Her rather whimsical maggot mischief, she realizes with regret, was a breach of something (she's not sure what), but without a doubt she should never have decided to give a gift, serious or otherwise, to the legendary forensic pathologist Dr. Kay Scarpetta. Nic's face heats up, and a cold sweat dampens her armpits as she watches for her hero's reaction, unable to read it, probably because Nic is stunned stupid by insecurity and embarrassment.

"So I'll call her Maggie, although we really can't determine gender yet," Scarpetta decides, her wire-rim glasses reflecting shifting candlelight. "But a good enough name for a maggot, I think." A ceiling fan snaps and whips the candle flame inside its glass globe as she holds up the vial. "Who's going to tell me which instar Maggie is? What life stage was she in before some-one"—she scans the faces at the table, pausing on Nic's again—"dropped her in this little bottle of ethanol? And by the way, I suspect Maggie aspirated and drowned. Maggots need air the same way we do."

"What asshole drowned a maggot?" one of the cops snipes.

"Yeah. Imagine inhaling alcohol . . ."

"What'cha talking about, Joey? You been inhaling it all night."

A dark, ominous humor begins to rumble like a distant storm, and Nic doesn't know how to duck out of it. She leans back in her chair, crossing her arms at her chest, doing her best to look indif-ferent as her mind unexpectedly plays one of her father's worn-out storm warnings: *Now, Nic, honey, when there's lightning, don't stand alone or think you'll be protected by hiding in the trees. Find the nearest ditch and lie as low in it as you can.* At the moment, she has no place to hide but in her own silence.

"Hey Doc, we already took our last test."

"Who brought homework to our party?"

"Yeah, we're off duty."

"Off duty, I see," Scarpetta muses. "So if you're off duty when the dead body of a missing person has just been found, you're not going to respond. Is that what you're saying?"

"I'd have to wait until my bourbon wears off," says a cop whose shaved head is so shiny it looks waxed.

"That's a thought," she says.

Now the cops are laughing—everyone but Nic.

"It can happen." Scarpetta sets the vial next to her wine glass. "At any given moment, we can get a call. It may prove to be the worst call of our careers, and here we are, slightly buzzed from a few drinks on our time off, or maybe sick, or in the middle of a fight with a lover, a friend, one of the kids."

She pushes away her half-eaten yellowfin tuna and folds her hands on top of the checkered tablecloth.

"But cases can't wait," she adds.

"Seriously. Isn't it true that some can?" asks a Chicago detective his classmates call Popeye because of the anchor tattooed on his left forearm. "Like bones in a well or buried in a basement. Or a body under a slab of concrete. I mean, they ain't going anywhere."

"The dead are impatient," Scarpetta says.

2

Night on the bayou reminds Jay Talley of a Cajun band of bull-frogs playing bass, and peepers screaming on electric guitars, and cicadas and crickets rasping washboards and sawing fiddles.

He shines a flashlight near the dark, arthritic shape of an old cypress tree, and alligator eyes flash and vanish beneath black water. The light simmers with the ominous soft sound of mos-quitoes as the BayStealth drifts, the outboard motor cut. Jay sits in the captain's chair and idly surveys the woman in the fish box not far below his feet. When he was boat shopping several years ago, this particular BayStealth excited him. The fish box beneath the floor is long and deep enough to hold more than a hundred and twenty pounds of ice and fish, or a woman built the way he likes.

Her wide, panicked eyes shine in the dark. In daylight, they are blue, a deep, beautiful blue. She painfully screws them shut as Jay caresses her with the beam of the flashlight, starting with her mature, pretty face, all the way down to her red painted toenails.

She is blonde, probably in her early- to mid-forties, but looks younger than that, petite but curvaceous. The fiberglass fish box is lined with orange boat cushions, dirty and stained black from old blood. Jay was thoughtful, even sweet when he bound her wrists and ankles loosely so the yellow nylon rope wouldn't cut off her circulation. He told her that the rope wouldn't abrade her soft flesh as long as she didn't struggle.

"No point in struggling, anyway," he said in a baritone voice that goes perfectly with his blond-god good looks. "And I'm not going to gag you. No point in screaming, either, right?"

She nodded her head, which made him laugh, because she was nodding as if answering *yes* when, of course, she meant *no*. But he understands how haywire people think and act when they are *terrified*, a word that has always struck him as so completely inadequate. He supposes that when Samuel Johnson was toiling at the many editions of his dictionary, he had no idea what a human being feels when he or she *anticipates* horror and death. The *anticipation* creates a frenzy of panic in every neuron, in every cell of the body, that goes far, far beyond mere terror, but even Jay, who is fluent in many languages, has no better word to describe what his victims suffer.

A *frisson* of horror.

No.

He studies the woman. She is a lamb. In life, there are only two types of people: wolves and lambs.

Jay's determination to perfectly describe the way his lambs feel has become a relentless, obsessive quest. The hormone epinephrine—adrenaline—is the alchemy that turns a normal person into a lower form of life with no more control or logic than a gigged frog. Added to the physiological response that precipitates what criminologists, psychologists and other so-called experts refer to as fight-or-flight are the additional elements of the lamb's past experiences and imagination. The more violence a lamb has experienced through books, television, movies or the news, for example, the more the lamb can imagine the nightmare of what might happen.

But the word. The *perfect word.* It eludes him tonight.

He gets down on the boat floor and listens to his lamb's rapid, shallow breaths. She trembles as the earthquake of horror (for lack of the *perfect word*) shifts her every molecule, creating unbearable havoc. He reaches down into the fish box and touches her hand. It is as cold as death. He presses two fingers against the side of her neck, finding her carotid artery and using the luminescent dial of his watch to take her pulse.

"One-eighty, more or less," he tells her. "Don't have a heart attack. I had one who did."

She stares at him with eyes bigger than a full moon, her lower lip twitching.

"I mean it. Don't have a heart attack." He is serious.

It is an order.

"Take a deep breath."

She does, her lungs shaky.

"Better?"

"Yes. Please . . ."

"Why is it that all of you little lambs are so fucking polite?"

Her dirty magenta cotton shirt had been torn open days ago, and he spreads the ripped front, exposing her more than ample breasts. They tremble and shimmer in the faint light, and he follows their round slopes down to her heaving rib cage, to the hollow of her flat abdomen, down to the unzipped fly of her jeans.

"I'm sorry," she tries to whisper as a tear rolls down her dirt-streaked face.

"Now, there you go again." He sits back in his throne of the captain's chair. "Do you really, *really* believe that being polite is going to change my plans?" The politeness sets off a slow burning rage. "Do you know what politeness means to me?"

He expects an answer.

She tries to wet her lips, her tongue as dry as paper. Her pulse visibly pounds in her neck, as if a tiny bird is trapped in there.

"No." She chokes on the word, tears flowing into her ears and hair.

"Weakness," he says.

Several frogs strike up the band. Jay studies his prisoner's nakedness, her pale skin shiny with bug repellent, a small humane act on his part, motivated by his distaste for red welts. Mosquitoes are a gray, chaotic storm around her but do not land. He gets down from his chair again and gives her a sip of bottled water. Most of it runs down her chin. Touching her sexually is of no interest to him. Three nights now he has brought her out here in his boat, because he wants the privacy to talk and stare at her nakedness, hoping that somehow her body will become Kay Scarpetta's, and finally becomes furious because it can't, furious because Scarpetta wouldn't be polite, furious because Scarpetta isn't weak. A rabid part of him fears he is a failure because Scarpetta is a wolf and he captures only lambs, and he can't find the perfect word, the *word*.

He realizes the word will not come to him with this lamb in the fish box, just as it hasn't come with the others.

"I'm getting bored," he tells his lamb. "I'll ask you again. One last chance. What is the *word*?"

She swallows hard, her voice reminding him of a broken axle as she tries to move her tongue to speak. He can hear it sticking to her upper palate.

"I don't understand. I'm sorry . . ."

"Fuck the politeness, do you hear me? How many times do I have to say it?"

The tiny bird inside her neck beats frantically, and her tears flow faster.

"What is the word? *Tell me what you feel.* And don't say *scared.* You're a goddamn schoolteacher. You must have a vocabulary with more than five words in it."

"I feel . . . I feel acceptance," she says, sobbing.

"You feel *what* ?"

"You're not going to let me go," she says. "I know it now."

3

Scarpetta's subtle wit reminds Nic of heat lightning. It doesn't rip and crack and show off like regular lightning but is a quiet, shimmering flash that her mother used to tell her meant God was taking pictures.

He takes pictures of everything you're doing, Nic, so you'd better behave yourself because one day there will be the Final Judgment, and those pictures are going to be passed around for all to see.

Nic stopped believing such nonsense by the time she reached high school, but her silent partner, as she thinks of her conscience, will probably never stop warning her that her sins will find her out. And Nic believes her sins are many.

"Investigator Robillard?" Scarpetta is saying.

Nic is startled by the sound of her own name. Her focus returns to the cozy, dark dining room and the cops who fill it.

"Tell us what you'd do if your phone rang at two a.m. and you'd had a few drinks but were needed at a bad, really bad, crime scene," Scarpetta presents to her. "Let me preface this by saying that no one wants to be left out when there's a bad, really bad, crime scene. Maybe we don't like to admit that, but it's true."

"I don't drink very much." Nic instantly regrets the remark as her classmates groan.

"Lordy, where'd you grow up, girlfriend, Sunday school?"

"What I mean is, I really can't because I have a five-year-old son . . ." Nic's voice trails off, and she feels like crying. This is the longest she's ever been away from him.

The table falls silent. Shame and awkwardness flatten the mood.

"Hey, Nic," Popeye says, "you got his picture with you? His name's Buddy," he tells Scarpetta. "You gotta see his picture. A really ass-kicking little hombre sitting on a pony . . ."

Nic is in no mood to pass around the wallet-size photograph that by now is worn soft, the writing on the back faded and smeared from her taking it out and looking at it all the time. She wishes Popeye would change the subject or give her the silent treatment again.

"How many of you have children?" Scarpetta asks the table.

About a dozen hands go up.

"One of the painful aspects of this work," she points out, "maybe the worst thing about this work—or shall I call it a mission—is what it does to the people we love, no matter how hard we try to protect them."

No heat lightning at all. Just a silky black darkness, cool and lovely to the touch, Nic thinks as she watches Scarpetta.

She's gentle. Behind that wall of fiery fearlessness and brilliance, she's kind and gentle.

"In this work, relationships can also become fatalities. Often they do," Scarpetta goes on, always trying to teach because it is easier for her to share her mind than to touch feelings she is masterful at keeping out of reach.

"So, Doc, you got kids?" Reba, a crime-scene technician from San Francisco, starts on another whiskey sour. She has begun to slur her words and has no tact.

Scarpetta hesitates. "I have a niece."

"Oh yeah! Now I 'member. Lucy. She's been in the news a lot. Or was, I mean . . ."

Stupid, drunk idiot, Nic silently protests with a flash of anger.

"Yes, Lucy is my niece," Scarpetta replies.

"FBI. Computer whiz." Reba won't stop. "Then what? Let me think. Something about flying helicopters and AFT."

ATF, you stupid drunk. Thunder cracks in the back of Nic's mind.

"I dunno. Wasn't there a big fire or something and someone got killed? So what's she doing now?" She drains her whiskey sour and looks for the waitress.

"That was a long time ago." Scarpetta doesn't answer her questions, and Nic detects a weariness, a sadness as immutable and maimed as the stumps and knees of cypress trees in the swamps and bayous of her South Louisiana home.

"Isn't that something, I forgot all about her being your niece. Now she's something, all right. Or was," Reba rudely says again, shoving her short dark hair out of her bloodshot eyes. "Got into some trouble, didn't she?"

Fucking dyke. Shut up.

Lightning rips the black curtain of night, and for an instant, Nic can see the white daylight on the other side. That's how her father always explained it. *You see, Nic,* he would say as they gazed out the window during angry storms, and lightning suddenly and without warning cut zigzags like a bright blade. *There's tomorrow, see? You got to look quick, Nic. There's tomorrow on the other side, that bright white light. And see how quick it heals. God heals just that fast.*

"Reba, go back to the hotel," Nic tells her in the same firm, controlled voice she uses when Buddy throws a tantrum. "You've had enough whiskey for one night."

"Well, 'scuse me, Miss Teacher's Pet." Reba is careening toward unconsciousness, and she talks as if she has rubber bands in her mouth.

Nic feels Scarpetta's eyes on her and wishes she could send her a signal that might be reassuring or serve as an apology for Reba's outrageous display.

Lucy has entered the room like a hologram, and Scarpetta's subtle but deeply emotional response shocks Nic with jealousy, with envy she didn't know she had. She feels inferior to her hero's super-cop niece, whose talents and world are enormous compared to Nic's. Her heart aches like a frozen joint that is finally unbent, the way her mother gently straightened out Nic's healing broken arm every time the splint came off.

Hurting's good, baby. If you didn't feel something, this little arm of yours would be dead and fall right off. You wouldn't want that, would you?

No, Mama. I'm sorry for what I did.

Why, Nicci, that's the silliest thing. You didn't hurt yourself on purpose!

But I didn't do what Papa said. I ran right into the woods and that's when I tripped . . .

We all make mistakes when we're scared, baby. Maybe it's a good thing you fell down—you were low to the ground when the lightning was flying all around.

4

Nic's memories of her childhood in the Deep South are full of storms.

It seems the heavens threw terrible fits every week, exploding in rageful thunder and trying to drown or electrocute every living creature on the Earth. Whenever thunderheads raised their ugly warnings and boomed their threats, her papa preached about safety, and her pretty blonde mother stood at the screen door, motioning for Nic to hurry into the house, hurry into a warm, dry place, hurry into her arms.

Papa always turned off the lights, and the three of them sat in the dark, telling Bible stories and seeing how many verses and psalms they could quote from memory. A perfect recitation was worth a quarter, but her father wouldn't pay out until the storm passed, because quarters are made of metal, and metal attracts lightning.

Thou shalt not covet.

Nic's excitement had been almost unbearable when she learned

14

that one of the Academy's visiting lecturers was Dr. Kay Scarpetta, who would teach death investigation the tenth and final week of training. Nic counted the days. She felt as though the first nine weeks would never pass. Then Scarpetta arrived here in Knoxville, and to Nic's acute embarrassment, she met her for the first time in the ladies' room, right after Nic flushed the toilet and emerged from a stall, zipping up the dark navy cargo pants of her Battle Dress Uniform.

Scarpetta was washing her hands at a sink, and Nic recalled the first time she had seen a photograph of her and how surprised she had been that Scarpetta wasn't of dark Spanish stock. That was about eight years ago, when Nic knew only Scarpetta's name and had no reason to expect that she would be a blue-eyed blonde whose ancestors came from Northern Italy, some of them farmers along the Austrian border and as Aryan in appearance as Germans.

"Hi, I'm Dr. Scarpetta," her hero said, as if oblivious that the flushing toilet and Nic were related. "And let me guess, you're Nicole Robillard."

Nic turned into a mute, her face bright red. "How . . ."

Before she could sputter the rest of the question, Scarpetta explained, "I requested copies of everyone's application, including photographs."

"You did?" Not only was Nic stunned that Scarpetta would have asked for their applications, but she couldn't fathom why she would have had the time or interest in looking at them. "Guess that means you know my Social Security number," Nic tried to be funny.

"Now, I don't remember that," Scarpetta said, drying her hands on paper towels. "But I know enough."

5

"Second instar." Nic shows off by answering the forgotten question about Maggie the maggot.

The cops around the table shake their heads and cut their eyes at one another. Nic has the capacity to irritate her comrades and has done so on and off for the past two and a half months. In some ways, she reminds Scarpetta of Lucy, who spent the first twenty years of her young life accusing people of slights they hadn't quite committed and flexing her gifts to the extreme of exhibitionism.

"That's very good, Nic," Scarpetta commends her.

"Who invited smarty pants?" Reba, who refuses to return to the Holiday Inn, is just plain obnoxious when she isn't nodding off into her plate.

"I think Nic hasn't been drinking enough and is having the D.T.s and seeing maggots crawling everywhere," says the detective with the shiny shaved head.

The way he looks at Nic is pretty obvious. Despite her being the class nerd, he is attracted to her.

"And you probably think an instar is a position on a baseball field." Nic wants to be funny but can't escape the gravity of her mood. "See that little maggot I gave Dr. Scarpetta . . . ?"

"Ah! At last she confesses."

"It's second instar." Nic knows she should stop. "Already shed its skin once since it hatched."

"Oh, yeah? How do you know? You an eyewitness? You actually see little Maggie shed her little skin?" the detective with the shaved head persists, winking at her.

"Nic's got a tent in the Body Farm, sleeps out there with all her creepy-crawly friends," someone else says.

"I would if I needed to."

No one argues with that. Nic is well known for her ventures into the two-acre, wooded decay research facility at the University of Tennessee, where the decomposition of donated human bodies is studied to determine many important facts of death, not the least of which is when death occurred. The joke is, she visits the Body Farm as if she's dropping by the old folks' home and checking on her relatives.

"Bet Nic's got a name for every maggot, fly, beetle and buzzard out there."

The quips and gross-out jokes continue until Reba drops her fork with a loud clatter.

"Not while I'm eating rare steak!" she protests much too loudly.

"The spinach adds a nice touch of green, girlfriend."

"Too bad you didn't get no rice . . ."

"Hey, it ain't too late! Waitress! Bring this lady a nice bowl of rice. With gravy."

"And what are these tiny black dots that look like Maggie's eyes?" Scarpetta lifts the vial to the candlelight again, hoping her students will settle down before they all get kicked out of the restaurant.

"Eyes," says the cop with the shaved head. "They're eyes, right?"

Reba begins to sway in her chair.

"No, they're not eyes," Scarpetta replies. "Come on. I already gave you a hint a few minutes ago."

"Look like eyes to me. Little beady black eyes like Magilla's."

In the past ten weeks, Sergeant Magil from Houston has become "Magilla the Gorilla" because of his hairy, muscle-bound body.

"Hey!" he protests. "You ask my girlfriend if I got maggot eyes. She looks deep into these eyes of mine"—he points to them—"and faints."

"Exactly what we're saying, Magilla. I looked into those eyes of yours, I'd pass out cold, too."

"They gotta be eyes. How the hell else does a maggot see where it's going?"

"They're spiracles, not eyes," Nic answers. "That's what the little black dots are. Like little snorkels so the maggot can breathe."

"Snorkels?"

"Wait a minute. Hey, hand that thing over, Dr. Scarpetta. I wanna see if Maggie's wearing a mask and fins."

A skinny state police investigator from Michigan has her head on the table, she is laughing so hard.

"Next time we find a ripe one, just look for little snorkels sticking up . . ."

The guffaws turn to fits, Magilla sliding off his chair, prone on the floor. "Oh, shit! I'm gonna throw up," he shrieks with laughter.

18

"Snorkels!"

Scarpetta surrenders, sitting back in silence, the situation out of her control.

"Hey, Nic! Didn't know you were a Navy SEAL!"

This goes on until the manager of Ye Old Steak House silently appears in the doorway—his way of indicating that the party in his back room is disturbing the other diners.

"Okay, boys and girls," Scarpetta says in a tone that is slightly scary. "Enough."

The hilarity is gone as quickly as a sonic boom, the maggot jokes end, and then there are other gifts for Scarpetta: a space pen that can supposedly write in "rain, blizzards, and if you accidentally drop it in a chest cavity while you're doing an autopsy"; a Mini Maglite "to see in those hard-to-reach places"; and a dark blue baseball cap embellished with enough gold braid for a general.

"General Dr. Scarpetta. Salute!"

Everybody does as they eagerly look for her response, irreverent remarks flying around again like shotgun pellets. Magilla tops off Scarpetta's wine glass from a gallon paper carton with a push-button spout. She figures the cheap Chardonnay is probably made from grapes grown at the lowest level of the slopes, where the drainage is terrible. If she's lucky, the vintage is four months old. She will be sick tomorrow. She is sure of it.

6

Early the next morning in New York's Kennedy Airport, a security guard recommends that Lucy Farinelli remove her oversized stainless-steel Breitling watch, empty her pockets of coins and place them in a tray.

It is not a suggestion but an order when she is asked to remove her running shoes, jacket and belt and place them and her briefcase on the conveyor that will carry them through the X-ray machine, where nothing but a cell phone, a hairbrush and a tube of lipstick will fluoresce. British Airways attendants are friendly enough in their dark blazers and navy blue dresses with red and white checks, but airport police are especially tense. Although she doesn't set off the doorframe-shaped scanner as she walks through in her athletic socks, her jeans hanging loose, she is searched with the hand scanner, and her underwire bra sets it off with a beep-beep-beep.

"Hold up your arms," the hefty female officer tells her.

Lucy smiles and holds out her arms crucifixion-style, and the officer pats her down quickly, her hands fluttering under Lucy's arms, under her breasts, up and down her thighs, all the way to her crotch—very professionally, of course. Other passengers pass by unmolested, and the men, in particular, find the good-looking young woman with arms and legs spread of keen interest. Lucy couldn't care less. She has lived through too much to waste energy in being modest and is tempted to unbutton her shirt and point out the underwire bra, assuring the officer that no battery and tiny—very tiny—explosive device are attached.

"It's my bra," she casually says to the startled guard, who is far more unnerved than her suspect. "Damn it, I always forget to wear a bra without wire in it, maybe a sports bra, or no bra. I'm really sorry to inconvenience you, Officer Washington." She's already read her name tag. "Thank you for doing your job so well. What a world we live in. I understand the terrorist alert is orange again."

Lucy leaves the bewildered guard and plucks her watch and coins out of the tray and collects her briefcase, jacket and belt. Sitting on the cold, hard floor, out of the way of traffic, she puts on her running shoes, not bothering to lace them. She gets up, still polite and sweet to any police or British Airways employees watching her. Reaching around to her back pocket, she slips out her ticket and passport, both of them issued to one of her many false names. She strolls nonchalantly, laces flopping, deep inside the winding carpeted gate 10, and ducks inside the small doorway of Concorde flight 01. A British Airways attendant smiles at her as she checks Lucy's boarding pass.

"Seat one-C." She points the way to the first row, the bulkhead aisle seat, as if Lucy has never traveled on Concorde before.

Last time she did, it was under yet another name, and she was wearing glasses and green contact lenses, her hair dyed funky blue and purple, easily washed out and matching the photograph on that particular passport. Her occupation was "musician." Although no one could possibly have been familiar with her non-existent techno band, Yellow Hell, there were plenty of people who said, "Oh yes, I've heard of it! Cool!"

Lucy counts on the dismal observation skills of the general masses. She counts on their fear of showing ignorance, on their accepting lies as familiar truths. She counts on her enemies noticing all that goes on around them, and like them, she notices all that goes on around her, too. For example, when the customs agent studied her passport at great length, she recognized his behavior and understood why security is at a feverish pitch. Interpol has sent a Red Notice screaming over the Internet to approximately 182 countries, alerting them to look out for a fugitive named Rocco Caggiano, wanted in Italy and France for murder. Rocco has no idea he is a fugitive. He has no idea that Lucy sent information to Interpol's Central Bureau in Washington, D.C., her credible tip thoroughly checked out before it was relayed through cyberspace to Interpol's headquarters in Lyon, France, where the Red Notice was issued and rocketed to law enforcement all around the world. All this in a matter of hours.

Rocco does not know Lucy, although he knows who she is. She knows him very well, although they have never met. At this moment, as she straps herself into her seat and the Concorde starts its Rolls Royce engines, she can't wait to see Rocco Caggiano, her anticipation fueled by intense anger that will evolve into a nervous dread by the time she finally gets to Eastern Europe.

7

"I sure hope you're not feeling as bad as I am," Nic says to Scarpetta.

They sit inside the living room of Scarpetta's suite at the Marriott, waiting for room service. It is nine a.m., and twice now Nic has inquired about Scarpetta's health, her banality partly due to her flattered disbelief that this woman she admires so intensely invited her to have breakfast.

Why me? The question bounces inside Nic's head like a bingo ball. *Maybe she feels sorry for me.*

"I've felt better," Scarpetta replies with a smile.

"Popeye and his wine. But he's brought worse poison than that."

"I don't know how anything could be worse," Scarpetta says as a knock sounds on the door. "Unless it really is poison. Excuse me."

She gets up from the couch. Room service has arrived on a table wheeled inside. Scarpetta signs the check and tips in cash. Nic notes that she is generous.

"Popeye's room—room one-oh-six—is the watering hole," Nic says. "Any night, just go on in with your six-pack and dump it in the bathtub. Starting around eight p.m., he does nothing but haul twenty-pound bags of ice to his room. Good thing he's on the first floor. I went once."

"Only once in ten weeks?" Scarpetta watches her closely, probing.

When Nic returns to Louisiana, she will face the worst homicide cases she may ever have in her life. So far, she hasn't said a word about them, and Scarpetta is concerned about her.

"When I was in medical school at Johns Hopkins," Scarpetta offers as she pours coffee, "I was one of three women in my class. If there was a bathtub full of beer anywhere, I can assure you I was never told. What do you take?"

"Lots of cream and sugar. You shouldn't be serving me. Here I am, just sitting." She pops up from her wing chair.

"Sit down, sit down." Scarpetta sets Nic's coffee on a table. "There are croissants and rather inedible-looking bagels. I'll let you help yourself."

"But when you were in medical school, you weren't a small-town . . ." Nic catches herself before saying *hick*. "Miami's not exactly some little mud puddle in Louisiana. All these guys in my class are from big cities."

She fixes her attention on Scarpetta's coffee cup, on how perfectly steady it is as she lifts it to her lips. She drinks her coffee black and seems uninterested in food.

"When my chief told me the department was offered a fully funded slot at the Academy and would I go, I can't tell you what I felt like," Nic goes on, worrying that she's talking too much about herself. "I really couldn't believe it and had to go to a world of trouble to make it possible for me to leave home for close to three months. Then I got here to Knoxville and found myself with Reba as a roommate.

"I can't say it's been fun, and I feel terrible sitting here and complaining." She nervously drinks her coffee, setting it down, then picking it up again, clenching her napkin tightly in her lap. "Especially to you."

"Why especially to me?"

"Truth is, I guess I was hoping to impress you."

"You have."

"And you don't seem the sort to appreciate whining." Nic looks up at her. "It's not like people are always nice to you, either."

Scarpetta laughs. "Shall I call that an understatement?"

"That didn't come out right. People are jealous out there. You've had your battles. What I'm saying is, you don't complain."

"Ask Rose about that." Scarpetta is quite amused.

Nic's mind locks, as if she should know who Rose is but can't make a connection.

"My secretary," Scarpetta explains, sipping her coffee.

An awkward silence follows, and Nic asks, "What happened to the other two?"

Scarpetta is confused.

"The other two women in your medical class."

"One dropped out. I think the other got married and never practiced medicine."

"I wonder what they're feeling now. Probably regret."

"They probably wonder about me, too," Scarpetta replies. "They probably think I feel regret."

Nic's lips part in disbelief. "You?"

"Everything comes with sacrifices. And it's human nature to have a hard time accepting anyone who's different. Usually, you don't figure that out until you get what you asked for in life and are shocked that in some instances your reward is hatred instead of applause."

"I don't see myself as different or hated. Maybe picked on a lot, but not back home," Nic quickly replies. "Just because I'm with a small department instead of LAPD doesn't mean I'm stupid." Her spirit rises, her voice heating up. "I'm not some mudbug swamp-rat redneck . . ."

"*Mudbug.*" Scarpetta frowns. "I don't believe I know what that is."

"A crawfish."

"Did someone in the class call you a crawfish?"

Nic can't help but lighten up. "Oh, hell. None of them have ever even eaten a crawfish. They probably think it's a fish that crawls along the bottom of the ocean or something."

"I see."

"I know what you mean, though. Sort of," Nic says. "In Zachary, only two street cops are women. I'm the only female investigator, and it's not that the chief dislikes women or anything like that. In fact, the mayor's a woman. But most times when I'm in the break room, getting coffee or eating or whatever, I'm the only woman in there. Truth is, I rarely think about it. But I have thought about it a lot here at the Academy. I realize I try too hard to prove I'm really not a hick, and then I annoy everyone. Well, I know you need to go. You probably have to pack, and I don't want you to miss your plane."

"Not so fast," Scarpetta replies. "I don't think we're finished talking."

Nic relaxes, her attractive face more animated, her slender body less rigid in the chair. When she speaks this time, she doesn't sound as nervous.

"I will tell you the nicest thing anybody's said to me during this entire ten weeks. Reba said I look a little bit like you. 'Course, it was when she was drunk. Hope I didn't just insult you."

"You may have insulted yourself," Scarpetta modestly replies. "I'm somewhat older than you, if what I read on your application is to be trusted."

"Thirty-six in August. It's amazing what you pick up about people."

"I make it my business to know as much about people as I can. It's important to listen. Most people are too busy making assumptions, too self-absorbed to listen. And in the morgue, my patients speak very quietly and are unforgiving if I don't listen and find out everything I can about them."

"Sometimes I don't listen to Buddy like I should—when I'm frantic or just too tired." Sadness crosses her eyes. "I of all people ought to know how that feels, since Ricky hardly ever listened to me, which is one reason we didn't get along. One of many reasons."

Scarpetta has suspected that Nic's marriage is in trouble or has ended. People who are unhappy in relationships carry about them a distinct air of discontent and isolation. In Nic's case, the signs are there, especially the anger that she thinks she hides.

"How bad?" Scarpetta asks her.

"Separated, well on our way to divorce." Nic reaches for her coffee cup again but changes her mind. "Thank God my father lives nearby in Baton Rouge or I don't know what I'd do about Buddy. I know damn well Ricky would take him from me just to pay me back."

"Pay you back? For what?" Scarpetta inquires, and she has a reason for all these questions.

"A long story. Been going on more than a year, from bad to worse, not that it was ever all that good."

"About as long as these women have been disappearing from your area." Scarpetta finally gets to her point. "I want to know how you're handling that, because it will get you if you let it. When you least expect it. It's not escaped my notice that you haven't brought up the cases once, not once, not while I've been here. Ten women in fourteen months. Vanished, from their homes, vehicles, parking lots, all in the Baton Rouge area. Presumed dead. I can assure you they are. I can assure you they were murdered by the same person, who is shrewd—very shrewd. Intelligent and experienced enough to gain trust, then abduct, then dispose of the bodies. He's killed before, and he'll kill again. The latest disappearance was just four days ago—in Zachary. That makes two cases in Zachary, the first one several months ago. So you're going home to that, Nic. Serial murders. Ten of them."

"Not ten. Just the two in Zachary. I'm not on the task force," Nic replies with restrained resentment. "I don't run with the big boys. They don't need help from little country cops like me, at least that's the way the U.S. Attorney looks at it."

"What's the U.S. Attorney got to do with it?" Scarpetta asks. "These cases aren't the jurisdiction of the feds."

"Weldon Winn's not only an egotistical asshole, but he's stupid. Nothing worse than someone who's stupid and arrogant and has power. The cases are high-profile, all over the news. He wants to be part of them, maybe end up a federal judge or senator someday.

"And you're right. I know what I'm going home to, but all I can do is work the two disappearances we've had in Zachary, even if I know damn well they're connected to the other eight."

"Interesting the abductions are now happening farther north of Baton Rouge," Scarpetta says. "He may be finding his earlier killing field too risky."

"The only thing good I can say about that is Zachary may be in the East Baton Rouge Parish, but at least it isn't the jurisdiction of the Baton Rouge police. So the high and mighty task force can't boss me around about my cases."

"Tell me about them."

"Let's see. The most recent one. What I know about it. What anybody knows about it. Two days after Easter, just four nights ago," she begins. "A forty-year-old schoolteacher named Glenda Marler. She's a teacher at the high school—same high school I went to. Blonde, blue-eyed, pretty, very smart. Divorced, no children. This past Tuesday night, she goes to the Road Side Bar Be Q, gets pulled pork, hush puppies and slaw to go. She has a '94 Honda Accord, blue, and is observed driving away from the restaurant, south on Main Street, right through the middle of town. She vanishes, her car found abandoned in the parking lot of the high school where she taught. Of course, the task force is suggesting she was having a rendezvous with one of her students, that the case isn't related to the others, that it's a copycat. Bullshit."

"Her own high school parking lot," Scarpetta thoughtfully observes. "So he talked to her, found out about her after he had her in his car, maybe asked her where she worked, and she told him. Or else he stalked her."

"Which do you think it is?"

"I don't know. Most serial killers stalk their victims. But there's no set rule, despite what most profilers would like to think."

"The other victim," Nic continues, "vanished right before I came here. Ivy Ford. Forty-two years old, blonde, blue-eyed, attractive, worked as a bank teller. Kids are off in college, and her husband was up in Jackson, Mississippi, on a business trip, so she was home alone when someone must have showed up at her door.

As usual, no sign of a struggle. No nothing. And she's gone without a trace."

"Nothing is ever without a trace," Scarpetta says as she envisions each scenario, contemplating the obvious: The victim has no reason to fear her attacker until it is too late.

"Is Ivy Ford's house still secured?" Scarpetta doubts it after all this time.

"Family's still living in it. I don't know how people return to homes where such awful things have happened."

Nic starts to say that she wouldn't. But that isn't true. Earlier in her life, she did.

"The car in this most recent case, Glenda Marler's case, is impounded and was thoroughly examined?" Scarpetta asks.

"Hours and hours we . . . well, as you know, I was here." This detail disappoints her. "But I've gotten the full report, and I know we spent a lot of time on it. My guys lifted every print they could find. Entered the useable ones in AFIS, and no matches. Personally, I don't think that matters because I believe that whoever grabbed Glenda Marler was never inside her car. So his prints wouldn't be in there, anyway. And the only prints on the door handles were hers."

"What about her keys and wallet and any other personal effects?"

"Keys in the ignition, her pocketbook and wallet in the high school parking lot about twenty feet from the car."

"Money in the wallet?" Scarpetta asks.

Nic shakes her head. "But her checkbook and charge cards weren't touched. She wasn't one to carry much cash. Whatever she had, it was gone, and I know she had at least six dollars and thirty-two cents because that was the change she got when she gave the guy at the barbecue a ten-dollar bill to pay for her food. I had my guys check, because oddly, the bag of food wasn't inside her car.

So there was no receipt. We had to go back to the barbecue and have him pull her receipt."

"Then it would appear that the perpetrator took her food, too."

This is odd, more typical of a burglary or robbery, certainly not the usual in a psychopathic violent crime.

"As far as you know, is robbery involved in the cases of the other eight missing women?" Scarpetta asks.

"Rumor has it that their billfolds were cleaned out of cash and tossed not far from where they were snatched."

"No fingerprints in any of the cases, as far as you know?"

"I don't know for a fact."

"Perhaps DNA from skin cells where the perpetrator touched the billfold?"

"I don't know what the Baton Rouge police have done, because they don't tell anybody shit. But the guys at my department swabbed everything they could, including Ivy Ford's wallet, and did get her DNA profile—and another one that isn't in the FBI's database, CODIS. Louisiana, as you know, is just getting started on a DNA database and is so backed up on entering samples, you may as well forget it."

"But you do have an unknown profile," Scarpetta says with interest. "Although we have to accept right off that it could be anybody's. What about her children, her husband?"

"The DNA's not theirs."

Scarpetta nods. "Then you have to start wondering who else would have had good reason to touch Ivy Ford's wallet. Who else besides the killer."

"I wonder about that twenty-four hours a day."

"And this most recent case, Glenda Marler?"

"The state police labs have the evidence. The tests results will be a while, even though there's a rush on them."

"An alternate light source used on the inside of the car?"

"Yes. Nothing, nothing, nothing, nothing," Nic says in frustration. "No crime scenes, no bodies, like it's all a bad dream. If even just one body would show up. The coroner's great. You've heard of him? Dr. Sam Lanier."

Scarpetta doesn't know him.

8

The east Baton Rouge parish Coroner's Office overlooks a long straight reach of the Mississippi River and the former art deco state capitol where the wily, fearless and despotic Huey Long was assassinated.

Muddy, sluggish water carries Dr. Sam Lanier's eye to a riverboat casino and past the USS *Kidd* battleship to the distant Old Mississippi Bridge, as he stands before his office window on the fifth floor of the Governmental Building. He is a fit man in his early sixties with a head of gray hair that naturally parts neatly on the right side. Unlike most men of his power, he shuns suits except when he is in court or attending the political functions he cannot avoid.

His may be a political office, but he despises politics and virtually all people involved in it. Contrary by nature, Dr. Lanier wears the same outfit pretty much every day, even if he's meeting with the mayor: comfortable shoes capable of walking him into unpleasant places, dark slacks and a polo shirt embroidered with the East Baton Rouge Parish coroner's crest.

Deliberate man that he is, he ponders how to handle the bizarre communication he received yesterday morning, a letter enclosed in a National Academy of Justice postage-paid mailing. Dr. Lanier has been a member of the organization for years. The large white NAJ envelope was sealed. It did not look tampered with in any way until Dr. Lanier opened it and found another envelope, also sealed. It was addressed to him by hand in block printing, the return address the Texas Department of Criminal Justice, Polunsky Unit. A search on the Internet revealed that the Polunsky Unit is death row. The letter, also written by hand in block printing, reads:

GREETINGS MONSIEUR LANIER,

OF COURSE YOU REMEMBER MADAME CHARLOTTE DARD, WHOSE UNTIMELY, SAD DEATH OCCURRED ON 14 SEPTEMBER 1995. YOU WITNESSED HER AUTOPSY, AND I DO ENVY YOU FOR THAT DELICIOUS EXPERIENCE, HAVING NEVER SEEN ONE MYSELF, NOT IN PERSON. I WILL BE EXECUTED SOON AND AM RELIEVING MYSELF OF SECRETS.

MADAME DARD WAS MURDERED VERY CLEVERLY.

MAIS NON! NOT BY ME.

A PERSON OF INTEREST, AS THEY STUPIDLY REFER TO POSSIBLE SUSPECTS THESE DAYS, FLED TO PALM DESERT SHORTLY AFTER MADAME DARD'S DEATH. THIS PERSON IS NOT THERE NOW. THIS PERSON'S LOCATION AND IDENTITY YOU MUST DISCOVER FOR YOURSELF. I VERY MUCH ENCOURAGE YOU TO SEEK ASSISTANCE. MIGHT I SUGGEST THE GREAT SKILLS OF DETECTIVE PETE MARINO? HE KNOWS ME VERY WELL FROM MY JOYOUS RICHMOND DAYS. SURELY YOU MUST HAVE HEARD OF THE GREAT MARINO?

YOUR SURNAME, MON CHER MONSIEUR, IMPLIES YOU ARE OF FRENCH DESCENT. PERHAPS WE ARE RELATED.

À BIENTÔT,

JEAN-BAPTISTE CHANDONNE

Dr. Lanier has heard of Jean-Baptiste Chandonne. He has not heard of Pete Marino but is introduced to him easily enough by sending out a few search engines to chug through cyberspace and find him. It is true. Marino led the investigation when Chandonne was murdering women in Richmond. What interests Dr. Lanier more, however, is that Marino is best known for his close professional relationship with Dr. Kay Scarpetta, a gifted forensic pathologist. Dr. Lanier has always respected her and was more than a little impressed when he heard her lecture at a regional meeting of coroners. Most forensic pathologists, particularly ones with her status, look down on coroners, think they're all funeral home directors who got voted into office. Of course, some of them are.

Trouble stuck out its big foot and tripped Dr. Scarpetta, hurting her badly, several years back. For that she has Dr. Lanier's sympathy. Not a day goes by when trouble doesn't stomp around looking for him, too.

Now some notorious serial killer seems to think Dr. Lanier needs the help of her colleague Marino. Maybe he does. Maybe he's being set up. With the election not even six months away, Dr. Lanier is suspicious of any deviation from routine, and a letter from Jean-Baptiste Chandonne makes him as leery as hell. The only reason he can't dismiss it is simple: Jean-Baptiste Chandonne, if the letter is really from him, knows about Charlotte Dard. Her case has been forgotten by the public and was never all that newsworthy outside of Baton Rouge. Her cause of death was undetermined. Dr. Lanier has always entertained the possibility that she was murdered.

He's always believed that the best way to identify a cottonmouth is to poke at it. If the inside of its mouth is white, whack off its head. Otherwise, the critter's nothing more than a harmless water snake.

He may as well poke at the truth and see what he finds. While sitting at his desk, he picks up the phone and discovers Marino doesn't care who finds him—he has what Dr. Lanier calls a bring-'em-on attitude. He envisions Marino as the type who would ride a Fat Boy Harley, probably without a helmet. The cop's answering machine doesn't say he *can't* answer the phone because he's *not in* or is *on the other line*, which is what most professional, polite people record as greetings. The recorded gruff male voice says, "Don't call me at home," and offers another number for the person to try.

Dr. Lanier tries the other number. The voice that answers sounds like the recorded one.

"Detective Marino?"

"Who wants to know?"

He's from New Jersey and doesn't trust anyone, probably doesn't like hardly anyone, either.

Dr. Lanier introduces himself, and he's careful about what he says, too. In the trust and like department, Marino's met his match.

"We had a death down here about eight years ago. You ever heard of a woman named Charlotte Dard?"

"Nope."

Dr. Lanier gives him a few details of the case.

"Nope."

Dr. Lanier gives him a few more.

"Let me ask you something. Why the hell would I know anything about some drug overdose in Baton Rouge?" Marino's not at all nice about it.

"Same question I have."

36

"Huh? What is this? Are you some asshole bullshitting me?"

"A lot of people think I'm an asshole," Dr. Lanier replies. "But I'm not bullshitting you."

He debates whether he should tell Marino about the letter from Jean-Baptiste Chandonne. He decides that no useful purpose would be served. He's already found out what he needed to know: Marino is clueless about Charlotte Dard and annoyed at being bothered by some coroner.

"One other quick question, and then I won't take up any more of your time," Dr. Lanier says. "You have a long history with Dr. Kay Scarpetta . . ."

"What's she got to do with this?" Marino's entire demeanor changes. Now he's just plain hostile.

"I understand she's doing private consulting." Dr. Lanier had read a brief mention of it on the Internet.

Marino doesn't respond.

"What do you think of her?" Dr. Lanier asks the question that he feels sure will trigger a volcanic temper.

"Tell you what, asshole. I think enough of her not to talk about her with some shitbag stranger!"

The call ends with a dial tone.

In Sam Lanier's mind, he couldn't have gotten a stronger validation of Dr. Kay Scarpetta's character. She's welcome down here.

9

Scarpetta waits in line at the Marriott's front desk, her head throbbing, her central nervous system shorted out by wine so terrible it ought to have a skull and crossbones on the label.

Her malady, her malaise, is far more serious than she ever let on to Nic, and with each passing minute, her physical condition and mood worsen. She refuses to diagnose her illness as a hangover (after all, she barely had two glasses of that goddamn wine), and she refuses to forgive herself for even considering an alcoholic beverage sold in a cardboard box.

Painful experience has proven for years that when she suffers such merry misadventures, the more coffee she drinks, the more awful she's going to feel, but this never stops her from ordering a large pot in her room and flying by the seat of her pants instead of trusting her instruments, as Lucy likes to say when her aunt ignores what she knows and does what she feels and crash-lands.

When she finally reaches the front desk, she asks for her bill and is handed an envelope.

"This just came in for you, ma'am," the harried receptionist says as he tears off the printout of her room charges and hands it to her.

Inside the envelope is a fax. Scarpetta walks behind the bellman pushing her cart. It is loaded with bags and three very large hard cases containing carousels of slides that she has not bothered to convert to PowerPoint presentations because she can't stand them. Showing a picture of a man who has blown off the top of his head with a shotgun or a child scalded to death does not require a computer and special effects. Slide presentations and handouts serve her purposes just as well now as they did when she started her career.

The fax is from her secretary, Rose, who must have called about the same time Scarpetta was miserably making her way from the elevator to the lobby. All Rose says is that Dr. Sam Lanier, the coroner of East Baton Rouge Parish, very much needs to speak to her. Rose includes his home, office and cell telephone numbers. Immediately, Scarpetta thinks of Nic Robillard, of their conversation not even an hour ago.

She waits until she is inside her taxi before calling Dr. Lanier's office number. He answers himself.

"How did you know who my secretary is and where to reach her?" she asks right off.

"Your former office in Richmond was kind enough to give me your number in Florida. Rose is quite charming, by the way."

"I see," she replies as the taxi drives away from the hotel. "I'm in a taxi on the way to the airport. Can we make this quick?"

Her abruptness is more about her annoyance with her former office than with him. Giving out her unlisted phone number is blatant harassment—not that it hasn't happened before. Some people who still work at the Chief Medical Examiner's Office remain loyal to their boss. Others are traitors and bend in the direction that power pulls.

"Quick it will be," Dr. Lanier says. "I'm wondering if you would review a case for me, Dr. Scarpetta—an eight-year-old case that was never successfully resolved. A woman died under suspicious circumstances, apparently from a drug overdose. You ever heard of Charlotte Dard?"

"No."

"I've just gotten information—don't know if it's good or not—but I don't want to discuss it while you're on a cell phone."

"This is a Baton Rouge case?" Scarpetta digs in her handbag for a notepad and pen.

"Another story for another day. But yes, it's a Baton Rouge case."

"Your case?"

"It was. I'd like to send you the reports, slides and all the rest. Looks like I'd better dig back into this thing." He hesitates. "And as you might suspect, I don't have much of a budget . . ."

"Nobody who calls me has consultants built into the budget," she interrupts him. "I didn't either when I was in Virginia."

She tells him to FedEx her the case and gives him her address. She adds, "Do you happen to know an investigator in Zachary named Nic Robillard?"

A pause, then, "Believe I talked to her on the phone a few months back. I'm sure you know what's going on down here."

"I can't help but know. It's all over the news," Scarpetta cautiously replies over the noise of the taxi and rush-hour traffic.

Neither her tone nor her words betray that she has any personal information about the cases, and her trust of Nic slips several notches as she frets that perhaps Nic called Dr. Lanier and talked about her. Why she might have done that is hard to say, unless she simply volunteered that Scarpetta could be a very useful resource for him, should he ever need her. Maybe he really does need her for this cold case he's just told her about. Maybe he's trying to develop a relationship with her because he's not equipped to handle these serial murders by himself.

"How many forensic pathologists work for you?" Scarpetta asks him.

"One."

"Did Nic Robillard call you about me?" She doesn't have time for subtlety.

"Why would she?"

"That's no answer."

"Hell no," he says.

10

An air-conditioning unit rattles in a dusty window, the afternoon hotter than usual for April, as Jay Talley hacks meat into small pieces and drops them into a bloody plastic bucket below the scarred wooden table where he sits.

The table, like everything else inside his fishing shack, is old and ugly, the sort of household objects people leave at the edges of their driveways to be picked up by garbage collectors or spirited away by scavengers. His work space is his special place, and he is patient as he repeatedly adjusts torn bits of clothing that he jams under several of the table legs in his ongoing attempt to keep the table level. He prefers not to chop on a surface that moves, but balance is virtually impossible in his warped little world, and the graying wood floor slopes enough to roll an egg from the kitchenette right out to the dock, where some planks are rotted, others curled like dull dead hair flipped up at the ends.

Swatting at sea gnats, he finishes a Budweiser, crushes the can and hurls it out the open screen door, pleased that it sails twenty feet past his boat and plops into the water. Boredom gives pleasure to the most mundane activities, including checking on the crab pots suspended below floats in the murky freshwater. It doesn't matter that crabs aren't found in freshwater. Crawfish are, and they're in season, and if they don't pick the pots clean, something bigger usually comes along.

Last month, a large log turned into an alligator gar weighing at least a hundred pounds. It moved like a torpedo, speeding off with a trotline and its makeshift float of an empty Clorox bottle. Jay sat calmly in his boat and tipped his baseball cap to the carnivorous creature. Jay doesn't eat what he catches in the pots, but out here in the middle of this hellish nowhere he now calls home, his only acceptable fresh choices are catfish, bass, turtles and as many frogs as he can gig at night. Otherwise, his food comes in bags and cans from various grocery stores on the mainland.

He brings down a meat cleaver, cutting through muscle and bone. More pieces of foul flesh land in the bucket. It doesn't take long for meat to rot in this heat.

"Guess who I'm thinking about right now," he says to Bev Kiffin, his woman.

"Shut up. You just say that to get to me."

"No, *ma chérie*, I say it because I'm remembering fucking her in Paris."

Jealousy flares. Bev can't control herself when she is forced to think of Kay Scarpetta, who is fine-looking and smart—plenty fine-looking, and smart enough for Jay. Rarely does it occur to Bev that she has no good reason to compete with a woman Jay fantasizes about chopping up and feeding to the alligators and crawfish in the bayou outside their door. If Bev could cut Scarpetta's throat, she sure as hell would, and her own dream is to one day get her chance. Then Jay wouldn't talk about the bitch anymore. He wouldn't stare out at the bayou half the night, thinking about her.

"How come you have to always talk about her?"

Bev moves closer to him and watches sweat trickle down his perfectly sculpted, smooth chest, soaking the waistband of his tight cutoff jeans. She stares at his muscular thighs, the hair on them fine and shiny as gold. Her fury heats to flashover and erupts.

"You got a damn hard-on. You chop away and get a stiff dick! Put down that meat ax!"

"It's a *cleaver*, honey. If only you weren't so stupid." His handsome face and blond hair are wet with sweat, his cold blue eyes bright against his tan.

She bends over and cups her thick, stubby hand around the bulge between his thighs as he calmly spreads his legs wide and leans back in the chair long enough for her to get started on his zipper. She wears no bra, her cheap flower-printed blouse halfway unbuttoned, offering him a view of heavy, flaccid breasts that arouse nothing beyond his need to manipulate and control. He rips open her blouse, buttons lightly clattering against wood, and begins fondling her the way she craves.

"Oh," she moans. "Don't stop," she begs, moving his head closer.

"Want more, baby?"

"Oh."

He sucks her, disgusted by her salty, sour taste, and shoves her hard with his bare feet.

The thud of her body hitting the floor, her shocked gasp, are familiar sounds in the fishing shack.

11

Blood seeps from a scrape on Bev's dimpled left knee, and she stares at the wound.

"How come you don't want me no more, baby?" she says. "You used to want me so bad I couldn't keep you off me."

Her nose runs. She shoves back her short, frizzy, graying brown hair and pulls her torn blouse together, suddenly humiliated by her ugly nakedness.

"Want is when *I* want."

He resumes the blows with the meat cleaver. Tiny bits of flesh and bone fly out from the thick, shiny blade and stick to the stained wooden table and to Jay's sweaty bare chest. The sweet, sour stench of rotting flesh is heavy in the stifling air, and flies drone in lazy zigzags, lumbering airborne like fat cargo planes. They hover over the gory mother lode inside the bucket, their black and green swarming bodies shimmering like spilled gasoline.

Bev collects herself off the floor. She watches Jay hacking and tossing flesh into the bucket, flies darting up and greedily dive-bombing back to their feast. They buzz loudly, bumping against the side of the bucket.

"And now we're supposed to eat off that table." Hers is an old line. They never eat off it. The table is Jay's private space and she knows not to touch it.

He swats furiously at the sea gnats. "Goddamn, I hate these fucking things! When the fuck are you going shopping? And next time, don't come back here with only two bottles of insect repellent and no pups."

Bev disappears into the lavatory. It is no bigger than the head on a small boat, and there is no tank to chemically store and treat human waste, which slops through a hole into a washtub between pilings that support the shack. Once a day, she empties the tub into the bayou. Her persistent nightmare is that a water moccasin or alligator is going to get her while she sits on the wooden box toilet, and at especially uneasy times, she squats above it, peering down at the black hole, her fat thighs shaking from fear and the strain of supporting her weight.

She was fleshy when Jay first met her at a campsite near Williamsburg, Virginia, where his family business brought them together by accident, really. He needed a place, and hers was out of the way, an overgrown, garbage-strewn, densely wooded property with abandoned, rusting campers and a motel mostly patronized by prostitutes and drug dealers. When Jay appeared at Bev's door, she was thrilled by his power and was instantly attracted to him. She came on to him the same way she did with all men, rough raw sex her only means of gratifying her lonely, angry needs.

The rain was driving down that night, reminding her of shiny nails, and she fixed Jay a bowl of Campbell's vegetable beef soup and a grilled cheese sandwich while her young children hid and watched their mother involving herself with yet another stranger. Bev paid her little ones no mind at the time. She tries not to think about them now or wonder how big they're getting. They are wards of the state and far better off without her. Ironically, Jay was nicer to them than she was. He was so different then, when he took her to bed that first night.

Three years ago she was more attractive and had not gained weight from eating snack foods and processed cheeses and meats that don't spoil. She can't do push-ups and squats all day long the way Jay does, and she gets no exercise. Behind the shack, grass flats thick with mussels and rich black muck stretch for miles. There is no dry ground to walk on except the pier. Maneuvering Jay's boat through narrow waterways burns few calories.

A small outboard motor would do, but Jay will have nothing less than a 200-horsepower Evinrude with a stainless-steel prop to speed through channels, heading to his secret spots, and drift silently beneath cypress trees, waiting perfectly still like a possum if a helicopter or small plane flies low overhead. He helps Bev with nothing, his distinctive looks impossible to disguise because he is too vain to ruin his beauty. When he goes to shore, it is to get money at a family hideaway and not to run errands. Bev can venture out for provisions because she scarcely resembles her photograph on the FBI's most-wanted list, her skin withered by the sun, her body overblown, her face puffy and hair cut short.

"Why can't we close the door?" Bev asks as she walks out of the tiny, dirty bathroom.

He goes to the refrigerator, rounded and white with spots of rust, left over from the sixties. Swinging open the door, he grabs another beer.

"I like being hot," he says, his footsteps heavy on the old planking.

"The air-conditioning's going right out the door." Hers is the usual complaint. "We only got so much gasoline for the generator."

"Then you'll just have to go out and get more. How many times do I have to tell you to get your fat ass out to get more?"

He stares at her, his eyes weird, the way they get when he is engrossed in his ritual. His arousal strains against his zipper, and soon he will relieve it—again, at a time of his choosing. Body odor and a rotten stench waft past her as he carries the bucket outside, flies storming after it in a loud buzzing blitzkrieg. He busies himself, pulling up crab pots by their yellow nylon ropes. He has dozens of pots. He simply tosses pieces too big to fit inside them into the water, where gators will drag them to the bottom and feed off them at their pleasure. Skulls pose the biggest problem, because they make identity certain. Another ritual of his is to pound skulls into dust, which he mixes with powdered white chalk that he stores in empty paint cans. Chalky, bony dust reminds him of the catacombs that wind twenty-five meters below the streets of Paris.

Now inside and flopping on the narrow bed against a wall, he puts his hands behind his head.

Bev slips out of her torn blouse, teasing him like a stripper. A master at the waiting game, he does not react as she brushes against his lips. She throbs unbearably. This might go on for a very long time, never mind her begging, and when he is ready, and only then, he bites, but not hard enough to leave a mark because he can't abide the idea of being anything like Jean-Baptiste, his brother.

Jay used to smell and taste so good. Now that he is a fugitive, he rarely bathes, and when he does, he simply dumps buckets of bayou water over his body. Bev dares not complain or react in the slightest way to the strong stench of his breath and groin. The one and only time she gagged, he broke her nose and forced her to finish, her blood and small cries of pain giving him pleasure.

When she cleans the shack, she obsessively scrubs that spot below the bed, but the bloodstains are stubborn, like something out of a horror movie, she thinks. Bleach has left a mottled whitish-brown area the size of a doormat that Jay constantly complains about, as if he had nothing to do with how it got there.

12

Jean-Baptiste Chandonne is Rodin's *The Thinker* on the stainless-steel toilet, his white pants drooping around his furry knees.

Corrections officers make fun of him. It never stops. He can sense it as he perches on the toilet, staring at the locked steel door of his cell. The iron bars in its tiny window are drawn to the iron in Jean-Baptiste's blood. Animal magnetism is a scientific fact scarcely heard of now and, for the most part, not accepted centuries ago, even though there are documented cases of magnetized materials having been applied to diseased and damaged parts of the body, causing all symptoms to cease, the patient's health restored. Jean-Baptiste is well schooled in the doctrine of the famous Dr. Mesmer, whose system of treatment is eloquently laid out in his *Mémoire sur la Découverte du Magnétisme Animal*.

The original work, first published in French in 1779, is Jean-Baptiste's Bible. Before his books and radio were confiscated, he memorized long sections of Mesmer, and he is devout in his belief that a universal magnetic fluid influences the tides and people.

"I possessed the usual knowledge about the magnet: its action on iron, the ability of our body fluids to receive that mineral . . ." Mesmer wrote, and Jean-Baptiste quotes under his breath as he thinks on the toilet. "I prepared the patient by the continuous use of chalybeates."

A chalybeate is an iron tonic, and who but Jean-Baptiste knows this? If only he could find a chalybeate, just the right one, he would be healed. Before he was in prison, he tried soaking iron nails in drinking water, eating rust, sleeping with pieces of iron under his bed and pillow, and carrying nuts and bolts and magnets in the pockets of his pants. He came to believe that his chalybeate is the iron in human blood, but he could not get enough of it before he went to prison, and he can't get it at all now. When, on rare occasion, he bites himself and sucks, it makes no difference but is the equivalent of one drinking his own blood to cure himself of anemia.

Franz Anton Mesmer was mocked by the religious and scientific community, just as Jean-Baptiste has always been mocked. True believers publicly feigned skepticism—or if they were believers, used pseudonyms to avoid being labeled as quacks. *The Philosophy of Animal Magnetism*, published in 1837, for example, was written by "A Gentleman in Philadelphia," who some suspect was Edgar Allan Poe. Such books ended up in universities and were eventually discarded by their libraries, allowing Jean-Baptiste to acquire a small but amazing collection for a pittance.

He obsesses about what has happened to his books. His pulse pounds in his neck as he strains on the toilet. The books he brought here from France were taken from him as punishment when the prison's classification team demoted him from a level-one status to a level-three, supposedly because he masturbates and commits food infractions. Jean-Baptiste spends much of the time on the toilet, and the officers call this masturbating.

Twice in one day—he forgets how long ago—he fumbled his meal trays as they were shoved through the slot at the bottom of his door. Food splattered everywhere, and the incidents were deemed deliberate. He has been deprived of all commissaries, including, of course, his books. He is allowed only one hour of recreation per week. It doesn't matter. He can write letters. The guards are baffled.

"He can write fucking letters when he's blind?" they say.

"Don't know for sure he is. Seems like sometimes he is, and sometimes he ain't."

"Faking?"

"Fucking crazy, man."

Jean-Baptiste can do push-ups, sit-ups and jumping jacks whenever he pleases inside his sixty-four-square-foot cell. His number of visits from the outside world has been limited. That doesn't matter, either. Who asks to see him except reporters and those physicians, profilers and academic types who wish to study him as if he is a new strain of virus? Jean-Baptiste's incarceration, abuse and imminent death have condensed his soul into a bright light scattered with white specks.

He's perpetually magnetized and somnambulant, and his clairvoyance gives him clear-sightedness without eyes. He has ears but does not need them to hear. He can know without knowing and go anywhere without the body that has punished him since birth. Jean-Baptiste has never known anything but hate. Before he attempted to murder the lady forensic pathologist in Virginia and was finally captured by police, intense hatred flowed through others, through him, and returned to others, the circuit complete and infinite. His violent rampages were inevitable, and he does not hold his body responsible for them and suffers no remorse.

After two years on death row, Jean-Baptiste exists in a perpetual state of magnetism and no longer suffers from negativity toward any living being. This does not imply that he would no longer kill. Given the opportunity, he would rip women apart as he did in the past, but his electricity is not charged by hate and lust. He would destroy beautiful females to answer his higher calling, to complete a pure circuit that is necessary and godly. His delicious ecstasy would flow through his chosen ones. Their pain and deaths would be beautiful, and his chosen ones would be eternally grateful to him as their minds detached from their bodies.

"Who's there?" he demands of the stale, foul air.

He pushes the roll of toilet paper toward his small bunk, watching the unfurling of a soft white highway that will take him beyond his cinder-block walls. Today, perhaps, he will go to Beaune and visit his favorite twelfth-century cave at the domain of Monsieur Cambrai and taste Burgundies from casks of his choosing and not bother pulling air into his mouth and spitting the wine into a stone bowl, as is proper when tasting the treasures of *le terroire.* He cannot waste a drop! Ha! Let's see, which grand *vins de Bourgogne* this time? He touches an index finger to his deformed lips.

His father, Monsieur Chandonne, owns vineyards in Beaune. He owns wine makers and exporters. Jean-Baptiste is very knowledgeable about wines, even if they were denied him when he was confined to the basement and then banished from his family home. His intimacy with Beaune is a rich fantasy projected from his charming brother's detailed stories of wines to remind Jean-Baptiste of his deprivation and nonexistence. Ha! Jean-Baptiste does not need a tongue to taste. He knows the confident Clos de Vougeot, and the soft, complex and elegant red Clos de Mouches.

Nineteen ninety-seven was a very good year for red Clos de Mouches, and the 1980 white wine hints of hazelnuts and is so special. And, oh, the harmony of the Echezeaux! But it is the king of Burgundies that he loves most, the muscular and bigger-built Chambertins. Of the 280 bottles produced in 1999, Monsieur Chandonne acquired 150 for his cave. Of those 150, Jean-Baptiste got not a sip. But after one of his murders in Paris, he robbed her and celebrated with a 1998 Chambertin that tasted of roses and minerals and reminded him of her blood. As for Bordeaux? A Premier Grand Cru Classé, perhaps the 1984 Château Haut-Brion.

"Who's there?" he calls out.

"Shut up and quit fucking with the toilet paper! Pick it up."

Jean-Baptiste does not have to look to see the angry eyes peering through the bars in the door.

"Roll it up nice and neat, and quit playing with your Mini-Me dick!"

The eyes disappear, leaving cool air. Jean-Baptiste must leave for Beaune, where there are no eyes. He must find his next chosen one and rip away her flawed sight and beat her brains into forgetfulness so she will not remember her revulsion when she saw him. Then her domain is his. Her hillsides and luscious clusters of grapes belong to him. Her cave is his to explore, to feel his way along dark, damp walls that become cooler the longer he takes. Her blood is fine red wine, whichever vintage he craves. Reds, reds, splashing and running down his arms, turning his hair red and sticky, making his teeth ache with joy!

"Who's there?"

Rarely is he answered.

After two years, the corrections officers assigned to death row are weary of the mutant madman Jean-Baptiste Chandonne. They look forward to the end of him. The French wolfman with his deformed penis and hairy body is repulsive. His face is asymmetrical, as if the two sides were not lined up when they were put together in the womb, one eye lower than the other, his tiny baby teeth widely spaced and pointed. Until recently, he shaved daily. Jean-Baptiste doesn't shave now. This is his right. The last four months before execution, the condemned inmate doesn't have to shave. He can go to the death chamber with long hair and a beard.

Other inmates do not have baby-fine swirls of hair that cover every inch of their bodies except for the mucous membranes and the palms and the soles of their feet. Jean-Baptiste has not shaved himself in two months, and three-inch-long hair covers his lean, ropy body, his entire face and neck, even the back of his hands. Other death-row inmates joke that Jean-Baptiste's victims died of fright before he had a chance to beat and bite them into hamburger.

"Hamburger! Help her!"

The taunts are meant for Jean-Baptiste to hear, and he receives written cruelties, too, in the form of notes—or *kites*, as they are called—that are passed through cracks beneath the doors, cell to cell, like chain letters, until he is the final recipient. He chews the notes to pulp and swallows them. Some days as many as ten. He can taste each word, they say.

"Too bad we won't be strapping his hairy ass in a chair, then he'd be cooked well-done. Fried." He has overheard officers say words to that effect.

"The whole joint would smell like burning hair."

"It ain't right that we don't get to shave them bald as a cue ball before they get the needle."

"It ain't right they don't get fried anymore. Now it's too fuckin' easy. A little needle prick and nighty-night."

"We'll chill the juice extra good for the Wolfman."

13

Jean-Baptiste strains on the toilet, as if he is hearing these derisive comments now, although it is silent outside his door.

Chilling the juice is a dirty secret of tie-down and IV teams who want their little bit of sadistic fun at each execution. Whoever is in charge of the lethal drugs places them in an ice chest when transporting them from a locked refrigerator to the death chamber. Jean-Baptiste has overheard death-row inmates claim that the drugs are chilled beyond what's necessary, almost to the freezing point. The teams think it only fair that the condemned inmate feel the frigid intravenous hit, as enough poison to kill four horses rushes through the needle and shocks the blood. If the inmate doesn't exclaim, "Oh, God!" or, "Jesus!" or some utterance when he feels his icy, imminent death, the members of the execution teams are disappointed and a bit pissed off.

"That last ol' boy sure as hell had an ice-cream headache," voices yell and bounce off steel doors as inmates retell the stories.

"A screamin' one. You hear how he puckered when the shit hit?"

"No way that was on the radio."

"He begged for his mama."

"A lot of the whores I done begged for their mama. Last one screamed, 'Mama! Mama! Mama!'" The man the other inmates call Beast is bragging again.

He thinks his anecdotes are funny.

"You're a fucker. Can't believe the governor gave you another month, you fucker!"

Beast is the source of most of the execution stories circulating through the cells in the death-row pod. Beast was transported by van the forty-three miles to Huntsville and was already eating his last meal of fried shrimp, steak, fries and pecan pie in the barred cage next to the death chamber when the governor suddenly granted him a stay of execution so further DNA tests could be run. Beast knows damn well the tests are a waste of time, but he continues to milk what he can out of his last days on Earth now that he has been returned to the Polunsky Unit. He goes on and on about a process that is supposed to be secret. He even knows the names of the members of the tie-down and IV teams and the doctor who was scheduled to start the IV and pronounce Beast dead.

"If I ever get out, I'm going to do every one of the bitches and videotape it!" Beast brags some more.

"Wish I videotaped the ones I did. Hell, I'd pay all I got for even one videotape. Don't know why I didn't think of it at the time. Give those shrinks and FBI assholes an eyeful to worry about when they go home to their little wives and kiddies."

Jean-Baptiste never filmed his murders. There wasn't time, and stupidly, the idea never occurred to him. For that he continually rebukes himself. How rare it is for him to be so stupid . . .

Espèce de sale gorille . . .

Stupid monkey mutant.

Jean-Baptiste covers his ears with his hands.

"Who's there?"

If only he had filmed his bloody art or at least had taken photographs. Oh, the longing, the longing, the anxiety he cannot relieve because he cannot relive, relive, relive their ecstasy as they died. The thought turns the key on an unbearable pressure in his groin. He can't relieve the misery. He was born with an ignition that doesn't work, sexual pistons that spark but will not fire. He breathes hard, straining on the toilet, sweat dripping from his face.

14

"What you doing in there?"

An officer bangs on the door. Two mocking dark eyes are there again, between the bars in the window.

"Playing ring-around-the-ass again. Man, your guts are gonna come out one of these days."

Jean-Baptiste hears footsteps on metal catwalks and other death-row inmates yelling their usual complaints and obscenities. Not including Jean-Baptiste, 245 men wait their turn while lawyers continue appeals and do what they can to persuade district supreme courts or the U.S. Supreme Court to overturn a sentence or at least convince a judge to rule in their favor and allow DNA tests or some other trickery. Jean-Baptiste knows what he did and pled guilty, despite the histrionics of his attorney, Rocco Caggiano, also owned by the Chandonne family.

Rocco Caggiano's feigned vigorous opposition to Jean-Baptiste's pleading guilty before the judge was very poor acting. Caggiano abides by his instructions, just as Jean-Baptiste seems to do, only Jean-Baptiste is a very good actor. The Chandonne family believes it best for their shameful, disgusting son to die.

Why would you want to sit on death row for ten years? they reasoned with him. *Why would you want to be released back into a society that will hunt you down like a monster?*

At first Jean-Baptiste could not accept that his family would want him to die. He accepts it now. It makes sense. Why would his family care if he dies when they never cared that he lived? He has no choice. It is clear. If he didn't plead guilty, his father would have seen to it that Jean-Baptiste was murdered while awaiting trial.

Prison is such a dangerous place, his father softly told him in French over the phone. *Remember what happened to the cannibal Jeffrey Dahmer? He was beaten to death with a mop, or maybe it was a broom.*

Jean-Baptiste was emotionally beaten to death, all hope gone, when his father said that. Jean-Baptiste relied on his mind and meticulously began to study his predicament as he was flown to Houston. He vividly remembers the *Welcome to Humble* sign and a Holiday Inn with a Hole in One Café, which made no sense, since he saw no golf courses in the area, only parched leaves and dead trees and what seemed to be an endless stretch of slack telephone lines, scrubby pines, feed stores, mobile homes, decapitated buildings and prefabricated houses on cinder blocks. His motorcade turned off North 59, all those federal and local agents treating Jean-Baptiste like Frankenstein.

He sat, perfectly well behaved, in the backseat of a white Ford LTD, manacled like Houdini. The motorcade turned onto a deserted road overgrown with brush that thickened into dense forests on either side, and when they reached the Texas Department of Criminal Justice's Polunsky Unit, he felt the sun reclaim gray skies, and the day turned bright. Jean-Baptiste took it as a sign.

He waits patiently. He imagines meteor showers and great battalions marching because he wills it. How simple! People are fools! They set up such foolish rules! Prison officials can take away his radio and punish him by grinding up his meals and cooking them into food loaves, but no one can neutralize his magnetism and legal right to send and receive uncensored mail. If he marks an envelope or package *Legal Mail* or *Media Mail*, no prison employee can open it. Jean-Baptiste sends mail to Rocco Caggiano whenever he pleases. Now and then he receives mail the same way. That is the most special treat of all, especially when Madame Scarpetta wrote him recently because she cannot forget him. She was so close to ecstasy and by her own foolishness robbed herself, cheated herself, of Jean-Baptiste's benevolence. His selfless intention was to make her lovely body let go of her soul. Her passing would have been perfect. Finally, she realizes her terrible mistake and now makes an excuse to see him.

I will see you again.

Jean-Baptiste has enough information to topple the entire Chandonne cartel.

If that is what she wants, why not? When she comes, he will find a way to finish her release, to bless her with what she wants. The ecstasy. The ecstasy!

He tore her letter into small pieces and ate each word, chewing so hard he cut his gums.

Jean-Baptiste lifts himself off the toilet and doesn't bother flushing. He yanks up his pants.

"Who's there?"

The white V-neck shirt has *DR* for Death Row in large letters stenciled in black on the back. It is the abbreviation for doctor. Another sign. He is hers for now, and she is his forever. His prison fatigues are soaking wet with sweat. They stink. He sweats constantly and smells like a dirty animal. He smiles as he thinks of the last inmate executed several weeks ago, an old man named Pitt who killed a policeman in Atlanta. Pitt murdered prostitutes for years without mishap, dumping his victims in parking lots or the middle of the road. He broke the code when he stabbed a policeman thirteen times.

The rumor in the pod is that when the doctor sent the fatal cocktail speeding through Pitt's IV tube like a train through a tunnel, death occurred in exactly two minutes and fifty-six seconds. Three physicians take turns working the executions—again, more stories from the media and from inmates who have returned from Huntsville after stays of execution. There is a pediatrician, a heart surgeon, and a woman who set up a family practice in Lufkin a few years ago. She is the coldest executioner of all. She comes in with her black bag, does her job and leaves, indifferent and arrogant, speaking to no one.

It arouses Jean-Baptiste to fantasize about a woman doctor invisible in a small secret room, waiting for the signal to kill his strapped-down body. He does not fear the death of his body, for his mind is his soul and cannot be destroyed. He is electric. He is a fluid. He can detach his mind from his body. He is part of God. Jean-Baptiste sighs in his bunk, where he lies on his back, staring up at a ceiling that is incapable of preventing his clairvoyant journeys. Most of the time, he transports his spirit back to Paris and flies unnoticed, acutely aware of sounds in a way he never was before. He visited Paris just the other day, right after a light rain, and tires swished on wet pavement, and distant traffic was surprisingly guttural, reminding him of his stomach growling. Raindrops were diamonds scattered over the seats of parked motorcycles, and a woman carrying lilies walked past him, and he floated in perfume.

How observant he has become! Whenever his soul visits Paris, the most beautiful city on Earth, he discovers another old building wrapped in green netting, and men blasting limestone with air hoses to clean away centuries of pollution. It has taken years to restore Notre Dame's creamy complexion. Monitoring the work is how Jean-Baptiste measures time. He never stays in Paris more than a few days, and each night he sets out toward the Gare de Lyon, then to the Quai de la Rapée to gaze at the Institut Médico-Légal, where some of his earlier chosen ones were autopsied. He can see the women's faces and bodies, and he remembers their names. He waits until the last Bateau-Mouche thrums by, until the last ripple of wake laps over his shoes before he strips naked on the cold stones of the Quai de Bourbon.

All his life he has braved the murky cold currents of the Seine to wash away the curse of le Loup-Garou.

The werewolf.

His nocturnal bathing has not cured his hypertrichosis, the extremely rare birth defect that causes babylike hair to cover his body, and continues its cruelty by adding a deformed face, abnormal teeth and stunted genitalia. Jean-Baptiste immerses himself in the river. He drifts along the Quai d'Orléans and the Quai de Béthune to the eastern tip of the Ile St.-Louis. There on the Quai d'Anjou is the seventeenth-century four-story town house with its carved front doors and gilded drainpipes, the *hôtel particulier* where his prominent parents live in obscene luxury. When chandeliers are ablaze with crystal and silver, his parents are in, but often they socialize with friends or drink their nightcaps in a sitting room that cannot be seen from the street.

During Jean-Baptiste's disembodied travels, he can go into any room of the *hôtel particulier*. He moves about as he pleases. The other night when he visited the Ile St.-Louis, his obese mother had several more folds of fat beneath her chin, and her eyes were as small as raisins in her bloated face. She had wrapped herself in a black silk robe and wore matching slippers on her stubby feet. She smoked strong French cigarettes nonstop as she complained and chattered to her husband while he watched the news, talked on the phone and went through paperwork.

Just as Jean-Baptiste can hear without ears, his father can become deaf at will. It is no wonder he seeks relief and pleasure in the arms of many beautiful young women and only remains married to Madame Chandonne because that is the way it must be. At a young age, Jean-Baptiste was told hypertrichosis is congenital, but he is certain it was caused by his mother's alcoholism. She made no effort to curtail her drunkenness while she was pregnant with him and his twin brother, who calls himself Jay Talley and had the good fortune to emerge from their mother's womb less than three minutes after Jean-Baptiste. His brother was born a perfect specimen of maleness, a golden sculpture with an exquisite body touched by blond hair that catches light, his face formed by a master. He dazzles everyone he meets, and the only satisfaction Jean-Baptiste finds in the injustice of their births is that Jay Talley, whose real name is Jean-Paul Chandonne, does not look like what he is. For that reason, he is worse than Jean-Baptiste.

It is not lost on Jean-Baptiste that the several minutes separating his birth from his brother's is how long it is supposed to take for Jean-Baptiste to die on May 7. Several minutes is about how long his chosen ones lived, as blood spattered walls in peaks and valleys that looked very much like an abstract painting he once saw and wished badly he could buy, but had no money and no place to hang it.

"Who's there!" he screams.

15

The Charles River reflects the fledgling green of spring along Boston's embankment, and Benton Wesley watches young men row a racing shell in perfect rhythm.

Muscles ripple like the gentle current, paddles dip in whispered plashes. He could watch and say nothing all afternoon. The day is perfect, without a cloud, the temperature seventy-five degrees. Benton has become a close companion of isolation and silence, and craves them to the extreme that conversation fatigues him and is weighted by long pauses that intimidate some people and irritate others. He rarely has more to say than the homeless people who sleep in rag piles beneath the Arthur Fiedler footbridge. He even managed to offend the loud, gregarious Max, who works in the Café Esplanade, where Benton on occasion buys rootbeer and Cracker Jacks or a soft pretzel. The first comment Benton ever made to Max was taken the wrong way.

"Change." That was all Benton muttered with a shake of his head.

Max, who is German and often mistranslates English and takes umbrage easily, interpreted the cryptic remark to mean that that smart-ass in running clothes and dark sunglasses thinks all foreigners are inferior and dishonest and was demanding the change due him from the five-dollar bill Max tucked inside the till. In other words, the hardworking Max is a thief.

What Benton meant was that Cracker Jacks at the Café Esplanade are served in bags, not boxes, and cost a dollar instead of a quarter. The toy surprises inside are games printed on folded white paper, cheap as hell, and require the IQ of a pigeon. Gone are the days of Benton's childhood, when his sticky fingers dug through caramel-glazed popcorn and peanuts for treasure, such as a plastic whistle or BB game or, best of all, the magic decoding ring that little Benton wore on his index finger, pretending it empowered him to know what people thought, what they would do and which monster he would defeat on his next secret mission.

The irony isn't lost on him that he grew up to wear a special ring—this one gold and engraved with the FBI crest—and became the champion of decoding the thoughts, motivations and actions of people the public calls monsters. Benton was born with a special gift for channeling his intuition and intellect into the neurological and spiritual abysses of the worst of the worst. His quarry was the elusive offenders whose violent sexual acts were so heinous that panicking police from the United States and abroad used to wait in line to review their cases with him in the FBI Academy's Profiling Unit in Quantico, Virginia. Benton Wesley was the legendary unit chief who wore conservative suits and a large gold ring.

It was believed that from reports and nightmarish photographs, he could divine some clue that investigators missed, as if there was a magic prize to be rooted out during sessions inside the dank, windowless space where the only sounds were grim voices, papers sliding across the conference room table, and distant muffled shots from the indoor firing range. Benton's world for most of his FBI career was J. Edgar Hoover's former bomb shelter, an airless bunker belowground where pipes from the Academy's upper-level toilets sometimes leaked on worn carpet or ran in stinking trickles down cinder-block walls.

Benton is fifty and has reached the bitter belief that psychological profiling isn't psychological in the least, but is nothing more than forms and assumptions based on decades-old data. Profiling is propaganda and marketing. It is hype. It is just one more sales pitch that helps rake in federal dollars as FBI lobbyists stalk Capitol Hill. The very word *profiling* makes Wesley grit his teeth, and he can't abide the way what he used to do is misunderstood, abused, has become a hackneyed Hollywood device drawn from worn-out and faulty behavioral science, anecdotes and deductive assumptions. Modern profiling is not inductive. It is as specious and misleading as physiognomy and anthropometry—or the dangerous and ridiculous beliefs from centuries past that murderers looked like cavemen and could be unequivocally identified by the circumference of their heads or the length of their arms. Profiling is fool's gold, and for Benton to come around to that conviction is akin to a priest deciding there is no God.

No matter what anybody says, no matter what statistics and epidemiological studies suggest and intellectual gurus pontificate, the only constant anymore is *change*. Human beings today commit more murders, rapes, pedophilia, kidnapings, hate crimes, acts of terrorism and just plain dishonest, dishonorable, self-serving sins against all forms of life than the free world has ever seen. Benton obsesses about it a lot. He has plenty of time to do so. Max thinks Benton, whose name he does not know, is a wacko intellectual snob, probably a professor at Harvard or MIT, and a humorless one at that. Max does not catch the occasional irony or dry-ice wit that Benton was known for when he was known, and he is known by virtually no one anymore.

Max no longer speaks a word to him, just takes his money and makes a big production of counting Benton's change before shoving it and a slice of cheese pizza or a soda or a bag of Cracker Jacks to the "Scheiße Arsch."

He talks about Benton every chance he gets.

"The other day he buy a pretzel," Max told Nosmo King, the delivery man whose mystical-sounding name is the mundane result of his mother seeing *No Smoking* divided into *No Smo king* when double doors parted as she was being rolled into the delivery room to give birth to him.

"He eats his pretzel there"—Max stabbed his cigarette toward a canopy of old oaks—"and schtared up like some schzombie at that schtuck kite"—pointing the cigarette again and nodding at the tattered red kite high in the branches of an oak tree—"like it some schientific phenomenal or a schymbol from God. Maybe a UFO!"

Nosmo King was stacking cases of Fiji bottled water inside the Café Esplanade kiosk and paused, shielding his eyes from the sun as he followed the line of Max's cigarette up to the wrecked kite.

"I remember how that used to piss me off as a kid," Nosmo King recalled. "Get yourself a brand new kite and five minutes later it's hung up in power lines or a fucking tree. That sure is life.

One minute things are moving along good, the next, the wind blows your ass to ruination."

Dark preoccupations and shadows from the past are what Benton feels and sees, no matter where he is or what he does. He lives inside a steel box of isolation that depresses and frustrates him so profoundly that there are moments, hours, days and weeks when he does not care about anything, has no appetite and sleeps too much. He needs sun and dreads winter. He is grateful that this early afternoon is polished so brightly that he cannot look across the Charles or up at the intense blue sky unless his eyes are blacked out, as they usually are, by sunglasses. He casually turns away from the young athletes who rule the river, pained that half a century has passed and he is no longer consumed by courage and conquest but by nonexistence, powerlessness and irrevocable loss.

I am dead, he says to himself every morning as he shaves. *No matter what, I am dead.*

My name is Tom. Tom Haviland. Tom Speck Haviland, born in Greenwich, Connecticut, on February 20, 1955, parents both from Salem, Massachusetts. A psychologist, retired, sick of listening to people's problems, Social Security number yada yada yada, unmarried, homosexual, HIV-positive, like to eye gorgeous boys eying themselves in the mirrors at the gym but don't pursue, don't strike up conversations, don't cruise gay bars or date. Ever, ever, ever.

It is all a lie.

Benton Wesley has lived with falsehoods and exile for six years.

He walks to a picnic table and sits on top of it, rests his arms on his knees, tightly laces his tapered fingers. His heart begins to beat rapidly with excitement and fear. Decades of a well-meant pursuit of justice have been rewarded by banishment, by a forced acceptance of the nonexistence of himself and all he has ever known. Some days, he can scarcely remember who he used to be, as he spends most of his time living in his mind, distracted by and even content with reading philosophical and spiritual books, history and poetry, and feeding the pigeons in the Public Garden, around the Frog Pond, or wherever he can blend with the locals and tourists.

He no longer owns a suit. He shaves his thick, silver hair to the scalp and wears a neatly trimmed mustache and beard, but his body and bearing belie his attempt to look sloppy and older than his years. His face is tan but smooth, his posture military-straight. He is fit and muscular, with so little body fat that his veins run under his flesh like slender tree roots pushing through soil. Boston has many health clubs and places to jog and run sprints, and he is relentless about fitness and staying light on his feet. Physical pain reminds him that he is alive. He does not allow himself patterns for when and where he runs or works out or shops or eats in restaurants.

He turns to his right as his keen peripheral vision catches the lumbering form of Pete Marino strolling in his direction. Benton's breath catches. He is electrified by anxiety and joy but does not wave or smile. He has not communicated with his old friend and former colleague since he supposedly died and vanished into what is called a level-one protected-witness program designed uniquely for him and jointly controlled by London's Metropolitan Police, Washington and Interpol.

Marino settles next to Benton on top of the picnic table, checking first for bird shit as he taps an unfiltered Lucky Strike from a soft pack and lights up after several sparked attempts with a disposable lighter low on fluid. Benton notes that Marino's hands are shaking. The two men are hunched over, staring out at a sailboat gliding away from the boathouse.

"You ever go to the band shell here?" Marino asks, overcome by emotions he strangles in his throat with repeated coughs and loud sucks of smoke.

"I heard the Boston Pops on the Fourth of July," Benton softly says. "You can't help but hear them from where I live. How are you?"

"But you don't come down in person." Marino does his best to sound normal, just like the old days. "Yeah, I can understand that. Me, I probably wouldn't, either, all those mobs of idiots, and I hate mobs of people. Like in the malls. It's gotten to where I can't take shopping malls no more." He blows out a large volume of smoke, the unfiltered cigarette trembling in his thick fingers. "Least you ain't so far away you can't hear the music, pal. Could be worse. That's what I always say, *could be worse.*"

Benton's lean, handsome face does not register the volatile mix of thoughts and feelings inside his hidden places. His hands betray nothing. He controls his nerves and facial expressions. He is nobody's pal and never has been, and acute grief and anger heat up powerfully. Marino called him *pal* because he doesn't know what else to call him.

"I suppose I should ask you not to call me *pal*," Benton comments in a bland voice.

"Sure. What the fuck." Marino shrugs, stung.

For a big, tough cop, he is overly sensitive and takes the world personally. His capacity for interpreting an honest remark as an insult wearies those who know him and terrifies those who don't. Marino has a temper from hell, and his fury knows no bounds when he is sufficiently pissed off. The only reason he hasn't been killed during one of his outbursts is that his physical strength and survival skills are mixed with a strong dose of experience and luck. Even so, chance is never favorable forever. As Benton takes in every

73

detail of Marino's appearance, he entertains the same worries from the past. He's going to be dropped by a bullet or a stroke one of these days.

"I sure as hell can't call you *Tom*," Marino counters. "Not to your face."

"Be my guest. I'm used to it."

Marino's jaw muscles flex as he smokes.

"You taking care of yourself better or worse since I saw you last?" Benton stares down at his relaxed hands between his knees. His fingers slowly toy with a splinter he picks off the picnic table. "Although I think the answer is obvious," he adds with a slight smile.

Sweat rolls down Marino's balding head. He shifts his position, conscious of the 40-caliber Glock pistol strapped under his huge left arm and his desire to snatch off his bowling team windbreaker. Beneath it he is soaking wet, his heart beating hard, the dark blue nylon absorbing sunlight like a sponge. He exhales a cloud of smoke, hopes it doesn't drift in Benton's direction. It does. Right in his face.

"Thanks."

"Don't mention it. I can't call you Tom."

Marino ogles a young woman in spandex shorts and sports bra trotting by, breasts bobbing. He can't get used to females running around in bras, and for a veteran homicide detective who has seen hundreds of naked women in his day—most of them in strip joints or on top of autopsy tables—he is surprisingly awed when he sees a female so scantily clad in public that he knows exactly what she looks like naked, right down to the size of her nipples.

"My daughter ran around like that, I'd kill her," he mutters, staring at the retreating pumping buttocks.

"The world is grateful you don't have a daughter, Pete," Benton remarks.

"No shit. Especially if she got my looks. Probably would've ended up some dyke professional wrestler."

"I don't know about that. Rumor has it, you used to be quite the hunk."

Benton has seen photographs of Marino when he was a uniformed cop for NYPD in the long-ago days of his fledgling career. He was broad-shouldered and fine-looking, a real stud, before he let himself go to hell, unrelenting in his self-abuse, as if he hates his own flesh, as if he wants to kill it off and get it out of his way.

Benton climbs down from the picnic table. He and Marino start walking toward the footbridge.

"Oops." Marino smiles slyly. "Forgot you was gay. Guess I should be more sensitive about queers and dyke wrestlers, huh? But you try to hold my hand, I'll tear your head off."

Marino has always been homophobic, but never as uncomfortable and confused as he is at this stage in his life. His conviction that gay men are perverts and that lesbians can be cured by sex with men has evolved from clear as air to dark as ink. He can see neither in nor out of what he believes about people who lust for their own gender, and his cynical, ugly comments have the flat ring of a bell cast in lead. Not much is plain to him anymore. Not much seems unquestionably true. At least when he was devoutly bigoted, he didn't have to question. In the beginning, he lived by the gospel according to Marino. Over recent years, he has become an agnostic, a compass with no magnetic north. His convictions wobble all over the place.

"So what's it feel like to have people think you're . . . you know?" Marino asks. "Hope nobody's tried to beat you up or nothing."

"I feel nothing about what people think of me," Benton says under his breath, conscious of people passing them on the footbridge, of cars speeding below them on Storrow Drive, as if any person within a hundred feet of them might be watching and listening. "When's the last time you went fishing?"

16

Marino's demeanor sours as they follow a cobblestone walk in the shade of double rows of Japanese cherry trees, maples and blue spruce.

During his most venomous moods, usually late at night when he is alone and throwing back beers or shots of bourbon, he resents Benton Wesley, almost despises him for how much he has damaged the lives of everyone who matters. If Benton really were dead, it would be easier. Marino tells himself he would have gotten over it by now. But how does he recover from a loss that didn't happen and live with its secrets?

So when Marino is alone and drunk and has worked himself into a rabid state, he swears out loud at Benton while crushing one beer can after another and hurling them across his small, slovenly living room.

"Look what you've done to her!" he rails to the walls. "Look what you've done to her, you fucking son of a bitch!"

Dr. Kay Scarpetta is an apparition between Marino and Benton as they walk. She is one of the most brilliant and remarkable women Marino has ever met, and Benton's torture and murder ripped off her skin. She stumbles over Benton's dead body everywhere she goes, and all along—from day one—Marino has known that Benton's gruesome homicide was faked right down to the autopsy and lab reports, death certificate and the ashes Scarpetta scattered into the wind at Hilton Head Island, a seaside resort she and Benton loved.

The ashes and bits of bone were scraped from the bottom of a crematorium oven in Philadelphia. Leftovers. God knows whose. Marino presented them to Scarpetta in a cheap little urn given to him at the Philadelphia Medical Examiner's Office, and all he could think to say was, "Sorry, Doc. I sure am sorry, Doc." Sweating in a suit and tie and standing on wet sand, he watched her fling those ashes into the wind of a hovering helicopter piloted by Lucy. In a hurricane of churning water and flying blades, the supposed remains of Scarpetta's lover were hurled as far out of reach as her pain. Marino stared at Lucy's hard face staring back at him through Plexiglas as she did exactly what her aunt had asked her to do, and all the while, Lucy knew, too.

Scarpetta trusts Lucy and Marino more than anyone else in her life. They helped plan Benton's staged murder and disappearance, and that truth is a brain infection, a sickness they battle daily, while Benton lives his life as a nobody named Tom.

"I guess no fishing," Benton goes on in the same light tone.

"They ain't biting." But Marino's anger is. His fury bares its fangs.

"I see. Not a single fish. And bowling? Last I remember, you were second in your league. The Firing Pins. I believe that was the name of your team."

"Last century, yeah. I don't spend time in Virginia. Only when

I get dragged back down to Richmond for court. I'm not with their PD anymore. In the process of moving to Florida and signing on with the Hollywood PD, south of Lauderdale."

"If you're in Florida," Benton points out, "when you go to Richmond, it's *up* to Richmond, not *down* to Richmond. One thing you've always had is an amazing sense of direction, Pete."

Marino's caught in a lie, and he knows it. He constantly thinks of moving from Richmond. It shames him that he doesn't have the nerve. It is all he knows, even if there is nothing left for him in that city of old battles that continue to rage.

"I didn't come here to bother you with long stories," Marino says.

Benton's dark glasses glance in his direction as the two of them continue their leisurely pace.

"Well, I can tell you've missed me," Benton comments, a splinter of ice in his tone.

"It ain't fucking fair," Marino hisses, his fists clenched by his sides. "And I can't take it no more, *pal*. Lucy can't take it no more, *pal*. I wish you could be a fucking fly on the wall and see what you done to her. The Doc. Scarpetta. Or maybe you don't remember her, either."

"Did you come here to project your own anger onto me?"

"I just thought while I was in the neighborhood I'd point out, now that I got your attention, that I don't see how dying can be worse than the way you live."

"Be quiet," Benton quietly says with flinty self-control. "We'll talk inside."

17

In an area of Beacon Hill lined with proud old brick homes and graceful trees, Benton Wesley managed to find an address to suit his present, peculiar needs.

His apartment building is ugly beige precast with plastic lawn chairs on balconies and a rusting wrought-iron fence that encloses a front yard, overgrown and depressingly dark. He and Marino take dimly lit stairs that smell of urine and stale cigarette smoke.

"Shit!" Marino gasps for breath. "Couldn'tcha at least find a joint with an elevator? I didn't mean nothing by what I said. About dying. Nobody wants you to die."

On the fifth landing, Benton unlocks the scratched gray metal door to apartment 56.

"Most people already think I did."

"Shit. I can't say anything right." Marino wipes sweat off his face.

"I've got Dos Equis and limes." Benton's voice seems to mimic the flip of the dead-bolt lock. "And, of course, fresh juice."

"No Budweiser?"

"Please make yourself comfortable."

"You got Budweiser, don't you?" Pain sounds in Marino's voice. Benton doesn't remember anything about him.

"Since I knew you were coming, of course I have Budweiser," Benton says from the kitchen. "An entire refrigerator full of it."

Marino looks around and decides on a floral printed couch, not a nice one. The apartment is furnished and bears the dingy patina of many threadbare and careless lives that have come and gone. Benton probably hasn't lived in a decent place since he died and became Tom, and Marino sometimes wonders how the meticulous, refined man stands it. Benton is from a wealthy New England family and has always enjoyed a privileged life, although no amount of money would be enough ransom to free him from the horrors of his career. To see Benton living in an apartment typically occupied by partying college students or the lower middle class—to see him with a shaved head, facial hair, baggy jeans and sweatshirt, and to know he doesn't even own a car—is unimaginable to Marino.

"At least you're in good shape," Marino remarks with a yawn.

"*At least*, meaning that's the best you can say about me." Benton ducks inside the old white refrigerator and emerges with two beers.

The cold bottles clank together in one hand as he opens a drawer, rooting around for a church key, as Marino calls any gadget that flips the cap off a beer.

"Mind if I smoke?" Marino asks.

"Yes." Benton opens and shuts a cabinet door.

"Okay, so I'll go into fits and swallow my tongue."

"I didn't say you couldn't smoke." Benton walks across the dim, shabby living room and hands Marino a Budweiser. "I said I minded."

He hands him a water glass that will have to do for an ashtray.

"Yeah, so maybe you're in shape and don't smoke and all the rest"—Marino gets back to that as he takes a slug of beer and sighs contentedly—"but your life sucks."

Benton takes a seat across from Marino, the space between them occupied by a scratched Formica-topped coffee table neatly lined with news magazines and the television remote control.

"I don't need you to drop out of the sky to tell me my life sucks," he says. "If that's why you're here, I wish to hell you'd never come. You've violated the program, put me at risk . . ."

"And put myself at risk," Marino snaps.

"I was about to point that out." Benton's voice heats up, his eyes burning. "We know damn well my being *Tom* isn't just about me. If it was just about me, I would let them take their best shot."

Marino begins picking at his beer bottle label. "No-Nuts Wolfman has agreed to spill the beans on his family, the great Chandonnes."

Benton reads the papers several times a day, excavating the Internet, sending out queries on search engines to recover pieces of his past life. He knows all about Jean-Baptiste, the deformed, murderous son of Chandonne—the great Monsieur Chandonne, intimate friend of the *noblesse* in Paris, the head of the largest, most dangerous organized crime cartel in the world. Jean-Baptiste knows enough about his family business and those who carry out its terrible tasks to put everyone who matters behind bars or on a death-chamber gurney.

So far, Jean-Baptiste has bided his time in a maximum-security Texas prison, saying nothing to anyone. It was the Chandonne family and its massive web that Benton tangled with, and now, from thousands of miles away, Monsieur Chandonne sips his fine wines and never doubts that Benton has paid the ultimate price, a terrible price. Monsieur Chandonne was foiled, but in a way, he wasn't. Benton died a fake death to save himself and others from dying real ones. But the price he pays is Promethean. He may as well be chained to rocks. He cannot heal because his guts are torn out daily.

"Wolfman," as Marino usually refers to Jean-Baptiste, "says he'll finger everyone from his daddy on down to the butlers, but only under certain conditions." He hesitates. "He ain't fucking with us, either, Benton. He means it."

"You know that for a fact," Benton blandly says.

"Yeah. A fact."

"How has he communicated this to you?" Benton's eyes take on a familiar intensity as he goes into his mode.

"Letters."

"Do we know who he's been writing, besides you?"

"The Doc. Her letter was sent to me. I haven't given it to her, see no point."

"Who else?"

"Lucy."

"Hers also sent to you?"

"No. Directly to her office. I got no idea how he got the address or knew the name The Last Precinct, when she doesn't list it. Everybody thinks her business is called Infosearch Solutions."

"Why would he know that people like Lucy and you refer to her business as The Last Precinct? If I logged on to the Internet right now, would I find any mention of The Last Precinct?"

"Not the one we're talking about, you wouldn't."

"Would I find Infosearch Solutions?"

"Sure."

"Is her office phone number listed?" Benton asks.

"Infosearch Solutions is."

"So maybe he also knows the listed name of her business. Called directory assistance and got the address that way. Actually, you can find just about anything on the Internet these days and for less than fifty bucks, even buy unlisted and cell phone numbers."

"I don't think Wolfman has a computer in his death-row cell," Marino says in annoyance.

"Rocco Caggiano could have fed him all kinds of information," Benton reminds him. "At one time he had to have Lucy's business number, since he planned to depose her. Then, of course, Jean-Baptiste pled."

"Sounds like you keep up with the news." Marino tries to divert the conversation away from the subject of Rocco Caggiano.

"Did you read the letter he wrote to Lucy?"

"She told me about it. Didn't want to fax or e-mail it." This bothers Marino, too. Lucy didn't want him to see the letter.

"Any letters to anybody else?"

Marino shrugs, sips his beer. "Not a clue. Obviously, he ain't writing to you." He thinks this is funny.

Benton doesn't smile.

"Because you're dead, right?" Marino assumes Benton doesn't catch the joke. "Well, in prison, if an inmate marks his outgoing letters *Legal Mail* or *Media Mail*, it's illegal for officials to open them. So if Wolfman's got any legal and media pen pals, the information's privileged."

He begins picking at the label on his beer bottle, talking on as if Benton knows nothing about the inner workings of penitentiaries, where he has interviewed hundreds of violent criminals during his career.

"The only place to look is his visitors list, since a lot of the people these squirrels write also come visit. Wolfman's got a list. Let's see, the governor of Texas, the president . . ."

"As in president of the United States?" Benton's trademark is to take all information seriously.

Marino says, "Yup."

It unnerves him to see gestures and reactions that are the Benton of the past, the Benton he worked with, the Benton who was his friend.

"Who else?" Benton gets up and collects a legal pad and pen from tidy stacks of paperwork and magazines next to the computer on the kitchen table.

He slips on a pair of wire-rim glasses, very small, John Lennon-style, nothing he would have worn in his former life. Sitting back down, he writes the time, date and location on a clean sheet of paper. From where Marino sits, he makes out the word "offender," but beyond that, he can't read Benton's small scrawl, especially upside down.

Marino answers, "His father and mother are on the list. Now that's a real joke, right?"

Benton's pen pauses. He glances up. "What about his lawyer? Rocco Caggiano?"

Marino swills beer in the bottom of the bottle.

"Rocco?" Benton says with more emphasis. "You going to tell me?"

Fury and shame dart across Marino's face. "Just remember, he ain't mine, didn't grow up with me, don't know him, don't want to know him, would blow his fuckin' brains out just as easy as any other dirtbag's."

"Genetically, he's your son, whether you like it or not," Benton replies matter-of-factly.

"I don't even remember when his birthday is." Marino dismisses his only child with a wave of a hand and a last slug of Budweiser.

Rocco Marino, who changed his surname to Caggiano, was born bad. He was Marino's shameful, dirty secret, an abscess he showed to no one until Jean-Baptiste Chandonne loped onto the scene. For most of Marino's life, he believed that Rocco's curdled choices were personal—the harshest punishment he could levy on the father he despises. Oddly, Marino found some comfort in that. A personal vendetta was better than the humiliating and painful truth that Rocco is indifferent to Marino. Rocco's choices have nothing to do with Marino. If anything, Rocco laughs at Marino, his father, and thinks he is a Keystone-Kop loser who dresses like a pig, lives like a pig and is a pig.

Rocco's reappearance in Marino's world was a coincidence—"a funny as hell coincidence," in Rocco's own words—when he stopped long enough to speak to his father outside the courtroom door after Jean-Baptiste Chandonne's arraignment. Rocco has been in deep with organized crime since he was old enough to shave. He was a toady, scumbag lawyer for the Chandonnes long before Marino had ever heard of them.

"We know where Rocco's spending his time these days?" Benton asks.

Marino's eyes turn as dark and flat as old pennies. "Possibly— *very possibly*—we will soon enough."

"Meaning?"

Marino leans back against the couch, as if the conversation pleases him and pumps up his ego. "Meaning he's got tin cans tied to his ass this time and don't know it."

"Meaning?" Benton asks again.

"Interpol's flagged him as a fugitive, and he ain't aware of it. Lucy told me. I'm confident we're going to find him and a lot of other assholes."

"*We?*"

Marino shrugs again, tries to take another swallow of beer and gulps air. He belches, thinks about getting up for a refill.

"*We* is collectively speaking," he explains. "*We* as in us good guys. Rocco's going down because he's gonna traipse through an airport and his little Red Notice is gonna pop up on a computer and next thing, he's got a nice pair of shiny handcuffs on and maybe an AR-fifteen pointed at his head."

"For what crimes? He's always gotten away with his dirty work. That's part of his charm."

"All I know is there are warrants on him in Italy."

"Says who?"

"Lucy. I'd give anything to be the one who points that AR-fifteen at his head, only I'd pull the trigger for sure," Marino says, believing he means it, but unable to envision it. The images won't come.

"He's your son," Benton quietly reminds him. "I suggest you get yourself ready for how it will feel if you have *anything at all* to do with whatever might happen to him. I'm not aware that your pursuit of him or any other Chandonne operatives is your legal jurisdictional right. Or are you now working undercover for the feds?"

A pause. Marino hates the feds. "I won't feel nothing." He tries to keep his demeanor flat, but his nerves have begun to fizz with fury and fear. "Besides, I don't even know where the hell he is. Someone else out there will catch him, and he'll be extradited to Italy if he lives that long. I got no doubt the Chandonnes will take him out before he has a chance to open his mouth."

"Who else?" Benton moves on. "Who else is on the list?"

"A couple reporters. Never heard of 'em, and for all I know, they don't exist. Oh yeah, and here's a good one. Wolfman's pretty-boy brother, Jean-Paul Chandonne, aka Jay Talley. Wish the bastard would drop by the prison for a visit so we could arrest his ass and he could join his ugly-ass twin on death row."

Benton stops writing, a fleeting emotion passing through his eyes at the mention of Jay Talley's name. "You're assuming he's still alive. Do you know that?"

"Got no reason to think otherwise. My guess is his family's protecting him and he's living the good life somewhere while he carries on with the family business."

It occurs to Marino as he says all this that Benton probably knows Talley is a Chandonne who passed himself off as an American, became an ATF agent and managed to get himself assigned as a liaison to Interpol's headquarters in France. Marino mentally scans everything that has been made public about the Jean-Baptiste case. He's not sure if there was any mention of Scarpetta's relationship with Talley when she and half the world believed he was the handsome big-shot agent who spoke dozens of languages and had gone to Harvard. Benton doesn't need to know what went on between Scarpetta and Talley. Marino hopes like hell Benton never finds out.

"I've read about Jay Talley," Benton says. "He's very smart, very smooth, extremely sadistic and dangerous. I seriously doubt he's dead."

"Uhhhh . . ." Marino's thoughts scatter like startled birds. "Like what have you read?"

"It's no secret that he's Jean-Baptiste's twin brother. Fraternal twin." Benton's face is impassive.

"Weirdest thing I ever heard of." Marino shakes his head. "Imagine. He and Wolfman born a few minutes apart. Talk about one brother getting the bad luck of the draw, while the other, Talley, gets dealt all aces."

"He is a violent psychopath," Benton replies. "I wouldn't exactly call that *aces*."

"Their DNA's so much alike," Marino goes on, "you've got to

use a lot of probes to figure out you're looking at the DNA of two different people." Marino pauses, slightly exasperated, as he continues picking at his beer label. "Don't ask me to explain probes and DNA shit. The Doc figured it all . . ."

"Who else is on the list?" Benton interrupts him.

Marino's face goes blank.

"The visitors list."

"The list is garbage. I'm sure no one on it has ever come to see John the Baptist except his lawyer."

"Your son, Rocco Caggiano." He won't let Marino evade that fact. "Anyone else?" Benton persists, taking notes.

"Turns out I am. Isn't that sweet? And then my new pen pal Wolfman sends me mail. A letter for me, and the one for the Doc that I didn't give to her."

Marino gets up to help himself to another beer.

"Need one?"

Benton tells him, "No."

Retrieving his jacket, Marino digs in one pocket, then another, finding folded pieces of paper.

"I just happen to have them with me. Photocopies, including the envelopes."

"The list." Benton won't stray from that subject. "Certainly you brought a copy of the list with you."

"I don't need a copy of that goddamn list." Marino's annoyance shows. "What is it about you and that fucking list? I can tell you exactly who's on it. The people I've already mentioned, plus two reporters. Carlos Guarino and Emmanuel La Fleur."

His pronunciation is unintelligible and Benton asks him to spell the names.

"Supposedly, they live in Sicily and Paris."

"Real people?"

"No sign of their bylines on the Internet, and Lucy's looked."

"If Lucy can't find them, they don't exist," Benton decides.

"Also on Wolfman's guest list," Marino adds, "is none other than Jaime Berger, who would have prosecuted his ass had he gone to trial in New York for the newslady he mauled up there. Berger's a piece of work, has a history with the Doc. They're friends."

Benton knows all this and doesn't react. He takes notes.

"And last and probably least, some guy named Robert Lee."

"His name sounds real enough. By chance is his middle initial E?" Benton wryly comments. "Any correspondence between Jean-Baptiste and this Robert Lee, on the outside chance Mr. Lee didn't die a hundred-some years ago?"

"All I can tell you is he's on the visitors list. Any mail that's privileged, the prison won't talk about, so I got no idea who else Wolfman writes to or gets love notes from."

18

Marino smooths open his letter from Jean-Baptiste and begins to read: " *'Bonjour, mon cher ami,* Pete . . .' "

He interrupts himself and looks up, scowling. "Can you believe he calls me Pete? Now that really pisses me off."

"More than being called *mon cher ami*?" Benton asks dryly.

"I don't like dirtbags calling me by my first name. It's just one of my things."

"Please read," Benton says with a touch of impatience, "and I hope there is nothing more in French for you to mangle. What's the date of this letter?"

"Not even a week ago. I arranged things to get here as quick as I could. To see you . . . oh, for shit's sake, I'm gonna call you *Benton.*"

"Actually, you're not. Please read."

Marino lights another cigarette, inhales deeply and continues:

JUST A NOTE TO TELL YOU I AM GROWING MY HAIR. WHY?
BUT OF COURSE IT IS BECAUSE THEY HAVE GIVEN ME MY

DATE TO DIE. IT IS MAY SEVENTH AT TEN P.M. NOT A MINUTE LATER, SO I HOPE YOU WILL BE THERE AS MY SPECIAL GUEST. BEFORE THEN, MON AMI, I HAVE BUSINESS TO CONCLUDE, SO I MAKE YOU AN OFFER YOU CAN'T REFUSE (AS THEY SAY IN THE MOVIES).

YOU WILL NEVER CATCH THEM WITHOUT ME, JEAN-BAPTISTE. IT WOULD BE LIKE CATCHING A THOUSAND FISH WITHOUT A VERY BIG NET. I AM THE NET. THERE ARE TWO CONDITIONS. THEY ARE SIMPLE.

I WILL ADMIT NOTHING EXCEPT TO MADAME SCARPETTA, WHO HAS ASKED MY PERMISSION TO SEE HER AND TELL HER WHAT I KNOW.

NO ONE ELSE CAN BE PRESENT.

I HAVE YET ANOTHER CONDITION THAT SHE DOES NOT KNOW. SHE MUST BE THE DOCTOR WHO ADMINISTERS MY LETHAL COCKTAIL, AS THEY SAY. MADAME SCARPETTA MUST KILL ME. I FULLY TRUST IF SHE AGREES, SHE WILL NOT BREAK HER PROMISE TO ME. YOU SEE HOW WELL I KNOW HER.

À BIENTÔT, JEAN-BAPTISTE CHANDONNE

"And the letter to her?" Benton abruptly asks, unwilling to say Scarpetta's name.

"The same thing. More or less." Marino does not want to read it to him.

"You have it in your hand. Read it."

Marino taps ash into the water glass, squinting an eye as he blows out smoke. "I'll give you the upshot."

"Don't protect me, Pete," Benton softly says.

"Sure. If you want to hear it, I'll read it. But I don't think it's necessary, and maybe you ought . . ."

"Please read it." Now Benton sounds weary. His eyes are not as intense, and he leans back in the chair.

Marino clears his throat as he unfolds another plain white sheet of paper. He begins:

MON CHER AMOUR, KAY . . .

He glances up at Benton's expressionless face. The color has drained from it, his complexion sallow beneath his tan.

MY HEART IS IN GREAT PAIN BECAUSE YOU HAVE NOT MADE
AN APPOINTMENT TO COME TO SEE ME YET. I DO NOT UNDER-
STAND. OF COURSE, YOU FEEL AS I DO. I AM YOUR THIEF IN
THE NIGHT, THE GREAT LOVER WHO CAME TO STEAL YOU
AWAY, YET YOU REFUSED. YOU SHUNNED ME AND WOUNDED
ME. NOW YOU MUST BE EMPTY, SO BORED, LANGUISHING FOR
ME, MADAME SCARPETTA.
  AS FOR ME? I AM NOT BORED. YOU ARE HERE WITH ME IN
MY CELL, WITHOUT A WILL, COMPLETELY UNDER MY SPELL.
YOU MUST KNOW IT. YOU MUST FEEL IT. LET ME SEE, CAN I
COUNT? IS IT FOUR, FIVE OR FIFTEEN TIMES A DAY I RIP OPEN
THOSE VERY NICE SUITS YOU WEAR—THE HAUTE COUTURE
OF MADAME SCARPETTA, THE DOCTOR, THE LAWYER, THE
CHIEF. I TEAR OFF EVERYTHING WITH MY BARE HANDS AND
BITE INTO THOSE BIG TITS WHILE YOU SHIVER AND DIE WITH
DELIGHT . . .

"Is there a point to this?" Benton's voice snaps like a pistol slide racking back. "I'm not interested in his pornographic drivel. What does he want?"

Marino looks hard at him, pauses, then turns over the letter.

Sweat beads on his balding head and rolls down his temples. He reads what is on the back of the plain white sheet of paper:

> I MUST SEE YOU! YOU CANNOT ESCAPE UNLESS YOU DO NOT
> CARE IF MORE INNOCENT PEOPLE DIE. NOT THAT ANYONE IS
> INNOCENT. I WILL TELL YOU ALL THAT IS NECESSARY. BUT I
> MUST LOOK AT YOU IN THE FLESH AS I SPEAK THE TRUTH.
> AND THEN YOU WILL KILL ME.

Marino stops reading. "More shit you don't need to hear . . ."

"And she knows nothing about this?"

"Well," Marino equivocates, "not really. Like I said, I didn't show it to her. All I told her is I got a letter and Wolfman wants to see her and will exchange information for her visit. And he wants her to be the one who gives him the needle."

"Typically, penitentiaries use free-world doctors, regular physicians from the outside to administer the lethal cocktail," Benton oddly comments, as if what Marino just said has no impact on him. "Did you use ninhydrin on the letters?" Now he changes the subject. "Obviously I can't tell, since these are photocopies."

The chemical ninhydrin would have reacted to the amino acid in fingerprints, turning portions of the original letters a deep violet.

"Didn't want to damage them," Marino replies.

"What about an alternate light source? Something nondestructive, such as a crime scope?"

When Marino doesn't respond, Benton pierces him with the obvious point.

"You did nothing to prove these letters are from Jean-Baptiste Chandonne? You just assume? Jesus." Benton rubs his face with his hands. "Jesus Christ. You come here—*here*—take a risk like that and don't even know for a fact that these letters came from him? And let me guess. You didn't have the backs of the stamps and envelope flaps swabbed for DNA, either. What about postmarks? What about return addresses?"

"There's no return address—not for him, I mean—and no postmark that might tell us where he sent it from," Marino admits, and he is sweating profusely now.

Benton leans forward. "What? He hand-delivered the letters? The return address isn't his? What the hell are you talking about? How could he mail something to you and there's no postmark?"

Marino unfolds another piece of paper and hands it to him. The photocopy is of an eight-and-a-half-by-eleven-inch white envelope, preprinted, U.S. postage paid for the nonprofit organization the National Academy of Justice.

"Well, I guess we've both seen this before," Benton says, looking at the photocopy, "since we've been members of the NAJ for most of our lives. Or at least I used to be. Sorry to say, but I'm not on their mailing list anymore." He pauses, noting that *First-class mail* has been x-ed through just below the preprinted postage-paid stamp.

"For once, I'm blanking out on any possible explanation," he says.

"This is what came in the mail to me," Marino explains. "The NAJ envelope, and when I opened it, the two letters were inside. One to me, one to the Doc. Sealed, marked *Legal Mail*, I guess in case someone at the prison was curious about the NAJ envelope and decided to tear into it. Only other thing written on the envelopes was our names."

Both men are silent for a moment. Marino smokes and drinks beer.

"Well, I do have a possibility, the only thing I can think of," Marino then says. "I checked with the NAJ, and from the warden on down, there are fifty-six officers who are members. It wouldn't be unusual to see one of these envelopes lying around somewhere."

Benton is shaking his head. "But your address is printed, *machine-printed*. How could Chandonne manage to do that?"

"How the hell do you stand this joint? Don't you even got air-conditioning? And we did swab the envelopes the letters came in, but it's that self-stick adhesive. So he didn't have to lick nothing."

This is evasion and Marino knows it. Sloughed-off skin cells can adhere to self-sticking adhesives. He doesn't want to answer Benton's question.

"How did Chandonne pull off sending you letters inside an envelope like this?" Benton shakes the photocopy at Marino. "And don't you find it just a little odd that *first-class mail* is x-ed out? Why might that be?"

"I guess we'll just have to get Wolfman to explain," Marino rudely replies. "I got no fucking idea."

"Yet you seem to know for a fact that the letters are from Jean-Baptiste." Benton measures each word. *"Pete. You're better than this."*

Marino wipes his forehead on his sleeve. "Look, so the fact is, we don't got scientific evidence to prove nothing. But it's not because we didn't take a shot at it. We did use the Luma-Lite, and we did try for DNA, and everything's whistle-clean as of this moment."

"Mitochondrial DNA? You trying for that?"

"Why bother? It would take months, and by then he'll be dead. And there's no way in hell we're going to get a goddamn thing anyway. For crying out loud, don't you think the asshole gets off on somehow using a National Academy of Justice envelope? How's that for a fuck-you? Don't you think he gets off on making us do all these tests when he knows we'll come up with zip? All he had to do was cover his hands with toilet paper or whatever when he touched anything."

"Maybe," Benton says.

Marino is about to erupt. He is exasperated beyond his limit.

"Easy, Pete," Benton says. "You would think less of me if I didn't ask."

Marino stares off without blinking.

"My opinion?" Benton goes on. "He wrote the letters and was deliberate about not leaving evidence. I don't know how he managed to use a National Academy of Justice envelope, and yes, that is a huge fuck-you. Frankly, I'm surprised you haven't heard from him before now. The letters sound authentic. They do not have the off-key ring of a crank. We know Jean-Baptiste has a breast fetish." He says this clinically. "We know it is very likely he has information that could destroy his criminal family and the cartel. It fits with his insatiable need to dominate and control that he presents the conditions he has."

"And what about him saying the Doc wants to see him?"

"You tell me."

"She never wrote him. I asked her point-blank. Why the hell would she write that piece of shit? I told her about the National Academy of Justice envelopes, that the letter to her and me came in one. I showed her a photocopy . . ."

"Of what?" Benton interrupts.

"*A photocopy of the National Academy of Justice envelope.*" Marino is getting exasperated. "The one her and my letters from Wolfman came in. I told her if she gets one of these goddamn National Academy of Justice letters herself, not to open it, not to even touch it. Do you really believe he wants her to be his executioner?"

"If he intends to die . . ."

"Intends?" Marino interrupts him. "I don't believe ol' Wolfie Boy's got much to say about that."

"A lot can happen between now and then, Pete. Remember who his connections are. I wouldn't be too sure of anything. And by the way, when Lucy got her letter, was it also sent in a postage-paid National Academy of Justice envelope?"

"Yup."

"The fantasy of a woman doctor administering the lethal injection and watching him die would be erotic to him," Benton muses.

"Not just any doctor. We're talking about Scarpetta!"

"He victimizes to the end, dominates and controls another human being to the end, forces a person to commit an act that will scar forever." Benton pauses before he adds, "You kill someone, you never forget him, now do you? We have to take the letters seriously. I do believe they are from him—fingerprints, DNA or not."

"Yeah, well I believe they're from him, too, and that he means what he says, and that's why I'm here, if you ain't figured it out yet. If we can get Wolfman to sing, we move in on all his daddy's lieutenants and put the Chandonne cartel out of business. And you got nothing to worry about anymore."

"Who is *we*?"

"I wish you'd quit saying that!" Marino gets up to help himself to another beer. Anger and frustration flare again. "Don't you get it?" he calls out, rummaging inside the refrigerator. "After May seventh, after we got the goods and Wolfman's dead, there ain't no reason for you to be Tom what's-his-name anymore!"

"Who is we?"

Marino snorts like a bull as he pops open a bottle of Dos Equis this time. *"We* is me. *We* is Lucy."

"Does Lucy know you came to see me today?"

"No. I didn't tell no one and won't."

"Good." Benton doesn't move in his chair.

"Wolfman gives us pawns to knock off the board," Marino plans on without him. "Maybe he's already given us our first pawn by ratting out Rocco. I can only figure that somebody must have ratted him out if he's suddenly a fugitive."

"I see. How honorable of Chandonne, if your son is his first pawn. Will you visit Rocco in prison, Pete?"

Marino suddenly smashes the beer bottle in the sink. Glass shatters. He strides over to Benton and gets in his face.

"Shut up about him, you hear me? I hope he gets fucking AIDS in prison and dies! All the suffering he's caused! Now it should be his goddamn turn!"

"Whose suffering?" Benton doesn't flinch at Marino's hot, beery breath. "Your suffering?"

"Start with his mother's suffering. And keep on going." Marino still has a hard time thinking about Doris, his ex-wife and Rocco's mother.

She was Marino's sweetheart when he was in his prime. He still thought of her as his sweetheart long after he stopped paying attention to her. He was stunned when she left him for another man.

While this is crossing Marino's mind, he is yelling at Benton, "You can come home, you fucking idiot! You can live your life again!"

Marino sits down on the couch, breathing hard, his face a deep red that reminds Benton of the 575M Maranello Ferrari he has seen around Cambridge. Its color is a deep burgundy called Barcetta, and thinking of that car reminds him of Lucy, who has always been in love with fast, powerful machines.

"You can see the Doc, and Lucy, and . . ."

"Untrue," Benton whispers. "Jean-Baptiste Chandonne has manipulated himself into this position. He is exactly where he wants to be. Connect the dots, Pete. Go back to how it started after he was arrested. He shocked everyone by offering an unsolicited confession to yet another murder, this one in Texas, and then, of all things, pled guilty. Why? Because he *wanted* to be extradited to Texas. It was *his* choice, not the governor of Virginia's."

"No way," Marino challenges. "Our ambitious Virginia governor didn't want to piss off Washington by pissing off France—the anti-death penalty capital of the world. So we gave Chandonne to Texas."

Benton shakes his head. "Not so. Jean-Baptiste gave Jean-Baptiste to Texas."

"And how the hell would you know, anyway? You talking to people? I thought you didn't talk to no one."

Benton doesn't reply.

"I don't get it," Marino goes on. "Why would Wolfman give a shit about Texas?"

"He knew he would die quickly there, and he wanted to die quickly. It was part of his master plan. He had no intention of rotting on death row for ten or fifteen years. And his chances of gamesmanship are much greater in Texas. Virginia might very well fold to political pressure and stay his execution.

"Virginia is also claustrophobic. His every move would be watched. He would get away with much less, because law-enforcement and corrections officers would make it their mission to ensure his safety and good behavior. He would be monitored to the extreme. Don't tell me that if he were in Virginia, his mail wouldn't be secretly checked. The hell with his legal rights."

"Virginia would want to fry his ass," Marino argues. "After what he done."

"He killed a store clerk. He killed a cop. He almost killed the chief medical examiner. The governor at that time is now a senator and chairman of the Democratic National Committee. He didn't piss off Washington because he wasn't about to piss off the French. The governor of Texas, now in his second term and a trigger-happy Republican, by the way, doesn't give a damn who he pisses off."

"The chief medical examiner? You just can't bring yourself to say her name, can you?" Marino exclaims, incredulous.

19

A few years back, Lucy Farinelli's Aunt Kay recalled an anecdote about the decapitated head of a German soldier who died in World War II.

His body was discovered buried in sand somewhere in Poland, she recounted to Lucy, and arid conditions remarkably preserved his Aryan short blond hair, attractive features and even the stubble on his chin. When Scarpetta saw the head in a Polish forensic medical institute showcase while visiting as a forensic lecturer, she thought of Madame Tussaud's, she said.

"His front teeth are broken," Scarpetta went on with the story, explaining that she didn't think the damaged teeth were a post-mortem artifact or due to an antemortem injury that had occurred at or around the boyish Nazi's death. He simply had poor dental care. "Loose-contact gunshot wound to the right temple," she cited the Nazi's cause of death. "The angle of the wound points the way the gun was directed—in this case, *downward*. Often in a suicide, the muzzle will be straight on or directed *upward*. There's no soot in this case, because the wound was cleaned, the hair around it shaved at the morgue, where the mummified remains were sent to make certain the death wasn't recent, or so I was told when I was lecturing at the Pomorska Akademia Medyczna."

The only reason Lucy is reminded of the decapitated Nazi as her car is being searched at Germany's northeast border is that the German guard is a handsome, blue-eyed blond and seems much too young to be infected with ennui as he leans inside her black rental Mercedes and sweeps the leather seats with a flashlight. Next he sweeps the black carpeted floor, the strong beam illuminating Lucy's scuffed leather briefcase and red Nike duffel bags in back. He makes several bright stabs at the front passenger seat, then moves around to the trunk, popping it open. He shuts it with scarcely a glance.

Had he bothered to unzip those two duffel bags and dig through clothing, he would have discovered a tactical baton. It looks rather much like a black rubber fishing pole handle, but with a quick flip of the wrist extends into a two-foot-long thin rod of carbonized steel capable of shattering bone and shearing soft tissue, including the internal organs of the belly.

Lucy is prepared to explain the weapon, which is relatively unknown and unused except by law enforcement. She would claim that her overly protective boyfriend gave her the baton for self-defense because she is a businesswoman and often travels alone. She really isn't quite sure how to use the thing, she would sheepishly explain, but he insisted and promised it was perfectly all right to pack it. If police confiscated the baton, so what? But Lucy is relieved that it is not discovered and that the officer in his pale green uniform checking her passport from inside his booth does not seem curious about this young American woman driving alone late at night in a Mercedes.

"What is the purpose of your visit?" he asks in awkward English.

"Geschäft." She doesn't tell him what kind of business, but has an answer prepared, if necessary.

He picks up the phone and says something Lucy is unable to decipher, but she senses he isn't talking about her or, if he is, it is nothing. She expected her belongings to be riffled through and was ready for it. She expected to be quizzed. But the guard who reminds her of the decapitated head returns her passport.

"Danke," she politely says as she silently labels him a *trag Narr.* The world is full of lazy fools like him.

He waves her on.

She creeps forward, crossing the border into Poland, and now another guard, this one Polish, puts her through the same routine. There is no ordeal, no thorough search, not a hint of anything but sleepiness and boredom. This is too easy. Paranoia sets in. She remembers she should never trust anything that is too easy, and she imagines the Gestapo and SS soldiers, cruel specters from the past. Fear rises like body odor, a fear that is baseless and irrational. Sweat rolls down her sides, beneath her windbreaker, as she thinks of Poles overpowered and disenfranchised from their own names and lives during a war she knows about only from history books.

It is not so different from the way Benton Wesley exists, and Lucy wonders what he would think and feel if he knew she was in Poland and why. Not a day goes by when he doesn't shadow her life.

20

Her career experience does not show unless she intentionally displays it like a weapon.

She was still in high school when she began interning for the FBI and designed their Criminal Artificial Intelligence Network, known as CAIN. When she graduated from the University of Virginia, she became an FBI special agent and was given free rein as a computer and technical expert. She learned to fly helicopters and became the first female member of the FBI Special Forces Hostage Rescue Team. Hostility, harassment and crude innuendos followed her on every deployment, raid and punishing training session. Rarely was she invited to join the men for a beer in the Academy bar called the Boardroom. They did not confide in her about raids gone wrong or their wives and children or girlfriends. But they watched her. There was talk about her in the showers.

Her career with the FBI was aborted on a dewy October morning when she and her HRT partner, Rudy Musil, were shooting live nine-millimeter rounds inside the FBI Academy's Tire House. As its name implies, the highly dangerous indoor range was filled with old tires that tactical agents could dive over, duck under, dart around and hide behind as they practiced maniacal maneuvers. Rudy was breathing hard and sweating as he crouched behind a mound of tires and smacked another magazine into his Glock, peeking around a threadbare Michelin as he looked for Lucy, his partner.

"All right. Come clean," he yelled at her through gun smoke. "What's your sexual preference?"

"To have it as often as possible!" She reloaded and snapped back the slide while rolling between stacks of tires before firing five rounds at a pop-up target thirty feet away. The cluster of head shots was so tight, it looked like a small flower.

"Oh yeah?" Two bullets loudly clinked a pop-up thug holding a machine gun. "Me and the guys got bets on it." Rudy's voice came closer as he crawled on his belly across the filthy concrete floor.

He pounced through towers of sooty tires and grabbed an unsuspecting Lucy by her steel-reinforced Red Wing boots.

"Gotcha!" He laughed, setting his pistol on top of a tire.

"Are you fucking crazy?" Lucy cleared a round from the chamber of her pistol, the ejected cartridge bouncing off the floor. "We're using live ammo, you fucking idiot!"

"Let me see that thing." Rudy got serious. "It doesn't sound right."

He took the pistol from her, dropped out the magazine. "Loose spring." He shook the pistol before setting it next to his gun on the tire. "Aha. Rule number one: Never lose your weapon."

He got on top of her, laughing as he wrestled with her, somehow believing this was what she had been waiting for, and that she was excited and didn't mean it when she continued screaming, "Get off of me, asshole!"

Finally, he restrained both her wrists in one of his powerful hands. He plunged the other inside her shirt and shoved his tongue inside her mouth as he pushed up her bra. "The guys only say," he panted, "you're a dyke 'cause"——he fumbled with her belt buckle—"they can't have you . . ."

Lucy bit through Rudy's bottom lip and knocked her forehead hard against the bridge of his nose. He spent the rest of the day in the emergency room.

FBI attorneys reminded her that litigation benefitted no one, especially since Rudy believed that she "wanted it" and had probable cause to believe it. Lucy told Rudy she wanted it "as often as possible," he reluctantly stated in the forms he was forced to complete for Internal Affairs.

"It's true," Lucy calmly agreed during a sworn statement before a panel of five lawyers, not one of whom represented her. "I said that, but I didn't say I wanted it *with him* or with anyone *right then* in the middle of live fire in the middle of the Tire House in the middle of a maneuver in the middle of my period."

"But you'd led him on in the past. You'd given Agent Musil reason to think you were attracted to him."

"What reason?" Lucy was baffled under oath. "Offering him a stick of gum now and then, helping him clean his guns, hanging with him to run the Yellow Brick Road and other obstacle courses, the worst one at the Marine Corps base, joking around, that sort of thing?"

"Quite a bit of togetherness," the lawyers agreed with one another.

"He's my partner. Partners have quite a bit of togetherness."

"Nonetheless, you seemed to devote quite a lot of your time

and attention to Agent Musil, including personal attention, such as asking him about his weekends and holidays, and calling him at home when he was out sick."

"Perhaps *joking around*, as you put it, might have been interpreted as flirting. Some people joke around when they flirt."

The lawyers agreed once again, and what was worse, two of them were women—women in masculine skirt suits and high-heel shoes, women whose eyes reflected an identification with the aggressor, as if their irises were glued on to their eyeballs backward and were dull instead of bright, and blind to what was in front of them. The women lawyers had the dead eyes of people who kill themselves off to get what they want or to become what they fear.

"I'm sorry," Lucy said as her attention sharpened and she avoided the dead eyes. "You stepped on me. Please repeat," she muttered aviation jargon.

"I'm sorry? Who stepped on you?" Frowns.

"You interfered with my transmission to the tower. Oops, there is no tower. This is uncontrolled air space and you get to do whatever you want. Right?"

More frowns. The lawyers glanced at one another as if Lucy was very weird.

"Never mind," she added.

"You're an attractive single woman. Can you see how Agent Musil might have misinterpreted joking around, phone calls at home, et cetera, as your being sexually interested in him, Agent Farinelli?"

"It has also been stated that you often referred to Agent Musil and yourself as 'yin and ylang.'"

"I've told Rudy a hundred times that ylang is a Malayan tree. Ylang-ylang, to be more precise. A tree with yellow flowers that perfume is distilled from . . . but he doesn't always tune his ears to the right frequency." Lucy fought a smile.

The lawyers were taking notes.

"I never called Rudy 'ylang.' Now and then I did call him 'yang' and he called me 'ying,' no matter how many times I told him the word was *yin*," Lucy explained further.

Silence, pens poised.

"It has to do with Chinese philosophy." Lucy might as well have been talking to a chalkboard. "Balance, counterparts."

"Why did you call each other . . . whatever?"

"Because we're two peas in a pod. Do you know *that* expression?"

"I think we're familiar with the term *two peas in a pod*. Again, such nicknames suggest a relationship . . ."

"Not the kind you're talking about," Lucy replied without rancor, because she did not hate Rudy in the least. "He and I are two peas in a pod because neither of us fit in. He's Austrian and the other guys call him Musili because he's, quote, *full of shit*, which he doesn't think is the least bit funny. And I'm a lesbian, a man-hater, because no *normal* woman *who likes men* would want to be HRT and make the cut. According to the laws of machismo."

Lucy scanned the women's dead eyes and decided the male attorneys' eyes were dead, too. The only sign of life in them was the glint of small, miserable creatures who hated someone like Lucy because she dared to resist being overpowered and frightened by them.

"This interview, deposition, inquisition, whatever the hell it is, is bullshit," Lucy told them. "I have no interest in suing the Fucking Bureau of Investigation. I took care of myself in the Tire House. I didn't report the incident. Rudy did. He had to explain his injuries. He claimed responsibility. He could have lied. But he didn't, and the two of us are eye to eye." She used the word *eye* to remind the lawyers of their dead eyes, as if somehow the lawyers knew their eyes were dead and incapable of seeing a reality that flexed with truth and possibilities and begged humans to partake of it and war against the dead-eyed people who were ruining the world.

"Rudy and I have acted as our own mediator," Lucy went on, calmly. "We have reestablished that we are partners, and one partner doesn't do what the other doesn't want or commit any act that might betray the other partner or place him or her in harm's way. And he told me he was sorry. And he meant it. He was crying."

"Spies say they are sorry. They also cry." A flush was climbing up the throat of a hostile woman attorney in pinstripes and skinny high heels that reminded Lucy of bound feet. "And your accepting his apology isn't an option, Agent Farinelli. He attempted to rape you." She emphasized the point, assuming it would humiliate and victimize Lucy again by inviting the male attorneys to envision her naked and sexually assaulted on the sooty concrete floor of the Tire House.

"I didn't know Rudy was accused of being a spy," Lucy replied.

She resigned from the FBI and was hired by the Bureau of Alcohol, Tobacco, Firearms and Explosives, which the FBI unfairly considers a collection of backwoods boys who bust up moonshine stills and wear tool belts and guns.

She became an expert fire investigator in Philadelphia, where she helped stage Benton Wesley's murder, which included procuring the body of an anatomical donation bound for dissection at a medical school. The dead man was elderly, with thick silver hair, and after he was incinerated inside a torched building, a visual identification was unreliable if not impossible. All a shocked

Scarpetta saw at the filthy, water-soaked, smoking scene was a charred body and a faceless skull with silver hair and a titanium wristwatch that had belonged to Benton Wesley. Under secret orders from Washington, the chief medical examiner in Philadelphia was ordered to falsify all reports. On paper, Benton was dead, just one more homicide added to the FBI's crime statistics for 1997.

After he vanished into the black hole of the witness protection program, ATF immediately transferred Lucy to the Miami Field Office where she volunteered for dangerous undercover work and talked her way into it, despite reservations on the part of the Special Agent in Charge. Lucy had an attitude. She was volatile. No one close to her except Pete Marino understood why. Scarpetta didn't know or remotely suspect the truth. She assumed Lucy was going through a terrible phase because she couldn't cope with Benton being dead, when the truth was that Lucy couldn't cope with Benton being alive. Within a year of her new post in Miami, she shot and killed two drug dealers in a take-down that went bad.

Despite video surveillance tapes that clearly showed she had saved herself and the life of her undercover partner, there was talk. There was ugly gossip and disinformation, and one administrative investigation after another. Lucy quit ATF. She quit the feds. She cashed in her dot-com stocks before the economy destabilized and crashed after 9-11. She invested a portion of her wealth, along with her law enforcement experience and talent, into creating a private investigative agency she calls The Last Precinct. It's where you go when there's no place left. It isn't advertised or listed in any directory.

21

Benton gets up from the chair and slips his hands into his pockets.

"People from the past," he says. "We live many lives, Pete, and the past is a death. Something over. Something that can't come back. We move on and reinvent ourselves."

"What a load of crap. You've been spending too much time alone," Marino says in disgust as fear chills his heart. "You're making me sick. I'm glad as hell Scarpetta ain't here to see this. Or maybe she ought to, so she'd finally get over you like you've obviously gotten over her. Goddamn it, can't you turn up the air conditioner in this joint?"

Marino strides over to the window unit and turns it on high.

"You know what she's doing these days, or don't you give a flying fuck? Nothing. She's a goddamn consultant. Got fired as the Chief. Can you believe it? The fucking governor of Virginia got rid of her because of political shit.

"And getting fired in the middle of a scandal don't help you get much business," he rants on. "When it comes to her, no one's hiring, unless it's some pissant case in some place that can't afford anyone, so she does it for nothing. Like some stupid drug overdose in Baton Rouge. A stupid-ass drug OD . . ."

"Louisiana?" Benton wanders toward a window and looks out.

"Yeah, the coroner from there called me this morning before I left Richmond. Some guy named Lanier. An old drug OD. I knew nothing about it, so then he wanted to know if the Doc's doing private work and basically wanted me to vouch for her character. I was pretty fucking pissed. But that's what it's come down to. She needs fucking references."

"Louisiana?" Benton says again, as if there must be some mistake.

"You know any other state with a city named Baton Rouge?" Marino snidely asks above the noise of the air conditioner.

"Not a good place for her," Benton says oddly.

"Yeah, well, New York, D.C., L.A. ain't calling. It's just a damn good thing the Doc's got her own money, otherwise she'd be . . ."

"There are serial murders going on down there . . ." Benton starts to say.

"Well, the task force working them ain't the one calling her. This hasn't got nothing to do with those ladies disappearing. This is chicken shit. A cold case. And I'm just guessing the coroner will call her. And knowing her, she'll help him out."

"An area where ten women have vanished, and the coroner calls about a cold case? Why now?"

"I don't know. A tip."

"What tip?"

"I don't know!"

"I want to know why that drug OD's so important all of a sudden," Benton persists.

"Are your antennas in a knot?" Marino exclaims. "You're

missing the fucking point. The Doc's life has turned to shit. She's gone from being Babe Ruth to playing Little League."

"Louisiana's not a good place for her." Benton says it again. "Why did the coroner call you? Just for a reference?"

Marino shakes his head, as if trying to wake up. He rubs his face. Benton's losing his grip.

"The coroner called wanting *my* help with the case," he says.

"*Your* help?"

"Now what the hell is that supposed to mean? You don't think I could help somebody with a case? I could help any god-damn . . ."

"Of course you could. So why aren't you helping the Baton Rouge coroner?"

"Because I don't know anything about that case! Jesus, you're making me crazy!"

"The Last Precinct could help down there."

"Would you fucking give it a rest? The coroner didn't seem all that hot and bothered by it, just indicated he might want the Doc's medical opinion . . ."

"Their legal system is based on the Napoleonic Code."

Marino has no idea what he's talking about. "What's Napoleon got to do with anything!"

"The French legal system," Benton says. "The only state in America that has a legal system based on the French legal system instead of the English. Baton Rouge has more unsolved homicides of women per capita than any other city in America."

"All right, already. So it ain't a nice place."

"She should not go down there. Especially alone. Not under any circumstances. Make sure of it, Pete." Benton is still looking out the window. "Trust me on this one."

"Trust you. What a joke."

"The least you can do is take care of her."

Marino is incensed, staring at Benton's back.

"She can't go anywhere near him."

"Who the hell are you talking about?" Marino asks, his frustration intensifying.

Benton is a stranger. Marino doesn't know this man.

"Wolfieboy? Jesus. I thought we were talking about a drug overdose case in Cajun country," Marino complains.

"Keep her out of there."

"You got no right asking me anything, especially about her."

"He's fixated on her."

"What the hell does he have to do with Louisiana?" Marino steps closer to him and scrutinizes his face, as if straining to read something he can't quite see.

"This is a continuation of a power struggle he lost with her in the past. And he intends to win it now if it's the last thing he does."

"Don't sound to me like he's gonna win a goddamn thing when he gets pumped full of enough juice to kill a herd of horses."

"I'm not talking about Jean-Baptiste. Have you forgotten the other Chandonne, his brother? The Last Precinct should help the coroner. She shouldn't."

Marino doesn't listen. He feels as if he's sitting in the backseat of a moving car that has no one at the wheel.

"The Doc knows what Wolfman wants of her." Marino sticks with one subject—the one that interests him and makes sense. "She won't mind giving him the needle, and I'll be right there behind the smoky glass, smiling."

"Have you asked her if she minds?" Benton looks out at another spring day dying gently. Tender, vivid greens are dipped in golden sunlight, and shadows deepen closer to the ground.

"I don't need to ask."

"I see. So you haven't discussed it with her. I'm not surprised. It wouldn't be like her to discuss it with you."

The insult is subtle but stings Marino like a sea nettle. He has never been intimate with Kay Scarpetta. No one has ever been as intimate with her, not the way Benton was. She hasn't told Marino how she feels about being an executioner. She doesn't discuss her feelings with him.

"I've depended on you to take care of her," Benton says.

The air seems to heat up, both of them sweating and silent.

"I know how you feel, Pete," Benton softly says. "I've always known."

"You don't know nothing."

"Take care of her."

"I came here so you could start doing that," Marino says.

22

Carthage Bluff Landing is a good popular stop for groceries and gas, but Bev Kiffin never docks there.

She doesn't slow down as she motors past and approaches Tin Lizzy's Landing, a restaurant that cost a million dollars to build from torn-down shacks and what Bev calls *salvage shit*. Rich people from the mainland can access Lizzy's from the Springfield Bridge and eat all the Cajun steaks and seafood and drink all they want without having to go home after dark in a boat. Six months ago, Bev asked Jay to take her there for her birthday, and he just laughed, and then his face twisted in a snarl as he called her stupid and ugly and out of her mind to think he'd take her to a restaurant at all, much less an upper-class one accessible by a highway.

Jealousy smolders as Bev picks up speed, heading due west to Jack's Boat Landing. She imagines Jay touching other women.

She remembers her father lifting other little girls on his lap, demanding that Bev bring home playmates just so he could cuddle with them and make her watch. He was a handsome, successful businessman and, during her teenage years, the object of her friends' crushes. He touched them in ways that weren't obvious or reportable, just what he considered innocent contact between his hard penis and their buttocks as they sat on his lap. He never exposed himself or talked in a vulgar manner, never even swore. Worst of all, when he accidentally brushed against their breasts, her friends liked it, and sometimes they brushed against him first.

Bev walked out on him one day and never went back, the same way her mother had when Bev was three, leaving her with him and his needs. Bev grew up addicted to men, going from one to the next. Leaving Jay is another matter entirely, and she isn't sure why she hasn't done it yet. She isn't sure why she'll do whatever he demands, despite her fears for her own safety. The thought of him going off in the boat one day and never returning sears her with terror. It would serve her right, since that's what she did to her father, who was dropped by a heart attack in 1997. Bev didn't go to his funeral.

Now and then when she's headed to shore, she thinks of the Mississippi River. On a good day, she could make it there in less than six hours, and she senses Jay is onto her occasional impulse to escape to the Gulf Coast. He's told her more than once that the Mississippi is the biggest river in the United States, more than a million miles of rough, muddy water and tributaries that fan out into thousands of creeks, marshes and swamps, where a person could get so lost "she would end up a skeleton in her boat," as Jay puts it. Those are his words exactly, saying *she* and *her* instead of *he* and *his*, his choice of words no accident. Jay doesn't have accidents of the tongue or anything else.

All the same, when Bev is out in the boat, she fantasizes about the Mississippi, about riverboat cruises and casinos, about fruity cocktails and beer in frozen glasses and maybe watching Mardi Gras from the window of a nice air-conditioned hotel. She wonders if good food would make her sick now that she's gone so long without it. A comfortable bed would probably stiffen her up and make her sore because she's so accustomed to a stinking, broken-down mattress that not even Jay will sleep on anymore.

She motors around a semi-submerged log, worried at first that it might move and prove to have teeth, and she begins to itch, especially beneath the tight waistband of her jeans.

"Shit!" She steers with one hand and digs the other under her clothes, clawing at her flesh as her welts get bigger. "Goddamnit! Oh, shit, what the fuck's bit me now?"

Breathing hard and beginning to panic, she shoves the throttle lever into neutral, opens the hatch and rummages in her beach bag for the insect repellent, spraying herself all over, including under her clothes.

It's all in her head, Jay always says. The welts aren't bites, they're hives, because she has a nervous condition, because she's half-crazy. *Well, I wasn't half-crazy until I met you,* she answers him in her head. *I never got hives in my life, nothing like that, not even poison ivy.* Bev drifts in the creek for a minute or two, contemplating what she's about to do and imagining Jay's face when she brings him what he wants, then imagining his face if she doesn't.

She advances the throttle and trims out, speeding up to forty miles an hour, which is much too fast for this part of the Tickfaw and reckless in light of her fears of the dark water and what's beneath it. Sweeping left, she abruptly cuts back her speed and trims down, heeling into a turn that takes her into a narrow creek, where she runs slowly and quietly into marshland that smells like death. Reaching under the tarp, she slides out the shotgun and lays it across her lap.

23

Sunlight illuminates a sliver of Benton's face as he stares out the window.

Silence reigns for a long, tense moment. The air seems to shimmer ominously, and Marino rubs his eyes.

"I don't get it." His mouth quivers. "You could be free, go home, be alive again." His voice cracks. "I thought you'd at least thank my ass for going to all the trouble to come here and tell you that maybe Lucy and me ain't ever given up on getting you back . . ."

"By offering her?" Benton turns around and looks at him. "By offering Kay as bait?"

At last he says her name, but he is so calm, it is as if he has no feelings, and Marino is shocked. He wipes his eyes.

"Bait? What . . . ?"

"Isn't it enough what the bastard has already done to her?" Benton goes on. "He tried to kill her once." He's not talking about Jean-Baptiste. He's talking about Jay Talley.

"He ain't gonna kill her when he's sitting behind bulletproof glass, chatting away on a phone inside a maximum-security prison," Marino says as they continue to talk about two different people.

"You're not listening to me," Benton tells him.

"That's because you're not listening to me," Marino childishly retorts.

Benton turns off the air conditioner and slides up the window. He closes his eyes as a breeze touches his hot cheeks like cool fingers. He smells the burgeoning Earth. For an instant, he remembers being alive with her, and he begins to bleed inside like a hemophiliac.

"Does she know?" he asks.

Marino rubs his face. "Jesus. I'm so sick and tired of my blood pressure shooting up like I'm a damn thermometer."

"Tell me." Benton presses his palms against the window frame, leaning into the fresh air. He turns around and meets Marino's eyes. "Does she know?"

Marino gets his meaning and sighs. "No, hell no. She don't know. She'll never know unless you're the one who tells her. I wouldn't do that to her. Lucy wouldn't do that to her. See"—he angrily pulls himself to his feet—"some of us care too much about her to hurt her like that. Imagine how she'd feel if she knew you're alive and don't care a shit about her anymore."

He walks to the door, shaking with rage and grief. "I thought you might thank me."

"I do thank you. I know you mean well." Benton walks over to him, his calm demeanor uncanny. "I know you don't understand, but maybe someday you will. Good-bye, Pete. I don't ever want to see or hear from you again. Please don't take it personally."

Marino grabs the doorknob and almost yanks it out of the wood. "Good riddance and go fuck yourself. Don't take it personally."

They face each other like two men squaring off in a gun fight, neither wanting to be the first to move, neither really wanting the other to be gone from his life. Benton's hazel eyes are vacant, as if whoever lives behind them has vanished. Marino's pulse measures panic as he realizes that the Benton he knew is gone and nothing will ever bring him back.

And somehow Marino is going to have to tell Lucy. And somehow Marino will have to accept the fact that his dream of rescuing Benton and returning him to Scarpetta will always be a dream, only a dream.

"It don't make sense!" Marino shouts.

Benton touches an index finger to his lips. "Please go, Pete," he quietly says. "It doesn't have to make sense."

Marino hesitates in the dimly lit, stinking landing just beyond apartment 56. "Okay." He fumbles for his cigarettes and spills several on the filthy concrete. "Okay . . ." He starts to say *Benton* but catches himself as he squats to pick up the cigarettes, his thick fingers clumsily breaking two of them.

He wipes his eyes with the back of a big hand as Benton looks down at him from the apartment doorway, watching, not offering to help pick up the cigarettes, unable to move.

"Take care, Pete," Benton, the master of masks and self-control, says in a steady, reasonable voice.

Marino looks up with bloodshot eyes from his squatting position on the landing. The seam in the crotch of his wrinkled khakis is slightly ripped, his white briefs peeking through.

He blurts out, "Don't you get it, you can come back!"

"What *you* don't get is there is no *back* to go *back* to," Benton says in a voice so low it is almost inaudible. "I don't want to come *back*. Now please get the hell out of my life and leave me alone."

He pulls his apartment door shut and flips the dead bolt.

Inside, he collapses on the couch and covers his face with his hands while Marino's insistent knocking turns to violent thuds and kicks.

"Yeah, well, enjoy your great life, asshole!" his muffled voice sounds through the door. "I always knew you was cold and don't give a fuck about anybody, including *her*, you fucking psycho!" The banging and kicking suddenly stop.

Benton holds his breath, straining to hear. The sudden silence is worse than any tantrum. Pete Marino's silence is damning. It is final. His friend's heavy feet scuff down the stairs.

"I am dead," Benton mutters into his hands as he doubles over on the couch.

"No matter what, I am dead. I am Tom. Tom Haviland. Tom Speck Haviland . . ." His chest heaves and his heart seems to beat out of rhythm. "Born in Greenwich, Connecticut . . ."

He gets up, crushed by a depression that turns the room dark and the air as thick as oil. He smells Marino's lingering cigarette smoke, and it runs through him like a blade. Moving to the window, he stands to one side of it so he isn't visible from below, and he watches Pete Marino walking slowly away through intermittent shadows and dappled sunlight along uneven cobblestones.

Marino stops to light a Lucky Strike and turns around to stare up at Benton's depressing building until he finds apartment 56. Cheap sheer curtains are caught by a breeze and flutter out the open window like spirits leaving.

24

In Poland, it is a few minutes past midnight.

Lucy drives past caravans of World War II Russian Army trucks and speeds through miles of tiled tunnels and along the tree-lined E28. She can't stop thinking about the Red Notice, how easy it was for her to send computerized information that has law enforcement agencies around the world on guard. Of course, her information is legitimate. Rocco Caggiano is a criminal. She has known that for years. But until she recently received information that ties him to at least a few of his crimes, neither she nor other interested parties had probable cause to do anything more than hate him.

One simple phone call.

Lucy called Interpol's Central Bureau in Washington, D.C. She identified herself—her real identity, of course—and had a brief conversation with a U.S. Marshal liaison named McCord. The next step was a search of the Interpol database to see if Caggiano was known, and he wasn't, not even as a Green Notice, which simply means a person is of interest to Interpol and should be watched and subjected to extra scans and pat-downs when he or she crosses borders and passes through international airports.

Rocco Caggiano is in his mid-thirties. He has never been arrested and has made a fortune, ostensibly as a scumbag, ambulance-chasing lawyer, but his formidable wealth and power come from his real clients, the Chandonnes, although it isn't accurate to call them clients. They own him. They shield him. He is kept in high style and alive at their pleasure.

"Check out a murder in 1997," Lucy told McCord. "New Year's Day in Sicily. A journalist named Carlos Guarino. Shot in the head, his body dumped in a drainage ditch. He was working on an investigative story about the Chandonnes—a very risky thing to do, by the way. He had just interviewed a lawyer who represents Jean-Baptiste Chandonne . . ."

"Right, right. I know about that case. The Wolfman, or whatever they call him."

"The cover of *People* magazine, *Time* magazine, whatever. Who doesn't know about the Wolfman serial killer, I guess," Lucy replied. "Guarino was murdered hours after talking to Caggiano.

"Next, a journalist named Emmanuel La Fleur. Barbizon, France, February eleventh, 1997. Worked for *Le Monde.* He also was unwisely doing a story on the Chandonne family."

"Why all this interest in the Chandonnes, beyond their being Jean-Baptiste's unlucky parents?"

"Organized crime. A huge cartel. Never been proven that the father heads it, but he does. There are rumors. Investigative reporters are sometimes blinded by scoops and prizes. La Fleur had drinks with Caggiano hours before the journalist's body was found in a garden near the former château of the painter Jean François

Millet—don't bother looking for him. He's been dead more than a hundred years."

She wasn't being sarcastic. She would never assume that Millet was a household name and didn't want to find the artist was suddenly a person of interest.

"La Fleur was shot in the head, and the ten-millimeter bullet was fired from the same gun used to murder Guarino," she explained.

There was more. The information came from a letter written by Jean-Baptiste Chandonne.

"I'll e-mail you his letter immediately," Lucy said, a transmission that would have been unthinkable before Interpol began using the Internet.

But the International Police Agency's computerized communication network has more than enough firewalls, hieroglyphical encryptions and hacker-tracking systems to render any transmission secure. Lucy knows. When Interpol began to use the Internet, the secretary general personally invited her to hack her way in. She couldn't. She never made it past the first firewall and secretly was furious at being foiled, even though the last thing she should have wanted was success.

The secretary general called her, quite amused. He read to her a list of her usernames, passwords and the location of her computer.

"Don't worry, Lucy. I won't send the police," he said.

"Merci beaucoup, Monsieur Hartman," she replied to the secretary general, who is American.

From New York to London to Berlin and now crossing the border into Poland, police have been alert, she sensed that. But they didn't take her seriously, couldn't have cared less about this young American woman driving her rented Mercedes at a late hour on a cool spring night. To them she clearly doesn't look like a terrorist, and she isn't. But she could be—easily—and it is foolish not to take her seriously, for no reason beyond her nationality, youthfulness, appearance and a smile that can be warm and captivating when she chooses.

She is far too smart to carry a firearm. Her tactical baton will do if she runs into a problem, not from the police, but from some asshole along the way who might have singled her out for robbery or some other type of assault. The baton was easy for her to smuggle into Germany. She used her shopworn routine because it has never failed: overnighted it in a cosmetic bag filled with a jumble of accessories (curling iron, curling brush, blow-dryer, et cetera). The package arrived at a cheap hotel near the airport, addressed to one of Lucy's aliases; she also had a room reserved and paid for in that name. Lucy drove her rental car to the hotel, parked on a side street, picked up the package at check-in, messed up her room a bit and hung a *Do Not Disturb* sign on the door. She was back in her car in half an hour.

If a more serious weapon is imperative on a mission, a handgun and extra magazines of ammunition are tucked inside alleged lost baggage sloppily bound in airline tape and dumped at the hotel desk by one of Lucy's associates, dressed for the part. She has many associates. Most of them have never met her and don't know who she is. Only her core team knows her. She has them and they have her. It is enough.

She plucks her international cell phone from between her legs and presses redial.

"I'm on the go," she says when Rudy Musil answers. "An hour-fifteen out if I don't speed too much."

"Don't." A television plays loudly in the background.

Lucy eyes the speedometer as it eases past 120 kilometers per hour. She might be brazen, but never intentionally foolish. She has no intention of getting entangled with police as she heads toward the most prominent but beleaguered port city in Poland. Americans aren't often seen in Szczecin. Why would Americans go there? Certainly not for tourism, unless it is to look at nearby concentration camps. For years now, the Germans have been intercepting foreign vessels en route to the Szczecin port. Daily, the Germans steal business from a city where unemployment and economic depression continue to corrode what once was a jewel of architecture, culture and art.

Very little glory has been restored to Szczecin since World War II, when Hitler set out to bomb Poland off the map and exterminate its people. It is impossible to earn a decent living. Few people know what it is like to live in a nice house, drive a nice car, wear nice clothes, buy books or go on vacation. It is said that no one but members of the Russian Mafia and criminal cartels have money in Poland, and with rare exception, this is true.

Lucy constantly scans the highway and her smile fades, her eyes narrow.

"Taillights ahead. I don't like it," she says into the cell phone. "Someone slowing." She eases up on the accelerator. "Stopping in the middle of the fucking highway. No place to pull over."

"Don't stop. Go around it," Rudy tells her.

"Disabled limousine. Weird to see an American limo in these parts."

Lucy swerves around a white stretch Lincoln. The driver and a passenger are climbing out, and she resists the urge to stop and help.

"Shit," she mutters in frustration.

"Don't even think about it," Rudy warns, well aware of Lucy's high-risk personality and compulsion to save the world.

She pushes down the accelerator, and the limousine and its stranded passengers become part of the thick darkness behind her.

"The front desk is empty at this hour. You know where you're going," Rudy makes sure.

There can be no mistakes and no sightings.

Lucy repeatedly glances in the rearview mirror, worrying that the limousine might be gaining on her and turn out to be real trouble. Her stomach tightens. What if those people back there genuinely need help? She left them alone in the dark on E28, where there is no way to pull off the road. They'll probably get run over by a truck.

For several seconds she considers speeding to the next exit and turning around. She does it for lost dogs, for turtles crossing highways and streets. She always brakes for chipmunks and squirrels, and runs outside to check on birds that fly into her windows. But people are another matter. She can't afford to take the chance.

"You can't miss the Radisson," Rudy is saying. "Don't park in the courtyard for buses. They don't appreciate it."

He is joking. It goes without saying that Lucy will not park at the Radisson.

25

Delray Beach, Florida, is hot at six p.m., and Kay Scarpetta turns away from her kitchen window, deciding she will work another hour before venturing outside.

She has become an expert in judging shadows and light, monitoring them in her scientific manner before heading out to check on her fruit trees or walk on the beach. Making rather useless decisions based on analysis and calculations of how the sun moves across the sky helps her feel as though she has not lost complete control of her life.

Her two-story yellow stucco house is modest by her standards, just an old place with wobbly white railings, failing plumbing and wiring, and air-conditioning that seems to have a mean-spirited will of its own. Tiles sometimes fall out of the backsplash behind the electric stove, and yesterday the bathtub's cold-water handle pulled loose from the wall. For the sake of survival, she has read home-repair books and manages to keep her surroundings from falling on her head as she tries not to remember what days were like before she relocated hundreds of miles south of her former career, and barely an hour's drive north of Miami, where she was born. The past is dead, and death is just one more phase of existence. This is her creed. Most of the time she believes it.

Time on Earth is an opportunity to become more highly evolved, and then people move on or cross over—a concept that by no means is original to her, but she is not one to accept what isn't obvious without dissecting it first. After much contemplation, her findings about eternity are simple: No one good or evil ceases to exist; life is energy and energy cannot be created or destroyed; it is recycled. Therefore, it is possible that the pure of heart and the purely evil have been here before and will be here again. Scarpetta doesn't believe in heaven or hell, and she no longer goes to Mass, not even on religious holidays.

"What happened to your Catholic guilt?" Lucy asked her several Christmases ago when they were mixing a strong batch of eggnog and church was not on the agenda.

"I can't participate in something I no longer believe in," Scarpetta replied, reaching for freshly ground nutmeg. "Especially if I am at odds with it, which is worse than having a complete loss of faith in it."

"The question is, what is *it*? Are you talking about Catholicism or God?"

"Politics and power. They have an unmistakable stench, rather much like the inside of the morgue fridge. I can close my eyes and know what's there. Nothing alive."

"Thanks for sharing," Lucy said. "Maybe I'll just drink a little straight rum on the rocks. Raw eggs suddenly don't seem very appealing."

"You're not the least bit squeamish." Scarpetta poured Lucy a glass of eggnog, adding a sprinkle of nutmeg. "Drink up before Marino gets here and there's none left."

Lucy smiled. The only thing that makes her gag is walking into a ladies' room and finding someone in the middle of changing a baby's diaper. To Lucy, that stench is worse than a decomposing body buzzing with blow flies, and she has experienced her share of offensive horrors because of her and her aunt's unusual occupations.

"This mean you no longer believe in eternity?" Lucy challenged her.

"I believe in it more than ever."

Scarpetta has made the dead speak most of her life, but always through the silent language of injuries, trace evidence, diseases and investigative details that can be interpreted with medicine, science, experience and deduction that borders on the intuitive, a gift that cannot be learned or taught. But people change. She is no longer entirely clinical. She has come to accept that the dead continue to exist and intervene in the lives of their earthbound loved ones and enemies. It is a conviction that she conceals from her detractors and certainly never mentions in professional presentations or in journal articles or in court.

"I've seen psychics on TV talking about people dying and crossing over—I believe that's the term," Lucy observed, sipping her eggnog. "I don't know. It's pretty interesting. The older I get, the less certain I am of most things."

"I've noticed your advanced aging process," Scarpetta replied. "When you turn thirty, you will begin to have visions and see auras. Let's hope you don't get arthritis."

This conversation took place in Scarpetta's former home in Richmond, a fortress of stone she designed with love and an abandonment of financial reason, sparing no expense in her insistence on old woods, exposed beams, solid doors and plaster walls, and a kitchen and office that were perfect for her precise way of going about her business, whether it was over a microscope or a Viking gas stove.

Life was good. Then it wasn't and never would be again. So much went wrong. So much was spoiled and lost and could never be restored. Three years ago, she was well along her journey to disaster. She had resigned as president of the National Association of Medical Examiners. The governor of Virginia was about to fire her. One day, she cleared her office walls of scores of commendations, certifications and degrees that are now packed up somewhere in cardboard boxes. The pre-crash Scarpetta was impeccably, if not rigidly, intellectual, completely confident of her knowledge, her truthfulness and her ability to excavate for answers. She was a legend in law enforcement and criminal justice, and to some people unapproachable and cold. Now she has no staff except her secretary, Rose, who followed her to Florida with the excuse that it would be nice to "retire" near West Palm Beach.

Scarpetta can't get over Benton Wesley. She has tried. Several times she has dated perfectly acceptable men, only to recoil at their touch. A simple touch, and it isn't Benton's, and then she is reminded. Then she reviews her last images of him, burned, mutilated. She still regrets reading his autopsy report, and yet she doesn't. She regrets touching his ashes and scattering them, and yet she doesn't. It was crucial, it really was, she constantly tells herself when she remembers the feel of the silky, lumpy cremains, when she remembers returning him to the pure air and sea he loved.

She wanders out of the kitchen, clutching the same mug of coffee she has warmed up in the microwave at least four times since noon.

"Dr. Scarpetta, can I get you anything?" Rose calls out from a spare bedroom that serves as her office.

"Nothing would help," Scarpetta replies, halfway joking, as she heads in the direction of Rose's voice.

"Nonsense." It is her secretary's favorite rebuttal. "I told you if you went to work for yourself, you'd only be busier, if that was possible. And worn-out and overextended."

"And what did I tell you about retirement?"

Rose looks up from the autopsy report she is proofreading on her computer. She tabs to the space for *brain* and types *1,200 grams. Within normal limits* and corrects a typo.

Nails click across the wooden floor like Morse code as Scarpetta's bulldog hears voices and walks rather lazily, then pauses, then walks some more toward them, then sits.

"Come here, Billy-Billy," Scarpetta affectionately calls out.

He looks at her with drooping eyes.

"His name is Billy," Rose reminds her, although there is no point in doing so. "If you keep calling him Billy-Billy, he'll think he lives with an echo or has a split personality."

"Come here, Billy-Billy."

He gets up, takes his time. Click-click.

Rose is wearing a peach pantsuit. It is wool, as are all of Rose's suits. The house is on the beach. It is bloody hot and humid, and Rose doesn't hesitate to walk outside in a skirt and long-sleeved blouse and water the hibiscus, climb a ladder to pick bananas or key limes, or save baby frogs from drowning in the trap of the pool. It's a wonder that moths haven't carried off every bit of clothing Rose owns, but she is a proud woman, her dignity masking a fragile, gentle nature, and it is out of her respect for herself and her boss that she takes time each morning to make sure her choice of outfit for the day is pressed and clean.

135

If anything, she seems secretly pleased that her sense of style is dated, some of her suits so old that she was wearing them more than a decade ago when she first started working for Scarpetta. Rose hasn't changed her hair, either, still pinning it up in a fuss-budget French twist and refusing to get rid of the gray. Good structure makes the building, and her bones are exquisite. At the age of sixty-seven, men find her attractive, but she hasn't dated since her husband died. The only man Scarpetta has ever seen her flirt with is Pete Marino, and she doesn't mean it and he knows it, but they have tormented each other since Scarpetta was appointed chief medical examiner of Virginia, what now seems as though it were another incarnation.

Billy is panting as he appears at the desk. He is not quite a year old, white with a large brown spot on the middle of his back, and his underbite reminds Scarpetta of a backhoe. He sits at her feet, looking up.

"I don't have any . . ."

"Don't say that word!" Rose exclaims.

"I wasn't going to. I was going to spell it."

"He can spell now."

Billy suffers no language barrier with the words *bye-bye* and *treat*. He also recognizes *no* and *sit* but pretends he doesn't, stubbornness the right of his breed.

"You better not have been chewing on anything back there," Scarpetta warns him.

In the last month, Billy has taken a fancy to gnawing and ripping molding off doorframes and around the base of the walls, especially in Scarpetta's bedroom.

"This isn't your house, and I will have to pay for all repairs when I move out." She wags her finger at him.

"It would be worse if it was your house," Rose remarks as the dog continues to stare up at Scarpetta and wag his tail, which looks like a croissant.

She picks up a slim stack of mail from her desk and offers it to her boss.

"I've dealt with the bills. There are a couple personal letters. And the usual journals and so forth. And this, from Lucy."

She directs Scarpetta's attention to a large manila envelope, her name and address neatly written in black Magic Marker, the return address Lucy's New York office, also written in Magic Marker. The envelope is marked *Personal* in large letters and underlined twice. It is a die-hard habit for Scarpetta to look at postmarks, and this one is puzzling.

"The postal code isn't for her part of the city," Scarpetta says. "Lucy always mails things from her office, and as a matter of fact, she always overnights mail to me. I can't remember a single time she's ever sent me anything by regular mail, not since she was in college."

Rose doesn't seem concerned. "'A foolish consistency is the hobgoblin of little minds,'" she quotes Ralph Waldo Emerson. In fact, it is her favorite quote.

Rose shakes the envelope. "Doesn't sound like anything dangerous in there," she teases. "If you're feeling one of your bouts of paranoia coming on, I'll open it for you, but it's marked *Personal* . . ."

"Never mind." Scarpetta takes it and her other mail from Rose.

"And Dr. Lanier from Baton Rouge left a message." Rose pecks at the keyboard and corrects another typo. "It's regarding the Charlotte Dard case. He says you'll get it Monday, his reports and all that. He sounded stressed. He wants to know what you find, *immediately*."

She gives her boss a look that always reminds Scarpetta of a schoolteacher about to single out some unsuspecting student and put him or her on the spot. "I think something's going on in this case, something worse than a drug overdose."

Scarpetta massages Billy's soft, speckled ears. "Her cause of death isn't straightforward. That's plenty bad. What's worse, the case is eight years old."

"I don't understand why it's such a big deal right now, as if they don't have enough unsolved murders and suspicious deaths down there. Those abducted women. Lord."

"I don't know why it's suddenly become a priority, either," Scarpetta replies. "But the fact is, it has, and I feel obliged to do what I can."

"Because nobody else can be bothered."

"*I* can be bothered, can't I, Billy-Billy?"

"Well, let me tell you a thing or two, Dr. Echo. I think there's something the coroner down there has no intention of telling you."

"There had better not be," Scarpetta remarks as she walks off.

26

Lucy desperately needs a ladies' room.

Forget looking for a gas station or a rest stop. She pushes the Mercedes up to 160 kilometers per hour, despite Rudy's warning about speeding. Focusing on the dark road, she tries hard to concentrate and ignore her bladder. The drive seems to take twice as long as it should, but she makes excellent time and is ahead of schedule by thirty-five minutes. She redials Rudy's cell phone.

"On final," she says. "Just got to land this thing somewhere."

"Shut up," Rudy orders someone in the room, as the TV plays loudly. "Don't make me tell you again."

27

Rocco Caggiano's favorite form of relaxation is to sit for hours in beer gardens, drinking one *Gross Bier* after another.

The pale gold elixirs are served in tall, plain glasses, and he prefers clean-tasting lagers and will not touch wheat beers. Rocco has never understood how he can drink a gallon of beer in one sitting but not a gallon of water. He could not drink a gallon of water during an entire day, probably not even in three days, and he has always puzzled over how much beer, wine, champagne or mixed drinks he can put away when he can scarcely finish a single glass of water.

In fact, he hates water. Perhaps what a psychic once told him is true: He drowned in a former life. What a terrible way to die, and he often thinks of the killer in England who drowned one wife after another in the tub by grabbing her feet and yanking until her head was under water and she could do nothing but helplessly flop her arms like a fish on a dock. The scenario was a constant emotional itch when Caggiano began to hate his first wife, then his second. Alimony was cheaper than the price he would pay if some medical examiner discovered bruises or God knows what. But even if he did drown in a former life and thought drowning someone was a good way to commit murder, this, in his mind, would not explain the enigma—the purely biological phenomenon—of how much alcohol he can consume and why he cannot and will not finish even one glass of water.

No one has ever been able to settle his mind with an answer he accepts. Small conundrums have always worried him like a sandspur stuck to his sock.

"It must be 'cause you pee all the time when you drink beer," Caggiano introduces the question at virtually every social gathering. "When you pee, you make room for more, right?"

"You drink a gallon of water, you will be pissing all the time, too," a Dutch customs agent challenged him some months back when he, Rocco and several other friends of the Chandonne cartel were taking time out in a beer garden in Munich.

"I hate water," Rocco said.

"Then how do you know this about whether you would pee water as fast as beer?" a German container ship's captain asked.

"He doesn't know."

"Yes. You ought to test it out, Rocco."

"We'll drink beer, you drink water, and see who pees the most and the fastest."

The men laughed and clanked glasses in a drunken toast, slopping beer all over the wooden table. It had been a good day. Before they caroused at the beer garden, they had wandered into the nudist park where a naked man on a bicycle pedaled past and the Dutchman yelled at him in Dutch that he'd better be careful which gear he shifted, while the ship's captain yelled in German that his kickstand was very small. Rocco yelled in English that the man didn't have to worry about his dick getting caught in the spokes because it didn't even hang over the seat. The bicyclist pedaled on, ignoring them.

Women sunbathe in the nude in the park and do not seem to care if men stare at them. Rocco and his henchmen would get very brazen and hover right over a woman stretched out on her towel and make comments about her anatomical points of interest. Usually, the woman would turn over on her belly and go back to sleep or continue reading her magazine or book while the men went on to survey her buttocks, as if they were hills they might climb. Rocco's intense arousal would make him mean, and he would fire vile, lewd aspersions at the woman until his companions had to usher him away. Rocco is especially vicious with the homosexuals minding their own business in the park. He believes all homosexuals should be castrated and executed, and he would like to be the one to do it and watch them pee and defecate out of fright.

"It's a medical fact that when you're tortured or about to be snuffed, you piss and shit in your pants," he announced later in the beer garden.

"What medical fact? I thought you were a lawyer, not a doctor."

"So you know this, Rocco? And how do you know this? You take off their pants to see? Maybe you take their pants off to check for shit and piss?" Loud laughter. "Then you can know it as a fact. If this is true, I must come around to my important question. Do you go around taking the pants off dead bodies? I think all of us have a right to hear this. Because at least for me, if I die, I need to know if you will take my pants off."

"If you die," Rocco replied, "you won't know a fucking thing."

It is irrational that Rocco should remember this boozy

conversation and what his doctor has preached to him for years. Rocco has gastritis and cranky bowel syndrome due to stress, smoking and heavy drinking. *All ills in life are blamed on acute stress, smoking and heavy drinking,* Rocco always retorts on his way out of the examination room. He files for medical reimbursement and resumes his self-destructive life.

His bowels and bladder let loose as he sits in a chair inside his hotel room, a Colt .380 cocked and pointed at his head.

28

Jack's Boat Landing is a clutter of trailers, bateaux, bass and flat-bottom boats, and runabouts tied to pilings along a crisscross of rickety docks strung with old tires that serve as fenders.

Pulled up on the muddy shore are several pirogues—or Cajun canoes—and a rotting bow rider that won't be pulling water-skiers anymore. The parking lot is dirt, and on the fuel dock are two pumps—one for regular gas, the other for diesel. Jack works from five a.m. until nine p.m. in his one-room office with its mounted fish hanging at random angles on the wall with peeling paint. The calendar above his old metal desk features glossy photos of glitter-painted bass boats—the very expensive kind that can go up to sixty miles an hour.

Were it not for the window air-conditioning unit and the Port-a-John behind the building, Jack would lack all modern conveniences. Not that he would care, particularly. He was born into a hard life and raised to make any sacrifice that might keep him right where he is, in a world of water and the creatures in it, and trees draped in Spanish moss.

For those who frequent his boat landing, tying up for gas and making a trip into town for provisions is normal behavior. People who stay for weeks or longer in their fishing camps on the bayous and rivers are expected to leave vehicles and boat trailers parked at the landing. He never thinks twice about the white Jeep Cherokee tucked between trucks and other SUVs in a far corner of the lot near the water's edge. He minds his own business, even if he does have instincts about people that are as strong as his sense of smell. Swamp Woman sent strong signals to him from day one—and that's been some two years now. Her demeanor is no-nonsense about asking personal questions.

Bev Kiffin opens the hatch and pulls out her beach bag. She stands aft and drops in the plow anchor, then tosses two nylon lines up on the fuel dock as Jack waves, walking swiftly her way.

"Why if it isn't Swamp Woman!" he calls out. "Can I top you off?"

The landing is lit and bugs are thick, roiling clouds in the yellow glow of lamps. Jack tosses her the bowline.

"I'll be leaving her here for a few hours." Bev turns the rope and makes a half hitch over the horns of the cleat. She pulls back the tarp and sets empty gas cans on the dock. "Fill 'em up. What's your price these days?"

"One eighty-five."

"Shit." Bev hops up on the dock, moving nimbly for a woman her size. "That's highway robbery."

Jack laughs. "It ain't me who decides the price of oil."

He's tall and bald, as dark and strong as a cypress. Bev's never seen him once when he wasn't wearing his sweat-stained orange Harley-Davidson cap and chewing on a plug of tobacco.

"You comin' and goin'?" He spits and wipes his mouth on the back of a sunspotted, gnarled hand and helps her with the stern lines.

"Just to the store."

Bev dips into her beach bag for a single key attached to a small fishing bobber—in case she ever accidentally drops the key into the water. Her attention wanders around the crowded parking lot, fixing on the Cherokee.

"I guess I'd better crank her up to make sure the battery ain't dead."

"Well if it is," Jack says, lining up the four gas cans near the pump, "you know I'll jump 'er."

Bev watches him squat, sticking the gas nozzle into each can, the pump clicking away her cash. The back of his neck reminds her of alligator hide, and his elbows are big calluses. She's been coming to him at least ten times a year, more often of late, and he doesn't have a damn clue about her, which is a good thing for him. She heads to the SUV, suddenly worried about whether it needs gas, too. She can't remember if she filled it up last time.

Unlocking the driver's door, she slides in and turns the key in the ignition. The engine cranks after three tries, and she's relieved to see she has more than half a tank of gas. When she runs low, she'll fill up at a gas station. Turning the headlights on, she backs up and parks near the dock. While she is pulling cash out of her wallet and squinting to make out the bills, Jack wipes his hands on a rag and waits for her to roll down the window.

"That'll be forty-four dollars and forty cents," he tells her. "I'll get those cans back in your boat for ya and keep an eye on it. I noticed you got your friend with ya." He means the shotgun. "You plan on leaving it in the boat? I wouldn't. Watch out shooting at gators with that thing. All it does is make 'em rageful."

Bev can't believe she almost drove off and left her shotgun. She's not thinking clearly tonight, and her knee hurts.

"Last thing you do before you leave," she adds as he steps down into the boat, "is fill the fish box with ice."

"How much?" He fetches the shotgun, climbs back up on the dock and carefully places it on the backseat of the Cherokee.

"A hundred pounds will do."

"Must be doing a lot of shopping to need all that ice." He stuffs the rag in a back pocket of his old, soiled work pants.

"Stuff spoils quick out here."

"That'll be another twenty. I'm givin' you three bucks off."

She hands him two tens and doesn't thank him for the discount.

"I'm gone by nine." He looks past her, inside the beat-up Cherokee. "So if you ain't back by then . . ."

"Won't be," Bev tells him, shifting the SUV into reverse.

She never is and doesn't need the reminder.

He stares past her at the front passenger's door, at the rolled-up window and the missing crank and push-in lock.

"You know, girl, I could fix that if you're ever of a mind to leave the keys."

Bev glances at the door. "Don't matter," she says. "Nobody rides in this thing but me."

147

29

Upstairs in the north wing of the house is a guest bedroom overlooking the ocean, and in front of the bay window is Scarpetta's large desk, not an antique or anything special, just an inexpensive computer desk with a matching return.

Bookcases fill the walls so tightly that some light switches and electrical outlets are behind them, out of reach, and she has to get by with power strips. Her furniture is a light maple veneer, in depressing contrast to the beautiful antiques and artistic pieces, including Oriental rugs, fine stemware and china, that she spent most of her career collecting. Scarpetta's former life is locked up in a Connecticut storage warehouse, one secure enough for museum pieces.

She has not gone to see what she owns since Lucy took care of her aunt's chattel more than two years ago, choosing the location because of its proximity to New York, where Lucy has her headquarters and apartment. Scarpetta doesn't miss the furniture from her past. It is useless to care about it. Just the thought of it makes her tired for reasons she doesn't completely comprehend.

The office in her Delray rental house is a comfortable size, although nowhere near as spacious and organized as what she was accustomed to in her Richmond house, where she had cabinets of hanging files, miles of workspace and a massive desk custom-built of Brazilian cherry. Her house there was modern Italian country, put together stone by stone, the walls antiqued plaster, the exposed beams nineteenth-century black jarrah railroad ties from South Africa. If the house she built in Richmond wasn't beautiful before, it was spectacular by the time she remodeled it in an attempt to eradicate the past—a past haunted by Benton and Jean-Baptiste Chandonne. But she felt no better. The ghosts followed her from room to room.

Her denial of unbearable loss and her own near murder were fragmented dreams of horror that chilled her, no matter the temperature inside the house. Every creak of old wood and utterance of wind sends her hand reaching for the pistol she carried as her heart beat hard. One day she walked out of her magnificent home and never went back, not even to retrieve her belongings. Lucy handled that.

For one who had always walled her soul from a wicked world and unreachable pain, she found herself a wanderer, skipping from one hotel to another like a stone across water, making phone calls to set up private consulting, and quickly became so bound in the snarled chains of evidence, of investigative incompetence and carelessness of police and medical examiners all over the place, that she had no choice but to settle in another house because she had to settle somewhere. She could no longer review cases while sitting on a hotel bed.

"Go south, far south," Lucy told her quietly, lovingly, one

afternoon in Greenwich, Connecticut, where Scarpetta was in hiding at the Homestead Inn. "You aren't ready for New York yet, Aunt Kay, and you sure as hell aren't ready to work for me."

"I'll never work for you." Scarpetta meant it, shame pulling her eyes away from her niece.

"Well, you don't have to be insulting about it." Lucy was stung too, and within a minute, the two of them were arguing and fighting.

"I raised you," Scarpetta blurted out from the bed, where she sat rigidly and enraged. "My goddamn sister, the admired author of children's books who doesn't have a clue about raising her own goddamn child, dumped me on your doorstep . . . I mean, the other way around."

"Freudian slip! You needed me worse than I needed you."

"Not hardly. You were a monster. At ten, when you rolled into my life like the Trojan Horse, I was stupid enough to let you park, and then what? Then what?" The great Chief, the logical doctor-lawyer, was sputtering, tears rolling down her face. "You had to be a genius, didn't you? The worst brat on Earth . . ." Scarpetta's voice quavered. "And I couldn't give you up, you awful child." She could hardly speak. "If Dorothy had wanted you back, I would have taken the bitch to court and proved she wasn't a fit mother."

"She wasn't a fit mother and she isn't." Lucy was beginning to cry, too. "A bitch? That's charging her with a misdemeanor when she's a felon. A felon! A character disorder. For God's sake, how did you end up with a psycho for a sister?" Lucy weeps, sitting next to her aunt on the bed, their shoulders touching.

"She's the dragon you always fight, have spent your life

fighting," Scarpetta said. "You're really fighting Mom. She's too small a quarry for me. She's nothing more than a rabbit with sharp teeth that goes after your ankles. I don't waste my time on rabbits. I don't have time."

"Please go south," Lucy begged her, getting up from the bed and facing her with wet eyes and a red nose. "For now. Please. Go back to where you came from and start all over."

"I'm too old to start over."

"Shit!" Lucy laughed. "You're only forty-six, and men and women stare at you everywhere you go. And you don't even notice. You're one hell of a package."

The only time Scarpetta was ever called a *package* was when she was in worse trouble than usual and required off-duty police for security. On their radios, they referred to her as *the package*. Scarpetta wasn't entirely sure what they meant.

She moved south to Delray Beach, not exactly returning to her roots, but to an area near where her mother and sister live, yet safely far away.

Inside her weather-beaten 1950s rented house, her office is piled with paperwork and stiff cardboard slide folders, so much of it stacked on the floor that she has to make an effort not to trip over her work, making it impossible for her to be her usual prepossessed self when she walks in. Bookcases are crammed, some medical and legal tomes are double-shelved, while her rare antique books are protected from the sun and humidity in a tiny room next door that was probably intended to be the nursery.

She picks at Rose's fresh tuna salad as she goes through her mail, her letter opener a scalpel. She slices open the manila envelope first, apparently from her niece or perhaps someone else in her office, and is baffled to discover another envelope inside, this one plain white and addressed by hand in calligraphy to *Madame Kay Scarpetta, LLB.*

She drops the manila envelope on the table and hurries out of her office, rushing past Rose without speaking and into the kitchen for freezer paper.

30

Taxicabs remind Benton of insects.

And during his exile, he has grown fond of certain insects. Stick bugs look remarkably like twigs. Benton often loses himself in parks and along sidewalks, patiently searching shrubbery for a stick bug or, better yet, a praying mantis, which is extremely rare and a good omen, although he has never experienced a positive change in fortune directly after spotting a praying mantis. Maybe someday he will. Ladybugs are good luck. Everybody knows that. If one ends up wherever he is staying, he gently coaxes it onto his finger and takes it outside, no matter how many flights of stairs, and deposits it on a bush.

One week he did this ten times and enjoyed the thought that it was the same ladybug flirting with him. He believes that all kindnesses will be repaid. He also believes that evil will get its ugly reward, and until he began his nonexistence, he argued about that with Scarpetta often, because he didn't believe it at all back then. And she did.

We often don't know the reason for things, Benton. But I believe there is one, always.

He hears Scarpetta's voice in a remote cavern of his brain as he sits in the dark backseat of a southbound taxi.

How can you say that?

He hears his own voice answering her.

Because I've seen enough to say it. What reason *can there possibly be for a sister or a daughter or a brother or a son or a parent or a significant other to be raped, tortured and murdered?*

Silence. The taxi driver is listening to hip-hop.

"Turn that down, please," Benton calmly says, this time out loud.

Or what about the old woman struck by lightning because her umbrella frame was metal?

Scarpetta doesn't answer him.

Okay, then what about the entire family killed by carbon monoxide because no one told them not to cook with charcoal in the fireplace, especially with the windows closed? What reason, *Kay?*

His sense of her continues to linger like her favorite perfume.

So there's a reason I was murdered and am gone from your life forever?

The conversation has turned one-sided and won't stop. What reason has she assigned to what she believes happened to him, he asks, convinced she has come up with a reason, certainly by now.

You're rationalizing, Kay. You have forgotten our talks about denial.

Benton's facile mind moves on to another point as he rides in the taxi shortly after dark, en route to Manhattan, the trunk and every other space in the car piled with his belongings. The driver did not disguise his disgust when he realized that his fare came with a substantial pile of baggage. But Benton was clever. He hailed the cab from the street, and the driver didn't see the pile of luggage in the thick shadows of the sidewalk until he was faced with the choice of speeding off or accepting the lucrative job of driving a fare to New York.

The driver's name is Robert Leary, a white male with brown hair, brown eyes, approximately five-foot-ten and one hundred and eighty pounds. Those details and others, including the identification number on the photo ID clamped to the visor, are written in a refillable wallet-size leather notebook that Benton carries wherever he goes. As soon as he gets to his hotel room, he will, as is customary for him, transfer the notes to his laptop computer. Since he entered the witness protection program, Benton has recorded his every activity, his every location and every person he has met—especially if it is more than once—and even the weather and where he worked out and what he ate.

Several times now, Robert Leary has attempted to initiate a conversation, but Benton stares out the window and says nothing, the driver, of course, having no idea that the man with the tan, chiseled, bearded face and shaved head is silently making points and examining tactical requirements and possibilities and probabilities from every tilt imaginable. No doubt, the cabbie is thinking it is his sorry luck to have picked up a weirdo, who, based on the shabbiness of his luggage, has fallen on hard times, very hard times.

"You sure you can pay the fare?" he asks, or rather demands, for the third time. "It ain't gonna be cheap, you know, depending on what route I end up taking, depending on traffic and what streets they got closed off in the city. These days, ya never know what streets the cops will close off. Security. It's something. Me, I'm not a big fan of machine guns and guys in camouflage."

"I can pay the fare," Benton replies.

The headlights of passing cars slash his window, briefly lighting up his somber face. Of this he is certain: Jean-Baptiste

Chandonne's attempted murder of Scarpetta has no point or meaning beyond the remarkable fact that she used her wits and survived. Thank God, thank God. Other schemes to bring about her ruination have no meaning beyond the miracle that they, too, have failed. Benton is well versed in the details, perhaps not all of them, but what he has followed in the news is enough.

Every person involved in his plan is tangentially if not directly connected to the Chandonnes' evil, intricate network. Benton knows what empowers the Chandonnes and what robs them of their strength. He knows the receptacles, without whom the major conduits between drones and the higher order cannot function. The solution to the situation has always been far too complicated for anyone to work out, but for six years, Benton has had nothing to do but work it out.

The answer, he discovered, is simple: Surgically snip and strip the wires and disconnect, then splice, rewire and reconnect so that the criminals short-circuit and the Chandonne empire implodes. Meanwhile, Benton—the dead Benton—invisibly watches what he has designed and implemented as if it is a video game, and no player in his game has an inkling about what is going on, except that something is, and whatever it is must be instigated by traitors from inside. Main players must die. Other players, many of whom Benton does not know, will be blamed and labeled traitors. They will die.

By this method, Benton will manipulate his enemies and delete them, one by one. By his calculations, the coalition comprised of himself and others who do not even know they have been conscripted into his private army will complete his mission in a few months, perhaps weeks. By his calculations, Rocco Caggiano is already dead or soon will be dead, killed in cold blood, his murder staged, and Lucy and Rudy may know what they are doing or have done, but what they don't know is the video game. They don't know that they are in it.

What Benton did not calculate and would never have anticipated is that Kay Scarpetta would form a connection to Baton Rouge, the most strategic position on Benton's mental map. For some reason, this part of his near-perfect plan has failed. He doesn't know why. He doesn't know what happened. He reviews every detail repeatedly, but at the end of the routine, the screen is blank, a useless cursor blinking hypnotically at him. Now Benton must rush. It is against his nature to rush. Scarpetta was never supposed to have any contact whatsoever with anything or anybody in Baton Rouge. Marino was. The Last Precinct was.

Learning that his son is dead would inevitably result in Marino retracing Rocco's steps, which would lead Marino and his compatriots to Baton Rouge, where Rocco keeps an apartment and has for many years. The port in Baton Rouge is formidable. The Gulf Coast is gold. All manner of valuable and dangerous materials travels the Mississippi daily. Baton Rouge is yet another Chandonne holding, and Rocco has enjoyed many successes and gratifications there, including sovereign immunity from the police, and intrigues, including protecting Jay Talley and Jean-Baptiste Chandonne as they enjoyed their fair share of fun in the Baton Rouge area.

Jean-Baptiste and Jay were only sixteen the first time they visited Baton Rouge. Jean-Baptiste honed his murderous skills by killing prostitutes after Jay was serviced by them. Those cases have never been linked because the former coroner abdicated his investigative rights to other agencies, and the police didn't give a damn about prostitutes.

One step would lead to another until Marino discovered Jay Talley and Bev Kiffin in Baton Rouge and eliminated them. That was the plan. Scarpetta was never supposed to be part of it. His pulse beats rapidly in his temples.

He holds his wrist close to his face, unable to read the time on his cheap black plastic watch because the dial isn't luminescent. By design, it isn't. He wants nothing that glows in the dark.

"What time should we get there?" he asks in the same clipped tone.

"I dunno exactly," his driver replies. "Depends if the traffic stays light like this. Maybe another two, two and a half hours."

A car draws close to them from the rear, its high beams bouncing blinding white light off the taxi's rearview mirror. The driver curses as a black Porsche 911 passes, its receding red taillights reminding Benton of hell.

31

Scarpetta stares at the unopened letter, the warm, damp air moving freely through her open door.

Clouds are black flowers floating low on the horizon, and she senses that rain will come before dawn and she will wake up with all the windows fogged up, which is intolerable. No doubt the neighbors think she's obsessive and mad when they see her on her balcony with bath towels at seven a.m., vigorously wiping condensation off the outside of the glass. Then, because of her forced and despicable bond with *him*, she imagines him inside his death-row cell with no view, and her mission of scrubbing clean her dewy, opaque windows becomes all the more urgent.

The unopened letter addressed to *Madame Scarpetta, LLB* is centered on a square of clean white freezer paper. Female physicians in France are addressed as *Madame*. In America, referring to a female physician as anything but *Doctor* is an insult. She is unpleasantly reminded of crafty defense attorneys addressing her in court as Mrs. Scarpetta instead of Dr. Scarpetta, thereby stripping her of her credentials and expertise, in the hope that the jurors and perhaps even the judge would not take her as seriously as they would a *Medicinae Doctor* whose specialty of pathology and subspecialty of forensic pathology required six additional years of training after medical school.

While it is true that Scarpetta also has a law degree, virtually no one adds the abbreviation for *legum baccalaureus* after her surname, and for her to do so would be arrogant and misleading because she does not practice law. The three years she spent in law school at Georgetown were for the purpose of facilitating her eventual career in legal medicine, and that was all. To add the abbreviation LLB after her name is mocking in its pretentiousness and condescension.

Jean-Baptiste Chandonne.

She knows the letter is from him.

For an instant, she smells his horrible stench. An olfactory hallucination. The last time she had one was when she visited the Holocaust Museum and smelled death.

"I've been out in the yard with Billy. He's done his business and is very busy chasing lizards," Rose is saying. "Anything else I can do for you before I leave?"

"No thank you, Rose."

A pause, then, "Well, did you like my tuna salad?"

"You could open your own restaurant," Scarpetta says.

She puts on a fresh pair of white cotton examination gloves and picks up the letter and the scalpel, working the tip of the triangular blade into a top corner of the envelope. Stainless steel hisses through the cheap paper.

32

The chair Rocco sits on is a padded one.

Two—no, maybe it was three or four—surreal hours ago, he was in this same chair, eating dinner, when room service knocked on his door to bring him a bottle of champagne, a very nice Moët & Chandon, compliments of the management. Rocco, who is street-wise and chronically paranoid, was not the least bit suspicious. He is an important man who stays in the Radisson whenever he is in Szczecin. It is the only decent hotel in the city, and management routinely sends him gifts, including fine cognac and Cuban cigars, because he pays his bills in American cash instead of worthless zloty.

His habit of feeling secure in this hotel is how the intruder with the Colt pistol got inside Rocco's deluxe room. It happened so fast, he didn't have time to react to the tall waiter who wasn't wearing a uniform and shoved his way inside with an empty bottle of champagne on a service tray he obviously had picked up out-side another guest's room. This asshole—whoever he is—grabbed Rocco that easily.

Rocco pushes his plate as far away from him as possible. He worries that next he will vomit. He has soiled himself. The room smells so foul he cannot understand how his captor endures it, but the young, muscular man sitting on the bed doesn't seem to notice. He stares at Rocco, the stare of a man high on adrenaline and ready to kill. He will not allow Rocco to clean up. He won't allow Rocco to get out of the chair. He drops his cell phone on the bed after another brief conversation with someone, and goes over to the tray with its empty champagne bottle. Rocco watches the man carefully wipe off the bottle with a napkin. Rocco tries to place him. Maybe he has seen him before, or maybe the explanation is that he has that look—the look of a federal agent.

"Listen," Rocco says over the noise of the TV, "just tell me who and why, come on. You tell me who and why, maybe we can work something out you'll like better. You're an agent, aren't you? Some kinda agent. That don't mean we can't work something out."

He has said this at least six times since the agent walked in with the empty bottle on its tray, then slammed the door shut with a back kick and pulled his gun. Several times now, he has opened the door and slammed it shut. This makes Rocco increasingly nervous. Although he doesn't understand the agent's purpose, it has crossed his mind, even during previous stays, that the doors shut so loudly in this hotel that they sound like gunshots.

"Keep your voice down," the agent tells him.

He places the champagne bottle on Rocco's table.

"Pick it up." The agent nods at it.

Rocco stares at the bottle and swallows hard.

"Pick it up, Rocco."

"So I'll ask you again. How come you know my name?" Rocco

persists. "Come on. You know me, right? We can work things out . . ."

"Pick up the bottle."

He does. The agent wants Rocco's fingerprints on the bottle. This is not good. The agent wants it to appear as though Rocco ordered or somehow acquired the champagne and drank it. This is very bad. His fears gather in strength as the agent returns to the bed, picks up a jacket and pulls out a leather flask. He unscrews the cap and returns to Rocco's table, pouring a large amount of vodka in what is left of one of Rocco's cocktails.

"Drink up," the agent says.

Rocco swallows the vodka in several gulps, grateful as it burns its way down, warming him and sending its seductive, dulling agents along his blood and to his head. His confused thoughts float toward the hope that the agent is showing mercy, treating him decently, trying to make him relax. Maybe the agent's rethinking things, wants to make a deal.

Rocco speculates, but it is a fact that someone sent the man, someone who knows Rocco's business intimately and is aware that once a month he travels to Szczecin to handle Chandonne affairs at the port. Rocco's primary responsibility is to deal with police and other officials. This is business as usual. He can do it drunk, nothing more than routine legal finagling and the usual fees and, if necessary, reminders of what a dangerous world it is.

Only an insider would know Rocco's schedule and where he stays. The hotel staff doesn't know what he does, only that he is from New York, or so he says. No one cares what he does. He is generous. He is rich. Instead of passing off the usual zloty, he pays and lavishly tips in American cash, which is very hard to come by and very useful on the black market. Everyone likes him. The bartenders double the Chopin vodka in his drinks at the upstairs bar, where he frequently sits in the dark, smoking cigars.

His captor looks about twenty-eight, maybe early thirties. His black hair is short and styled with gel in that spiked look that a lot of young men like these days. Rocco notices the square jaw, straight nose, dark blue eyes, stubble and the veins standing out in the man's biceps and hands. He probably doesn't need a weapon to crush someone. Women like him. They probably stare at him, hit on him. Rocco has never been attractive. As a teenager, he was already suffering from pattern baldness, and he couldn't stay away from pizza and beer, and looked it. Envy possesses him. It always has. Women sleep with him only because he has power and money. Hatred toward his captor flares.

"You don't know what you're messing with here," Rocco says.

The agent doesn't bother answering him, his eyes darting around the room. Rocco wipes his face with his greasy napkin, his attention wandering to the steak knife on his plate.

"Try it," the agent says, looking at the steak knife. "Go ahead. Please try it. Make my life a hell of a lot easier."

"I wasn't gonna do nothing. Just let me go and we'll forget this ever happened."

"I can't let you go. Truth is, this isn't my idea of fun. So I'm in a bad mood already. Don't piss me off. You want to help yourself? Well, you know what they say about coming clean at the end."

"No. What the hell do they say?"

"Where's Jay Talley, and don't tell me another fucking lie, asshole."

"I don't know," Rocco whines. "I swear to God I don't. I'm scared of him, too. He's crazy. He don't play the game, and every one of us stay clear of him. He marches to his own beat, swear to God. Can't I please change my pants? You can watch me. I won't try nothing."

Rudy gets off the bed and opens the closet door, the Colt casually by his side, indicating to an increasingly defeated and terrified Rocco that this man is not afraid of anything. There are maybe half a dozen flashy suits hanging on the rod, and he pulls off a pair of pants and tosses them to Rocco.

"Go on." The agent opens the bathroom door and sits back down on the bed.

Rocco trembles as he walks inside the bathroom and peels off his pants and briefs. He tosses them into the tub, douses a towel with tap water and wipes himself.

"Jay Talley," the agent says again. "Real name, Jean-Paul Chandonne."

"Ask me something else." Rocco means it as he sits in a different chair.

"Okay. We'll get back to Talley later. You got plans to take out your father?" The agent's stare is cold. "It's no secret you hate him."

"I don't claim him."

"Doesn't matter, Rocco. You ran away from home. You changed your name from Marino to Caggiano. What's the plan and who's involved?"

Rocco hesitates for the longest time, thoughts jumping behind his bloodshot eyes. The agent gets up, breathing through his mouth as if to avoid the stench. He presses the barrel of the Colt against Rocco's right temple.

"Who, what, when and where?" he says, tapping the barrel of the pistol against Rocco's head with each word. "Don't fuck with me!"

"I was gonna do it. In a couple months when he goes fishing. He always goes fishing at Buggs Lake the first week of August. Nail him in his cabin, make it look like a burglary gone bad."

"So you would kill your own father when he's on a fishing trip. You know what you are, Rocco? You're the worst shit I ever met."

33

Whenever Nic Robillard drives past the Sno Depot in downtown Zachary, she feels like crying.

Tonight, the stand, with its handpainted signs advertising snow cones, is dark and deserted. If Buddy were with her, he'd be staring out the window and begging, not caring that the Sno Depot is closed and it isn't possible for his mother to buy him a treat. That boy loves snow cones more than anybody Nic's ever heard of, and despite her efforts to steer him away from sweets, he demands a snow cone—cherry or grape—every time she takes him anywhere in the car.

Buddy is with his grandfather in Baton Rouge right now, where he always is when Nic has to work late, and ever since she returned from Knoxville, she works constantly. Scarpetta inspired her. The need to impress Scarpetta dominates Nic's life. She is determined to bring about the arrest of the serial killer. She is frantic about the abducted women, knowing it absolutely will happen again if the maniac isn't caught. She is tormented by grief and guilt because she is neglecting her son after she was away from him for two and a half months.

If Buddy ever stopped loving her or turned out wrong, Nic would want to die. Some nights when she finally returns to her tiny Victorian house around the corner from St. John the Baptist Catholic Church on Lee Street, she lies in bed, staring at dark shapes inside her small room, and listens to the silence as she imagines Buddy sound asleep at her father's house in Baton Rouge. Thoughts about her son and ex-husband, Ricky, flit about like moths. She contemplates whether she would shoot herself in the heart or the head if she were to lose everything that matters.

Not one person has any idea that Nic gets depressed. Not one person would ever imagine that there are times when she entertains thoughts of suicide. What keeps her from the unthinkable is her belief that self-murder is one of the most selfish sins a person can commit, and she envisions the dire consequences of such an act, pushing the fatal fantasy far out of reach until the next time she dives into a dead man's spin of powerlessness, loneliness and despair.

"Shit," she whispers as she drives south on Main Street, leaving the Sno Depot behind in her emotional wake. "I'm so sorry, Buddy-Boy, my Buddy-Boy." What a decision she faces: choosing between doing nothing about women being murdered and doing nothing about her son.

34

"*Mon petit agneau prisé.*"

My little treasured lamb, Scarpetta translates as her heart freezes at the sight of Chandonne's handwriting and she feels his presence in his letter to her.

She has been sitting in the same position for so long—in the straight-backed wooden chair by her bedroom's open door—that her lower back aches and the small glass table is sweating from the humid sea air. As she remembers to breathe, she realizes that every muscle is tense, her entire body like a clenched fist.

The letter, the letter, the letter.

It stuns her that his handwriting is beautiful, a practiced calligraphy penned in black ink, not a single word crossed through, not a single mistake that she can see at a glance. He must have spent a lot of time writing this letter to her, as if it was a loving endeavor, and the idea of that just adds to the horror. He thinks of her. He is telling her so by the very act of his artistic penmanship.

She reads his words:

DO YOU KNOW ABOUT THE RED STICK YET AND THAT YOU
MUST GO THERE?

BUT NOT UNTIL YOU COME TO SEE ME FIRST. IN THE
LONGHORN STATE, AS THEY SAY!

YOU SEE, I DIRECT YOU.

YOU HAVE NO WILL OF YOUR OWN. YOU MAY THINK YOU
DO, BUT I AM THE CURRENT RUNNING THROUGH YOUR
BODY, EVERY IMPULSE COMING FROM ME. I AM INSIDE YOU.
FEEL IT!

DO YOU REMEMBER THAT NIGHT? YOU EAGERLY OPENED
YOUR DOOR AND THEN ATTACKED ME BECAUSE YOU COULD
NOT FACE YOUR LONGING FOR ME. I HAVE FORGIVEN YOU
FOR TAKING MY EYES, BUT YOU COULD NOT TAKE MY SOUL.
IT FOLLOWS YOU CONSTANTLY. IF YOU TRY, YOU CAN TOUCH
IT.

MAINTENANT! MAINTENANT! IT IS TIME. THE RED STICK
AWAITS YOU.

YOU MUST COME TO ME FIRST OR IT WILL BE TOO LATE TO
HEAR MY STORIES.

ONLY FOR YOU WILL I TELL THEM.

I KNOW WHAT YOU WANT, MON PETIT AGNEAU PRISÉ! I
HAVE WHAT YOU WANT.

IN TWO WEEKS I WILL BE DEAD AND HAVE NOTHING TO SAY. HA!

WILL YOU RELEASE ME TO THE ECSTASY?

OR WILL I RELEASE YOU? SINKING MY TEETH INTO YOUR
SOFT, ROUND LOVELINESS.

IF YOU DO NOT FIND ME, I WILL FIND YOU.

LOVE AND RAPTURE,

JEAN-BAPTISTE

In the old-style bathroom with its plain white toilet, its plain plastic shower curtain around the plain white tub, its mildew-stained white walls, Scarpetta vomits. She drinks a glass of water from the tap and returns to the bedroom, to the table, to that blighted piece of paper, which she suspects will offer her no evidence. He is too clever to leave evidence.

She sits in the chair, trying to fight the images of the filthy beast flying through her front door like an evil spirit crackling out of hell. Scarcely can she recall in detail the pursuit, that terrible pursuit around her living room, as he swung an iron hammer, the same iron hammer he had used before to shatter women's heads and bodies to battered flesh and splintered bone, especially their faces.

At the time she was the medical examiner for the Richmond murders, it never occurred to her that she might be the next one. Since that near-death experience, she struggles to will away her imagined destruction of her own body and face. He would not have raped her. He isn't capable of rape. Jean-Baptiste's revenge on the world is to cause death and disfigurement, to re-create others in his own image. He is the ultimate embodiment of self-hate.

If it is true that she saved her life by permanently blinding him, then he should be so lucky as to be spared his own reflection in the polished metal mirror he must look at every day inside his death-row cell.

Scarpetta goes to a hallway closet and moves the vacuum cleaner out of the way. She rolls out a suitcase.

35

"If you need anything, call me on my cell phone," Nic says, standing in the front doorway of her father's white brick house in the Old Garden District, where homes are large and spreading canopies of magnolias and live oaks keep much of the city's old establishment in the shade.

Even on the brightest days, Nic finds her childhood home dark and foreboding.

"Why, you know I'm not calling that newfangled little phone of yours," her father says, winking at her. "Even if you don't make the call, you have to pay for it, isn't that right? Or does unlimited mileage, I mean minutes, apply?"

"What?" Nic frowns, then laughs. "Never mind. My new number's taped to the refrigerator, whether you decide to call it or not. If I don't call back right away, you know it's because I'm busy. Now you be good, Buddy-Boy. You're my big man, right?"

Her five-year-old son peeks out from behind his grandfather and makes a face.

"Got it!" Nic pretends to snatch his nose and tries the old trick of sticking her thumb up between two fingers. "Do you want your nose back or not?"

Buddy looks like the proverbial towheaded choir boy, dressed in overalls that are an inch too short. He touches his nose and sticks out his tongue.

"You keep sticking out that tongue of yours and one day it won't fit in your mouth anymore," his grandfather warns him.

"Shhhh," Nic says. "Don't be saying things like that, Papa. He'll believe you."

She peeks around him and grabs her son. "Gotcha!" She lifts him up and covers his face with kisses. "Looks like it's time to go shopping, my big man. You're outgrowing your clothes again. How come you keep doing that, huh?"

"I dunno." He hugs her tightly around the neck.

"Do you think it's possible you might wear something besides overalls?" she whispers in his ear.

He vigorously shakes his head. She gently puts him down.

"Why can't I come?" Buddy pouts.

"Mama has to work. By the time you wake up, I'll be back, okay? You go on to bed like my big man and I'll bring you a surprise."

"What surprise?"

"If I told you, it wouldn't be a surprise, now would it?" Nic kisses the top of his head again, and he irritably musses his hair as if swatting away bugs. "Uh-oh," she says to her father. "I believe someone's getting grumpy."

Buddy gives her a look, a mixture of anger and hurt that never fails to make Nic feel as though she has betrayed and failed him. Ever since her salesman ex-husband Ricky got the promotion he always wanted, he got more impossible to live with, traveling all the time, complaining and unkind. He's gone, and Nic's glad, relieved, but deeply wounded in ways she can't define. Hardships in life are always for the best if you do God's will, according to the doctrine of her father, who loves her but won't take her side in her failed marriage.

"You ought to know that being a cop doesn't mix with holding on to a man, if you ever get married," he told her when she got accepted to the police academy eight years ago, after a dreary career of working as a bookkeeper at the Ford dealership in Zachary, where she eventually met Ricky. They dated three months and moved in together. Another sin. At last she was free of her haunted house.

"Mama had her own business," Nic reminded her father every time he made his comments.

"Honey, that's not the same. She didn't carry a gun."

"Maybe if she had . . ."

"Now, you hush your mouth!"

She finished the sentence only once. This was after she filed for divorce and her father berated her for an entire afternoon, pacing in his living room, his face a storm of disbelief, fear and anger. He's a big, lanky man, and every upset stride seemed to carry him from one wall to the other and jostled the antique crystal lamp on the table next to the couch until it finally fell over and broke.

"Now look what you did!" he cried out. "You broke your mother's lamp."

"You broke it."

"Girls don't need to be chasing criminals and shooting guns. That's why you lost Ricky. He married a pretty woman, not an Annie Oakley. And what kind of mother . . ."

That was when Nic said it. "If Mama had a gun, maybe she

wouldn't have been butchered by some fucking asshole right here in our own house!"

"Don't you dare use words like that," he told her, emphasizing each stony word with a violent stab of his finger, stabs that reminded her of what was done to her mother.

They never touched the subject again. It remains a stalled storm front between them. No matter how often they see each other, she can't feel his warmth or get too close. After two premature babies who didn't survive, Nic was born and is the only child her father has. After he retired from teaching high school sociology, he got bored and pretty much quit life. He spends his mornings working crossword puzzles when he's not babysitting, and taking obsessively long, brisk walks.

She knows he blames himself. Her mother was murdered eight years ago in the middle of the day while he and Nic were both at work. Maybe she blames herself, too, not so much for her mother's death, she tells herself, but because if Nic hadn't gone out with friends after work, her father might not have been the one to find his wife's body and blood all over the house, from where she fought her killer, running from room to room. By the time Nic got home, slightly drunk from beer, police were swarming the property, her mother's body already removed. Nic never saw it. It was a closed-casket funeral. She's never been able to bring herself to get a copy of the police report, and because the case remains unsolved, the coroner's office won't give her a copy of the autopsy records. All she knows is that her mother was stabbed and slashed and bled to death. Knowing that was enough. But for some reason, it isn't anymore.

On this particular night, Nic is determined to talk, but that can't happen unless Buddy is occupied.

"You want to watch TV for a few minutes before bed?" she asks him.

It is a special privilege indeed.

"Yes," he says, still pouting.

He runs inside the house, and the TV goes on.

She nods at her father, and he accompanies her outside.

"Come on," she whispers to him, and they pick their usual spot beneath the ancient live oak tree at the edge of the yard.

"This had better be good." He has his lines and never tires of reusing them.

She catches the gleam of his teeth as he talks and knows he's pleased when she drags him out in the middle of the night to have a secret conversation, one not meant for a toddler's ears.

"I know you don't want to talk about it," Nic begins, "but it's about Mama." She feels him jerk and withdraw, as if his spirit has suddenly fled from his body. "I need to know more, Papa. Not knowing is doing something to me. Maybe because of what's happening around here now, with these women disappearing. I'm feeling something. I don't know how else to say it, but I'm feeling something. Something terrible." Her voice trembles. "And it's scaring me, Papa. The way I'm feeling sometimes is scaring me bad."

His silence is as formidable as the tree they stand under.

"Remember when I got the ladder and propped it against this very tree." She looks heavenward, her vision caught in thick, dark branches and leaves. "Next thing I know, I'm stuck up there, too scared to climb higher or come back down. And you had to get me."

"I remember." His voice sounds as if nobody is home.

"Well, that's the way I feel right now," she goes on, trying to appeal to the part of him that shut down after his wife was murdered. "I can't climb up or down, and I need you to help me, Papa."

"There's nothing I can do," he says.

36

Szczecin's skyline is pierced by antennas, the streets quiet, the downtown shabby.

Not one of the stores looks inviting, especially at this late hour, and the few cars out are old and worse for wear. The Radisson is built of brick, the courtyard gray and red pavers, and a large blue banner out front welcomes a Methods and Models in Automation and Robotics meeting, and that is fortunate.

The more people in the hotel, the better, and Lucy used to program robots and can talk technology with anybody if need be. But it won't be necessary. She has a plan, a very good one in all respects. She finds a spot to park several streets down from a Fila store, just past a *delikatesy*.

Flipping down the mirror on the visor, she quickly applies makeup and puts on gold hoop earrings. She yanks off her tennis shoes and pulls on black satin cowboy boots that are disgustingly necessary should someone spot her inside the hotel. She struggles into a black blouse, linen and wrinkled, and tucks her tactical baton up its sleeve. She unbuttons it low enough to show off cleavage. Transformed into a sexy young woman who is staying in the hotel, Lucy is sufficiently disheveled and alluring to pass for a typical convention attendee who has been out having a good time half the night. Throwing on a windbreaker and cursing her boots, she walks quickly to the hotel beneath the dim auras of streetlights.

This Radisson is *self-service*, as Lucy calls hotels where she carries her own bags, uses her magnetized room key to let herself into the gym and fills her own ice bucket, and where the housekeepers are shocked when left a tip. There is no doorman or bellman at this hour, only a young woman reading a Polish magazine behind the front desk. Lucy stays outside in the dark, glancing around, making certain no one suddenly walks up and sees her. In that unlikely event, she will dig inside the small leather satchel looped over her shoulder, pretending to look for her room key. She waits restlessly for ten minutes before the bored, weary desk clerk gets up and walks off, perhaps to the ladies' room, perhaps to find coffee. Lucy strolls across the lobby and disappears inside the elevator, pushing the button for the fifth floor.

Rudy is in room 511. It is not his room. He got inside the hotel very much the same way Lucy did, only he got a good break, got to walk in with a crowd of businessmen returning from dinner. Fortunately, he was smart enough to wear a suit and tie. Rudy is an odd breed. Former HRT comrades envied his beautiful muscular body and accused him of taking steroids, which he has never touched. Lucy would know, because Rudy may have his flaws, but he is so honest and sincere that she sometimes calls him *girlfriend*. She knows every detail of his diet, vitamin and protein supplements, and grueling workout routines, and his favorite magazines and television shows. She can't remember the last time he read a book. She also understands why he sexually assaulted her in the Tire House and, if anything, feels bad that she broke his nose.

"I thought you were hot for me, too. I swear," he explained with the most pitiful expression on his face. "I guess I got all excited rolling around between tires and shooting, and you were right there with me with cartridge cases pinging everywhere, both of us dirty and sooty, and you looked so good I couldn't stand it, so I asked you that question—when I shouldn't have—and then you said you wanted sex whenever you could get it. I thought you meant with me."

"Right that minute?" Lucy said. "You really thought that?"

"Yeah. That you were hot and bothered too."

"Now and then you should watch something besides action movies," Lucy replied. "Walt Disney, maybe?"

They had this conversation inside her room at the FBI Academy, both of them sitting on her bed because she was not afraid of Rudy and never had been. He was the one with stitches below his lip and a broken nose that required the skills of a plastic surgeon.

"Besides, and I know this may sound like bullshit to you, Lucy, but I'd had it with what the other guys were saying. Maybe I wanted to prove something—prove you weren't what they've been saying."

"I get it. If we had sex, then you could go back and tell them all about it."

"No! I didn't mean it like that. I wouldn't have told them anything. It's none of their business!"

"Hmmm. Let me sort through this. Having sex in the Tire House would have proven to the other guys that I'm into guys—even though they wouldn't have known about our having sex in the Tire House because you're too honorable to kiss and tell."

179

"Ah, fuck." Rudy stared dejectedly at the floor. "I'm not saying it right. I wouldn't have told them a thing, but next time they bad-mouthed you, accused you of being gay or frigid or whatever, I could have given them a look, done something to indicate they didn't know what they were talking about."

"I appreciate that your intention was my welfare as you tried to rip off my clothes and rape me," Lucy replied.

"I wasn't trying to rape you! For Christ's sake, don't use a word like that! I thought you were turned on, too. Shit, Lucy. What do you want me to do?"

"Never try a stunt like that again. Or next time I'll break more than your nose."

"Fine. I won't ever do anything again unless you start it. Or change your mind."

He resigned from the Bureau and eventually came to work for her at The Last Precinct. Rudy is a perplexing mix. In some ways, he is the big, handsome dope incapable of making a commitment to any woman he has ever claimed to desperately love (and his choices, as far as Lucy knows, demonstrate appallingly bad judgment). But as a crime fighter, he is as meticulous and skillful as he is as a helicopter pilot. Rudy isn't selfish or narcissistic. He rarely drinks and never touches drugs, not even aspirin.

"One good thing about it." Rudy looked up at Lucy as they sat on her bed. "When the plastic surgeon was fixing my nose, he went ahead and shaved that little bump off it." He gently touched the splint on the bridge of his nose. "He says I'll have a perfect Roman nose. That's what he called it, a *Roman nose*."

He paused, slightly perplexed. "What exactly is a Roman nose?"

37

Lucy knocks on the door of room 511.

It has a *Do Not Disturb* sign hanging on the knob, and the TV is loud inside, hoofs pounding, guns firing. It sounds like Rudy is watching a Western. But what he's watching is Rocco.

"Yeah." After a pause, Rudy's voice sounds from inside.

"Down and secure," she uses helicopter talk and scans the hallway as she pulls latex gloves out of a pocket and works her hands into them.

The door opens wide enough for her to slip through, and she closes it behind her. Rudy is also wearing surgical gloves, and turns the lock and dead bolt. Lucy takes off her windbreaker and stares hard at Rocco Caggiano, at his flabby, fat body and his bloodshot eyes. She takes in every detail of the room. Draped over a chair is his black cashmere overcoat, and in a corner on the carpet are a plastic tray and an empty bottle of champagne next to a stainless-steel ice bucket filled with water. It would have taken hours for the ice to completely melt. The bed is king-size, and directly across from it in front of a window with the drapes drawn are a small glass table and two chairs. On the carpet are several British newspapers. He's recently been in England, maybe. But Rocco has never bothered to learn a second language. The papers could have come from anywhere along his route here.

Parked between the table and the bed is a room-service cart with nothing on it but four stainless-steel plate covers. Lucy can't help but think of Rocco's estranged father, Pete Marino, as she eyes a gnawed T-bone, the shredded skin of a baked potato, a plate with one pat of butter left (melted), an empty bread basket and a glass goblet filled with wilted lettuce, cocktail sauce, wedges of lemon and shrimp tails. He so completely devoured a slice of chocolate cake, nothing is left but smears made with Rocco's fingers.

"I gotta go."

"Be my guest."

She hurries into the bathroom. The stench is horrible.

"He sober?" Lucy asks Rudy when she returns.

"Sober enough."

"Must be in the genes."

"What?"

"The way father and son take care of themselves," she says. "But that's all he and Marino have in common." This to Rocco: "Drop by Szczecin to check on a few spare firearms? Maybe some ammunition, explosives, electronics, perfumes and designer clothing? How many phony bills of lading are in your briefcase?"

Rocco glares at her, his attention dropping to her cleavage.

"Keep your goddamn eyes to yourself," Lucy snaps, having forgotten about her appearance. She buttons up and resumes her interrogation. "Probably thousands of them floating around somewhere, right, Rocco?"

He says nothing. Lucy notices vomit on the carpet between his black crocodile loafers.

" 'Bout time you gagged on your own shit, Rocco." She sits on the edge of the bed.

"That a pickle up your sleeve, or you just happy to see me," Rudy says to Lucy without a smile, without taking his eyes off Rocco.

Lucy remembers the tactical baton up the sleeve of her linen blouse, slips it out and sets it on the bedside table. It is warm in the room. She glances at the thermostat, verifying that Rudy turned up the heat to seventy-four degrees. Any higher than that could arouse suspicion. Blowing heat moves the drapes drawn across the window on the other side of the room. The window is large and faces the front of the hotel. Rocco stares at the pistol, his eyes filling with tears.

"My, my," Lucy remarks, "you're quite a crybaby for someone so mean and tough. And by the way, your father doesn't cry." She looks at Rudy. "You ever seen Marino cry?"

"Nope."

"You ever seen him shit in his pants?"

"Nope. Did'cha know that Rocco here had plans to put a bullet in Marino's head on his fishing trip? You know, the one he always takes to Buggs Lake."

Lucy doesn't comment. A flush creeps up her neck. Hopefully, Marino will never know that she and Rudy came here and probably saved his life. Rocco won't be shooting anyone ever again.

"You could have killed your father years ago. Why this August?" Lucy asks him.

She knows when Marino takes his annual fishing trip.

Rocco shrugs. "Instructions."

"From whom?"

"My former client. He has scores to settle."

"Jean-Baptiste," Lucy says. "So the two of you have remained close. That's touching, because he's the reason you're about to die."

"I don't believe you!" Rocco exclaims. "He'd never . . . He needs me."

"For what?" Rudy asks.

"Outside work," Rocco replies. "I'm still his attorney. He can send me anything he wants. Contact me anytime he wants."

"What does he send you?" Rudy asks.

"Anything. All he's got to do is mark it *Legal Mail*, and no one can open it. So if he wants letters or shit sent to somebody who obviously ain't a lawyer, he sends it through me."

"The letter I got from him that ratted you out, Rocco, did he send it through you?" Lucy asks.

"No. He's never sent me a letter with your name on it. I never open them. Too risky. If he ever found out." He pauses, his eyes glassy. "I don't believe he sent you a letter!"

"We're here, aren't we?" Rudy says. "So how did that happen if Chandonne didn't send a letter and tell us everything we need to know?"

Rocco has no answer.

"Why would he want you to kill your father?" Lucy isn't about to forget that subject. "Especially now. What scores to settle?"

"Maybe Jean-Baptiste don't like him. I guess you could consider it a parting shot." Rocco briefly looks smug.

"Mind if I see that for a minute?" Lucy holds out her hand for Rudy's pistol.

He drops out the magazine and clears the round from the chamber. The cartridge bounces on the bed. Lucy picks it up and Rudy gives her the Colt. She walks close to Rocco and pushes the loose cartridge into the magazine with her thumb.

"Your father taught me how to drive," she tells Rocco in a conversational tone. "You ever seen those huge pickup trucks of his? Well, that's what I learned in when I was so little I had to sit on a pillow, even with the seat raised."

She racks back the slide and aims the pistol between his eyes.

"He taught me how to shoot, too."

She squeezes the trigger.

Click.

Rocco jumps violently.

"Oops." Lucy smacks the magazine back inside the handle. "Forgot it wasn't loaded. Get up, Rocco."

"You're cops." His voice trembles in fear and disbelief. "Cops don't kill people. They don't do this!"

"I'm not a cop," Rudy says to Lucy. "Are you a cop?"

"No. I'm not a cop. I don't see a single cop in this room, do you?"

"Some CIA paramilitary operatives. Bet they sent you into Iraq, didn't they? To take out Saddam Hussein. I know what people like you do."

"Never been to Iraq, have you?" Lucy says to Rudy.

"Not recently."

185

38

Another Western is playing on the TV.

Mouths move out of sync as two cowboys dismount their horses, voices dubbed in Polish.

"One last chance," Rudy says to Rocco. "Where's Jay Talley? Don't lie. I promise I'll know."

"He took a statement analysis course at the FBI Academy," Lucy says drolly. "Was the star of the class."

Rocco slowly shakes his head. It is apparent by now that if he knew, he would tell them. He is a self-serving, sniveling coward, and right now he is more afraid of them than he is of Jay Talley.

"Here's the deal. We're not going to kill you, Rocco." Lucy tosses the pistol back to Rudy. "You're going to commit suicide."

"No." He shakes as if he has Parkinson's disease.

"You're history, Rocco," Rudy says. "A fugitive. A Red Notice. You can't go anywhere anyway. You'll be grabbed. If you're lucky, you'll end up in prison, probably in Sicily, and I hear that's not a holiday. But you know better. The Chandonnes will take you out. Instantly. And perhaps not as humanely as you can end your own miserable, stinking life. Right now."

Lucy goes to the bed and digs an envelope out of her shoulder bag's back pocket. Inside it is a folded sheet of paper. She opens it.

"Here." She offers it to Rocco.

He makes no effort to touch it.

"Take it. A hard copy of your Red Notice. Hot off the press. You must be curious."

Rocco doesn't respond. Even his eyeballs seem to be shaking.

"Take it," Lucy tells him.

Rocco does. The Red Notice shakes violently in his hands as he leaves his fingerprints on the paper, a detail he probably isn't thinking about.

"Now read it out loud. I think it's very important you see what it says. Because I'm confident you'll decide you have no choice but to kill yourself right here in this lovely hotel room," Lucy says.

The single page has Interpol's crest in the upper right corner, of course in bright red. Prominently displayed is Rocco's photograph, easily acquired. Egotist that he is, he has never ducked the camera when he's represented criminals in scandalous trials. The picture on the Red Notice is recent and a very good likeness.

"Read out loud," Lucy orders him again. "Story time, Rocco."

"Identity particulars." His voice wavers, and he continues to clear his throat. "Present family name, Rocco Caggiano. Name at birth, Peter Rocco Marino, Junior."

He pauses at this, and tears brighten his eyes. He bites his lower lip, then continues, reading on and on, all about himself. When he gets to the judicial information and reads that he is wanted for the murders of the Sicilian and French journalists, he rolls his eyes toward the ceiling.

"Jesus," he mutters, taking a deep breath.

"That's right," Lucy says. "Arrest warrant number seven-two-six-oh for poor Mr. Guarino. Arrest warrant number seven-two-six-one for poor Monsieur La Fleur. Issued April twenty-fourth, 2003. Two days ago."

"Jesus fucking Christ."

"Your faithful client, Jean-Baptiste," Lucy reminds him.

"The bastard," Rocco mutters. "After all I did for the ugly piece of shit."

"It's over, Rocco," Rudy says.

He drops the Red Notice on top of the table.

"I understand the Chandonnes can be pretty creative," Lucy says. "Torture. Remember how much Jay Talley liked to string people up with rope and eyebolts and burn them with heat guns? Burn them until their skin was charred black. While they were alive and conscious. Remember how he tried to do that to my aunt while his fucking accomplice Bev Kiffin tried to blow me away with a shotgun?"

Rocco stares off.

She steps closer to him, the thought of what almost happened to her aunt tempting her to whip open her tactical baton and beat Rocco to death. She glances at it on the bedside table, knows better.

"Drowning is another pet choice," she goes on.

Rocco jerks at this. "No," he begs.

"Remember Jean-Baptiste's cousin Thomas? Drowned. Not a nice way to die." She gives Rudy a look.

He carefully wipes off the Colt with a corner of the bedsheet as an extra precaution, his face hard, his eyes gleaming with a detachment and determination that makes it possible for him to block out the sudden wave of empathy he feels for Rocco, no matter how unworthy of life he is.

Rudy glances at Lucy and briefly their eyes touch like two sparks.

Sweat rolls down Lucy's face, wisps of hair plastered to her temples. She is pale, and Rudy knows that each of her attempts at dry humor and harshness are forced as she plays the most terrible role of her life.

He pulls back the slide, chambering a round, and approaches Rocco.

"Right-handed, you agree, partner?" Rudy calmly says to Lucy.

"I agree."

She doesn't take her eyes off Rocco. Her hands have begun to shake, and she wills herself to think of Jay Talley and his evil paramour Bev Kiffin.

Images.

Lucy envisions the grief on her aunt's face as she scattered what she believed were Benton Wesley's ashes over the water. Lucy's brain seems to slide inside her skull. She has never been seasick. It must feel something like this.

"Your choice," she says to Rocco. "I mean it. You can die now and feel no pain. No torture. No burns. No drowning. The Red Notice is found right where you dropped it, your suicide completely understandable. Or you can walk out of here, never knowing when you'll breathe your last breath and what nightmare you'll suffer when the Chandonnes get you. And they will."

He nods. Of course they will. It is a given.

"Put out your right hand," Rudy tells Rocco.

Rocco rolls his eyes toward the ceiling again.

"See? I'm holding the gun, I'm going to help you," Rudy goes on, lightly, indifferently, as sweat drips on the carpet.

"Make sure the barrel is pointed up," Lucy says, thinking of the decapitated Nazi's head.

"Come on, Rocco. Do what I say. It won't hurt. You won't even know it."

Rudy touches the barrel against Rocco's right temple.

"Up," Lucy reminds him again.

"Your hand goes around the grips, and my hand goes around yours."

Rocco closes his eyes, and his hand jumps up and down. He closes his pudgy, short fingers around the grips, and Rudy's big, strong hand immediately clamps over his.

"I have to help you because you can't hold the gun still," Rudy tells him. "You don't shoot straight, and that could be ugly. And I can't let you hold the gun all by yourself, now can I? That would make me stupid." Rudy's voice is gentle now. "See, that's not so hard. Now press the barrel tight against your head."

Rocco gags, his chest heaving. He begins to hyperventilate.

"Pointed up," Lucy says it one more time, fixated on the decapitated Nazi's head, trying not to see Rocco's head.

He sways in his chair, grabbing shallow breaths, his face livid, his eyes squeezed shut. Rudy's gloved finger pulls the trigger.

The gun fires in a loud pop.

Rocco and his chair fall backward. His head lands on the British newspapers strewn over the carpet, his face turned toward the window. Blood gushing out of his head sounds like running water. Gunsmoke turns the air acrid.

Rudy squats to tuck Rocco's limp right arm and the pistol under his chest. Any prints or partial prints recovered on the blue steel Colt will be Rocco's.

Lucy opens a window a crack, no more than three inches, and yanks off her gloves as Rudy presses two fingers against Rocco Caggiano's carotid artery. His pulse beats faintly and stops. Rudy nods at Lucy and stands up. He digs inside a pocket of his jacket and pulls out a German mustard jar. Holes have been punched in the lid, and blow flies crawl along the inside of the glass, feeding on what is left of the rotting meat that yesterday baited them into captivity at a Dumpster crammed with garbage behind a Polish restaurant.

He opens the jar and shakes it. Several dozen flies lethargically lift off, buzzing to lamps and bouncing against illuminated shades. Sensing pheromones and the plume of an open wound, they greedily drone straight to Rocco's motionless body. Blow flies, the most common of carrion-feeding insects, alight on his bloody face. Several disappear inside his mouth.

39

It is only eight p.m. in Boston.

Pete Marino sits at the US Air gate, eating chocolate-dipped pretzels and listening to another apologetic announcement that promises his flight will depart after another minor delay of only two hours and ten minutes. This is after an earlier delay that has already held him hostage in Logan Airport for an hour and twenty-five minutes beyond his scheduled departure.

"Shit!" he exclaims, not caring who hears him. "I coulda walked by now!"

Rarely does he have plenty of time to ponder his life, and he thinks of Benton and diverts his misery and rage by focusing on Benton's physical conditioning and hard, manly body. He looks even better than he used to, Marino depressingly decides. How can that be possible after six years of what amounts to solitary confinement? Marino can't comprehend it. He starts on a brownie from the basket of Delicious Desserts of Gainesville that he happened upon in the airport gift shop and wonders what it would be like if he quit working for Lucy, just gave up going after dirtbags. They're cockroaches. Squash one, and five others take its place. Maybe Marino should go fishing, maybe become a professional bowler (he almost had a perfect score once), find him a nice woman and build a cabin in the woods.

Once, very long ago, Marino was admired, too, and the mirror did not hate him. Women—and men, he supposes with confusion and disgust—stare at Benton and lust for him. Marino is certain of this. They can't resist him when added to his good looks are his brain and his big-shot FBI status, or, more accurately, former FBI status. Marino pushes back strings of gray hair and wakes himself up to the fact that people don't meet Benton anymore and know his real name or admire his former FBI career. He is supposed to be dead or Tom or nobody. That Scarpetta could miss Benton so much causes Marino a sick pain somewhere around his heart and topples him into deeper despair. He hurts deeply for her. He hurts deeply for himself. If he died, she would grieve, but not forever. She has never been in love with him, never will be, and doesn't want his fat, hairy body in her bed.

Marino wanders into another gift shop and snatches a fitness magazine off a pile on the floor, an action as foreign to him as Hebrew. *Men's Workout* has a handsome young man on the cover who looks as if he's cut of smooth stone. He must have shaved his entire body except for his head and polished his tanned skin with oil. Marino returns to a nearby sports bar, orders another Budweiser on tap, finds his same table, brushes off pizza crumbs, and sets down the magazine, somewhat afraid of opening it. He finally musters the nerve to pick it up, and its slick cover sticks to the table.

"Hey!" Marino calls to the bartender. "Anyone ever wipe off a table in this joint?"

Everyone in the bar stares at Marino.

"I just paid three-fifty for this watered-down beer, and the table's so disgusting, my magazine's sticking to it."

Everyone in the bar stares at Marino's magazine. Several young men nudge one another and smile. The annoyed bartender, who would have to be an octopus to keep up with orders, tosses a wet bar towel to Marino. He wipes off his table and tosses it back, almost hitting an old woman in the head. She sips her white wine, oblivious. Marino starts flipping through his magazine. Maybe it isn't too late to reclaim his masculine plumage, to have muscles he can flex like a peacock fanning its tail. As a boy in New Jersey, he made himself strong from chin-ups, push-ups and maniacal repetitions with free weights he constructed from cinder blocks and mop or broom handles. He lifted the rear ends of cars to work on his back and biceps, clutched a laundry bag filled with bricks while doing squats or running up and down stairs. He boxed with laundry drying on the clothesline, always on windy days when the clothes and linens fought back.

"Peter Rocco! You stop fighting with the laundry! You knock it in the dirt and you get to wash it!"

His mother was a meshed figure behind the screen door, hands on her hips, trying to sound severe as her son's savage right hook yanked one of his father's wet undershirts from wooden clothespins and sent it sailing into a nearby bush. As Marino got older, he wrapped his fists in layers of rags and threw wicked punches at an old mattress he kept in the crawl space beneath the house. If it was possible to kill a mattress, this one died a thousand times, propped up against the porch, its ticking finally ripping and its dry-rotted foam rubber disintegrating with each blow. Marino scavenged neighborhood trash piles for discarded mattresses, and he battled his stained obtuse opponents as if he hated them for some unforgivable sin they had committed against him.

"Who you trying to kill, honey?" his mother asked him one afternoon when he was dripping with sweat and wobbly from exhaustion and flinging open the refrigerator door for the ice water his mother always kept there. "Don't drink out of the jug. How many times I gotta tell you? You know what germs are? They're little ugly bugs crawling out of your mouth right into the jug. Don't matter if you can't see 'em. Doesn't make them any less real, and those very germs are what gives you and everyone else the flu and polio, and you end up in an iron lung and . . ."

"Dad drinks outta the jug."

"Well."

"Well *what*, Mom?"

"He's the man of the house."

"Well, ain't that something. Guess he ain't got little ugly bugs crawling out him like everybody else, since he's the man of the house. Guess he don't give a rat's ass who ends up in an iron lung."

"Who you fighting out there when you beat up the mattress? Fight, fight, fight. You're always fighting."

Marino buys another beer and consoles himself with the thought that the male models in the workout magazine are not fighters, because they have the flexibility of a rock. They don't dance on their feet, boxing. They don't do anything but lift iron and pose for photographers and poison themselves with steroids. Still, Marino wouldn't mind having a stomach that looks like moguls in a ski run, and what he wouldn't give for his hair to come home to his head instead of continuing its relentless migration to other parts of his body. He smokes and drinks to the noise of a basketball dribbling, shoes squeaking and crowds yelling on the big-screen TV. Loudly flipping through a few more pages of his magazine, he begins to notice advertisements for aphrodisiacs, performance enhancements and invitations to skin parties and strip volleyball.

When he reaches a centerfold of hairless hunks wearing G-strings and fishnet bikini briefs, he slaps the magazine shut. A businessman sitting one table over gets up and moves to the other end of the bar. Marino takes his time finishing his beer and gets up and stretches and yawns. People in the bar watch him as he makes his way toward the businessman and drops the magazine on top of his *Wall Street Journal*.

"Call me," Marino says with a wink as he saunters out of the bar.

40

Back at the US Air gate, Marino is seized by agitation and impetuosity.

His flight has been delayed another hour due to weather. Suddenly, he doesn't want to go home to Trixie and get up in the morning and realize what happened in Boston. Thinking of his small house with its carport in its blue-collar neighborhood sinks his spirit lower into bitterness and a need to fight back. If only he could identify the enemy. Why he continues to live in Richmond makes no sense. Richmond is the past. Why he allowed Benton to blow him off makes no sense. He should never have walked away from Benton's apartment.

"You know what *due to weather* means?" Marino asks the young redheaded woman sitting next to him, filing her nails.

Two rude behaviors Marino simply can't tolerate are public farts and the scratching sound of manicures accompanied by drifting nail dust.

The file continues to rapidly scratch-scratch.

"It means they ain't decided *whether* to fly our asses outta Boston yet. See? There ain't enough passengers to make it worth their while. They lose money, they don't go nowhere and blame it on something else."

The file freezes and the woman looks around at dozens of empty plastic seats.

"You can sit here all night," Marino goes on, "or come find a motel room with me."

After a moment of disbelief, she gets up and walks off in a huff. "Pig," she says.

Marino smiles, civility restored, his boredom assuaged, if only briefly. He is not going to wait for a flight that probably will never happen, and then he thinks of Benton again. Anger and paranoia ooze into his skull. His feeling of powerlessness and rejection settle more closely around him, choking him with a depression that stalls his thoughts and fatigues him as if he hasn't slept in days. He can't stand it. He won't. He wishes he could call Lucy, but he doesn't know where she is. All she told him was that she had business to take care of that required traveling.

"What business?" Marino asked her.

"Just business."

"Sometimes I wonder why the hell I work for you."

"I don't wonder about it in the least. I never give it a thought," Lucy said over the phone from her office in Manhattan. "You adore me."

Outside Logan Airport, Marino flags down a Cambridge Checker cab, practically stepping in front of it and waving his arms, ignoring the taxi line and the dozens of weary, unhappy people in it.

"The Embankment," he tells the driver. "Near where the band shell is."

41

Scarpetta doesn't know where Lucy is, either.

Her niece doesn't answer her home or cell phones and hasn't returned numerous pages. Scarpetta can't reach Marino, and she has no intention of calling Rose and telling her about the letter. Her secretary worries too much already. Scarpetta sits on her bed, thinking. Billy makes his way up the dog ramp and plops down just far enough away to make her reach if she wants to pet him, and she does.

"Why do you always sit so far away from me?" she talks to him as she stretches out to stroke his soft, floppy ears. "Oh, I get it. I'm supposed to reposition myself and move closer to you."

She does.

"You're a very willful dog, you know."

Billy licks her hand.

"I have to go out of town for a few days," she tells him. "But Rose will take good care of you. Maybe you'll stay at her house and she'll take you to the beach. So promise you won't get upset that I'm leaving."

He never does. The only reason he comes running when she heads out on a trip is that he wants a ride in the car. He'd ride around in a car all day, given the choice. Scarpetta dials Lucy's office a second time. Although it is long past closing time, the phone is answered by an alive and awake human being twenty-four hours a day, seven days a week. Tonight, it is Zach Manham's turn.

"Okay, Zach," she says right off. "It's bad enough you won't tell me where Lucy is . . ."

"It's not that I won't tell . . ."

"Of course it is," she cuts him off. "You know, but you won't tell me."

"I swear to God I don't know," Manham replies. "Look, if I did, I'd call her on her international cell phone and at least tell her to call you."

"So she has her international cell phone with her. Then she's out of the country?"

"She always carries her international cell phone. You know, the one that takes photographs, videotapes, connects to the Internet. She's got the latest model. It makes pizza."

Nothing is funny to Scarpetta right now.

"I tried her cell phone. She's not answering," she says, "whether she's in this country or some other one. So what about Marino? You holding out on me about him, too?"

"I haven't talked to him in days," Manham says. "No, I don't know where he is. He not answering his cell phone or pages, either?"

"No."

"Want me to take a polygraph, Doc?"

"Yes."

Manham laughs.

"Okay, I quit. I'm too tired to keep this up all night," Scarpetta says as she rubs Billy's tummy. "If and when you ever hear from either one of them again, tell them to contact me immediately. It's urgent. Urgent enough that I'm flying to New York tomorrow."

"What? Are you in danger?" Manham asks, alarmed.

"I don't want to talk about it with you, Zach. No offense intended. Good night."

She locks her bedroom door, sets the alarm and places her pistol on the bedside table.

42

Marino doesn't like the taxi driver and asks him where he's from.

"Kabul."

"Kabul's where, exactly?" Marino asks. "I mean, I know what country" (he doesn't), "but not its exact geographical location."

"Kabul is the capital of Afghanistan."

Marino tries to envision Afghanistan. All that comes to mind are dictators, terrorists and camels.

"And you do what there?"

"I do nothing there. I live here." The driver's dark eyes glance at him in the rearview mirror. "My family worked in the wool mills, and I came here eight years ago. You should go to Kabul. It is very beautiful. Visit the old city. My name is Bābur. You have questions or need a cab, call my company and ask for me." He smiles, his teeth gleaming white in the dark.

Marino senses the driver is making fun of him, but he doesn't get the joke. The driver's identification card is fastened to the passenger's seat visor, and Marino tries to read it, but can't. His vision isn't what it used to be, and he refuses to wear glasses. Despite Scarpetta's urging, he also refuses laser surgery, which he adamantly claims will make him blind or damage his frontal lobe.

"This way don't look familiar," Marino comments in his usual grumpy tone as unrecognizable buildings flow past his window.

"We take a shortcut along the harbor, past the wharfs and then the causeway. Very pretty sights."

Marino leans forward on the hard bench seat, avoiding a spring that seems determined to work its way out of the vinyl upholstery and uncoil and bite his left buttock.

"You're heading north, you Mohammed scumbag! I may not be from Boston, but I know where the Embankment is, and you ain't even on the right side of the fucking river!"

The cabdriver who calls himself Bābur completely ignores his passenger and continues along his route, cheerfully pointing out the sights, including the Suffolk County Jail, the Massachusetts General Hospital and the Shriners Burn Center. By the time he drops Marino off on Storrow Drive, close but not too close to Benton Wesley's apartment building, the meter registers $68.35. Marino slings open the door and throws a crumpled one-dollar bill onto the front seat.

"You owe me sixty-seven dollars and thirty-five cents." The taxi driver smooths open the dollar bill on his leg. "I will call the police!"

"And I'll beat the shit out of you. And you can't do nothing about it, because you ain't legal, right? Show me your green card, asshole, and guess what, I'm the police and got a pistol strapped under my arm." He snatches out his wallet and flashes the badge he did not return to the Richmond Police Department after he retired.

He said he lost it.

Tires squeal as the taxi driver speeds off, screaming curses out his open window. Marino heads toward the Longfellow Bridge and veers off southeast, briefly following the same sidewalk he and Benton walked along earlier today. He takes a roundabout way beneath gas lamplight on Pinckney and Revere, constantly listening and checking his surroundings, making certain he isn't being followed, as is his habit. Marino isn't thinking about the Chandonne cartel. He is on the lookout for the usual street punks and lunatics, although he has seen no evidence of either in this section of Beacon Hill.

When Benton's building comes into view, Marino notices that the windows of unit 56 are dark.

"Shit," he mutters, tossing his cigarette, not bothering to stamp it out.

Benton must have gone out for a late dinner, or to the gym, or for a jog. But that isn't likely, and Marino's anxieties tighten his chest with his every step. He knows damn well that Benton would leave lights on when he goes out. He isn't the sort to walk into a completely dark house or apartment.

Climbing the stairs to the fifth floor is worse than last time, because adrenaline and beer quicken his straining heart until he can scarcely breathe. When he reaches unit 56, he bangs on the door. Not a sound comes from inside.

He pounds harder and calls out, "Yo, Tom!"

43

Lucy starts the Mercedes and suddenly stares at Rudy in the pitch dark.

"Oh my God! I can't believe it!" She pounds the steering wheel with her fist, accidentally blaring the horn.

"What!" Rudy jumps, startled and suddenly frantic. "What the hell? What the hell are you doing!"

"My tactical baton. Goddamn son of a bitch! I left it on the night table inside the room. It's going to have my fingerprints on it, Rudy."

How could she make such a brain-dead mistake? All went according to plan until she made an oversight, a mindless blunder, the very sort of blunder that catches people on the run all the time. The engine rumbles quietly on the side of the dark street, neither Lucy nor Rudy quite sure what to do. They are free. They got away with it. No one near or inside the hotel saw them, and now one of them must go back.

"I'm sorry," Lucy whispers. "I'm a fucking idiot," she says. "You stay here."

"No. I'll take care of it." Rudy's fear turns to the more manageable emotion of rage, and he resists taking it out on her.

"I fucked it up. I get to fix it." She swings open the car door.

44

Bev Kiffin runs her fingers through a rack of cheap acetate panties and bras.

The women's lingerie section of Wal-Mart is near arts and crafts and directly across from men's athletic shoes, a section of the store she frequently haunts. She is certain, however, that the clerks in their cheap blue vests and name tags don't recognize her. This is the type of business where tired, glazed employees don't pay much attention to common-looking people like Bev who root around for bargains in a discount store that is open twenty-four hours a day, seven days a week.

A red, lacy bra captivates her imagination, and she checks sizes, looking for a 38D. Finding one in black, she tucks it up a sleeve of her dark green rain slicker. The bra is followed by two pairs of bikini-cut panties, size large. Stealing lingerie and other items that do not have security sensors is so easy. She wonders why everybody doesn't do it. Bev has no fear of consequences. No frontal-lobe alarm sounds when she contemplates committing a crime, no matter how serious. Opportunities come and go on her radar screen, some bigger and brighter than others, such as the woman who has just wandered into the arts and crafts section, interested in needlepoint.

The thought of such a stupid domestic hobby fills Bev with contempt as she instantly deduces that the attractive blonde dressed in jeans and a light blue jacket is naïve.

A lamb.

Bev continues rummaging through the lingerie rack, the target on her radar flashing brighter with each passing second, her pulse picking up, her palms getting clammy.

The woman drops skeins of colorful floss and a needlepoint pattern of an eagle and a flag into her cart. *So she's patriotic,* Bev thinks. Maybe she has a husband or boyfriend in the military, might be gone, maybe still in Iraq. She's at least thirty-five, maybe close to forty. Could be her man's in the National Guard.

The cart rolls forward, getting closer.

Bev detects cologne. The scent is unfamiliar and probably expensive. The woman's legs are slender, her posture good. She works out in the gym. She's got free time on her hands. If she has children, she must be able to afford having someone take care of them while she's trotting off to the gym or maybe the hair salon.

Bev scans a scrap of paper, a shopping list, feigning that she is unaware of the woman, who pauses in the aisle, looking directly at the rack of lingerie. She wants to keep her man happy.

A lamb.

Good-looking.

An air about her that Bev associates with intelligence.

She can sense when people are smart. They don't have to say one word, because the rest of them is talking. The woman pushes her cart straight to the rack, not even a foot from where Bev is standing, and the perfume crawls up Bev's sinuses, burrowing way up inside her skull, and her focus sharpens to a point as the woman unzips her jacket, picks a sheer red bra off the rack and holds it up to firm, ample breasts.

Hatred and envy electrify every nerve and muscle in Bev's matronly body, her upper lip breaking out in a cold sweat. She wanders in the direction of men's running shoes as the woman dials a cell phone. It rings somewhere for several seconds.

"Honey?" she sweetly, happily says. "Still here. I know. Such a big place." She laughs. "I like the Wal-Mart off Acadian better." She laughs again. "Well, maybe I will if you're sure you don't mind."

She holds out her left arm, glancing at the watch peeking out of her sleeve, the sort of watch runners wear. Bev expected something fancier.

45

A light, misty rain dampens the streets of Szczecin as Lucy nears the Radisson Hotel.

This time she doesn't have to wait for the clerk to leave the front desk. The lobby is deserted. She walks inside, casually but briskly, and heads to the elevators. Her finger is about to make contact with the elevator button when the doors part and a very intoxicated man lurches out, knocking into her.

" 'Scussssse me!" he says loudly, startling Lucy and jerking her mind out of gear.

What to do? What to do?

"Now, aren't you the prettiest thing I've seen forever!"

His words slur as if his mouth is numb with lidocaine, and he is almost yelling as he leers at her, checking her out from her hair to her cleavage to her satin cowboy boots. He announces that his party is going strong in room 301 and she must come. He goes on and on. My, my, how beautiful and sexy she is, and obviously American, and he was from Chicago, transferred recently to

Germany, and is lonely and separated from his wife, who is a bitch.

The desk clerk rushes back to the lobby, and not a minute later a security guard follows and speaks in English to the drunk.

"Perhaps you should go back to your room. It is late, and you should go to sleep," the guard says stiffly, eyeing Lucy with distaste and suspicion, as if assuming she is the vulgar man's girlfriend, or perhaps a prostitute, and is probably drunk, too.

She stabs at the elevator button, missing it several times, swaying and clutching the drunk man's arm.

"Come on, baby, let's go," she slurs with a Russian accent, leaning against him.

"Now ain't that sweet . . ." He is about to show besotted surprise and pleasure in her company when she reaches up and kisses him hard on the mouth.

The elevator doors open and she pulls him inside, wrapping herself around him and continuing a long, tongue-groping kiss that tastes like garlic and whiskey. The security guard stares stonily at them as the doors shut.

Mistake.

The guard will remember her face. Lucy's face is hard to forget, and the guard had plenty of time to look at it because Lucy was trapped with the drunk asshole.

Big mistake.

She hits button 2 as the man paws her. He doesn't seem to notice that the elevator is stopping at the wrong floor, but suddenly his new lover is running away, clutching at her clothes. He tries to chase after her, wildly waving his arms, cursing, catching his toe on the carpet and stumbling.

Lucy follows exit signs, turning into another hallway, then into a stairway. She silently makes her way up three flights and waits on the dimly lit landing, holding her breath and listening, sweat rolling down her face and soaking her sexy black blouse. Possibly, it was habit more than instinct that caused her to pluck up a plastic hotel key from the table in Caggiano's room and tuck it in a pocket of her windbreaker. Whenever she checks out of a hotel, she always keeps a key, if it is a disposable one, in the event she suddenly realizes she has forgotten something. Once, and she doesn't like to remember this, she left her gun in a bedside drawer and didn't realize it until she was climbing into a taxi. Thank God she still had a key.

The *Do Not Disturb* sign hangs ominously from the doorknob of room 511, and Lucy searches the hallway, desperately hoping she is not surprised by anyone else. As she makes her approach, she faintly hears the television inside Rocco's room, and a sick pain stabs her stomach. Fear burns. Recalling what she and Rudy just did is awful, and now she must confront their sin again.

A green light flickers, and she pushes open the door with her elbows because she has no fresh gloves, having raced off without them. She runs into a wall of rank smell from Rocco's last greasy meal and detects his alcohol-saturated blood. It coagulates like pudding under his head, his eyes half open and dull, the chair overturned, the gun under his chest, every detail exactly as she and Rudy had left it. Blow flies buzz around his body, searching for the perfect piece of moist human real estate to appropriate for their eggs. Lucy stares, transfixed, at the frenzied insects.

She focuses on her tactical baton. It, too, is exactly as she left it, on the table to the left of the bed.

"Oh, thank God," she mutters.

The baton is safely back up her sleeve as she cautiously opens the door, wiping the knob with her blouse. This time she takes the stairs all the way down to the service level, where she hears the murmur of voices, possibly from the kitchen. Along walls are carts loaded with dirty dishes, wilted flowers in bud vases, empty wine bottles and what is left from cocktails and other beverages. Food is hardened on hotel china and stains white cloths and wadded napkins. There are no flies down here. Not one.

She swallows repeatedly, suddenly nauseous as she envisions the blow flies crawling all over Rocco and feeding on his gore. She thinks about what will happen next. Inside his warm room, blow fly eggs will hatch into maggots that, depending on how long he remains undiscovered, will teem over his decomposing body, especially inside his wound and other orifices. Blow flies love deep, dark, moist crevices and passageways.

The intense presence of carrion predators will throw off Rocco's time of death, as intended when Rudy introduced the flies into the room. The forensic pathologist who examines Rocco's body will be confused by the story of when room service delivered his late dinner and the advanced stage of maggot infestation and decomposition. His blood-alcohol level will indicate that Caggiano was intoxicated when he died of a self-inflicted gunshot wound that penetrated his temple and tore through his brain in a storm of lead shrapnel and the ragged razor-sharp copper edges of a semi-jacketed hollow-point bullet. Prints on the gun will be his.

The warmth of the room will be factored in but should not arouse suspicion. The empty champagne bottle has Caggiano's prints on it, should the police bother to check, although there will be no record of his ordering the champagne or receiving it compliments of the manager. He could have bought it elsewhere. The Red Notice will have his prints on it, should anyone bother to check, and she must assume someone will.

She wishes Rocco had not ordered room service, but she planned for that possibility, realizing that whoever delivered his dinner will recall the tip and not want to reveal that it was American cash. He or she will not want to be implicated in any sort of scandal that involves the police. In addition, if Rocco's time of death, as determined by the forensic pathologist, doesn't jibe at all with what the hotel employee who delivered the room service has to say—assuming the person talks—then it may very well be assumed that the person is mistaken about the time, possibly even the day. Or is lying. No one in that hotel will want to admit to accepting American money and who knows what other favors and contraband that Rocco, a fugitive, has probably bestowed on them over the many years he has stayed in that hotel.

Who will care that Rocco Caggiano is dead? Perhaps no one except the Chandonne family. They will wonder. Lucy plotted with the expectation that they will press hard to know the facts. Maybe they will. Maybe they won't. Suicide will be accepted, and no one will feel grief or even give a damn.

46

Lucy sprints through the dark, her aching chest not due to physical exertion.

The Mercedes is quiet on the side of the street, and she can't see Rudy through the tinted windows. The locks click free and she opens the driver's door.

"Mission accomplished?" he grimly asks in the dark. "Don't start the car yet."

She tells him about her encounter with the drunk and the hotel staff and explains the way she handled it. He says nothing. She feels his disapproval and irritation with her.

"Give me some credit. I think we're fine."

"As fine as you could be under the circumstances," he has to admit.

"There's no reason for anyone to connect me with Rocco's room, with his death," she goes on. "I guarantee that hotel staff won't touch his room with that *Do Not Disturb* sign on the door. More flies will come in through the opening in the window. Say he's found in three or four days, maggots will have devoured him to the point he won't be recognizable. And in case you didn't know it, blow flies are attracted to shit, too.

"And his blood alcohol will be high, no reason in the world for anyone to think anything but suicide, and the hotel will want his rotting body and maggots out of there as quickly as possible. And the medical examiner will think he's been dead longer than room service says—assuming there is an exact time associated with Rocco's dinner order, and there probably won't be. Orders aren't handled by computer. I know that for a fact."

"For a fact?" Rudy asks. "How the hell can you know that for a fact?"

"What do you think I am, fucking stupid? I called. Days ago. Said I was a Hewlett-Packard rep checking on their computers and that the one the kitchen used for room service needed a software upgrade. And they didn't know what I was talking about, said they didn't use computers for room service, only for inventory. Then I talked about the advantages of using an hp pavilion 753n with an Intel Pentium processor and eighty-gigabyte hard drive and CD-ROM and all the rest for room service orders . . . Point is, there is no computer record of what time Rocco ordered dinner, okay?"

Rudy was silent, then said, "They use Hewlett-Packards at that hotel?"

"Easy enough to find out by calling the business office. Yes," she replied.

"Okay. Good job on that one. So even if the drunk or anyone else paid any attention to you, the way we've staged Rocco's crime scene will make it appear he was dead long before you went off to party with the drunk."

"That's right, Rudy. We're fine. We're fine. Rocco's already being infested. Masses of maggots will produce heat and speed up decomposition, and it looks like a suicide, anyway—one committed earlier—much earlier—than anyone will imagine."

She starts the car, laying a hand on his arm. "Now, can we get the hell out of here?"

"We can't make any more mistakes, Lucy," he says in a defeated way. "We just can't."

She pulls away from the sidewalk, angry.

"The fact is, at least two people in that hotel think you might be a drunk conventiongoer or maybe even a prostitute, and you aren't easy to forget, no matter what they think you are. It probably doesn't matter one goddamn bit, but . . ." He doesn't finish.

"But it could have." Lucy drives carefully, checking her mirrors and the sidewalks, dark with shadows.

"Right. It could have."

She feels his eyes and the shifting of his moods. He is softening toward her, sorry he was so rough.

"Hey, you-Rudy-you." She reaches out and affectionately touches his cheek, his stubble reminding her of a cat's tongue. "We're on the go and we're okay."

She reaches for his hand and holds it tightly.

"This went down bad, Rudy, really bad, but it's going to turn out fine. We're fine," she says again.

When one or the other or both of them are scared, they never admit it, but they know because they need each other. Each becomes desperate for the other's warm flesh. Lucy lifts his hand to her mouth, resting his arm against her.

"Don't," he says. "We're both tired, strung-out. Not a good time to . . . to not have both hands on the wheel. Lucy, don't," he mutters as she deeply kisses his fingers, his knuckles, his palm.

She makes love to one hand and slides the other inside her black linen blouse.

"Lucy, stop . . . oh, Jesus . . . it's not fair." He unfastens his seat belt. "I don't want to feel this way about you, goddamn it."

Lucy drives.

"You do feel it for me. At least sometimes, don't you?"

Lucy pets his hair, his neck, slips her hand into his collar and traces the muscles of his upper back. She doesn't look at him as she drives fast.

47

Several times, Nic sent memos to the Baton Rouge Task Force, reminding the men and women—mostly men—that a Wal-Mart or other huge store like it would be a very good place for a killer to stalk his victims.

No one would pay any attention to a vehicle in the parking lot, no matter the hour, and based on charge-card receipts, every one of the missing women shopped at Wal-Mart, if not the one closest to the Louisiana State University campus, then at others in Baton Rouge and New Orleans. Ivy Ford did. The Saturday before she disappeared, she drove from Zachary and shopped at this very Wal-Mart, the one near LSU.

The task force never responded directly to Nic, but someone associated with it must have called her chief because he found her in the breakroom before she took off to Knoxville and said, out of nowhere, "Most everybody in the world shops at Wal-Marts, Sam's Clubs, Kmarts, Costcos and so on, Nic."

"Yes, sir," she replied. "Most everybody does."

Baton Rouge isn't her jurisdiction, and the only way she might change that fact would be for the attorney general to say the hell with boundaries. She has no good reason to request this, and he would have no good reason to grant it. Nic has never been the sort to ask permission unless the subject rises before her like a drawbridge, giving her no choice but to put on the brakes or turn around. These days, she works undercover wherever her instincts take her, which frequently is the Wal-Mart near LSU, close to where her father lives in the Old Garden District. It isn't difficult to intuit which area of the store a killer might frequent if he is looking for prey. Women's lingerie would excite him, especially if a potential victim was holding up bras and panties, checking out styles and sizes, as that fleshy woman with short graying hair was doing moments earlier before leaving the store with stolen merchandise tucked up the sleeve of her raincoat. The petty thievery will go unreported because Nic has a much bigger agenda. She leaves her shopping cart in the aisle and walks out of the store, aware of every man she spots, aware of his awareness and activity, and acutely conscious of the pistol in her fanny pack.

Outside, the parking lot is fairly well lit by tall lamps. What few cars there are—less than a hundred—are parked close together, as if to keep one another company. She spots the heavy-set petty thief walking swiftly toward a dark blue Chevrolet with Louisiana tags. Nic memorizes the plate number as she heads in the woman's general direction without appearing to notice her. In fact, Nic doesn't notice anyone in the area who might be a potential serial killer. If the woman is being stalked, and of course that was a long shot to begin with, there is no hint of it.

Once again, Nic is prodded by guilt because she is disappointed. The idea that she could possibly feel regret that a woman is not about to become another victim is so abhorrent that Nic will not acknowledge her sinful hopes to anyone and scarcely to herself. She represses that truth so completely that she would probably pass a polygraph test if the examiner asked her, "Do you feel disappointed when you tail a potential victim and the killer doesn't try to abduct her or succeed in abducting her?" Nic wouldn't get tense or hesitate. Her pulse rate would stay the same as she replied, "No." The shorter the answer, the less chance of her nervous system betraying her.

She does not walk anywhere near her own car, a five-year-old forest-green Ford Explorer that is clandestinely equipped with a portable dash-mounted flashing beacon, a shotgun, a first-aid kit, jumper cables, flares, a fire extinguisher, a jump-out bag containing Battle Dress Uniforms, boots, extra magazines and other tactical gear, a handheld scanner tucked under the dash and a charger for her international cell phone, which also works as a two-way radio. A lot of her equipment she bought with her own money. In life, she is always overprepared for the worst.

The woman digs inside a dirty canvas beach bag, maybe ten feet from the Chevrolet. Certainly she doesn't fit the victimology, not in the least. But Nic doesn't trust so-called patterns or MOs. She remembers Scarpetta emphasizing that profiles are dangerous, because they're fraught with errors. Not everybody does everything the same way every time, and, if nothing else, the woman is a loner in a dark, relatively deserted parking lot at the edge of a major university campus, and that makes her vulnerable to predators.

The woman fumbles with keys and drops them. Stooping to pick them up, she loses her balance and falls, suddenly crying out and clutching her left knee.

She casts about helplessly, spots Nic and begs, "Help me!"

Nic sprints and squats by the woman.

"Don't move," she tells her. "What hurts?"

She smells insect repellent and body odor. It vaguely brushes against her thoughts that the car keys on the pavement don't look as if they belong to a relatively new Chevrolet.

"I think I pulled something in my knee," the woman says, her eyes fixed on Nic's. "It's my bad knee."

Her accent is Southern with a distinct lilt. She is not native to the area, and her hands are rough and raw as if she is accustomed to hard, physical work such as cleaning or shucking shellfish. Nic notices no jewelry, not even a watch. The woman pulls up her pant leg and looks at an angry purple bruise centered on her kneecap. The bruise isn't fresh. Instinctively, Nic is repulsed by the woman's unpleasant odor, her bad breath and something about her demeanor that she can't pinpoint but finds disturbing. She gets to her feet and steps back.

"I can call an ambulance," Nic says. "Not much else I can do, ma'am. I'm not a doctor."

A look takes over the woman's face, making it harsher in the glow of the parking lot lamps.

"No, I don't need an ambulance. Like I said, I have this happen all the time." She tries to get up.

"Then why do you have just one bruise?"

"I always fall the same way."

Nic keeps her distance. She has no intention of offering further assistance. The woman is dirty, maybe mentally ill, and Nic knows better than to tangle with that type. They can be contagious, unpredictable, even violent if one has physical contact with them. The woman is on her feet now, favoring her left leg.

"Believe I'll get me a coffee and rest for a bit," she says. "I'll be fine, just fine."

Slowly, she limps away from the Chevrolet, back toward the store.

Nic softens. She digs in a pocket of her jeans as she trots after the woman.

"Here." She hands her a five-dollar bill.

The woman smiles, her quick dark eyes hot on Nic's.

"God bless you." She clutches the money. "You're a lamb," she says.

48

The door across the hallway opens and an older man in an undershirt and sweatpants studies Marino suspiciously.

"What's all the racket about?" he inquires, his gray hair sticking up like the bristles of a hedgehog, his wrinkled face patchy with stubble, his eyes puffy and bloodshot.

Marino knows the look all too well. The man's been drinking, probably since he got up and downed his first eye-opener.

"You seen Tom?" Marino asks, sweating and struggling for air.

"Can't say I really know him. Don't have a heart attack. I can't do CPR, although I am familiar with the Heimlich maneuver."

"He promised to meet me"—Marino catches a breath—"and I came all the friggin' way from California."

"You did?" The man is very curious now and steps out into the hallway. "What for?"

"What do you mean, what for?" Marino recovers enough to

snap at him, as if it is any of the man's business. " 'Cause the friggin' gold rush's over. 'Cause I'm tired of sittin' on the friggin' dock of the bay. 'Cause I got bored being a friggin' movie star."

"If you were in the movies, I've never seen you, and I rent movies all the time. What else is there to do around here?"

"Have you seen Tom?" Marino persists, trying in vain to force the knob by turning it hard and shaking the door.

"I was asleep when you started all the racket," says the man, who looks at least sixty and a bit deranged. "I haven't seen Tom and don't care for the likes of him, if you get my drift."

He scrutinizes Marino.

"What do you mean, *the likes of him?*"

"Homo."

"That's news to me, not that I give a shit what people do, as long as I ain't around to see it. He bringing men to his apartment or something? 'Cause I'm not sure I want to get in if . . ."

"Oh, no. Never saw him bring anybody to his apartment. But another homo in the building who wears leather and earrings told me he's seen Tom in some of those bars where homos go and pick each other up for a quick visit to the bathroom."

"Listen, jerkface, I'm supposed to be subletting this dump from the son of a bitch," Marino heatedly informs the man. "Already paid him the first three months' rent, and drove from California to get the key and move in. All my stuff's down there in my damn truck."

"That would really piss me off."

"No joke, Sherlock."

"I mean, really piss me off. Who's Sherlock? Oh, yes. That detective with the hat and pipe. I don't read violent books."

"So if you hear any noise coming from this apartment, ignore it. If I have to use dynamite, I'm getting in."

"You don't really mean that," the old man worries.

"Right," Marino says sarcastically. "I walk around with dynamite in my pockets. I'm a suicide bomber with a New Jersey accent. Know how to fly planes, just can't take off or land."

The old man disappears inside his apartment, and a burglar chain rattles.

49

Marino studies the hollow metal door of unit 56.

Some twelve inches above the knob is a dead-bolt lock. He lights a cigarette, squinting through smoke at the enemy: a cheap brass knob with a push-button lock and the more problematic single cylinder dead bolt. None of the other doors along the hallway have dead bolts, confirming Marino's suspicion that Benton installed the lock himself. Knowing him, he opted for a jimmy-proof dead bolt that neither a thief nor a hit man nor an aggravated Marino can drill through without a spring-actuated plate sliding shut like a bank window and foiling the drill bit. One security risk that Benton couldn't have done much about was the door frame, which is a thin strip of metal screwed into wood.

Piece of cake, Marino says to himself as he unsnaps a bucktool from his belt and slides it out of its worn leather sheath.

The hinges are the common loose-pin variety, and Marino unfolds a pair of pliers from his all-purpose tool, attacks the pin and works it out of the hinge like a cork out of a bottle. Soon, three pins are on the floor, the door free on the left side. With two powerful yanks, Marino breaks the locks loose from the metal jamb. Inside the apartment, he props the door against the opening to give himself a little privacy. He flips on the overhead lights.

Benton had moved out, leaving nothing behind but food in the cupboards, a refrigerator full of Budweiser and half a bag of trash in the kitchen. *May as well grab a beer while I'm here,* Marino thinks. The bottle opener is on the counter where Marino saw it last, seeming to welcome him in a generous, affectionate way, like a Christmas stocking. Nothing else is out of place. Even the dishwasher is empty.

Strange.

Benton was careful not to offer so much as a partial fingerprint on windowpanes, tabletops or drinking glasses, dishes, cookware or silverware. Marino continues to hold up objects and look at them in oblique light. Sweep marks of the vacuum cleaner are visible on the carpet. Benton wiped down the entire place, and when Marino digs through the garbage bag, he finds nothing but his own empty Budweiser bottles and the broken glass from the Dos Equis he smashed in the sink. Every piece of glass is clean, the labels wet and soapy.

"What the hell is going on?" Marino asks the living room.

"I don't know," a male voice answers from behind the propped-up door. "Everything all right in there?"

Marino recognizes the neighbor from across the hall. "Go to bed," he gruffly tells him. "And if you and me are gonna get along, you need to mind your own business . . . what's your name?"

"Dave."

"That's funny, I'm Dave, too, as in t-o, not t-w-o."

"T-o-o."

"Sorry, I forgot to bring spell-check with me." Marino glares through the space between the propped-up door and the frame.

Dave appears more curious than frightened, peering in, trying to look around the room. Marino's considerable size blocks the nosy neighbor's view.

"Can't believe the bastard left like this," Marino says. "How'd you like to break into your own damn apartment?"

"I wouldn't."

"Not only that, the joint's a pigpen, and he made off with the silverware, pots and pans, and every bar of soap and roll of toilet paper."

"Silverware and cookware belong to the apartment," Dave says disapprovingly. "But from where I'm looking, the place looks quite tidy."

"Yeah, *from where you're looking*."

"I always thought he was an odd man. I wonder why he took the toilet paper."

"I only hooked up with him a couple months back, answering his ad for subletting," Marino comments.

He straightens up and steps away from the door, scanning the inside of the apartment again as Dave peers in. His eyes are red-rimmed and glassy, his cheeks sagging and rosy with broken blood vessels, probably from years of living inside a whiskey bottle.

"Yup," he says. "He never talked, I mean never, not even when he passed me in the hall or we both just happened to open our doors at the same time. There we are, face-to-face, and the most he ever did was sort of give me a little smile and a jerk of his chin."

Marino isn't a great believer in coincidences and suspects Dave listened for Benton to come and go and just happened to open his door when Benton was opening his.

"Where were you this afternoon?" Marino wonders if Dave heard the altercation, a loud one, coming from Benton's apartment.

"Oh, I don't know. After lunch, I sleep a lot."

Drunk, Marino thinks.

"He's the sort who didn't have friends," Dave goes on.

Marino continues looking around, standing near the door while Dave peers through the crack.

"Never saw him have a single visitor, and I've been living here five years. Five years and two months. Hate this place. He seemed to go away sometimes. Since I retired from being the head chef at the Lobster House, I have to watch my pennies."

Marino has no idea how watching pennies has anything to do with the man's mysterious neighbor.

"You was the head chef there? Every time I come to Boston, I eat at the Lobster House."

This isn't true, nor is Marino a frequent visitor to Boston.

"You and the rest of the world, yessir. Well, I wasn't the head chef, but I damn well should've been. I'll cook for you one of these days."

"How long did the weirdo live here?"

"Oh." Dave sighs, his eyes shining through the space as he watches Marino. "I'd say goin' on two years. On and off. What was your favorite dish at the Lobster House?"

"Two damn years. That's interesting. Told me he'd just moved in and gotten transferred or something, which is why he had to give up the apartment."

"Well, probably lobster," Dave remarks. "All tourists get the lobster and sop it in so much butter it's a wonder they taste anything but butter, so I was always commenting to the other workers in the kitchen, what was the point of bringing in nice fresh lobsters if nobody tastes anything but the butter?"

"I hate seafood," Marino says.

"Well, we do have mighty fine steaks. Aged one-hundred-percent-prime Angus."

"*Aged* always worries me. In the grocery store, *aged* means spoiled. You know, clearance buggy shit."

"Now, he wasn't here all the time," Dave says. "In and out, sometimes gone for weeks. But no way he'd just moved in. I've seen him coming in and out for two years, like I said."

"Anything else you can tell me about this homo who locked me out and made off with half the stuff in the joint?" Marino asks. "When I find him, I'm gonna kick his ass."

Dave shakes his head and disappointment glints. "Sure wish I could help you out, but like I've been saying, I didn't know the man and I'm glad he's gone, and it's looking like you and me will be great neighbors, *Dave Too*."

"Thick as thieves. Now you go on to bed. Let me get a few things done in here, and I'll catch you later."

"So nice to meet you. I guess I'll be calling you *Dave Too* from now on, if that's okay with you."

"Nighty-night."

50

Benton lived here two years and nobody knew him, not even his lonely, busybody neighbor Dave.

Not that Marino is really surprised, but the realization is a reminder of Benton's desolate, confining life, which is all the more reason his refusal to return to himself, his friends and those who love him makes no sense. Marino sits on Benton's perfectly made bed, staring in a glazed way at the mirror over the dresser. As well as Benton knows him, he must have suspected that Marino would come back and rant and rail at him again. Not much could be more wounding than for him to have said he doesn't want to see Marino again—ever.

He focuses on his big, unhealthy self in the mirror, sweat rolling down his face, and it occurs to him that Benton turned off the air-conditioning in the living room when he and Benton were arguing. But when Marino just broke in, the air-conditioning was back on in that room but turned off in this one. Virtually every move Benton makes is deliberate. That's the way he is, and for him to crank the air-conditioning on high in the living area and turn it off in the bedroom was for a reason. Marino gets off the bed and walks to the window unit, noticing an envelope taped to the side of it.

Perfectly centered on it in block letters are the initials PM.

Excitement kicks in but is tempered by Marino's wariness. He returns to the kitchen for a sharp knife. Back in the bedroom, he sets it on top of the air-conditioning unit. Then he heads to the bathroom and yanks off several long sections of toilet paper, wrapping it around his fingers. He returns to the window unit and carefully removes the envelope, noticing that both ends of the tape are folded over so that they adhere to themselves, the same technique police use to prevent fingerprint tape from sticking to their gloves.

He slits the top of the envelope and pulls out a folded sheet of plain white paper and smooths it open. Written in the same block printing that's on the envelope is: PLEASE KEEP ON.

Baffled, Marino considers for a moment that the note wasn't intended for him and wasn't written by Benton. He considers that neither the tape nor the paper is old, and they are very clean, and the folded ends of the tape hint that whoever used it might have been wearing latex gloves. Marino's initials are PM, and Benton knows that handwriting comparisons are usually foiled by block printing unless a documents examiner is comparing block printing exemplars written by the same individual. Benton also knows that Marino would be hot as hell in this room and would turn on the air conditioner. Or if nothing else, Marino would notice the inconsistency of one window unit left on while the other wasn't and would wonder about it.

"Keep on the air conditioner?" Marino says out loud, frustrated and exhausted.

He returns to the kitchen and snatches open a cupboard where a few minutes earlier he noticed a neat, tidy stack of small paper grocery bags. Shaking one open, he drops the envelope inside it.

"What the hell are you talking about? Are you just fucking with me, you son of a bitch?"

Frustration tightens his chest as he thinks of the way Benton treated him, as if the two of them hadn't been lifelong friends, buddies, almost like brothers, sharing the same woman but in entirely different ways. In a fantastic and secret part of Marino's mind, he and Benton were married to Scarpetta—at the same time. Now Marino has exclusive rights to her. But she doesn't long for him, and that repressed anguish adds to his volatility, his upset. A flutter of panic stirs in his stomach and floats up his throat.

Outside in the dark without a cab in sight, Marino lights a cigarette and weakly sits on a brick wall, breathing hard, his heart pounding violently against his ribs like a boxer pounding him, battering him, knocking the wind out of him. Pain shoots through the left side of his chest, terrifying him, and he takes slow, deep, sharp breaths but can't get enough air.

An empty taxicab drives by, seems to drift by, as sweat drips from Marino's face while he sits perfectly still on the wall, eyes wide, hands on his knees. The cigarette drops from his clamped fingers and rolls on cobblestones, stopping in a crack.

51

Bev can't stop thinking about her.

She should stay far away from that lamb who just gave her five dollars in the Wal-Mart parking lot. But she can't. Bev can't control the compulsion, and although her reaction defies any rational explanation, there is a cause and effect in her black, ugly thoughts. The lamb spurned her. The woman backed away from Bev as if she was repulsive and then dared to degrade her further by giving her money.

Inside Wal-Mart, Bev lingers near a display of insect repellents, picking up bottles, pretending to read the labels as she watches the parking lot through the plate glass. To her surprise, the lamb isn't driving a new car, but an old forest-green Explorer that for some reason doesn't seem in character for a spoiled, rich housewife or girlfriend. More interesting yet, she's sitting inside the SUV with the engine running and the headlights off. Bev is in and out of a dressing room in five minutes, outfitted in a loud Hawaiian shirt and Bermuda shorts—none of it paid for and the sensors cut off with her buck knife. Her rain slicker is inside out and draped over her arm, a cheap plastic rain bonnet over her hair, even though the night is clear. If people notice her at all, they will assume she is either crazy or processing her hair.

The Explorer hasn't moved. Bev walks directly to Jay's beat-up, filthy white SUV, confident the lamb doesn't notice her or at least doesn't connect her with the woman she encountered and gave money to not even half an hour ago. Driving off, Bev turns left onto Perkins, then crosses Acadian and parks in a small parking lot filled with cars because Caterie is a popular restaurant, especially with university students. She turns off her engine and headlights, waiting, her desire burning hotter the longer the lamb sits in the forest-green Explorer in the Wal-Mart parking lot across the street.

Maybe she is on the phone. Maybe this time she is fighting with her man instead of sounding so disgustingly sweet. Bev is an expert at tailing people. She does it regularly when she is driving Jay's Cherokee. Before she began biding her time as a fugitive at a fishing camp, she followed people, depending on what needed to be done or just for the hell of it. But in those days, her activities had a purpose, or at least were a means directed toward a useful end. Whatever Bev did, she was following orders.

To some extent, she is following Jay's orders now, but methods and emotions change when one is asked repeatedly to perform the same task. Bev has begun to indulge herself, entertain her own fantasies and have her own fun. It's her right.

The Explorer heads into the heart of the Old Garden District. The pretty blonde driver has no idea that the woman with the bad knee is not far behind. This amuses Bev. She smiles as the Explorer slows down and makes a right turn into a dark driveway bordered by tall shrubs. Bev drives past, pulls off the road and gets out. She quickly covers herself in her dark rain slicker and backtracks to the white brick house just in time to see its front door close, the woman safely inside. Bev returns to her Cherokee, writes down the address and cuts across a side road so she doesn't pass the house again. She waits.

52

More than anything, Jean-Baptiste Chandonne wants a dipole antenna, but he is not allowed commissary privileges, and the commissary is where the antennas are sold.

Inmates who enjoy favored status can buy dipole antennas, headphones, portable radios, an AM/FM booster and a religious medal with a chain. At least some inmates can. Beast, in particular, loves to boast about his portable radio, but he does not own a dipole antenna because inmates are allowed only one item from a special list of the Big Ten, as they call it. On death row, privileges are limited out of fear of inmates fashioning weapons.

Jean-Baptiste does not care about a weapon. His body is his weapon, should he ever decide to uncoil it. Uncoiling it is of no interest, not now. When he is led in restraints to the shower, he has no need to attack officers, which he could most assuredly do because of his magnetism, which is only enhanced when he is led past multiple metal doors with iron bars. His power builds. It throbs in his groin and lifts the top of his skull to a hover above his head. He leaves a visible trail of sparks. The corrections officers never understand what he smiles about, and his demeanor greatly annoys them.

Lights-out was at nine. The officer in the control booth enjoys flipping every switch and throwing the inmates into complete darkness in the pod. Jean-Baptiste has overheard officers comment that darkness gives the "dirtbags" time to think hard about their impending executions, the punishment for what they did when they were on the outside, free and able to satisfy their love. Those who do not kill do not understand that the ultimate union with a woman is to release her, to hear her scream and moan, to cover himself with her blood as he ravishes her body and then poses her, that all people might see, and therefore share in her ecstasy and the marriage of her magnetism to him for all eternity.

He lies on his bunk, sweat soaking through the sheets, his odor filling his small, airless cell, the stainless-steel toilet a toadstool shape against the right side of the back wall. The condemned inmates are quiet, with the exception of Beast. He talks quietly to himself, almost whispers, not realizing that Jean-Baptiste can hear without ears. Beast is transformed at night into the powerless, weak entity that he really is. He will be so much better off when the cocktail settles him to sleep and he no longer needs his weak, flawed flesh.

". . . Hold still. It's nice, isn't it? Feels so nice. Stop it, please stop it. Stop it! That hurts! Don't cry. This feels good. Don't you understand, you little bitch. It feels good! I want my mommy! So do I. But she's a whore. Now you quit crying, you hear me! You scream one more time . . ."

"Who's there?" Jean-Baptiste asks the foul-smelling air.

"Shut up. Shut the fuck up. It's your fault. You had to scream, didn't you. When I told you not to. Well, no more chewing gum for you. Cinnamon. Dropping the wrapper by the swingset so I know what flavor you like. Stupid little cunt. You stay right here in the shade, okay? I've gotta run, gotta run. How's that for a good one, I gotta run, gotta run, gotta run." He begins to softly sing. "Gotta run, gotta run, gotta run-run-run . . ."

"Who's there?"

"Knock, knock, who's there?" Beast calls back in a searing, mocking tone. "Hairy, hairy, quite contrary, how does your dickie grow? With little nuts hiding in your butt and a weenie smaller than your nose." Softly, softly singing, but loud enough. "I'm a poet, don'cha know it? You know that, dickless wonder? A real sensitive guy, I am, I am. Green eggs and ham. Cat in the hat. I like 'em meaty but not too fat. A drumroll please."

"Who's there?" Jean-Baptiste bares his widely spaced, tiny, pointed teeth. He licks them hard and tastes the salty metallic flavor of his own blood.

"Just me, Hair Ball. Your best pal in the world. Your only pal in the world. You got nobody but me, you know that? You must. Who else talks to you and sends little love notes door to door to door until it's slid under yours, all dirty and read by everybody?"

Jean-Baptiste listens, sucking blood out of his tongue.

"You got this pow-er-ful family. I heard all about it on my radio. More'an once I heard it."

Silence. Jean-Baptiste's ears are satellite dishes.

"Con-nec-tions. Where are those fucking guards when you need 'em?" he mocks the darkness.

His hateful voice flies like tiny bats through the iron bars in Jean-Baptiste's door. Words flutter around him, and he waves them off with sweeps of his hairy hands.

"Did ya know ya get crazy in here, Hair Ball? If you don't get out, you're crazy as a cat with M40s up its ass. You know that, Hair Ball?"

"Je ne comprends pas," Jean-Baptiste whispers, a drop of blood running down his chin and disappearing in his baby-fine hair.

He feels for the blood and licks his finger.

"Oh, you *comprendez vous*, all right. Maybe they stick something up your ass, huh? And kaboom!" Beast softly laughs. "See, once they get you over there in that cage, they can do whatever the fuck they like, and who's gonna know? You snitch and they hurt you more and say you did it to yourself."

"Who's there?"

"I'm so fucking sick of you saying that, knock-knock-shit, Mini-Me Dick! You know damn well who's there. 'Tis me. Your bud-dy."

Jean-Baptiste hears Beast breathing. His air travels past two cells and Jean-Baptiste smells garlic and red Burgundy, a young Clos des Mouches, what he calls a stupid wine because it has not slept long enough in dark, damp places to become brilliant and wise. In the dark, Jean-Baptiste's death-row cell is his cave.

"But here's the thing, my special pal, your only pal. They gotta transport me in this van to where they do me. Huntsville. What a name. Hunted and a villain, right? Takes an hour, the ride. What if something happens between point A and B?"

At Place Dauphine, chestnut trees, azaleas and roses are blossoming and blooming. Jean-Baptiste does not need to see, only to smell to know where he is: Bar du Caveau and Restaurant Paul, which is a good one. People are disconnected from him, eating and drinking behind glass, smiling and laughing or intensely leaning into candlelight. Some of them will leave and make love, not knowing they are watched. Jean-Baptiste glides through the night to the tip of the Ile St.-Louis, and the lights of Paris are caught in the current of the Seine and shimmer like fine hair. In but a few minutes, he is a mile or so from the morgue.

"Now I ain't got the wherewithal to do nothing. Bet you do, though. You get that van stopped when I'm on my way to the needle, and I'll come back for you, Hair Ball. My time's up. Three days. You hear that? Three goddamn days. I know you can figure out a way. You can arrange it, save my ass and then we'll be partners."

Inside a brasserie on the Ile St.-Louis, he sat in a corner and stared out at a balcony crowded with flowerpots, and a woman stepped out to look, perhaps at the blue sky and the river. She was very beautiful, and her windows were open to the fresh, fall air. He remembered that she smelled like lavender. He thought she did.

"You can have her when I'm done," Jay said as he sipped a Clos de Bèze of the Domaine Prieuré Roch. The wine hinted of smoked almonds.

He slowly swirled the red Burgundy, and it licked around the wide bowl of the glass like a warm tongue slowly licking in circles.

"I know you want some." Jay lifted the glass and laughed at the double entendre. "But you know how you get, *mon frère.*"

"You listening, Hair Ball? Three fucking days, just a week before you, I'll make sure you got all the bitches you want out there. I'll bring 'em to you, long as you don't mind if I have my piece of 'em first. Since you can't, right? So why shouldn't you share?" A pause, and Beast's voice turns sinister. "You listening to me, Hair Ball? Free as a bird!"

"So here we go," Jay said with a wink.

He set down his wine glass and said he'd be right back. Jean-Baptiste, clean-shaven with a cap pulled low over his face, was not to speak to anyone while Jay . . . He can't call him Jay. Jean-Paul,

Jean-Paul was gone. Through the window, Jean-Baptiste watched his beautiful brother call up to the woman on the balcony. He was motioning, pointing, as if in need of directions, and she smiled and began to laugh at his antics. Instantly, she was overcome by his spell and disappeared back inside her apartment.

Then his blessed brother was magically sitting in the booth again. "Leave," he commanded Jean-Baptiste. "Her apartment is on the third floor." He nodded toward it. "You see where it is. Hide while she and I have a drink. She will be simple enough. You know what to do. Now get out of here and don't frighten anyone."

"You fucking ugly piece of hairy shit." Beast's hideous whisper drifts inside Jean-Baptiste's cell. "You don't want to die, do ya? Nobody wants to die except the people we *do*, when they can't take no more and start begging, right? Free as a bird. Just think of that. *Free as a bird.*"

Jean-Baptiste envisions the woman doctor named Scarpetta. She will fall asleep in his arms, his eyes never leaving her, and she will be with him always. He strokes the letter she sent him, typed and brief, begging to come see him, asking for his help. He wishes she had written it by hand so he could study every curve and contour of her sensual penmanship. Jean-Baptiste imagines her naked and sucks his tongue.

53

Thunder sounds like kettledrums in the distance, and clouds roll past the waning moon.

Bev will not head back to Dutch Bayou until the storm passes if it moves this far southeast, and the forecast on the car radio doesn't call for that. But she isn't ready to return to the boat landing. The lamb in the forest-green Ford Explorer has followed an interesting route for the past two hours, and Bev can't figure it out. She—whoever she is—has cruised streets and especially parking lots for no reason that Bev can tell.

Her guess is that the lamb had a fight with her man and refuses to go home right now, probably to worry him sick, one of those little games. Bev has been careful to keep her distance, to turn up side streets, to pull off in gas stations along Highway 19, then speed up. Several times, Bev has passed the Explorer in the left lane, going ahead at least ten miles, pulling off the highway and waiting for her prey to get ahead of her again. Soon enough, they pass through Baker, a tiny town with businesses that have strange names: Raif's Po-Boy, Money Flash Cash, Crawfish Depot.

The town vanishes like a mirage, and the stretch of highway becomes pitch dark. There is nothing out here, no lights, only trees, and a billboard that reads: *You Need Jesus.*

54

Gator eyes remind Bev of periscopes fixing her in their sights before vanishing under water the color of weak coffee.

Jay told her gators won't bother her unless she bothers them. He says the same about cottonmouths.

"Did you ask them their opinion? And if it's the truth, then how come cottonmouths come crashing out of the trees, trying to get in the boat? And remember that movie we watched? Oh, what was it called . . . ?"

"*Faces of Death*," he replied, on this occasion amused instead of annoyed by her questions.

"Remember that game warden who fell in the lake and right there on camera, this huge gator got him?"

"Cottonmouths don't fall into the boat unless you startle them," Jay explained. "And the gator got the game warden because the game warden was trying to get him."

That sounded reasonable enough, and Bev felt slightly reassured until Jay smiled that cruel smile of his and did a complete about-face and explained how she can tell if an animal or reptile is a predator, and therefore an aggressor, and therefore the fearless hunter.

"It's all in the eyes, baby," he said. "The eyes of predators are in front of the head, like mine." He pointed to his beautiful blue eyes. "Like a gator's, like a cottonmouth's, like a tiger's. Us predators are going to look straight-on for something to attack. The eyes of non-predators are more on the sides of the head, because how the hell is a rabbit going to defend itself against a gator, right? So the little bunny needs peripheral vision to see what's coming and run like hell."

"I've got predator eyes," Bev said, pleased to know it but not at all happy to hear that gators and cottonmouths are predators.

Eyes like that, she realized, meant something's on the prowl, looking to hurt or kill. Predators, especially reptiles, aren't afraid of people. Shit! As far as Bev's concerned, she's no match for a gator or a snake. If she falls in the water or steps on a cotton-mouth, who's going to win? Not her.

"Humans are the ultimate predator," Jay said. "But we're complicated. A gator is always a gator. A snake's always a snake. A human can be a wolf or a lamb."

Bev is a wolf.

She feels her wolfish hot blood stirring as she glides past cypress knees jutting from the bayou like the ridges of a sea monster's back. The pretty blonde woman hog-tied on the floor of the boat squints in intermittent early morning sunlight. Wherever cypress roots break the surface, the water isn't deep, and Bev is vigilant as she motors slowly toward the fishing shack. Now and then her prisoner tries to shift her position to ease the terrible pain in her joints, and her labored breathing flares her nostrils, the gag around her mouth wetly sucking in and out.

Bev doesn't know her name and warned her not to say it. This was hours ago, inside the Cherokee, after the lamb realized she couldn't get out the passenger door, and if she tried to climb over the seat, Bev was going to shoot her. Then the lamb got chatty, trying to be friendly, trying to make Bev like her, going so far as to politely ask Bev's name. They all do that, and Bev always says the same thing: "My name is none of your fucking business, and I don't want to know yours or a damn thing about you."

The woman was instantly powerless, realizing that she wasn't going to talk her way out of whatever horror was in store for her.

Names have only two purposes: use them to manipulate people into feeling that their lives have value, and refuse to use them, to cause people to feel that their lives have no value. Besides, Bev will learn a lot about this pretty little lamb soon enough, when Jay monitors the news on his battery-powered radio.

"Please don't hurt me," the lamb begs. "I have family."

"I'm not listening," Bev tells her. "You know why? Because you're nothing but the catch of the day."

Bev laughs, enjoying the strength of her own voice, because very soon, she won't have a voice. Jay will. Once he takes possession of the lamb, there will be nothing left for Bev to do, except what he orders her to do or not to do. Mostly, Bev will watch, and thoughts of that overwhelm her with a compulsion to control and abuse while she can. She binds the lambs tighter than Jay does, tying ankles to wrists behind the back so the body is bowed, making it all the more difficult for the lamb's diaphragm to relax and contract as she struggles to breathe.

"Tell you what, honey," Bev says as she steers. "We're going to anchor right over there under those shade trees, and I'm gonna cover you good with skeeter spray, every inch of you, because my man ain't gonna want you swelled up and itching."

She laughs as her prisoner's eyes widen and tears flood her puffy red lids. This is the first the lamb's heard mention of a man.

"Now you quit your bawling, honey. You need to look pretty, and right now you're looking like shit."

The lamb blinks hard, the gag making wet noises with each agonizing, rapid, shallow breath. Bev steers the boat closer to shore, cuts the engine and drops anchor. She picks up the shotgun and scans the trees, checking for snakes. Satisfied that the only one in harm's way is her prisoner, she lays the pump-action shotgun on top of the tarp and places a boat cushion on the floor just inches from her "cute little catch of the day," as she continues to call her. Bev digs in her beach bag and pulls out a plastic squirt bottle of insect repellent.

"What I'm going to do now is take off your gag and untie you," Bev says. "You know why I can be that nice, honey? Because you ain't got nowhere to go but overboard, and if you think about what's in these waters, you ain't likely to want to go for a little swim. Or how about the fish box?"

Bev opens the lid of the coffin-sized fish box. It is filled with ice.

"That'll keep you nice and fresh if you decide to get rowdy. And you're not gonna do that, are you?"

The woman vigorously shakes her head and dryly says "No" as the gag comes off. "Thank you, thank you," she says in a shaking voice, wetting her lips.

"Bet your joints are hurting like hell," Bev says, taking her time untying her. "My man Jay tied me up once, my ankles and wrists tied up tight together behind my back until I was bent like a pretzel, just like you. It turned him on, you know." She tosses the rope on top of the tarp. "Well, you'll find out soon enough."

The woman rubs her raw ankles and wrists, trying to catch her breath. She reminds Bev of a cheerleader, one of those athletic blondes with pure prettiness, like those in *Seventeen* magazine. She wears small horn-rimmed glasses that make her look smart, and she's the right age, late thirties, maybe forty.

"You go to college?" Bev asks her.

"Yes."

"Good. That's real good." She disappears inside her thoughts for a moment, a slack expression on her fleshy, weathered face.

"Please take me back. We've got money. We'll pay you whatever you want."

Bev's meanness snaps back into her eyes. Jay's smart and has money. The woman is smart and has money. She leans close to the woman, the whine of mosquitoes loud beneath the trees. Not far away, a fish splashes. The higher the sun gets, the hotter it is, and Bev's Hawaiian shirt is damp with sweat.

"Money's not what this is about," Bev says as the woman stares at her, hope fading from her light blue eyes. "Don't you know what this is about?"

"I didn't do anything to you. Please just let me go home and I'll never tell anyone. I won't ever do anything to get you into trouble. How could I, anyway? I don't know you."

"Well, you're getting ready to know me, honey," Bev says, laying a rough, dry hand on the woman's neck and stroking it with her thumb. "We're getting ready to know each other real good."

The woman blinks, wetting her chapped lips as Bev's hand works its way down, touching the hollow of her neck, then down lower, exploring wherever she pleases. The woman sits rigidly and shuts her eyes. She jerks when Bev reaches under her clothing, unhooking her bra in back. Bev starts squeezing the insect repellent, rubbing it on the lamb's naked body, feeling her luscious, firm flesh tremble like Jell-O. Bev thinks of Jay and the bleached area of the floor beneath the bed, and she shoves the lamb hard, slamming her head into the outboard motor.

55

At the corner of 83rd and Lexington, a delivery truck struck a pedestrian—an elderly woman.

Benton Wesley overhears excited talk in the gawking crowd as emergency lights flash, the block cordoned off in yellow crime-scene tape. The fatal accident occurred less than an hour earlier, and Benton has seen enough gore in his life to walk swiftly past and respectfully avert his eyes from the body trapped under one of the truck's back tires.

He catches the words *brains* and *decapitated*, and something about *dentures* lying on the street. If the public had its way, every death scene would be pay-per-view: Five dollars for a ticket, and you can stare at blood and guts to your heart's content. When he used to arrive at crime scenes and all the cops would move out of the way to allow his expert eye to take in every detail, he had the right to order unauthorized people to leave. He could vent his disgust as he pleased—sometimes calmly, sometimes not.

He surveys the area from behind his dark glasses, his lean body moving along the crowded sidewalk, cutting in and out with the agility of a lynx. A plain black baseball cap covers his shaved head, and he backtracks toward Lucy's headquarters, having gotten out of a taxi ten blocks north instead of directly in front of her building or even near it. Benton probably could walk right past Lucy and say "excuse me," and she would not recognize him. Six years it has been since he has seen or talked to her, and he is desperate to know what she looks like, sounds like, acts like. Anxiety presses him onward at his determined pace until he nears the modern polished granite building on 75th Street. A doorman stands in front, hands behind his back. He is hot in his gray uniform and shifts his weight from leg to leg, indicating that his feet hurt.

"I'm looking for The Last Precinct," Benton says to him.

"The what?" The doorman looks at him as if he's crazy.

Benton repeats himself.

"You talking about some kind of police precinct?" The doorman scrutinizes him, and *homeless* and *wacko* register on his jaded Irish face. "Maybe you mean the precinct on Sixty-ninth."

"Twenty-first floor, suite twenty-one-oh-three," Benton replies.

"Yeah, now I know what you're talking about, but it ain't called The Last Precinct. Twenty-one-oh-three's a software company—you know, computer stuff."

"You sure?"

"Hell, I work here, don't I?" The doorman is getting impatient, and he glares at a woman whose dog is sniffing too close to the planter in front of the building. "Hey," he says to her. "No dogs doing their business in the hedge."

"She's just sniffing," the woman indignantly replies, jerking the leash, tugging her hapless toy poodle back to the middle of the sidewalk.

Having asserted himself, the doorman ignores the woman and

her dog. Benton digs in a pocket of his faded jeans and pulls out a folded piece of paper. He smooths it open and glances at an address and phone number that have nothing to do with Lucy or her building or the office that really is called The Last Precinct, despite what the doorman thinks. If the doorman happens to relay to her, perhaps in jest, that some weirdo stopped by asking for The Last Precinct, she will go on the alert, get very worried. Marino believes that Jean-Baptiste knows Lucy's company by that name. Benton wants Marino and Lucy on the alert and worried.

"Says here, twenty-one-oh-three," Benton tells the doorman, shoving the piece of paper back in his pocket. "What's the name of the company? Maybe the information I was given is wrong."

The doorman steps inside and picks up a clipboard. Running his finger down a page, he replies, "Okay, okay, twenty-one-oh-three. Like I said, some computer outfit. Infosearch Solutions. You want to go up, I gotta call 'em and see an ID."

An ID, yes, but calling isn't necessary, and Benton is amused. The doorman is openly rude and prejudiced toward the scruffy stranger before him, no longer mindful—as many New Yorkers aren't—that the city's greatest virtue in the past was to welcome scruffy strangers, desperately poor immigrants who barely spoke English. Benton speaks English exquisitely when he chooses, and he isn't poor, although his funds are regulated.

He reaches inside his jacket for his wallet and produces a driver's license: Steven Leonard Glover, age forty-four, born in Ithaca, New York, no longer Tom Haviland because Marino knows him by that alias. Whenever Benton has to change his identity, which he does whenever needed, he suffers a period of depression and meaninglessness, finding himself once again angrier than is necessary and all the more determined to prevail without burning with hate.

Hate destroys the vessel that holds it. To hate is to lose clarity of mind and vision. Throughout his life he has resisted hate, and it would be all too easy and appropriate to hate the hate-filled sadistic and unremorseful offenders he has relentlessly tracked and trapped beyond what was appropriate while he was with the FBI. Benton's gift at evasion and imperviousness would not be possible if he hated or gave in to any extreme of emotion.

He became Scarpetta's lover while he was still married, and perhaps that is his only sin he won't forgive. He can't bear to imagine the anguish Connie and their daughters suffered when they believed he was murdered. At times he considers his exile punishment for what he did to his family, because he was weak and gave in to an extreme of an emotion that he still feels. Scarpetta has that effect on him, and he would commit the same sin again—he knows it—were he to go back in time to when they first realized what they were feeling for each other. His only excuse—a weak one, he knows—is that their lust and falling in love wasn't premeditated by either one of them. It happened. It simply happened.

"I'll call 'em up for you," the doorman says, returning the fraudulent ID to Benton.

"Thank you . . . what is your name?"

"Jim."

"Thank you, Jim, but that won't be necessary."

Benton walks off, ignoring a *Don't Walk* sign, crossing 75th Street and becoming part of the anonymous flow of pedestrians along Lexington Avenue. Swerving under scaffolding, he pulls his cap lower, but behind his dark glasses, his eyes miss nothing. Were any of the same oblivious people to pass him again on another block, he would recognize their faces, always aware and on guard. Three times, and he will tail whoever it is and capture him or her on his pocket-size video camera. He has amassed hundreds of tapes in the past six years, and so far they mean nothing beyond demonstrating that he lives in a very small world, no matter how big the city.

Cops have an obvious presence in New York, sitting in their cruisers, talking to one another on sidewalks and street corners. Benton passes them, stoically looking straight ahead, his pistol strapped around his ankle, a violation so serious he would probably be tackled or slammed against a building, were a cop to spot the gun. He would be handcuffed, stuffed inside a police car, interrogated, run through the FBI computer system, fingerprinted and arraigned in court, all to no avail, really. When he worked crime scenes, his prints were stored in AFIS, the automated fingerprint identification system. After his alleged death, his prints—including his ten-print card in cold storage—were altered, swapped with a man who had died of natural causes and was surreptitiously fingerprinted in the embalming room of a Philadelphia funeral home. Benton's DNA profile is in no automated system anywhere on Earth.

He steps into a doorway and dials directory assistance on a cell phone that has the billing address of a phone number at the Texas Department of Criminal Justice. Programming the billing address was not so difficult. Benton has had years to become adept on the computer, using and violating cyberspace to his advantage. An occasional collect call added to the Texas penitentiary's telephone bills is likely to escape notice and could not be traced to anyone, certainly never to him.

Benton knows that when he makes his call to Lucy's office, the Texas penitentiary's name and number will show up on whatever sophisticated security system she has. Of course, all calls are taped. Of course, Lucy will have her own forensic voice analysis computer system. Of course, Benton has Jean-Baptiste's voice on tape and has had it for years, reaching back to the very dangerous days of an undercover operation that did not bring down the Chandonne cartel, but instead annihilated Benton's identity and life. For this, Benton has not yet forgiven himself. He doesn't believe he will ever be able to give up his guilt and humiliation. He underestimated those whose trust was synonymous with his life.

As a child, Benton and his magic ring made mistakes in his fantasy investigations. As an adult, he and his gold FBI ring have also made mistakes, errors in judgment, and flat-out wrong psychological assessments of murderers. But the one time in his career when he needed his acumen and wits the most, he slipped, and the thought of it still enrages him, sickens him, fills him with self-recrimination.

He tells himself during his most despondent moments, *No one else is to blame. Not even the Chandonnes and their minions are to blame. You dug your pit, and now you must get out of it.*

56

"Just plain-Jane copying paper," Polunsky's public information officer, Wayne Reeve, explains to Scarpetta over the phone.

"We buy it by the ream and sell it to the inmates for a penny a sheet. Envelopes are cheap white dime-store variety, three for a quarter," he adds. "If you don't mind my asking, why are you interested?"

"Research."

"Oh." His curiosity lingers.

"Forensic paper analysis. I'm a scientist. What if the inmate doesn't have commissary privileges?" Scarpetta inquires from her office in Delray Beach.

She was rushing out of the house with her suitcase when the phone rang. Rose answered it. Scarpetta eagerly took the call. She will miss her flight to New York.

"He—or she—can get writing paper, envelopes, stamps and so on. No one is denied that privilege, no matter what. You can understand it. Lawyers," Reeve says.

Scarpetta doesn't ask him if Jean-Baptiste Chandonne is still on death row. She doesn't hint that she's gotten a letter from him and is no longer certain Chandonne is safely locked up.

Enough, you son of a bitch.

I've had enough, you son of a bitch.

You want to see me, you'll see me, you son of a bitch.

You want to talk, we'll talk all right, you son of a bitch.

If you've escaped, I'm going to find out, you son of a bitch.

If you did or didn't write this letter, I'm going to find out, you son of a bitch.

You're not going to hurt anybody else, you son of a bitch.

I want you dead, you son of a bitch.

"Can you send me samples of commissary paper?" she asks Reeve.

"You'll get them tomorrow," he promises.

57

Turkey buzzards swoop low in the blue sky, the smell of death and decay drawing them to the marsh beyond the gray, weathered pier.

"What'd you do, throw meat in the saw grass?" Bev complains to Jay as she loops a rope over a piling. "You know how much I hate those damn buzzards."

Jay smiles, his attention on the lamb cowering in the stern of the boat. She rubs her wrists and ankles, her clothing partially unbuttoned and in disarray. For an instant, relief passes through her terrified eyes, as if the handsome blond man on the dock couldn't possibly be evil. Jay wears nothing but threadbare cutoff jeans, the muscles in his sculpted, tan body popping out with every move he makes. He lightly steps down into the boat.

"Get inside," he orders Bev. "Hi," he says to the woman. "I'm Jay. You can relax now."

Her wide, glassy eyes are riveted to him. She keeps rubbing her wrists and wetting her lips.

"Where am I?" she asks. "I don't understand . . ."

Jay reaches out to help her up, and her legs won't work, so he grabs her around the waist.

"There we go. A little stiff, are we?" He touches the dried bloody clumps of hair matted to the back of her head and his eyes burn. "She wasn't supposed to hurt you. You're hurt, aren't you? Okay. Hold on. I'm going to pick you up, just like this." He lifts her as if she weighs nothing. "Put your arms around my neck. Good." He places her on the dock and climbs out after her. Helping her to her feet again, he picks her up and carries her inside the shack.

Bev sits on the narrow, sour-smelling bed. It has no covers, just a dingy, rumpled white form-fitted sheet and a stained pillow that has lost its shape and is almost flat. Bev's eyes follow Jay as he lowers the woman to the floor, holding her around the waist while she struggles for balance.

"I can't seem to stand up," she says, avoiding Bev, pretending Bev isn't there. "My feet are numb."

"She tied you too tight, didn't she?" Jay says as his eyes burn brighter. "What'd you do to her?" he asks Bev.

Bev stares at him.

"Get off the bed," he says to her. "We need to let her lie down. She's hurt. Get a wet towel." To the lamb he says as he helps her on the bed, "I don't have any ice. I'm sorry. Ice would be good for your head."

"There's ice in the fish box. And groceries," Bev says in a flat tone.

"You didn't bring me any pups," Jay comments.

"I was busy, and nothing was open."

"Plenty of strays out there, if you aren't too lazy to look for them."

She opens the refrigerator and pours cold water on a dish towel.

261

"That's all right," the lamb meekly replies, relaxing a little.

Jay is handsome and sweet. He is a friend. Not horrid, like that ugly beast of a woman.

"I'll be fine. I don't need any ice."

"It's not all right." Jay gently arranges the pillow under her head, and she cries out in pain. "No, it's not all right."

He slips a hand under her neck, moving her head so he can feel the back of it. The pressure of his fingers is too much, and the woman cries out again.

"What'd you do to her?" he asks Bev.

"She fell in the boat."

The woman says nothing and refuses to look at Bev.

"Fell with a little help, maybe?" Jay asks in a tone of perfect self-control.

He gathers the lamb's blouse together and buttons it without touching her.

58

Benton takes off his jacket and drops it in a trash can.

A block south, he tosses his baseball cap into another trash can and ducks into the shadows of scaffolding to unfasten his canvas knapsack. Inside is a black do-rag, and he ties it tightly around his head. He slips on a denim vest that has an American flag embroidered on the back. During a brief lull in pedestrian traffic, he substitutes his sunglasses for amber-tinted ones in different frames. Rolling up the knapsack, he tucks it under his arm and cuts left on 73rd Street, then left again on Third and back on 75th, where he stands at the corner of Lucy's building. Jim the doorman ignores him and wanders inside the lobby for a welcome rush of air-conditioning.

New technology is Benton's ally and enemy. Cell phone calls can be traced by more than caller ID. Signals bounce off satellites and boomerang to where the caller is located geographically when the call is made, and to date, it is impossible to foil this technology. Benton has no choice but somehow to work around it. While caller ID will erroneously indicate that the call is being made from a Texas prison, the satellite transmission will reveal that the call was made in Manhattan, pinpointed to an area that is smaller than a city block.

He uses this to his advantage, however. All obstacles can be steps to a higher benefit.

Benton makes the call from Lucy's address at Lexington and 75th Street. Jean-Baptiste is on death row, and that is easy enough to check. Logic would dictate that Jean-Baptiste could not have called collect from Manhattan. Then who did? Lucy will puzzle over the call made in the immediate area of her office building, and knowing her as well as Benton does, he is certain she will make a call from her own address and see that the same coordinates are pinpointed by the satellite.

This will lead her to the conclusion that there must have been a technical glitch, that somehow the transmission traced back to where the call was received instead of where it was initiated. She will not understand how this could have happened when it has never happened before. Lucy will be paranoid. Without a doubt, she will be angry, because she does not forgive sloppy work or technical screwups. She will blame the snafu on the telephone company or her staff. Probably the latter.

As for Jim the doorman, when asked, he will say that at the precise moment the call was made, he saw no one on a cell phone in front of the building or close to it. This will be a lie. Almost everybody in New York walks around with a cell phone to his or her ear. The truth is, even if Jim remembers the precise time he left his post for the air-conditioned lobby, he won't want to admit it.

The last obstacle is voice analysis, which Lucy will conduct immediately to verify that the caller was Jean-Baptiste

Chandonne. That is no threat. Benton has spent several years meticulously studying, transcribing and editing recordings of Jean-Baptiste's voice, then rerecording them into digital files with a single directional microphone that, when used in a high-sensitivity mode, picks up multidirectional sound, or background noise—in this case, the inside of a prison. He edited and spliced it on a computer, and the results are seamless, each file a blitz of sound bites intended for voicemail or a live recipient who has no chance for a response that would force a mental engagement that is impossible. Switching from *Menu* to a folder he named *Redstick* for Baton Rouge, he verifies the time stamp on the LCD and double-checks that all details of the setup are in order.

He plugs the microphone into a speaker port and tucks in the earpiece.

The phone at Infosearch Solutions—The Last Precinct—is picked up.

"Manhattan. Collect call to Infosearch Solutions on Seventy-fifth," he says into the microphone.

"Your name?"

"Polunksy Unit."

"Please hold."

The operator connects the call.

"Collect call from Polunksy Unit. Will you accept charges?"

"Yes," without pause or change of inflection.

"Good afternoon. May I ask who's calling?" a male voice continues, the caller ID showing the Texas Department of Criminal Justice.

Benton sets noise cancel on high to eradicate the live feedback of New York traffic and other sounds that would be ruinous for a call supposedly made from the interior of a penitentiary. He presses *Play*. The indicator light glows green, and *File One* begins.

"When Mademoiselle Farinelli returns, tell her Baton Rouge." Jean-Baptiste's recorded voice is as natural as if he himself is speaking in real time.

"She's out of the office. Who's calling? Who is this?" The man in Lucy's office tries to talk to what is nothing more than a memory chip on the line. "May I give her a message?"

The call ended seven seconds ago. Benton erases *File One* from *Redstick*, to ensure that Jean-Baptiste's faked message cannot be played again, ever, by anyone.

He walks swiftly along the congested sidewalk again, head bent, missing nothing.

59

"Please don't hurt me," the lamb says.

Jay helps the woman sit up. She cries and moans as he gently cleans her bloody hair, worrying about the split in her scalp, caused by the blunt-force trauma of her head cracking against the outboard motor. He reassures her that the injury isn't serious and didn't fracture her skull. She's not seeing double, is she?

"No," she says, her breath catching as he touches her hair again with the wet, bloody towel. "I can see fine."

Jay's sweetness, his protectiveness, has the usual effect, and the woman's attention is fixed only on him. She identifies with him to the extent that she feels she can tell him that Bev—whose name the woman doesn't know—pushed her into the outboard motor.

"That's how I hit my head," she confides to Jay.

He tosses the bloody towel to Bev. She hasn't moved, just stands in the middle of the small room, staring at him like a cottonmouth coiled to strike. The towel lands at her feet, and she doesn't pick it up.

He tells her to pick it up.

Bev doesn't.

"Pick it up and wash it in the sink," he says. "I don't want to look at that thing on the floor. You shouldn't have hurt her. Clean the towel and get all this insect repellent off her."

"I don't need her to get it off me," the woman pleads. "Maybe it's good to keep it on because of all the bugs."

"No. You need it washed off," Jay says, leaning close and smelling her neck. "You have too much on. It's toxic. She must have soaked you with an entire bottle. That's not good."

"I don't want her touching me again!"

"She hurt you?"

The lamb doesn't answer.

"I'm here. She won't hurt you."

Jay gets up from the edge of the bed, and Bev collects the wet, gory towel.

"We don't need to waste water," she says. "The tank's low."

"It's supposed to rain, eventually," Jay replies, studying the woman as if she's a car he might buy. "The tank's got plenty, anyway. Wash the towel and bring it back in here."

"Please don't hurt me."

The woman lifts her head up from the pillow. It is pinkish and wet, and a bright red spot indicates that her laceration has begun to bleed again.

"Just take me home and I won't tell anybody. Not anybody, I swear to God."

Her eyes plead with Jay, her only hope because he's glorious to look at, and so far he's been nice.

"Won't tell anybody what?" Jay asks her, moving closer, sitting on the edge of the iron-frame bed with its foul, broken-down mattress. "What's there to tell? You hurt yourself, now, didn't you, and we're Good Samaritans, taking care of you."

She nods, uncertainty, then fear contorting her face.

"Make it quick. Please," she whispers between convulsions, sobs and hiccups jerking her body. "If you aren't going to let me go. Make it quick."

Bev returns with the towel and hands it to Jay. Water drips on the bed and trickles down his bare, muscular arm. Bev runs her fingers through his hair and kisses the back of his neck, then presses close to him as he opens the woman's blouse.

"Ah. No bra," he says. "She wasn't wearing one?" He cranes his head around, demanding an answer in a soft voice that by now has become scary.

Bev slides her hands down his sweaty chest.

The woman's eyes are wide with the same glassy terror that Bev saw in the boat. She trembles violently, her naked breasts quivering. A drop of saliva slips out of the side of her mouth, and Jay stands up, disgusted.

"Get the rest of her clothes off and clean her up," he orders Bev. "You touch her again, you know what I'll do to you."

Bev smiles. Theirs is a well-rehearsed, long-running drama.

60

The next morning, Scarpetta is still in Florida.

Once again, she was about to leave and was waylaid, this time by FedEx delivering two packages, one from the Polunsky Prison Information Office, the other a thick package containing Charlotte Dard's case, mostly copies of autopsy and lab reports and histological slides.

Scarpetta places a slide of the left ventricular free wall on the compound microscope's stage. If she could add up the hours she's spent looking at slides throughout her career, the number would be in the tens of thousands. Although she respects the histologist, whose devotion is to the minuscule structures of tissues and the tales their cells can tell, she has never been able to comprehend sitting inside a tiny lab day in and day out, surrounded by sections of heart, lung, liver, brain and other organs, and injuries and stigmata of diseases that are cut into sections and turn rubbery inside bottles of a fixative such as formalin. Each tissue section is embedded in paraffin wax or a plastic resin and shaved into slices thin enough for light to pass through them. After they are mounted on glass slides, they are stained with a variety of dyes that were developed by the nineteenth-century textile industry.

Mostly, Scarpetta sees a lot of pinks and blues, but there are a profusion of colors used, depending on the tissue and the cellular structure and possible defects that need to give up their secrets to her at the other end of the lens. Dyes, like diseases, are often named for whoever discovered or invented them, and this is where histology becomes unnecessarily complicated, if not annoying. It isn't enough for dyes or dyeing techniques to be called blue or violet; they must be Cresyl blue, Cresyl violet, or Perl's Prussian blue, or Heidenhain's haematoxylin (purplish red), or Masson's trichrome (blue and green), or Bielschowsky (neutral red), or her favorite mundanity: Jones's methenamine silver. A typical egocentric pathological legacy is a van Gieson staining of Schwann cell nuclei from a Schwannoma, and Scarpetta fails to understand why German naturalist Theodor Schwann would have wanted a tumor named after him.

She peers into the lens at the contraction bands in the pink-stained tissue shaved from a section of Charlotte Dard's heart at autopsy. Some fibers are missing their nuclei, indicating necrosis, or the death of tissue, and other slides reveal pink-and-blue-stained inflammation and old scarring, and narrowing of the coronary arteries. The Louisiana woman was only thirty-two when she dropped dead at the door of a motel room in Baton Rouge, dressed to go out, keys in hand.

It was suspected eight years ago, at the time of her death, that her family pharmacist illegally gave her the powerful pain medication OxyContin, found in her pocketbook. She didn't have a prescription for the drug. In a letter to Scarpetta, Dr. Lanier suggests that this pharmacist might have fled to Palm Desert,

California. Dr. Lanier doesn't indicate what he bases this possibility on or offer further details for his reopening Charlotte Dard's case.

It is a mess for multiple reasons: The case is old; there is no evidence the drug came from the pharmacist, and even if it did, unless he premeditated killing her with OxyContin, he is not guilty of first-degree murder; at the time of Charlotte Dard's death, he would not talk to the police but through his attorney claimed that a family friend with a ruptured disk must have given Charlotte Dard OxyContin, and she accidentally overdosed on it.

Several copies of letters sent eight years ago to Dr. Lanier are from the pharmacist's attorney, Rocco Caggiano.

61

Beyond the window in front of Scarpetta's desk, shadows crawl over sand dunes as the sun moves.

Palm fronds rattle lightly, and a man walking his yellow lab on the beach leans into a headwind. Far off on the hazy blue horizon, a container ship forges south, probably to Miami. If Scarpetta is too caught up in her work, she will forget the time and where she is and soon will miss another flight to New York.

Dr. Lanier answers his phone and is hoarse as he says, "Hello."

"You sound terrible," Scarpetta says sympathetically.

"I don't know what I caught, but I feel like hell. Thanks for getting back to me."

"What meds are you taking? I hope it's decongestants and a cough suppressant with an expectorant, and that you're staying away from antihistamines. Try the daytime or nondrowsy formulas that don't list antihistamines or doxylamine succinate on the label—unless you want to dry yourself out and get a bacterial infection. And stay away from alcohol. It lowers your immunities."

He blows his nose. "I'm a real medical doctor, just so you know. And an addictionologist, meaning I do know a thing or two about drugs." He says this without a trace of defensiveness. "Thought you might be relieved to hear that."

Scarpetta is embarrassed for making assumptions. Coroners are elected officials and unfortunately, nationwide, many of them are not physicians.

"I didn't mean to insult you, Dr. Lanier."

"You didn't. By the way, your sidekick Pete Marino thinks you walk on water."

"You checked me out." She is nonplussed. "Good. Now hopefully we can get down to business. I've been through Charlotte Dard's case."

"An oldie but goodie, and I don't mean that literally. There's nothing good about it. Hold on. Let me get something to write with. Unquestionably, there's a Bermuda Triangle for pens, and in my home it's my beloved wife. All right."

"Mrs. Dard's case is definitely perplexing," Scarpetta begins. "As you know from her tox reports, oxymorphone—the metabolite of OxyContin—is only four milligrams per liter of blood, which puts her in the low lethal range. Her gastric is negative, and the level in her liver's no higher than the level in her blood. In other words, death from an overdose of OxyContin is equivocal. Clearly, her drug level isn't as critical as her clinical findings."

"I agree. My thought all along. If you interpret her tox in light of the histological findings, it's possible she didn't need as high a level for an accidental overdose. Although her reports and body diagrams don't indicate any cutaneous stigmata of past intravenous drug abuse," he adds. "So I'm guessing she was a pill-popper but didn't shoot up."

"Certainly she was a chronic drug abuser," Scarpetta says. "Her heart tells us that. Patchy necrosis and fibrosis of varying age, and chronic ischemia, plus an absence of coronary artery disease or cardiomegaly. Basically, a coke heart."

It is a catch-all phrase that does not necessarily mean the person was a cocaine addict. Drugs such as narcotics, synthetic narcotics, OxyContin, hydrocodone, Percocet, Percodan and whatever else the addict can get his or her hands on will destroy the heart just as completely as cocaine will. Elvis Presley is a sad example.

"I need to ask you about blackouts," Dr. Lanier says, after a pause.

"What about them?" This must be what he so urgently wanted to talk to her about. "I saw nothing in the case file you sent me that mentions blackouts."

She checks her irritation. As a private consultant, she is limited by the medicolegal information presented to her, and the absence of pertinent findings—or the presence of incorrect findings—is intolerable. Until she gave up working her own cases or supervising those worked by her other forensic pathologists throughout the Commonwealth of Virginia, she did not have to rely on the competence or veracity of virtual strangers.

"Charlotte Dard suffered occasional blackouts," Dr. Lanier explains. "Or at least this is what I was told at the time."

"Who told you?"

"Her sister. It appears," he goes on, "or let me qualify this by saying it is *alleged*, that she suffered from retrograde amnesia . . ."

"I certainly would think her family would know that, unless no one was ever home."

"Problem is, her husband Jason Dard's a rather shady character. Nobody around here knows much, maybe nothing about him, except he's rich as hell and lives on an old plantation. I wouldn't call Mrs. Guidon a reliable witness. Although she certainly could be telling the truth about her sister's condition prior to her death."

"I've read the police narrative, which is brief. Tell me what you know," Scarpetta says.

After a coughing bout, Dr. Lanier replies, "The hotel where she died is in a not-so-nice part of the city, in my jurisdiction. A housekeeper found her body."

"What about blood tests? In the paperwork you sent me, all I got were postmortem levels. So I don't know whether she might have had the elevated GGTP or CDT associated with alcohol abuse."

"Since I first contacted you, I have managed to track down premortem blood test results, because she was in the hospital about two weeks before her death. Misfiled, I'm embarrassed to say. I've got a particular clerk I'd pay heaven and earth to get rid of. But she's the sort to sue for one thing or another. The answer to your question is no—no elevated GGTP or CDT."

"In the hospital for what?"

"Tests after her most recent blackout. So, obviously, she had one of these blackouts two weeks before she died. Again, I say *allegedly.*"

"Well, if she didn't have elevated GGTP or CDT, it would seem to me that we can rule out alcohol as the cause of her blackouts," Scarpetta replies. "And Dr. Lanier, I can't offer you a second opinion if I'm not supplied with all of the information."

"Be nice if I was supplied all the information, too. Don't get me started on the police down here."

"What was Mrs. Dard's behavior during her blackouts?"

"Supposedly violent, throwing things, trashing the house or wherever she was staying. On one occasion, she vandalized her

Maserati by smashing the windows, doors and hood with a hammer. She poured bleach all over the leather seats."

"A record of this with a body shop?"

"It happened in May of 1995 and required two months to repair the damage, then her husband traded it in on a new one for her."

"That wasn't her last blackout, though." Scarpetta flips to another page in her legal pad, writing quickly and illegibly.

"No, the last one—two weeks before her death—was in the fall. September first, 1995. On that occasion, she took a razor of some sort to paintings valued at more than a million dollars. Supposedly."

"This was in her home?"

"In a parlor, as I understand it."

"Witnessed?"

"Only the aftermath, based on what I'm told. Again, this is according to what her sister and husband said way back when."

"Certainly her drug abuse could cause blackouts. Another possibility is temporal lobe epilepsy. Any record of her having suffered a head injury?"

"None that I'm aware of, and no old fractures or scarring showed up on X ray and gross examination. Hospital records indicate that after her second blackout, which, as I've said, was September first, 1995, she went through the gamut of tests: MRI, PET scan and so on. Nothing. Of course, temporal lobe epilepsy doesn't always show up, and maybe she did suffer some sort of head injury and we just don't know about it. Hard to imagine. I'm inclined to think her drug abuse was to blame."

"Based on the information I have, I agree. Her findings correlate with chronic abuse and not from one single overdose of OxyContin. Sounds like the only answer as to manner of death is investigation."

"Jesus God. That's the problem. The cops who worked the case didn't do shit and sure as hell aren't going to do shit now. Hell, everything's a problem down here. Except the food."

"Mrs. Dard is probably a heart death with chronic drug abuse as a contributing factor," Scarpetta tells him. "That's the most I can offer you."

"Doesn't help that we've got an idiot of a U.S. Attorney, Weldon Winn," Dr. Lanier continues to complain. "Since this damn serial killer's been on the loose, a lot of people are sticking their noses in everything. Politics."

"I presume you're on the task force," Scarpetta interrupts him.

"No. They say I'm not needed, since no bodies have turned up."

"And if a body does turn up, you don't need to know anything about the investigation? Even though it's believed that each of the women was murdered? Everything you're telling me goes from bad to worse," Scarpetta says.

"You're absolutely right. I haven't been invited to look at the scenes of their abductions. I haven't looked at their homes, cars, not a single crime scene."

"Well, you should have," Scarpetta replies. "When a person is abducted and assumed to be a homicide, the police should ask you to look at everything and know every detail. You should be fully informed."

"*Should* doesn't mean crap down here."

"How many of the abducted women are—or were—from your parish?"

"So far, seven."

"And you haven't been to a single scene of an abduction? I'm sorry to keep asking you the same questions. But I'm incredulous. And now those scenes no longer exist, am I right?"

"Cases are as cold as an ice block," he replies. "I guess the cars are still impounded, and at least that's a good thing. But you can't secure a parking lot or house forever, and I have no idea what's happened with their homes." He pauses to cough. "It's going to happen again. Soon. He's escalating."

62

The sky is turning a dirty blue with haze, and the wind picks up.

Scarpetta picks through paperwork as she talks to Dr. Lanier. Just now she finds a copy of the death certificate, folded up inside an envelope. The document isn't certified and should not have been released by Dr. Lanier's office. Only vital records would be authorized to send Scarpetta or any other requesting party a copy—a certified one. When Scarpetta was Chief, it would have been unthinkable for one of her clerks to make such an egregious error.

She mentions the problematic copy of the death certificate, adding, "I'm not trying to interfere with how you run your office, but thought you should know . . ."

"Goddamn!" he exclaims. "Let me guess which clerk. And don't assume it was a *mistake.* Some people around here would love nothing better than to get me into serious trouble."

The maiden name on her death certificate is De Nardi, her father Bernard De Nardi, her mother Sylvie Gaillot De Nardi.

Charlotte De Nardi Dard was born in Paris.

"Dr. Scarpetta?"

She vaguely hears his hoarse voice and coughing. Her mind locks on the abducted women, on Charlotte Dard's suspicious death and the information blackout that keeps the coroner clueless. The Louisiana legal system is infamous for corruption.

"Dr. Scarpetta? You there? Did I lose you?"

Jean-Baptiste Chandonne is scheduled to die soon.

"Hello?"

"Dr. Lanier," she finally says. "Let me ask you something. How did you hear about me?"

"Oh, good. I thought we'd gotten disconnected. An indirect referral. A rather unorthodox one suggesting I contact Pete Marino. That led me to you."

"An unorthodox referral from whom?"

He waits for another coughing fit to pass. "A guy on death row."

"Let me guess. Jean-Baptiste Chandonne."

"I'm not surprised you would figure that out. I've been checking, I admit it. You have a pretty scary history with him."

"Let's don't go into that," she says. "I also assume he's the source of information about Charlotte Dard. And by the way, Rocco Caggiano, the lawyer who represented our mysterious pharmacist who allegedly fled to Palm Desert? He's also Chandonne's lawyer."

"Now that I didn't know. You think Chandonne had something to do with Charlotte Dard's death?"

"I'm betting that he or someone either in his family or associated with it did," she says.

63

Lucy isn't showered, her usual demeanor in the office fractured by exhaustion and by post-traumatic stress that she will not acknowledge.

Her clothes look slept in because they were—twice. Once in Berlin, when the flight was cancelled, and the next time at Heathrow, when she and Rudy had to wait three hours to board an eight-hour flight that landed them at Kennedy Airport not even an hour ago. At least they had no baggage to lose, their few belongings stuffed into one small carry-on duffel bag. Before leaving Germany, they showered and disposed of the clothing they had worn in room 511 of the Szczecin Radisson Hotel.

Lucy wiped all prints off her tactical baton, and without a pause in her step, tossed it through the slightly open window of a dented Mercedes on the side of a quiet, narrow street crowded with parked cars. Certainly the Mercedes's owner would puzzle over the baton and wonder who deposited it on his or her front seat and why.

"Merry Christmas," Lucy muttered, and she and Rudy briskly walked off into the dawn.

The morning was too dark and cool for blow flies, but with the afternoon, when Rudy and Lucy were long gone, the flies would awaken in Poland. More of the filthy winged insects would find Rocco Caggiano's slightly open window and heavily drone inside to feed on his cold, stiff body. The flies should be busy depositing hundreds—maybe thousands—of eggs.

Lucy's chief of staff, Zach Manham, needs but one piece of evidence to deduce that his boss is not herself and that something very bad happened wherever she's just been. She reeks of body odor. Even when Manham has spent hours in the gym or run miles with Lucy, she doesn't stink, not like this. Hers is the strong odor of fear and stress. Its secretion requires little perspiration, which is clammy and concentrated in the armpits and strongly permeates clothing, becoming more unpleasant and noticeable with time. Accompanying this acute reaction is an elevated heartbeat, shallow breathing, pallor and constricted pupils. Manham doesn't know the physiology of a response he learned to recognize early in his former career as a detective for the New York District Attorney's Office, but he doesn't need to know.

"Go home and get some rest," he repeatedly says to Lucy.

"Cut it out," she finally barks at him, interested in the large digital recorder on Manham's desk.

She slips on headphones and presses the *Play* button again, manipulating the volume.

For the third time, she listens to the cryptic message that their highly technical caller-identification system has narrowed down to the Polunsky Unit, while a satellite tracking system indicates the call was made from virtually the front door of Lucy's office building, or perhaps even inside it. Hitting the *Off* button, she sits down, worn-out and beside herself.

"Goddamn, goddamn it!" she exclaims. "I don't get it! You screw up something, Zach?"

She rubs her face, a residue of mascara sticky on her eyelashes and driving her crazy. When she played the role of pretty young thing who seemed perfectly in place at the Radisson in Szczecin, she somehow grabbed a tube of waterproof mascara, and she hates mascara, and she had no makeup remover because she's rather much a stranger to cosmetics. So she scrubbed her face hard, succeeding only in getting soap in her eyes, which are bloodshot and puffy, as if she had been drinking all night. With rare exception, alcohol on the job is forbidden, and the first words out of her mouth when she appeared in her office not even an hour ago, leaving a jet stream of stench whenever she moved, was that she had not been on a bender, as if Manham or anybody else would have suspected, for even two seconds, that she had been.

"I didn't screw up anything, Lucy," Manham patiently replies, looking at her with concern.

He is moving closer to fifty years old, fit, six feet tall, with thick brown hair and a brush of gray at the temples, his former thick Bronx accent neutralized or altered when necessary. Manham is a natural mimic. Amazingly, he can fit into virtually any environment. Women find him irresistibly attractive and entertaining, and he uses this to his professional advantage. Moral judgments do not exist at The Last Precinct, unless an investigator is foolish and selfish enough to violate an unbending code of impeccable behavior. One's personal choices must never, absolutely never, come within miles of the boundaries of missions that place lives at risk daily.

"I honestly have no idea what happened here, why the satellite tracking system pinpoints the immediate area of this building," Manham tells her. "I contacted Polunsky, and Jean-Baptiste is there. They say he's there. He could not have been here. That would be impossible, unless he can levitate, for Christ's sake."

"I think what you mean is travel out of body," Lucy retorts, and her unfairness and arrogance are uncontrollable right now, and she feels terrible about it. "Levitate means to hover off the ground."

She feels powerless because her usually brilliant and logical mind cannot decipher what has happened, and she wasn't here when it happened.

Manham politely looks at her. "It's him. You're sure?"

Lucy knows Jean-Baptiste's voice, soft, almost sweet, with a heavy French accent. His is a voice she will never forget.

"It's him, all right," she says. "Go ahead and run voice analysis, but I already know what it's going to show. And I think Polunsky needs to prove that the asshole they've got on death row is really Chandonne—as in proving it with DNA. Maybe his fucking family's pulled something. If need be, I'll go there and look at his ugly face myself."

She hates that she hates him. No competent investigator can give in to emotions, or judgment is obscured, even deadly. But Jean-Baptiste tried to kill Lucy's aunt. For that, she despises him. For that, he should die. Painfully, Lucy wishes. For what he intended and attempted, he should feel the abject terror he inflicted on others and lusted to inflict on Scarpetta.

"Demand a new DNA test? Lucy, we need a court order." Manham is aware of jurisdictional and legal limitations and has lived by their standards for so long that he is programmed to at least worry when Lucy suggests a plan that in the past would have been unthinkable and impossible and, if nothing else, would have resulted in a suppression of evidence that would destroy a case in court.

Patricia Cornwell

"Berger can request it." Lucy refers to Assistant DA Jaime Berger. "Give her a call and ask her to come over here as soon as she can. Like right now."

Manham has to smile. "I'm sure she has nothing to do and will welcome the diversion."

286

64

Scarpetta spreads out dozens of eight-by-ten color photographs she made by placing each sheet of the Polunsky commissary paper on a lightbox and photographing all of them under ultraviolet light, and then again at a magnification of 50x.

She compares them to photographs of the Chandonne letter she received. The paper has no watermarks and is composed of closely matted wood fibers, common in cheap paper as opposed to fine papers that include rag.

Visually, the paper has a smooth, shiny surface, typical in typing paper, and she sees no irregularities that might suggest it came from the same manufacturer's batch, which doesn't matter, really. Even if the paper did come from the same batch, that scientific evidence would be weak in court because the defense would instantly insist that because of the enormous size of a manufacturer's batch, inexpensive grades of paper such as this are produced with *untold millions and millions of sheets to a batch.*

The eight-and-a-half-by-eleven, twenty-pound paper is no

different from what Scarpetta uses in her printer. Ironically, the defense might make a case that *she* wrote the Chandonne letter and mailed it to herself.

She has been subjected to more ridiculously bizarre accusations than that. She doesn't fool herself. Once accused, always accused, and she has been accused of too many professional, legal and moral breaches to survive the intense scrutiny of anyone who might wish to destroy her again.

Rose peeks her head into Scarpetta's office. "If you don't leave right this minute, you're going to miss another flight."

65

Buying coffee on the street is an old routine that gives Jaime Berger a temporary escape from mayhem.

She takes her change from Raul, thanks him, and he nods, busy, aware of the long line behind her, and asks if she wants butter, even though she has refused butter for all the years she has patronized his kiosk across Centre Street from the District Attorney's office. She walks off with her coffee and usual high-carbohydrate lunch of a bagel—this one poppyseed—and two packets of Philadelphia cream cheese in a white paper bag with a napkin and a plastic knife. The cell phone on her belt vibrates like a stinging insect.

"Yes," she answers, pausing on the sidewalk across from her granite building downtown, close to Ground Zero, where on September 11, 2001, she was looking out her office window when the second plane crashed into the World Trade Center.

That empty hole along the Hudson has left an empty hole in her, too. Staring at blank air, at what is no longer there, makes her feel older than her forty-eight years, and with every passing era in her life, she has lost a part of herself that can never be resurrected.

"What are you doing?" Lucy asks. "I hear street chaos, so you're in the midst of cops, lawyers and thugs swarming around the courthouse. How quickly can you get to the Upper East Side, where things are more civilized?"

Typically, Lucy doesn't give Berger an opportunity to get in a word until it is too late for her to say no.

"You're not scheduled for court, are you?"

Berger says that she's not. "I suppose you want me *now*."

Realistically speaking, *now* is more like forty-five minutes, due to sluggish traffic. It is close to one p.m. when Berger is keyed up to the twenty-first floor of Lucy's building. The elevator doors open to a mahogany reception area with *Infosearch Solutions* in brass letters on the wall behind the curved glass desk. There is no area for clients to wait, and the desk is flanked by two opaque glass doors. The left one electronically unlocks as the elevator doors shut, an invisible camera in the chandelier broadcasting Berger and every sound she makes on platinum-screen TVs in every interior office.

"You look like holy hell. But what matters is how I look," she dryly says as Lucy greets her.

"You're very photogenic," Lucy replies with a quip she's used before. "You could have had a brilliant acting career in Hollywood."

Berger is a dark-haired woman with sharp features and pretty teeth. She is always dressed impeccably in power suits accented by expensive accessories, and although she might not think of herself as an actor, any good prosecutor is theatrical during interviews and certainly in the courtroom. Berger looks around at a wall of closed mahogany doors. One opens, and Zach Manham walks out, holding a stack of CDs.

"Step into my parlor," Lucy says to Berger. "A spider's turned up."

"A tarantula," Manham gravely adds. "How'ya doin', Boss?" He shakes Berger's hand.

"Still miss the good ol' days?" Berger smiles at him, but her eyes belie her light demeanor.

Losing Manham from the DA's detective squad, or from her A Team, as she calls it, still hurts, even though it is for the best and she continues to work with him at times such as this one.

Another era passed.

"Step this way," Manham says.

Berger follows him and Lucy inside what is simply referred to as *the lab*. The room is large and soundproof, like a professional recording studio. Overhead shelves are stacked with sophisticated audio, video and global-positioning and various tracking systems that defy Berger's expertise and never cease to amaze her when she comes to Lucy's office. Everywhere, lights blink and video screens flash from one image to another, some of them the interior of the building, others monitoring locations that make no sense to Berger.

She notices what looks like a bundle of tiny microphones on top of a desk crowded with modems and monitors.

"What's this latest contraption?" she asks.

"Your latest piece of jewelry. An ultramicro transmitter," Lucy replies, picking up the bundle and pulling loose one of the transmitters, no bigger than a quarter and attached to a long, thin cord. "It goes with this." She taps what looks like a black box with jacks and an LCD. "We can disappear this baby in the hem of one of your Armani jackets, and if you get snatched, the quasi-Doppler direction finder can locate your exact position by VHF and UHF signals.

"Frequency range, twenty-seven to five hundred megahertz. Channels selected on a simple keyboard, and this other thing you're looking at"—she pats the black box—"is a tracking system we can use to monitor wherever the hell you are in your car, on your motorcycle, your bicycle. Nothing more than a crystal oscillator powered by a nicad battery. Can monitor up to ten targets at a time, supposing your husband's screwing around on you with multiple women."

Berger doesn't react to a subtlety that is anything but subtle.

"Water-resistant," Lucy goes on. "A nice carrying case with a shoulder strap; could probably get Gurkha or Hermès to design a special one—perhaps in ostrich or kangaroo—just for you. Aircraft antenna available if you want to feel secure when you fly on a Learjet, a Gulf Stream, however you get about, woman-on-the-go that you are."

"Another time," Berger says. "I hope you didn't bring me uptown to show me what happens if I get lost or kidnaped."

"Actually, I didn't."

Lucy sits before a large monitor. Her fingers rapidly tap on the keyboard as she flies through windows, moving deeper into a forensic scientific software application that Berger doesn't recognize.

"You get this from NASA?" she asks.

"Maybe," Lucy replies, pointing the cursor at a folder labeled with a number that, again, is meaningless to Berger. "NASA does a lot more than bring home moon rocks. Put it this way"—Lucy pauses, hovering over a key, staring intently at the screen—"I've got rocket-scientist buddies at the Langley Research Center." She rolls the mouse around. "Lot of nice people there who don't get the credit they deserve"—tap-tap-tap. "We've got some pretty amazing projects going on. Okay." She clicks on a file labeled with an accession number and today's date.

"Here we go." She looks up at Berger. "Listen."

"Good afternoon. May I ask who's calling?" The male voice on the tape is Zach Manham's.

"When Mademoiselle Farinelli returns, tell her Baton Rouge."

66

Berger pulls up a chair and sits down, riveted to the computer screen.

Frozen on it are two voiceprints or spectrograms—2.5-second digital cuts—of a taped human voice converted into electrical frequencies. The resulting patterns are black and white vertical and horizontal bands that, like Rorschach inkblots, evoke different imaginative associations, depending on who is looking at them. In this case, the voiceprints remind Lucy of a black-and-white abstract painting of tornadoes.

She mentions this to Berger and adds, "That figures, doesn't it? What I've done here—or, should I say, what the computer's done here—is find Chandonne's speech sounds from another source. In this case, your videotaped interview of him after his arrest in Richmond. The computer looked for matching words.

"Of course, the bastard didn't make that easy when you look at the words used in the call we got. Nowhere in his interview with you," Lucy goes on, "does he say Baton Rouge, for example. Nor does he ever mention me—Lucy Farinelli—by name. That leaves *when*, *returns* and *tell her*. Nowhere near as many sounds as I'd like for comparison. We'd like at least twenty matching speech sounds for a positive match. However, what we've got is a significant similarity. The darkest areas on the known and questioned voiceprints correspond to the intensity of the frequencies." She points out black areas of the voiceprints on the computer screen.

"Looks the same to me," Berger remarks.

"Definitely. In the four words *when*, *returns* and *tell her*, yes, I agree."

"Hey, I'm convinced," Manham says. "But in court, we'd have a hard time, for the reason Lucy said. We don't have enough matching sounds to convince a jury."

"Forget court for the moment," says New York's most respected prosecutor.

Lucy strikes other keys and activates a second file.

"*I begin to touch her breasts and unhook her bra,*" says Jean-Baptiste's voice—that soft, polite voice.

Then Lucy says, "Here we go, three other fragments of an interview that contains words for comparison."

"*I was a bit confused at first when I tried to touch her and couldn't pull out her top.*"

Next is, "*But I can tell you are pretty,*" Jean-Baptiste Chandonne says.

"More," says Lucy: "*It was a return ticket, coach, to New York.*"

Lucy explains: "Our four words, Jaime, close enough. As I indicated, these phrases are from your videotaped interview with him prior to his arraignment, when you were brought in as a special prosecutor."

It is difficult for Lucy to hear segments of this interview. Vaguely, she resents Berger for forcing Scarpetta to watch the videotape, although it was necessary, completely necessary, to subject her to hours of what was nothing more than manipulative, violent pornography after he had almost murdered her. Jean-Baptiste lied and enjoyed it. No doubt, he was sexually aroused by the thought that Scarpetta, a victim and key witness, was his audience. For hours, she watched and listened to him fabricate in detail not only what he did in Richmond but his 1997 so-called romantic encounter with Susan Pless, a television meteorologist for CNBC whose savaged dead body was found inside her apartment in New York's Upper East Side.

She was twenty-eight years old, a beautiful African-American beaten and bitten in the same grotesque fashion as Chandonne's other victims. Only in her murder, seminal fluid was recovered. In Jean-Baptiste's more recent slayings, the ones in Richmond, the victims were nude only from the waist up, and no seminal fluid was recovered, only saliva. That fact led to conclusions, based in part on DNA analysis, that the Chandonne web is a tight weave of organized crime for profit and violent aberrance committed for sadistic sport. Jean-Baptiste and Jay Talley enjoy their nonprofit sport. In the sexual slaying of Susan Pless, the two brothers tag-teamed, the debonair Jay seducing and raping Susan, then handing her off to his hideous, impotent twin.

Lucy, Berger and Manham look at the sound spectrograms on the computer screen. Although voice analysis is not an exact science, the three of them are convinced that the man who left the message and Jean-Baptiste Chandonne are one and the same.

"As if I needed this." Berger swipes her finger across the video screen, leaving a faint trail. "I'd know the fucker's voice anywhere. *Tornado.* You got it. That's the damn truth. The way he tears through lives, and damn if it doesn't look like he's doing it again."

Lucy explained the satellite tracking that pointed to the immediate area around her building while caller ID showed that the call was made from across the country, at the Polunsky Unit in Texas. "How do we make sense of this?"

Berger shakes her head. "Unless there's some sort of technical glitch or some other explanation that eludes me, at least, at the moment."

"Most important, I want to know for a fact that Jean-Baptiste Chandonne is still on death row in Texas and is scheduled to get the needle on May seventh," Lucy says.

"No kidding," Manham mutters, repeatedly clicking a pen, a nervous habit that annoys all who know him.

"Zach?" Berger cocks an eyebrow, staring at the pen.

"Sorry." He slides it into the breast pocket of his starched white shirt. "Unless you two need me, I've got some calls to make." He looks at both of them.

"We're fine. Will fill you in later," Lucy says. "And if anybody calls looking for me, the word is that nobody knows where I am."

"Not ready to come up for air?" Manham smiles.

"No."

He leaves, the muffled sound of the heavily padded door barely audible.

"And Rudy?" Berger asks. "Hopefully in his apartment, taking a shower or a nap? Looks like you should be doing the same."

"Nope. We're both working. He's in his office down the hall, lost in cyberspace. Rudy the Internet junkie, which is a good thing. He has more search engines running all over the universe than England has tubes."

"For me to get a search warrant to have Chandonne swabbed for DNA," Berger says, "I have to show probable cause, Lucy. And a taped phone call not only isn't going to do it, but I'm not sure how much you want leaked outside this office. Especially since we really don't know what the phone call means . . ."

"Nothing," Lucy interrupts. "You know that's all I ever want leaking outside this office. Absolutely nothing."

"The unforgivable sin." Berger smiles, her eyes touched by a gentle sadness as she looks at Lucy's stern, determined face, a face still smooth and bright with youth, a face with sensuously full lips the hue of dark red earth.

If it is true that people begin to die the day they are born, then Lucy seems an exception. She is an exception to all things human, it often seems to Berger, and for this reason alone, she fears that Lucy will not live long. She envisions her compelling young face and strong body on top of a stainless-steel autopsy table, a bullet through her brain, and no matter how she struggles to strike that image from her imagination, she can't.

"Disloyalty, even born of weakness, is the unforgivable sin," Lucy agrees, puzzled and unsettled by the way Berger is looking at her. "What's the matter, Jaime? You think we've got a leak? Jesus, it's what I have nightmares about. The nightmare I live with. I fear it more than death." She is getting riled up. "I catch anybody betraying . . . well, one Judas in this organization, and we're all cooked. And so I have to be hard."

"Yes, you're hard, Lucy." Berger gets up, barely glancing at Chandonne's captured voice patterns on the monitor. "We have an active unsolved case here in New York: Susan Pless."

Lucy gets up, too, her eyes intense on Berger's, anticipating what she's about to say next.

"Chandonne is charged with her murder, and you know all the reasons why I gave in, folded up my tent, decided not to prosecute and let Texas have him instead."

"Because of the death penalty," Lucy says.

67

The two of them pause by the soundproof door, monitors glowing, images from closed-circuit cameras flashing from one to the next, and small, bright lights winking white, green and red, as if Lucy and Berger are in the cockpit of a spacecraft.

"I knew he'd be sentenced to death in Texas, and he was. May seventh," Berger mutters. "But no death penalty for him here, never in New York."

She stuffs her legal pad inside her briefcase and snaps it shut. "One of these days the DA might allow the needle, but probably not during my tenure. But I suppose the question now, Lucy, is do we want Chandonne to die? And more to the point, do we want whoever's in his cell in Polunsky to be executed when we can't be certain who that person is, now that we've gotten these communications from the infamous Loup-Garou?"

Berger says *we*, although she has gotten no communication from Jean-Baptiste Chandonne. As far as Lucy knows, only she, Marino and Scarpetta have: letters, and now a phone call that

300

seems to have been made from the Upper East Side of Manhattan, unless technology has failed or human programmers have.

"No judge is going to grant me a court order to get his DNA," Berger says again in her usual, calm, self-assured tone. "Not without probable cause for a search warrant. I get it, and I'll try to extradite him to New York and put him on trial for the murder of Susan Pless. Based on the DNA from his saliva, we'll get a conviction even if we know that the seminal fluid in her vagina wasn't his, was in fact Jay Talley's, his twin brother's. Chandonne's attorney, Rocco Caggiano, is going to throw in every dirty trick he can think of if we bring this case back to life—so to speak."

Lucy avoids the subject of Rocco Caggiano. Her expression registers nothing. Waves of nausea roll through her again. She wills them to pass. *I will not get sick,* she silently orders herself.

"I certainly would introduce Talley's seminal fluid into evidence, and there the case gets dicey. The defense will argue that Jay Talley, now a fugitive, raped and murdered Susan, and all I can prove without a doubt is that Chandonne sank his teeth into her. In summary," she is in courtroom mode, "hopefully, the donor of the seminal fluid will be of no consequence to jurors, who will be horrified that saliva found in bite marks virtually all over Susan's upper body will prove that Chandonne tortured her. But I can't prove he murdered her or that she was even alive when he started biting her."

"Shit," Lucy says.

"Maybe he gets convicted. Maybe the jurors believe she suffered extreme physical pain, that the murder was vicious and wanton. It's possible he would get the death penalty, but it's never carried out in New York. So, *if convicted*, he'd probably get life without possibility of parole, and then we have to live with him until he dies in prison."

Lucy places her hand on the doorknob and leans against thick acoustic foam rubber padding. "I've always wanted him dead."

"And I was glad he ended up in Texas," Berger replies. "But I also want his DNA so we know for a fact that he isn't roaming the streets somewhere, his eyes on his next victim . . ."

"Which could be one of us," Lucy says.

"Let me make some calls. The first step is for me to tell a judge I intend to reopen Susan Pless's murder and want a court order for Chandonne's DNA. Then I'll contact the governor of Texas. Without his sanction, Chandonne's not going anywhere. I know enough about Governor Corley to expect serious obstinance on his part, but at least I think he'll listen to me. It does his state proud to free the Earth of murderers. I'll have to make a deal with him."

"Nothing like justice to help them out at election time," Lucy says cynically as she opens the door.

68

Mid-morning in Poland, a maintenance worker named George Skrzypek is sent to room 513 of the Radisson Hotel to fix a stuck drain in a bathtub that is causing an unpleasant odor.

He knocks on the door and calls out "maintenance" several times. When no one answers, he lets himself in, noticing right away that the guests have checked out, leaving a bed of tangled sheets spotted with seminal fluid and numerous empty wine bottles and ashtrays filthy with cigarette butts on the bedside tables.

The closet door is open, coat hangers on the floor, and when he walks into the bathroom with his box of tools, he discovers the usual mess of toothpaste crusted on the sink and splattered on the mirror. The toilet isn't flushed, the tub filled with scummy water, and large flies crawl on a plate of partially eaten chocolates set on the counter next to the sink. Flies drone and butt against the light over the mirror and dive-bomb Skrzypek's head.

Pigs.

So many people are pigs.

He pulls on large rubber gloves and dips his hands into the cold, greasy bathwater, feeling for the drain. It is clogged with clumps of long black hair.

Pigs.

Water begins to drain from the tub. He tosses the wet, matted hair into the toilet and waves flies away from his face, disgusted as he watches them moil over the plate of chocolates. Taking off his rubber gloves, he flaps them at the fat, black, filthy pests.

Of course, flies are not exotic insects to him, and he sees them on the job, but never this many in a room and not this time of year when the weather is cool. He moves past the bed and notes the open window, a typical sight, even in the winter, because so many guests smoke. As he reaches to shut it, he notices another fly crawling on the sill. It lifts up like a dirigible and buzzes past him into the room. An odor seeps in with the outside air, a very faint odor that reminds him of sour milk or rotten meat. He sticks his head out the window. The stench is coming from the room directly to the right. Room 511.

69

The car is parked at a meter on East 114th Street in Harlem, within a block of Rao's.

In Benton's former life, he could get a coveted table at Rao's because he was FBI and had special status with the family who has owned the famous, if not notorious, Italian restaurant for a hundred years. It was a hangout for the mob, and there is no telling who dines there now. Celebrities frequent its few checked cloth-covered tables. Cops love the place. The mayor of New York stays away. Parked on East 114th, in a beat-up black Cadillac that Benton bought for $2,500 cash, is probably as close to Rao's as he will ever get again.

He plugs a cell phone into the cigarette lighter, engine and air-conditioning running, doors locked, his scan never leaving the mirrors as he eyes rough people who have nothing better to do than walk the streets, looking for trouble. The billing address of this phone is the P.O. Box number of a woman in Washington who does not exist. The satellite location of where Benton's call is made is of no consequence, and within two minutes, he hears U.S. Senator Frank Lord talking to a staff member who is unaware that the senator has activated mode two of his international cell phone and will now receive calls and actually transmit his conversation without any alert that can be detected by anyone other than himself.

While the senator was testifying on live TV, he checked his watch and suddenly called for a break. Without touching the phone clipped on his belt, the caller—in this case, Benton—can hear everything the senator says.

He hears muffled footsteps and voices.

". . . World's greatest obstructionist body. If that isn't the truth," says Senator Lord, who is always reserved, but as tough as they come. "Damn Stevens."

"He's raised filibuster to an art form, that's certain," another male voice sounds in Benton's earpiece.

When Benton left a text message on the senator's cell phone with the exact time he would make this call, it was the first time Benton had made any contact with him in almost a year. Senator Lord knows Benton is listening, unless he has forgotten or didn't get the message. Doubts wrestle with Benton's confidence. He tries to envision the senator, dressed as always in a crisp conservative suit, his posture as straight as a four-star general's.

But the remote one-sided meeting must be on track. The senator walked out of a hearing that was probably being aired live on C-SPAN. He wouldn't do that without a good reason, and it would be coincidental, to say the least, if he just happened to step out at the precise time Benton let him know he would call the number in mode two.

Also, it occurs to Benton with relief, the senator obviously has set his phone on mode two. Otherwise, Benton could not over-hear his conversation. *Don't be stupid and so damn jumpy,* he silently tells himself. *You are not stupid. Senator Lord is not stupid. Think clearly.*

He is reminded of how much he misses seeing his old friends and acquaintances in the flesh. Hearing the voice of Senator Lord, Scarpetta's trusted friend, a man who would do anything for her, tightens Benton's throat. He clenches his hands, gripping his phone so tightly that his knuckles blanch.

The man, probably a staff member, asks, "Can I get you some-thing to drink?"

"Not now," Senator Lord says.

Benton notices a muscular, bare-chested youth casually moving closer to his rusting, dented Cadillac, a hunk of junk so caked with Bondo, the car looks as if it has pigment disorder. Benton stares him down, a universal warning, and the youth veers off in another direction.

"He's not going to get appointed, sir," the staff member replies, oblivious that every word he says is being broadcast to a Nokia cell phone in Harlem.

"I'm always more optimistic than you are, Jeff. Things can turn around, surprise you," says Senator Lord, the chairman of the Judiciary Committee and the most powerful politician in federal law enforcement, because he controls funding, and everything is about funding, even solving the most heinous crimes.

"I want you to leave and call Sabat." Senator Lord refers to Don Sabat, the director of the FBI. "Assure him he'll get what he needs for his new cyber-crime unit."

"Yes, sir." The staff member sounds surprised. "Well, you'll make his day."

"He's done all the right things and needs my help."

"I'm not sure I agree with you, Chairman, in the sense that we have some other pretty big issues, and this is going to set off a lot of . . ."

"Thank you for taking care of it," Senator Lord cuts him off. "I've got to get back in there and make these idiots think about people instead of damn political power games."

"And punishment. There are those who aren't too fond of you."

The senator laughs. "Means I'm doing something right. Give Sabat my regards, tell him things are moving along well now, are in the works. Reassure him, I know he's been unsettled. But we've really got to be diligent now, more than ever."

The line goes dead. Within hours, money will be wired into various accounts at The Bank of New York at Madison and 63rd, and Benton can begin withdrawals with bank cards issued in other fictitious names.

70

Inside Lucy's office, a light begins to flash on a computer.

The news has hit the wire service. The infamous trial lawyer Rocco Caggiano appears to have committed suicide in a hotel in Poland, his body discovered by a maintenance worker who noticed a foul odor coming from one of the rooms.

"How in the hell . . . ?" Lucy strikes a key to deactivate the flashing light. She clicks the mouse on *Print*.

Search engines are her specialty, and a posse of them have been dedicated to finding any information that might be related to Rocco Caggiano. There is plenty. Rocco loved to read about himself, was a news hog, and every time Lucy has scanned some article about him or a client he represented, she has felt an uneasiness she has never experienced before. She can't muster enough self-control to stop imagining Rudy helping Rocco shoot himself in the head.

Pointed up.

The barrel should be pointed up.

A tip she learned from her Aunt Kay, whose reaction Lucy can't imagine were she to find out what her precious niece and Rudy have done.

"Not even forty-eight hours?" Rudy leans over her shoulder, his breath on her neck smelling like the cinnamon gum he has a habit of smacking away on when he's not in public.

"Sounds like our luck has continued to turn bad in Szczecin. Thanks to a maintenance worker and a stuck drain." Lucy continues reading an AP report.

Rudy sits next to her and leans an elbow on the desk, his chin in his hand. He reminds her of a boy who has just lost his first Little League baseball game.

"After all that planning. Fuck. Now what? You pulled up the medical examiner's report? Christ, don't tell me it's in Polish."

"Hold on. Let me jump out of this . . ." She clicks the mouse. "Into something else . . . I *love* Interpol . . ."

The Last Precinct is a very select client, one of those entities considered part of Interpol's massive international web. For the privilege, Lucy must pass security clearance, of course, and pay the same yearly subscription fee as a small country. She executes a search, and Rocco Caggiano's death records are on the screen in seconds. Police and autopsy reports have been translated from Polish into French.

"Oh, no," Lucy says with a sigh as she swivels around in the chair and looks up at Rudy. "How's your French?"

"You know how my French is. Limited to my tongue."

"You're so vulgar. Just a single-tasking computer. You boys. One thing on the mind."

"I don't always think about *only* one thing."

"You're right. I apologize. You think about the one thing, except you do it two, three, a million times a day."

"And you, *Mam-ouzelle* Farinelli?"

"Oh, God, your French is bad."

She glances at her watch, this one a formidable titanium Breitling that includes an Emergency Locator Transmitter, or ELT.

"I thought you weren't supposed to wear that thing unless you're flying." Rudy taps her watch.

"Don't touch it. You'll set it off," she teases him.

He holds on to her arm, studying the watch, frowning at the bright blue face, tilting his head this way and that, pretending he's stupid. Lucy starts laughing.

"One of these days I'm gonna unscrew this big knob right here"—he taps her watch again, still holding on to her arm—"and pull the antenna all the way out. And then run like hell . . ."

Lucy's cell phone vibrates, and she slips it out of the case on her belt.

"And laugh my ass off when the Coast Guard, the F-15s come roaring in . . ."

"Yes," she bluntly answers the phone.

"You have such a sweet manner with people," Rudy whispers in her ear. "If I die, will you marry me?"

Static on the other end is bad. "Who is this?" she asks, loudly. "I can't hear you." The static gets worse. Lucy shrugs and ends the call. "Don't recognize the number, do you?"

She holds up her phone, showing Rudy the number that someone just used to call her.

"Nope. Nine-three-six . . . ? What area code is that?"

"Easy enough to find out."

It doesn't require special search engines or Interpol to type in a telephone number and find out whose it is. Lucy logs on to Google. The name that comes up on the computer screen is the Texas Department of Criminal Justice, Polunsky Unit. Included is a map.

"You didn't answer my question," Rudy says, still flirting but completely cognizant of the importance of a call from Polunsky.

"Why would I marry you if you're dead?" she mutters, scarcely listening to him.

"Because you can't live without me."

"I can't believe this." She stares at the screen. "What the hell is going on? Get Zach to call my aunt, make sure she is safe. Have him tell her it's possible Chandonne might be out. Goddamn it! He's fucking with us!"

"Why don't you call her yourself?" Rudy puzzles.

"That piece of shit is fucking with us!" Her eyes blaze.

"Why don't *you* call Scarpetta?" Rudy asks again.

Lucy instantly becomes somber.

"I can't talk to her right now. I just can't." She looks at him. "How are you doing?"

"Awful," he says.

71

Benton did not call on a landline, because he did not want the inaudible conversation taped.

The technical tools that Lucy most likely has and can't live without would not include a cell phone that automatically tapes a live conversation, especially since very few people have her cell phone number, and those who do are not the sort she would secretly tape. This ploy was far simpler than the last one, and there is no risk that Lucy can try voice analysis to decipher what Jean-Baptiste's nonsensical taped voice had to say, which was nothing.

Benton simply spliced fragments of Jean-Baptiste's taped voice with static, to give the impression of an attempt to talk when one is in a very bad cell. Already she will have traced the call—just as she did the last one—to Polunsky. She will have no satellite capabilities, because the garbled call is gone, lost in space—again, because Benton did not call any of her office lines.

She will be angry. When she gets sufficiently irritated, nothing can stop her. Jean-Baptiste Chandonne is fucking with her.

This is what she will think, and Benton knows Lucy well enough to be certain she has made the mistake of hating Chandonne. Hate interferes with clear thinking. She will wonder how Chandonne can be calling her from Polunsky *and* from New York, if her satellite technology is to be trusted.

In the end, Lucy always trusts her technology.

A second call from Polunsky, and now she will begin to believe, seriously believe, that Chandonne must have a phone with a Texas Department of Criminal Justice billing address. She is no more than a breath away from believing that Jean-Baptiste Chandonne has escaped.

Scarpetta will decide she must encounter him face-to-face, behind protective glass, inside the Polunsky Unit. Chandonne will refuse to see anybody else, and that is his right.

Yes, Kay, yes. It's for you, it's for you. Please. Face him before it's too late. Let him talk!

Benton is getting frantic.

Baton Rouge, Lucy!

Chandonne said Baton Rouge, *Lucy!*

Are you listening to me, Lucy?

72

A radio with a dipole antenna is not required for Jean-Baptiste
Chandonne to know the breaking news.

"Hey, Hair Ball!" Beast yells. "You heard? Guess not, since you
don't got no fucking radio, like I do. Guess what? Guess what I
just heard? Your lawyer ate his gun in Poland."

Jean-Baptiste carefully moves his pen with the skilled hand of
a surgeon, tracing over the words *on death row and on the front row
of life.* He brushes his fingertips over the indentations on white
paper as he composes a letter to Scarpetta that will be forwarded
to her by his lawyer, who now Jean-Baptiste learns is supposedly
dead. If Rocco is dead, Jean-Baptiste has no emotions about it,
but he is curious to know whether the death is significant or
simply a random suicidal whim that carried Rocco away.

The news of the suicide creates an uproar of the usual obscenities, cruel remarks and questions.

Information.

On death row, information is precious. Anything new to hear

is devoured. The men are starved for rumors, gossip, information, information. So this is a big day for them. None of the inmates ever met Rocco Caggiano, but whenever Jean-Baptiste's name has been mentioned on the news, Rocco has been mentioned too, and vice versa. A simple deduction is enough for Jean-Baptiste to accept that Rocco's death is of interest to the press only because he represents the notorious Jean-Baptiste, alias Le Loup-Garou, alias Hair Ball, Mini-Me Dick and Wolfman and oh . . . What was the newest appellation that Beast—the ever-clever Beast— conjured up earlier today?

PUBIC Enemy Number One.

He wrote it on a folded note that was slid under Jean-Baptiste's door, complete with a pubic hair, Beast's pubic hair. Jean-Baptiste ate the note, tasting the words, and blew the pubic hair out his barred window. It drifted to the floor outside his cell.

"If I was Wolfman's lawyer, I'd eat my gun, too!" Beast calls out.

Laughter, and the *bang, bang* of inmates kicking their steel doors.

"Shut up! What the hell's going on in here?"

The mayhem doesn't last long. Corrections officers restore order to the pod immediately, and a pair of brown eyes appear in the barred window of Jean-Baptiste's door.

Jean-Baptiste feels the low energy of the stare. He never stares back.

73

"You need to make a phone call, Chandonne?" the voice belonging to the eyes asks. "Your lawyer's dead, committed suicide. They found his body in a hotel room in some Polish city I can't pronounce. Looks like he'd been dead a while. Killed himself because he was a fugitive. Figures that you'd be represented by a criminal. That's all I know."

Jean-Baptiste sits on his bunk, tracing over words on white paper. "Who are you?"

"Officer Duck."

"Monsieur Canard? *Coin-coin.* That is French for quack-quack, Monsieur Duck."

"You want to make a phone call or not?"

"No, *merci.*"

Officer Duck is never sure how to describe or define the subtleties that ignite his temper every time Jean-Baptiste speaks, but the result is belittlement and powerlessness, as if the mutant murderer is superior and indifferent to death row and those who have complete control of him. The Wolfman manages to make

Officer Duck feel as though he is nothing but a shadow in a uniform. He looks forward to Jean-Baptiste's execution and wishes it could be painful.

"Got that right. *No mercy*'s what your ass is gonna get in ten short days," Officer Duck mouths off. "Sorry about your lawyer's blowing his brains out and rotting inside a hotel room. I can tell you feel real bad about it."

"Lies," Jean-Baptiste replies as he gets up from his bunk and moves to the door, wrapping fingers with their swirls of pale, downy hair around the iron bars in the tiny window.

His Halloween face fills the space and startles Officer Duck, who almost panics at the close proximity of his inch-long filthy thumbnail—the only nail that, for some reason, Jean-Baptiste never cuts.

"Lies," Jean-Baptiste repeats.

It is never easy to know where his asymmetrical eyes are directed or how much they see, and the hair covering his forehead and neck and protruding in tufts from his ears overwhelms Officer Duck with fright.

"Move back. Goddamn, you stink worse than a dog that's been rolling around in the juice of something dead. We're gonna cut that fucking thumbnail of yours."

"It's my legal right to grow my nails and my hair," Jean-Baptiste replies softly, with a gaping smile that reminds the officer of a wide-mouthed fish.

He imagines those widely spaced, pointed baby teeth ripping into female flesh, biting breasts like a frenzied shark while hairy fists pound beautiful faces to pulp. Chandonne targeted only gorgeous, successful women with sexy bodies. He has a fetish for large breasts and nipples that, according to a forensic psychologist who is in and out of the pod, denotes an obsession with a body part that compels Jean-Baptiste to annihilate it.

"For some offenders, it's shoes and feet," the forensic psychologist explained over coffee, perhaps a month ago.

"Yeah, I know about the shoe thing. These wackos break into houses and steal some lady's shoes."

"It happens more than you might expect. The shoe itself is sexually arousing to the offender. Frequently, he then feels the need to kill the woman wearing the fetish or whose body part is the fetish. Many serial killers got their starts as fetish burglars, going into homes, stealing shoes, underwear, other objects that mean something to them sexually."

"So Wolfman was probably stealing bras when he was a hairy little kid."

"Could very well have been. He certainly enters homes with ease, and that is consistent with a serial burglar who has progressed to a serial murderer. The problem with fetish burglary is often the victim has no clue that her home has been entered and that anything was taken. How many women who can't find a shoe or even several shoes, or lingerie, would assume a burglar has been inside her home?"

Officer Duck shrugged. "Hell, my wife can't find nothing half the time she looks. You ought to see her closet. If anybody's got a shoe fetish, Sally does. But it's not like some guy can break in to a lady's home and walk off with a breast. Well, I guess some of them are into the dismemberment thing."

"It's like hair color, eye color or anything else. An offender has a fetish about whatever triggers sexual arousal that in some cases gives rise to a sadistic need to destroy that fetish. Which, in this instance, is the woman with the size and shape of breasts that are a fetish to Jean-Baptiste Chandonne."

Officer Duck understands in a limited way. He likes breasts, too. He is perversely, shamefully aroused by images, even violent ones.

74

The ringing of the officer's feet on the catwalk fades.

Jean-Baptiste resettles on his bunk, a stack of clean white paper on his lap. He taps his pen and composes another poetic phrase, unfurling it from his unique mind like a brilliant red flag that waves in rhythm with his pen. His soul brims with poetry. Molding words into images and profundities that roll together in perfect rhythm is effortless, so effortless.

Roll together in perfect rhythm. He traces his graceful calligraphy again and again, bearing down hard with the ballpoint pen.

Roiling *together in perfect rhythm.*

That is better, he thinks, tapping the pen on the paper again, in rhythm with his inner rhythm.

Tap-tap, tap-tap, tap-tap.

He can slow it down or make it faster or faint or strong, depending on the music of blood he remembers from each kill.

"*Rolling,*" he starts again. "*Mais non.*"

It all roils together in perfect rhythm.

320

"Mais non."

Tap, tap of the pen.

"Dear Rocco," Jean-Baptiste decides to write. "You did not dare to mention Poland to the wrong person, of this I can be sure. You are too much of a coward."

Tap, tap, tap.

"But who? Maybe Jean-Paul," he writes to his dead lawyer.

Tap tap tap tap tap tap tap . . .

"Hey, Hair Ball! I got my radio tuned in," Beast yells. "Ohhhh, too bad you can't hear it. Guess what? They're talking about your lawyer again. Another itty-bitty little news flash. He left a note, see? It said having you for a client *just killed him.* Get it?"

"Shut up, Beast."

"Get a life, Beast."

"Your jokes suck, man."

"I wanna smoke! Why the fuck don't they let me smoke!"

"Bad for your health, man."

"Smokin' will kill ya, dumb shit. Says so right on the pack."

75

The Atkins diet works fine for Lucy because she has never been keen on sweets and doesn't mind forgoing pasta and bread.

Her most dangerous indulgence is beer and wine, and she abstains from both at Jaime Berger's penthouse apartment on Central Park West.

"I won't force you," Berger says, returning the bottle of Pinot Grigio to the top shelf of the refrigerator inside her beautiful kitchen of wormy chestnut cupboards and granite countertops. "I'm better off without it myself. I can hardly remember anything anymore, as it is."

"I'd be better off if you would forget things now and then," Lucy says. "I'd be a lot better off if I would, too."

The last time she visited Berger's penthouse was at least three months ago. Berger's husband got drunk, and soon enough he and Lucy went at each other until Berger asked Lucy to please leave.

"It's forgotten," Berger says with a smile.

"He's not here, right?" Lucy makes sure. "You promised it was okay for me to come over."

"Would I lie to you?"

"Well . . ." Lucy kids her.

For the moment, their light exchange belies the horror of that event. Never has Berger witnessed such a display in what was supposed to be civilized socializing. She truly worried that Lucy and her husband would resort to blows. Lucy would win.

"He hates me," Lucy says, pulling a packet of folded paper out of the back pocket of her cutoff jeans.

Berger doesn't reply as she pours sparkling water into two tall beer glasses and goes back into the refrigerator for a bowl of freshly cut wedges of lime. Even when she is casual in a soft white cotton warm-up suit and socks, as she is now, she is anything but easygoing.

Lucy begins to fidget, stuffs the papers back into her pocket. "Do you think we can ever relax around each other, Jaime? It hasn't been the same . . ."

"It really can't be the same, now can it?"

Berger makes pennies as a prosecutor. Her husband is a real estate thief, maybe one notch more highly evolved than Rocco Caggiano, in Lucy's opinion.

"Seriously. When will he be home? Because if it's soon, I'm leaving," Lucy says, staring at her.

"You wouldn't be here right now if he was coming home soon. He's attending a meeting in Scottsdale. Scottsdale, Arizona. In the desert."

"With reptiles and cacti. Where he belongs."

"Stop it, Lucy," Berger says. "My bad marriage is not somehow related to all the awful men your mother chose over you when you were growing up. We've been through this before."

"I just don't understand why . . ."

"Please don't go there. The past is past." Berger sighs, returning the bottle of San Pellegrino to the refrigerator. "How many times do I have to tell you?"

"Yes, the past is past. So let's get on to what *does* matter."

"I never said it didn't—doesn't matter." Berger carries their drinks into the living room. "Come on now. You're here. I'm glad you're here. So let's make it all right, shall we?"

The view overlooks the Hudson, a side of the building considered less attractive than the front of it, which has the view of the park. But Berger loves water. She loves to watch the cruise ships docking. If she wanted trees, she has told Lucy many times, she wouldn't bother living in New York. If she wanted water, Lucy usually replies, she shouldn't have bothered living in New York.

"Nice view. Not bad for the cheap side of the building," Lucy says.

"You're impossible."

"That I know," Lucy replies.

"How does poor Rudy put up with you?"

"That I don't know. I guess he loves his job."

Lucy sprawls on an ostrich-skin couch, her bare legs crossed, her muscles speaking their own language, responding to movements and nerves while she lives on with little awareness of how she looks. Her workouts are an addictive release from demons.

324

76

Jean-Baptiste stretches out on the thin wool blanket he soaks with sweat each night.

He leans against the hard, cold wall. He has decided that Rocco isn't dead. Jean-Baptiste does not fall for yet another manipulation, although he is not certain what the purpose of this manipulation might be. Ah, of course, *fear*. His father must lurk behind this lie. He is warning Jean-Baptiste that suffering and death are the reward for betrayal, even if the traitor is the mighty Monsieur Chandonne's son.

A warning.

Jean-Baptiste had better not talk now that he is about to die. *Ha.*

Every hour of every day, the enemy attempts to make Jean-Baptiste suffer and die.

Don't talk.

I will if I want. Ha! It is me, Jean-Baptiste, who rules death.

He could kill himself easily. In minutes he could twist a sheet and tie it around his neck and a leg of the steel bed. People are misinformed about hangings. No height is necessary, only a position—such as sitting cross-legged on the floor and leaning forward with all his weight, thus putting pressure on the blood vessels. Unconsciousness happens in seconds, then death. Fear would not touch him, and were he to end his biological life, he would transcend it first, and his soul would direct all that he would do from that point on.

Jean-Baptiste would not end his biological life in this manner. He has too much to look forward to, and he joyfully leaves his small death-row cell and transports his soul into the future, where he sits behind Plexiglas and stares at the lady doctor Scarpetta, hungrily takes in her entire being, relives his brilliance at tricking his way into her lovely château and raising his hammer to crush her head. She denied herself the ecstasy. She denied Jean-Baptiste by depriving him of her blood. Now she will come to him in humility and love, realizing what she did, the foolishness of it, the joy she denied herself when she further maimed him and burned his eyes with formalin, the chemical of the dead. Scarpetta dashed it into Jean-Baptiste's face. The evil fluid demagnetized him briefly, and ever so briefly, pain forced him to suffer the hell of living only in his body.

Madame Scarpetta will spend eternity worshipping his higher state. His higher being will direct its superiority over other humans throughout the universe, as Poe wrote under the guise of a Philadelphia Gentleman. Of course, the anonymous author is Poe. The invisible agent that is the transcendent Poe came to Jean-Baptiste in a delirium as he was restrained in the Richmond Hospital. Richmond was where Poe grew up. His soul remains there.

Poe told Jean-Baptiste, "Read my inspired words and you will be independent of an intellect you will no longer need, my friend. You will be animated by the force and no longer distracted by pain and internal sensations."

Pages 56 and 57. The end of Jean-Baptiste's *limited march of reasoning powers*. No more diseases or peculiar complaints. The internal voice and glorious luminosity.

Who's there?

Jean-Baptiste's hairy hand moves faster beneath the blanket. A stronger stench rises from his profuse perspiration, and he screams in furious frustration.

77

Lucy slips the folded papers out of her back pocket as Berger sits next to her on the couch.

"Police reports, autopsy reports," Lucy tells her.

Berger takes the computer printouts from her and goes through them carefully but quickly. "Wealthy American lawyer, frequently in Szczecin on business, frequently stayed at the Radisson. Apparently shot himself in the right temple with a small-caliber pistol. Clothed, had defecated on himself, a STAT alcohol of point-two-six." She glances up at Lucy.

"For a boozer like him," Lucy says, "that was probably nothing."

Berger reads some more. The reports are detailed, noting the feces-stained cashmere pants, briefs and towels, the empty champagne bottle, the half-empty bottle of vodka.

"It appears he was sick. Let's see," Berger continues, "twenty-four hundred dollars in American cash inside a sock in the bottom drawer of a dresser. A gold watch, gold ring, a gold chain. No evidence of robbery. No one heard a gunshot, or at least never reported hearing one.

"Evidence of a meal. Steak, a baked potato, shrimp cocktail, chocolate cake, vodka. Someone—can't pronounce the name—working in the kitchen seems to think, but isn't sure, that Rocco had room service around eight p.m., the night of the twenty-sixth. Origin of a champagne bottle is unknown but is a brand the hotel carries. No fingerprints on the bottle except Rocco Caggiano's . . . Room was checked for prints, one cartridge case recovered—it and the pistol checked for prints. Again, Rocco's. His hands checked positive for gunshot residue, yada yada yada. They were thorough." She looks up at Lucy. "We're not even halfway through the police report."

"What about witnesses?" Lucy asks. "Anybody suspicious . . ."

"No." Berger slides one page behind another. "Autopsy stuff . . . uh . . . heart and liver disease, why am I not surprised? Atherosclerosis, et cetera, et cetera. Gunshot wound, contact with charred lacerated margins and no stippling. Instantly fatal—that would make your aunt crazy. You know how she hates it when someone says that a person died instantly. Nobody dies instantly, right, Lucy?" Berger peers over the top of her reading glasses and meets Lucy's eyes. "You think Rocco died in seconds, minutes, maybe an hour?"

Lucy doesn't answer her.

"His body was found at nine-fifteen a.m., April twenty-eighth . . ." Berger looks quizzically at her. "By then he'd been dead less than forty hours. Not even two days." She frowns. "Body found by . . . I can't pronounce his name, a maintenance guy. Body badly decomposed." She pauses. "Infested with maggots." She glances up. "That's a very advanced stage of decomposition for someone who's been dead such a short time in what sounds to me like a relatively cool room."

"Cool? The room temperature's in there?" Lucy cranes her neck to look at a printout she can't translate.

"Says the window was slightly opened, temperature in the room sixty-eight degrees, even though thermostat set on seventy-four degrees, but the weather was cool, temperature low sixties during the day, mid-fifties at night. Rain . . ." She is frowning. "My French is getting rusty. Ummm. No suspicion of foul play. Nothing unusual happened inside the hotel the night Rocco Caggiano ordered room service, the *alleged* night, if the room service guy has the date right. Ummm." She scans. "A prostitute made a scene in the lobby. There's a description. That's interesting. I'd love to depose her."

Berger looks up. Her eyes linger on Lucy's.

"Well," she says in a way that unsettles Lucy, "we all know how confusing time of death can be. And it appears that the police aren't sure of the time and date of Rocco's last meal, so to speak. Apparently, the hotel doesn't log room service orders on a computer."

She leans forward in her chair, a look on her face Lucy has seen before. It terrifies her.

"Shall I call your aunt about time of death? Want me to call our good detective friend Marino and ask his opinion about the disruptive *prostitute* in the lobby? The description in this report sounds a little bit like you. Only she was foreign. Maybe Russian."

Berger gets up from the couch and moves close to the windows, looking out. She starts shaking her head and running her fingers through her hair. When she turns around, her eyes are veiled with the protective curtain she keeps drawn virtually every hour of her every day.

The prosecutorial interview has begun.

78

Lucy may as well be shut off in a conference room on the fourth floor of the New York District Attorney's Office, looking out dusty windows at old downtown buildings pressing in from all sides, while Berger sips her black coffee from her paper cup with the Greek key trim around the lip, just like she has done in every interview Lucy has ever watched.

And she has observed many of them for many different reasons. She knows the noise and feel of Berger's shifting gears. She is intimately familiar with the modulations and revolutions of Berger's engine as she pursues, outruns or hits the perpetrator or lying witness head-on. Now the mighty machinery is directed at Lucy, and she is both relieved and petrified.

"You were just in Berlin, where you rented a black Mercedes sedan," Berger says. "Rudy was with you on the return flight to New York—at least I assume Frederick Mullins, supposedly your husband, was Rudy sitting next to you on Lufthansa and

331

then British Airways? Are you going to ask me how I know this, *Mrs. Mullins?*"

"An awful alias. One of the worst." Lucy feels herself breaking down. "Well, in terms of names, I mean . . ." She laughs inappropriately.

"Answer my question. Tell me about this Mrs. Mullins. Why she went to Berlin." Berger's face is metallic, her eyes reflecting anger born of fear. "I have a feeling that the story I'm about to hear is anything but funny."

Lucy stares at her sweating glass, at the lime sinking at the bottom of it, at bubbles.

"Your return ticket stubs and the rental car receipt were in your briefcase, and your briefcase—as usual—was wide open on top of your desk," Berger says.

Lucy's face remains expressionless. She knows damn well that Berger misses nothing and wanders at will in places she doesn't belong.

"Maybe you wanted me to see it."

"I don't know. I never thought I wanted you to see it," Lucy quietly replies.

Berger stares out at a cruise ship slowly being hauled in by a tugboat.

Lucy recrosses her legs nervously.

"So Rocco Caggiano committed suicide. I don't suppose you coincidentally happened to see him while you were in Europe? Not saying you happened to be in Szczecin, but I do know that most people traveling to that part of northern Poland would be quite likely to fly into Berlin, just like you and Rudy did."

"You'd make a great prosecutor," Lucy says drolly, still not looking up. "I would never have a chance under your direct or cross."

"A scenario I don't want to imagine. Jesus. Mr. Caggiano—Mr. Jean-Baptiste Chandonne's lawyer—former lawyer. Dead. A bullet in his head. I suppose that pleases you."

"He was going to kill Marino."

"Who told you that? Rocco or Marino?"

"Rocco," Lucy barely says.

She's in too deep. It's too late. She desperately needs to purge herself.

"Inside his hotel room," she adds.

"God," Berger mutters.

"We had to, Jaime. It's no different than, than what the soldiers did in Iraq, you get it?"

"No, I don't get it." Berger is shaking her head again. "How the hell you could do something like this."

"He wanted to die."

79

Lucy stands on the most beautiful Persian rug she has ever seen, one she has stood on many, many times during better moments with Jaime Berger.

They are far apart from each other in the living room.

"It's hard for me to imagine you dressed as a prostitute and getting into an altercation with a drunk," Berger goes on. "That was sloppy work on your part."

"I made a mistake."

"I'll say you did."

"I had to go back. For my tactical baton," Lucy tells her.

"Which one of you pulled the trigger?"

The question shocks Lucy. She doesn't want to remember.

"Rocco was planning on killing Marino, his own father," Lucy says again. "Next time Marino went on one of his fishing trips, Rocco was going to take him out. Rocco wanted to die. He *did* kill himself, sort of."

Berger looks out at the city, her hands tightly clasped. "He *sort of* killed himself. You *sort of* murdered him. *Sort of* dead. *Sort of* being pregnant. *Sort of* committing perjury."

"We had to."

Berger doesn't want to hear this. She has no choice.

"We did, I swear."

Berger remains silent.

"He was a Red Notice. He was going to die. The Chandonnes would have taken him out, and not in a nice way."

"Now the defense is mercy killing," Berger finally speaks.

"How is it different from what our soldiers did in Iraq?"

"Now the defense is world peace."

"Rocco's life was over, anyway."

"Now the defense is he was already dead."

"Please don't make fun of me, Jaime!"

"I'm supposed to congratulate you?" Berger goes on. "And now you've fucked me, too, because I know about it. *I know about it.*" Berger repeats each word slowly. "Am I stupid or what? Jesus! I sat right there"—she whirls around and jabs a finger at Lucy—"and translated those goddamn reports for you.

"You may as well have walked into my office and confessed to a murder, and had me say, *Don't worry about it, Lucy. We all make mistakes. Or It happened in Poland, so it's not my jurisdiction. It doesn't count. Or Tell me all about it if it will make you feel better.* See, I'm not a real district attorney when I'm with you. When we're alone, when we're inside my apartment, it's not professional."

80

"The fluid white as light and brilliant with sparks. Page forty-seven! Who's there!"

"Jesus Christ!" Eyes flash in the barred window, different eyes this time.

Jean-Baptiste feels the heat of the eyes. They are nothing more than small, weak embers.

"Chandonne, shut up, goddamn it! Shut up with this page-number shit. Goddamn, I'm sick and tired of this page-number shit. You hiding some book in there?" The eyes dart around the cell like sparks scattered by the wind. "And get your filthy hand out of your pants, Mini-Me Dick!"

That familiar hateful laughter. "Mini-Dick, Mini-Dick! Mini-Dick, Mini-Dick . . . !" Beast's is a voice from hell.

Jean-Baptiste has been within twenty feet of Beast. That's how far away the barred window in Jean-Baptiste's door is from the indoor recreation area one floor below him.

There is nothing to do during the one hour a death-row inmate with privileges is allowed to spend on the rectangular wooden floor that is securely enclosed by thick wire mesh, like a cage at the zoo. Shooting hoops is popular, or simply walking a mile, which by Jean-Baptiste's calculations requires approximately seventy laps that no one but he is motivated to do. If Jean-Baptiste runs the laps, which is his habit during the one hour per week he is allowed recreation, he doesn't mind the other men on his cell block who leer out at him, their eyes small hot spots from sun shining through a magnifying glass. They make their usual insolent remarks. The recreation hour is the only opportunity inmates have to chat with and see one another from a distance. Many of these conversations are friendly and even funny. Jean-Baptiste is beyond caring that no one is friendly with him, and that all fun is at his expense.

He is familiar with every detail about Beast, who is not considered a model prisoner but, unlike Jean-Baptiste, has privileges, including daily recreation and, of course, his radio. The first time Jean-Baptiste experienced every detail of Beast's presence was when two guards escorted Beast to the indoor recreation area, where he directed his diseased energy up to Jean-Baptiste's cell door.

Jean-Baptiste's hairy face looked out the bars of his window. It was time to see. One day, Beast might be useful.

"Watch this, No Nuts!" Beast yelled at him, pulling off his shirt and flexing bulging muscles that, like his thick forearms, are almost black with tattoos. He dropped to the concrete floor and fell into one-arm push-ups. Jean-Baptiste's face disappeared from the barred window, but not before he studied Beast carefully. He is smooth-skinned with a blaze of light brown hair that runs from his muscular chest down his belly and disappears into his groin. He is handsome, cruelly so, rather much like a swashbuckler, with a strong jaw, large, bright teeth, a straight nose and intensely cold hazel eyes.

He keeps his hair shorn close to his scalp, and although he appears quite capable of rough sex and beating his woman, one wouldn't be likely to suspect that his preference is abducting young girls, torturing them to death and committing acts of necrophilia on their dead bodies, in some instances returning to the shallow graves where he buried them and digging them up for further acts of perversion until they are too decomposed for even him to stand it.

Beast is called Beast not because he looks like a beast, but because he digs up carrion like a beast and is rumored to have cannibalized some of his victims, too. Necrophilia, cannibalism and pedophilia are transgressions that are repugnant to the typical violent offender on death row, who might have raped, strangled, slashed, dismembered or chained his victims in a basement (to mention but a few examples), but violating children or dead bodies and eating people are serious enough offenses that a number of the inmates on Beast's cell block would like nothing better than to kill him.

Jean-Baptiste doesn't bide his time imagining creative ways to smash Beast's bones or crush his windpipe—idle fantasies for those who can't get closer than ten feet to Beast. The necessity of keeping inmates separated is obvious. When people are sentenced to die, they obviously have nothing to lose by killing again, although in Jean-Baptiste's way of thinking, he has never had anything to lose, and with nothing to lose, there is nothing to gain, and life does not exist. References to those damned at birth are descriptive and dehumanizing and, in Jean-Baptiste's case, trace back as far as his earliest memories.

Let's see.

He thinks from his magnetizing metal toilet seat. He remembers being three. He remembers his mother roughly ushering him into the bathroom, where he could see the Seine from the window, and inevitably at a very young age connecting the river to bathing. He remembers his mother lathering his frail body with perfumed soap and ordering him to sit as still as a stone while she scraped baby-fine hair from his face, arms, neck, back, legs, feet and on and on with his father's sterling-silver-handled straight razor.

Sometimes she would scream at Jean-Baptiste if she accidentally nicked his finger or, occasionally, several fingers, as if her clumsiness was his fault. Knuckles, in particular, are very difficult. Madame Chandonne's tremors and drunken rages put an end to shaving her ugly son when she almost sliced off Jean-Baptiste's left nipple, and his father had to summon the family physician, Monsieur Raynaud, who coaxed Jean-Baptiste to be *un grand garçon* as the little boy shrieked each time the needle flashed in and out of bloody flesh, reattaching the pale nipple, which dangled by a thread of tissue from Jean-Baptiste's downy breast.

His drunken mother wept and wrung her hands and blamed *le petit monstre vilain* for not sitting still. A servant mopped up the little monster's blood while the little monster's father smoked French cigarettes and complained about the burden of having a son who was born wearing *un costume de singe*—a monkey suit.

Monsieur Chandonne could talk, joke and complain freely with Monsieur Raynaud, the only physician allowed contact with Jean-Baptiste when he, the little monster, *une espèce d'imbécile*, born in a monkey suit, lived in the family *hôtel particulier*, where his bedroom was in the basement. No medical records, including a birth certificate, exist. Monsieur Raynaud made sure of this and ministered to Jean-Baptiste only in emergencies, which did not include the usual illnesses or injuries, such as severe earaches, high fevers, burns, sprained ankles or wrists, a stepped-on nail and other medical misfortunes that send most children to the family doctor. Now Monsieur Raynaud is an old man. He will not dare speak of Jean-Baptiste, even if the press will pay large fees for secrets about his notorious former patient.

81

Shame and fear overwhelm Lucy.

She has told Berger in detail what happened in room 511 at the Radisson Hotel, but not who actually shot Rocco.

"Who pulled the trigger, Lucy?" Berger insists on knowing.

"It doesn't matter."

"Since you won't answer the question, I'll assume you did!"

Lucy says nothing.

Berger doesn't move as she looks out at dazzling city lights that give way to the darkness of the Hudson and become the flickering bright urban plains of New Jersey. The space between her and Lucy could not seem more impossible, as if Berger is on the other side of the expansive glass.

Lucy quietly steps closer, wanting to touch the curve of Berger's shoulder, terrified that should she dare, Berger might fall from reach forever, as if she is supported by nothing but air forty-five floors above the streets.

"Marino can't know. Not ever," Lucy says. "My aunt can't know. Not ever."

"I should hate you," Berger says.

She smells faintly of perfume, a strong scent, lightly applied, and it touches Lucy's thoughts that Berger didn't wear perfume for her husband. He isn't here.

"Call it what you want," Berger continues. "You and Rudy committed murder."

"Words," Lucy replies. "The casualties of war. Self-defense. Judicial homicide. Home protection. We have words, legal excuses for committing acts that should be inexcusable, Jaime. I promise you, there was no joy in it, no delicious flavor of revenge. He was a pitiful coward, blubbering and sorry about only one thing in his entire cruel, worthless life: that it was his turn to pay the price. How could Marino have a son like that? What markers in the human genome came together to spew out Rocco?"

"Who else knows?"

"Rudy. Now you . . ."

"Anyone else? Were you given instructions?" Berger presses on.

Lucy thinks about Benton's staged murder, about many events and conversations that she can never tell Berger. A tyrant of anguish and rage has ruled Lucy for years.

"There are others involved, indirectly involved. I can't talk about it. Really," Lucy says.

Berger doesn't know that Benton isn't dead.

"Oh, fuck. What *others*?"

"I said *indirectly*. I can't tell you anything else. I won't."

"People who give secret orders tend to vanish in the light of exposure. Are these your *others*? People who have given secret orders?"

"Not directly about Rocco." She thinks about Senator Lord, about the Chandonne cartel. "Let me just say that there are people who wanted Rocco dead. I just never had enough information to do anything about it until now. When Chandonne wrote to me, he told me what I needed to know."

"I see. And Jean-Baptiste Chandonne is credible. Of course, all psychopaths are. Whoever else is *indirectly* involved has already vanished. You can count on that."

"I don't know. There are instructions about the Chandonne cartel. Oh, yes. There have been for a long time. Years. I did what I could while I was ATF, down in Miami. But it wasn't working. Rules."

"That's right. You and rules," Berger says coldly.

"Until Rocco, I have been ineffective."

"Well, you certainly were effective this time. Tell me something, Lucy. Do you think you'll get away with it?"

"Yes."

"You and Rudy made mistakes," Berger says. "You left your tactical baton and had to go back to get it, and you were seen by several people. Never good, never good. And you staged the death scene—quite expertly, quite cleverly. Maybe too expertly, too cleverly. I would wonder about a room, a gun, a champagne bottle, et cetera, so clean that only Rocco's fingerprints are on them. I would wonder about advanced decomposition that seems to conflict with time of death. And flies, so damn many flies. Blow flies aren't terribly fond of cool weather."

"In Europe, they are more accustomed to cooler weather. As low as forty-eight degrees. The common bluebottle variety, blow fly. Of course, warmer temperatures are better."

"You must have learned that from your aunt Kay. She would be proud of you."

"You would wonder." Lucy gets back to mistakes. "You wonder about everything. That's why you're who you are."

"Don't underestimate the Polish authorities and medical experts, Lucy. You may not have heard the last of this. And if anything points back to you, I can't help you. I have to consider this conversation privileged. Right now, I am your lawyer. Not a prosecutor. It's a lie. But I will somehow live with it.

"But whoever has given you directives, I don't care how long ago, will not return your secret phone calls now, won't even know your name, will frown and shrug in some cabinet meeting or over drinks at the Palm, or worse, laugh it off. The story of some overzealous private investigator."

"It won't happen like that."

Berger slowly turns around and grabs Lucy's wrists. "Are you so goddamn sure of yourself that you're stupid? How can anyone so smart be so stupid?"

The blood rises to Lucy's cheeks.

"The world is full of users. They'll seduce you into the most outrageous acts for the sake of liberty and justice for all, and then they dissolve like mist. Prove to be fantasies. You begin to wonder if they were ever real, and as you rot away in a federal prison somewhere or, God forbid, are extradited to a foreign country, you will slowly but surely believe it was all a delusion, because everybody else believes you are delusional, some nutcase who committed murder because she was on some secret mission for the CIA, the FBI, the fucking Pentagon, Her Majesty's Secret Service, the Easter Bunny."

"Stop it," Lucy exclaims. "It's not like that."

Berger's hands move up to Lucy's shoulders. "For the first time in your life, *listen* to someone!"

Lucy blinks back tears.

"Who?" Berger demands to know. "Who sent you on this goddamn horrific mission? Is it someone I know?"

"Please stop it! I can't and won't ever tell you! There's so much . . . Jaime, you're better off not knowing. Please trust me."

"Jesus!" Berger's grip lightens, but she doesn't let go of her. "Jesus, Lucy. Look at you. You're shaking like a leaf."

"You can't do this." Lucy angrily steps away. "I'm not a child. When you touch me . . ." She steps back some more. "When you touch me, it means something different. It still does. So don't. Don't."

"I know what it means," Berger says. "I'm sorry."

82

At ten p.m., Scarpetta climbs out of a taxi in front of Jaime Berger's building.

Still unable to reach her niece, Scarpetta is pricked by anxiety that has worsened with each call she has made. Lucy doesn't answer her apartment or her cell phone. One of her associates at her office said he doesn't know where she is. Scarpetta begins to think about her reckless, fire-breathing niece and contemplates the worst. Her ambivalence about Lucy's new career has not abated. Hers is an unregimented, dangerous and highly secretive life that may suit her personality, but it frustrates Scarpetta and frightens her. She can be impossible to get hold of, and Scarpetta rarely knows what Lucy is doing.

Inside Jaime Berger's luxurious high-rise, a doorman greets Scarpetta.

"May I help you, ma'am?"

"Jaime Berger," Scarpetta replies. "The penthouse."

83

Lucy is tempted to dash from the building when she realizes that her aunt is headed up in the elevator.

"Calm down," Berger says.

"She doesn't know I'm here," Lucy says, upset. "I don't want her to know I'm here. I can't see her right now."

"You're going to have to see her at some point. May as well be now."

"But she doesn't know I'm here," Lucy repeats herself. "What am I going to tell her?"

Berger gives her an odd look as they hover near the door, waiting for the sound of the elevator.

"Is the truth such a bad thing?" Berger replies angrily. "You could tell her that. Now and then, telling the truth is very therapeutic."

"I'm not a liar," Lucy says. "That's one thing I'm not, unless it is for the sake of work, especially the undercover work."

"The problem is when the boundaries merge," Berger says as

347

the elevator arrives. "Go sit in the living room." As if Lucy is a child. "Let me talk to her first."

Berger's foyer is marble, a table centered with fresh flowers across from the spotless brass elevator. She hasn't seen Scarpetta in several years and is dismayed when she walks out of the elevator. Kay Scarpetta looks exhausted, her suit badly wrinkled, her eyes anxious.

"Does anybody on Earth answer the phone anymore?" she says first thing. "I've tried Marino, Lucy, you. In your case, your line was busy and has been busy for an hour. So at least I assumed someone was home."

"I had it off the hook . . . I wanted no interruptions."

This makes no sense to Scarpetta. "I'm so sorry to barge in on you like this. I'm frantic, Jaime."

"I can tell. Before you come in, I want you to know that Lucy is here." She states this matter-of-factly. "I didn't want to shock you. But I expect you are relieved."

"Not entirely. Her office stonewalled me, meaning Lucy did."

"Kay, please come in," Berger says.

They walk into the living room.

"Hi." Lucy hugs her aunt.

Her response is stiff. "Why are you treating me like this?" she asks, not caring if Berger hears.

"Treating you like what?" Lucy returns to the living room and sits on the couch. "Come on." She motions for Scarpetta to join her. "You, too, Jaime."

"Not unless you're going to tell her," Berger says. "Otherwise, I want no part in the conversation."

"Tell me what?" Scarpetta sits next to Lucy. "Tell me what, Lucy?"

"I guess you've heard that Rocco Caggiano allegedly committed suicide in Poland," Berger tells her.

"I haven't heard any news today about anything," Scarpetta replies. "Was either on the phone or in a plane, then a taxi. Now I'm here. What do you mean *allegedly*?"

Lucy stares down at her feet and says nothing. Berger stands at the edge of the living room and is silent.

"You disappeared for days. No one would tell me where you were," Scarpetta begins quietly. "Were you in Poland?"

A long pause, then Lucy lifts her eyes. "Yes, I was."

"Dear God," Scarpetta mutters. "Alleged suicide," she repeats.

Lucy explains the tip about the murdered journalists that Chandonne divulged to her in a letter. She explains further information from him about Rocco's whereabouts. Then she tells her aunt about the Red Notice.

"So Rudy and I found him, found him in the hotel he always stays in when he does his dirty business in Szczecin. We told him about the Red Notice, and he knew that was it. The end. Because, apprehended or not, the Chandonnes would make sure he didn't live very long."

"So he killed himself," Scarpetta says, looking straight into Lucy's eyes, searching them.

Lucy doesn't reply. Berger walks out of the room.

"Interpol has posted the information," Lucy then says, somewhat inanely. "The police say his death is a suicide."

This appeases Scarpetta temporarily, only because she doesn't have the strength to probe further.

She opens her briefcase and shows Lucy the letter from Chandonne, and then Lucy goes into Berger's office.

"Please come," Lucy starts to say.

"No," Berger replies, the look in her eyes one of disappointment, of judgment. "How can you lie to her?"

"I didn't and I haven't."

"By omission. The whole truth, Lucy."

"I'll get there. When it's time. Chandonne wrote her. You've got to see it. There's something really bizarre going on."

"There sure is." Berger gets up from her desk.

They return to the living room and look at the letter and envelopes through their protective plastic.

"That's not like the letter I got," Lucy says immediately. "It was block printing. It wasn't mailed regular post. I guess Rocco mailed it for him. Rocco mailed a lot of things for him. Why would Chandonne write Marino and me in block printing?"

"What did the paper look like?" Scarpetta asks.

"Notebook paper. Lined paper."

"The paper in the prison commissary is plain white, twenty-pound cheap stock. The same thing most of us use in our printers."

"If he didn't send those letters to Marino and me, then who did?" Lucy feels sluggish, her system overloaded.

Based on the information in the letter to her, she orchestrated Rocco Caggiano's death. When she and Rudy held him hostage in the hotel room, Rocco never actually admitted to murdering the journalists. Lucy recalls him rolling his eyes toward the ceiling— his only response. She can't know as fact what he really meant by that gesture. She can't know as fact that the information she sent to Interpol is correct. What she offered was enough for an arrest, but not necessarily a conviction because, in fact, Lucy doesn't know the facts. Did Rocco really meet with the two journalists mere hours before their murders? Even if he did, was he the one who shot them?

Lucy is responsible for the Red Notice. The Red Notice is why Rocco knew his life was over, no matter what he confessed or didn't confess. He became a fugitive, and if Lucy and Rudy hadn't brought about his death, the Chandonnes would have. He should be dead. He needed to be dead. Lucy tells herself the world is better off because Rocco isn't in it.

"Who wrote me that goddamn letter?" Lucy says. "Who wrote the one to Marino and the first one to you?" She looks at Scarpetta. "The ones that came in those National Academy of Justice postage-paid envelopes? They *sound* like they were written by Chandonne."

"I agree with that," Scarpetta says. "And the coroner in Baton Rouge got one, too."

"Maybe Chandonne changed his handwriting and paper when he wrote this one." Lucy indicates the letter with its beautiful calligraphy. "Maybe the bastard's not in prison at all."

"I heard about the phone calls to your office. Zach got hold of me on my cell phone. I think we can't assume at all that Chandonne is still in prison," Scarpetta replies.

"Seems to me," Berger says, "that he wouldn't have access to lined paper or National Academy of Justice envelopes if he's still in prison. How hard do you suppose it would be to create facsimiles of those postage-paid envelopes on a computer?"

"God, I feel so stupid," Lucy says. "I can't tell you what I feel. Of course it could be done. Just scan in an envelope, then type in the address you want, and print it on the same type of envelope. I could do it in five minutes."

Berger looks at her for a long time. "Did you, Lucy?"

She is stunned. "*Me* do it? Why would *I* do it?"

"You just admitted that you could," Berger somberly says. "It appears you're quite capable of doing a lot of things, Lucy. And it's convenient that information in the letter to you resulted in your going to Poland to find Rocco, who is now dead. I'm leaving the room. The prosecutor in me doesn't want to hear any further lies or confessions. If you and your aunt want to talk for a while, please help yourselves. I have to put the phone back on the hook. I have calls to make."

"I haven't lied," Lucy says.

352

84

"Sit down," Scarpetta says, as if Lucy is no longer a grown-up.

The lights are out in the living room, and the New York sky-line surrounds them with its brilliant possibilities and soaring power. Scarpetta could stare at it for hours, the way she does the sea. Lucy sits next to her on Berger's couch.

"This is a good place to be," Scarpetta says, gazing out at millions of lights.

She looks for the moon but can't find it behind buildings. Lucy is quietly crying.

"I've often wondered, Lucy, what would have happened had I been your real mother. Would you have adopted such a dangerous world and stormed through it so brazenly, so outrageously, so stunningly? Or would you be married with children?"

"I think you know the answer to that," Lucy mutters, wiping her eyes.

"Maybe you would have been a Rhodes scholar, gone to Oxford and become a famous poet."

Lucy looks at her to see if she's joking. She's not.

"A gentler life," her aunt says softly. "I raised you, or, better stated, I attended to you as best I could and can't imagine loving any child more than I did—and do—love you. But through my eyes, you found the ugliness in the world."

"Through your eyes I found decency, humanity and justice," Lucy replies. "I wouldn't change anything."

"Then why are you crying?" She picks out distant planes glowing like small planets.

"I don't know."

Scarpetta smiles. "That's what you used to say when you were a little girl. Whenever you were sad and I'd ask you why, you'd say *I don't know.* Therefore, my very astute diagnosis is that you are sad."

Lucy wipes more tears from her face.

"I don't know exactly what happened in Poland," her aunt then says.

Shifting her position on the couch, Scarpetta arranges pillows behind her back, as if inviting a long story. She continues to look past Lucy, out windows into the glittering night, because it is harder for people to have difficult conversations while they are looking at each other.

"I don't need you to tell me. But I think you need to tell me, Lucy."

Her niece stares out at the city crowded around them. She thinks of dark, high seas and ships lit up. Ships mean ports, and ports mean the Chandonnes. Ports are the arteries for their criminal commerce. Rocco may have been only one vessel, but his connection to Scarpetta, to all of them, had to be severed.

Yes. It had to be.

Please forgive me, Aunt Kay. Please say it's all right. Please don't lose your respect for me and think I've become one of them.

"Ever since Benton died, you've been a Fury, a spirit of

354

punishment, and there isn't enough power in this entire city to satisfy your hunger for it," Scarpetta talks on, still gently. "This is a good place for you to be," she says, as both of them stare out at the lights of the most powerful city on Earth. "Because one of these days when you're glutted with power, maybe you'll realize that too much of it is unbearable."

"You say that to explain yourself," Lucy comments with no trace of rancor. "You were the most powerful medical examiner in the country, perhaps in the world. You were the Chief. Maybe it was unbearable, that power and admiration."

Lucy's beautiful face is not quite as sad now.

"So much has seemed unbearable," Scarpetta replies. "So much. But no. I didn't find my power unbearable when I was the Chief. I have found losing my power unbearable. You and I feel differently about power. I am not proving anything. You are always proving something when it is so unnecessary."

"You haven't lost it," Lucy tells her. "Your removal from power was an illusion. Politics. Your true power has never been imposed by the outside world, and it follows that the outside world can't take it away from you."

"What has Benton done to us?"

Her question startles Lucy, as if Scarpetta somehow knows the truth.

"Since he died . . . I still can scarcely bring myself to say that word. *Died.*" She pauses. "Since then it seems the rest of us have gone to ruin. Like a country under siege. One city falling after another. You, Marino, me. Mostly you."

"Yes, I am a Fury." Lucy gets up, moves to the window and sits cross-legged on Jaime Berger's splendid antique rug. "I am the avenger. I admit it. I feel the world is safer, that you are safer, all of us are safer with Rocco dead."

"But you can't play God. You're not even a sworn law-enforcement officer anymore, Lucy. The Last Precinct is private."

"Not exactly. We are a satellite of international law enforcement, work with them, usually behind the curtain of Interpol. We are empowered by other high authorities I can't talk to you about."

"A high authority that empowered you to legally rid the world of Rocco Caggiano?" Scarpetta asks. "Did you pull the trigger, Lucy? I need to know that. At least that."

Lucy shakes her head. No, she didn't pull the trigger. Only because Rudy insisted on firing that round and having gunpowder and tiny drops of Rocco's blood blow back on his hands, not hers. Rocco's blood on Rudy's hands. That wasn't fair, Lucy tells her aunt.

"I shouldn't have allowed Rudy to put himself through that. I take equal responsibility for Rocco's death. Actually, I take full responsibility, because it was by my instigation that Rudy went on the mission to Poland."

They talk until late, and when Lucy has relayed all that happened in Szczecin, she awaits her aunt's condemnation. The worst punishment would be exile from Scarpetta's life, just as Benton has been exiled from it.

"I'm relieved that Rocco's dead," Scarpetta says. "What's done is done," she adds. "At some point, Marino will want to know what really happened to his son."

85

Dr. Lanier sounds as if he is on the mend, but he is as taut as a cocked catapult.

"You got a safe place for me to stay down there?" Scarpetta asks him over the phone inside her single room at the Melrose Hotel at 63rd and Lexington.

She opted not to spend the night with Lucy, resisting her niece's persistent urging. Staying with her would make it impossible for Scarpetta to leave for the airport in the morning without Lucy's knowing.

"The safest place in Louisiana. My guest house. It's small. Why? Now you know I can't afford consultants . . ."

"Listen," she cuts him off. "I've got to go to Houston first." She avoids being specific. "I can't get down your way for at least another day."

"I'll pick you up. Just tell me when."

"If you could arrange a rental car for me, that's what would work best. I have no idea about anything right now. I'm too tired.

But I'd rather take care of myself and not inconvenience you. I just need directions to your house."

She writes them down. They seem simple enough.

"Any particular kind of car?"

"A safe one."

"I know all about that," the coroner replies. "I've peeled enough people out of unsafe cars. I'll get my secretary on it first thing."

86

Trixie leans against the counter, smoking a menthol cigarette and glumly watching Marino pack a large ice chest with beer, luncheon meats, bottles of mustard and mayonnaise, and whatever his huge hands grab out of the refrigerator.

"It's way past midnight," Trixie complains, fumbling for a Corona in a longneck bottle that she clogged by stuffing in too large a slice of lime. "Come on to bed and then you can leave, can't you? Don't that make more sense than zooming out of here, half-lit and all upset, in the middle of the night?"

Marino has been drunk since he returned from Boston, sitting in front of the TV, refusing to answer the phone, refusing to talk to anyone, not even to Lucy or Scarpetta. About an hour ago, he was kicked hard by a message on his cell phone from Lucy's office. That sobered him enough to pry him out of his reclining chair.

Trixie holds the bottle straight up and tries to push the lime away with her tongue. She succeeds, and beer gushes into her mouth and over her chin. Not so long ago, Marino would have found this hilarious. Now nothing will make him smile. He jerks open the freezer door, pulling out the container of ice cubes and dumping them into the chest. Trixie, whose real name is Teresa, is thirty years old and not even a year ago moved into Marino's small house in its blue-collar neighborhood, right off Midlothian Turnpike on the wrong side of the James River in Richmond.

He lights a cigarette and looks at her, at her face, puffy from booze, the mascara so chronically smeared under her eyes that it looks tattooed on. Her platinum hair has been scalded by so many treatments that Marino hates to touch it, told her once while he was drunk that it felt like insulation. Some of her hurt feelings are permanently crippled, and when Marino catches a glimpse of them hobbling out of her eyes or mouth, he leaves the room, either with his thoughts or his feet.

"Please don't go." Trixie sucks hard on a cigarette and shoots the smoke out of the side of her mouth, barely inhaling. "I know what you're doing. You ain't coming back, that's what. I saw what you've been packing in your truck. Guns, your bowling ball, even your trophies and fishing poles. Not to mention your usual clothes, nothing nice like those suits that have been hanging in the closet since Jesus wrote the Ten Commandments."

She steps in front of him and grabs his arm as he rearranges ice in the chest, smoke making him squint.

"I'll call ya. I've got to get to Louisiana, and you know it. The Doc's down there, or is about to be down there. I know her. I know damn well what she's gonna do. She don't have to tell me. You don't want her dead, Trixie."

"I'm so fucking tired of the *Doc this* and the *Doc that*!" Her face darkens, and she shoves Marino's hand away, as if touching had been his idea, not hers. "Ever since I've known you, it's been the

Doc this and the *Doc that*. She's the only woman in your life, if you're honest about it. I'm just the second-draft choice in your basketball game of life."

Marino winces. He can't stand Trixie's colorful near-miss expressions, which remind him of a piano out of tune.

"I'm just the girl who sits out the dance in the prom that is your life," she continues the drama, and by now that's all it is.

A drama. Like a bad soap opera.

Their fights are by rote, for the most part, and although Marino has a special aversion to psychology, not even he can avoid an insight as big as a mountain. He and Trixie fight about everything because they fight about nothing.

Her fat bare feet with their chipped red-painted nails pat across the kitchen as she paces, wildly waving her plump arms, cigarette ashes snowing down on the stained linoleum floor. "Well, you just go on to Louisiana and get with the *Doc this and that*, and by the time you come back—if you ever do—maybe someone else will be living in this dump of yours and I'll be gone. Gone. Gone. Gone."

Half an hour ago, Marino asked her to put his house on the market. She can live in it until it sells.

Her flower-printed acetate robe flutters around her feet as she paces, her breasts sagging over the sash she keeps tightening around her thick waist. Marino feels pangs of anger and guilt. When Trixie nags him about Scarpetta, he flies out of control like a pissed-off bird out of a knothole, with no place to go, no way to defend himself, no way to counterattack, not really.

His wounded ego can't be assuaged by implying indiscretions with Scarpetta that unfortunately have never occurred. So the arrows of the jealous Trixies in his life find their spot and draw their blood. Marino isn't bothered that he's lost every woman he's ever had. He's bothered by the one he never got, and Trixie's tantrum is mounting dangerously close to the necessary crescendo that will bring about the necessary coda.

"You're so crazy for her it's disgusting," Trixie yells. "You're nothing but a big redneck to her. That's all you'll ever be. A big, fat, stupid redneck!" she shrieks. "And I don't care if she ends up dead! *Dead* is all she knows anyhow!"

Marino picks up the ice chest as if it weighs nothing and walks through his shabby, cluttered living room and stops at the front door. He looks around at the thirty-six-inch color TV—not a new one, but a Sony and plenty nice. He stares sadly at his favorite reclining chair, where it seems he has spent most of his life, and he feels an ache so deep it's a cramp in his bowels. He imagines how many hours he has spent half-drunk, watching football and wasting his time and efforts on the likes of Trixie.

She's not a bad woman. She's not evil. None of them have been. They're simply pitiful, and he is even more pitiful than any of them because he has never insisted on more for himself, and he could have.

"I won't be calling you after all," Marino tells her. "I don't even give a rat's ass what happens to the house. Sell it. Rent it. Live in it."

"You don't mean that, baby." Trixie begins to cry. "I love you."

"You don't know me," Marino says from the door, and he feels too tired to leave and too depressed to stay.

" 'Course I do, baby." She crushes out a cigarette in the sink and rummages in the refrigerator for another beer. "And you're going to miss me." Her face twists as she smiles, crying at the same time. "And you'll get your ass back here. I was just mad when I said you wouldn't. You will." She pops off the bottle cap. "One reason I know you'll be back is, what?" She points coyly at him.

"Can you guess what Detective Trixie noticed, huh? You're leaving without your Christmas decorations.

"All those millions of plastic Santas, reindeer, snowmen, jalapeno pepper lights and the rest of what you been collecting for a century? And you're gonna drive off and just leave 'em in the basement? Naw-uh. No way, naw-uh."

She talks herself into believing she's right. Marino wouldn't leave for good and not pack up his beloved Christmas decorations.

"Rocco's dead," he says.

"Who?" Trixie's face goes blank.

"See, that's what I mean. You don't know me," he says. "It's all right. It ain't your fault."

He shuts the door on her, shuts the door on Richmond for good.

87

The missing woman's name is Katherine Bruce.

She is now considered abducted, the latest victim of the serial killer, presumed dead. Her husband, a former Air Force pilot now employed by Continental, was out of town, and after trying to reach his wife for two days with no success, he became concerned. He sent a friend to the house. Katherine wasn't there, nor was her car, which was discovered parked at the Wal-Mart near LSU where it did not draw attention to itself, since the lot has cars in it twenty-four hours a day. Her keys were in the ignition, her doors unlocked, her purse and wallet gone.

The morning is barely materializing, as if its molecules are slowly gathering into a sky that promises to be clear and bright blue. Nic knew nothing about the abduction until yesterday's six o'clock news. She still can't believe it. Katherine Bruce's friend, according to what has been released to the media, called the Baton Rouge police immediately *yesterday morning*. The information should have been released immediately and nationally. What did the idiot task force do? Give the friend, whose identity has not been disclosed, a damn polygraph to make sure Katherine really is missing? Were they digging up the backyard to make sure the pilot husband didn't kill and bury his wife before flying out of town?

The killer got an extra eight hours. The public lost eight hours. Katherine lost eight hours. She might still have been alive, assuming she's not alive now. Someone might have spotted her and the killer. You never know. Nic obsessively walks the Wal-Mart parking lot, looking for any detail that might speak to her. The huge crime scene is mute, Katherine Bruce's car long gone, impounded somewhere. Nothing but bits of trash, chewing gum and millions of cigarette butts out here.

It's 7:16 when she makes her only find thus far, one that would have thrilled her as a child: two quarters. *Both of them heads.* That's always luckier than tails, and right now she'll nurture any fantasy of luck she can. After she heard the news last night, Nic rushed here right away. If the coins were on the tarmac at that time, her flashlight didn't pick them up. And she didn't see the coins first thing this morning, when she returned and it was still dark. She takes photographs with thirty-five-millimeter and Polaroid cameras and memorizes the coins' location, making notes, just as she was taught at the forensic academy. She pulls on surgical gloves and secures the coins in a paper evidence envelope, then trots into the store.

"I need to see the manager," she tells a checkout clerk who is busy ringing up a cartful of children's clothing while a tired-looking young woman—maybe a mother—pulls out a MasterCard.

Nic thinks of Buddy's overalls and feels terrible.

"That way." The clerk points to an office behind a swinging wooden door.

Thank God he's in.

Nic shows him her badge as she says, "I need to see the exact location where Katherine Bruce's car was found."

The manager is young and friendly. He is clearly upset.

"Glad to show you. I sure know where it is. The police were out here for hours, poking around, and then they towed it. This is really awful."

"It's awful, all right," Nic agrees as they leave the store and the sun begins to show its bright face in the east.

The location of Katherine Bruce's 1999 black Maxima was approximately twenty feet from where Nic found the quarters.

"You're sure this is where it was?"

"Oh, I'm sure, yes, ma'am. Parked right here five rows away. A lot of women who shop after dark park relatively close to the front door."

In her case, that didn't help. But she must have been at least somewhat security-conscious. Well, maybe not. Most people want to park as close to a store entrance as possible, unless they drive an expensive car and don't want anyone dinging the doors. Usually, it's men who worry about that. Nic has never understood why so many women don't seem to have much interest in cars or their upkeep. If she had a daughter, she'd make sure her little girl knew the name of every exotic car, and Nic would tell her if she works hard, maybe she'll drive a Lamborghini someday—the same thing she tells Buddy, who has numerous models of sports cars that he loves to roll into walls.

"Did anyone notice any unusual activity the night she drove her car into this lot? Did anyone spot Katherine Bruce? Did anyone see anything at all?" Nic asks the manager, both of them standing in the same spot and looking around.

"No. I don't think she ever made it inside the store," he says.

88

The Bell 407 has the most beautiful paint job Lucy has ever seen.

It should. It's her helicopter, and she designed its every detail, excluding those that came with it green, or straight out of the plant. Its four blades, smooth ride and maximum speed of 140 knots (damn good for non-military) and computerized fuel control are just a few of the basics. Added to that are leather seats, pop-out floats in case of an engine failure over water, which is very unlikely to occur, a wire strike for scud-running into power lines (Lucy's too safe a pilot for that), an auxiliary fuel tank, storm scope, traffic scope and GPS—all her instrumentation the best, of course.

The 34th Street heliport is on the Hudson, midway between the Statue of Liberty and the Intrepid. Out on pad 2, Lucy walks around her bird for the fourth time, having already checked inside the cowling and sight glasses for oil levels, oil drips, pop-out buttons on filters or hydraulic leaks that always remind her of dark red blood. One of many reasons she is fanatical about lifting weights in the gym is if she ever lost her hydraulics in flight, she'd have to muscle the controls. A weak woman would have a hard time with that.

She runs her hand lovingly along the tail boom, squatting again to check antennas on the underside. Then she climbs into the pilot's seat and wishes Rudy would hurry up. Her wish is granted as the door to the FBO swings open and Rudy appears with a duffel bag and trots to the helicopter, a hint of disappointment crossing his face when he spots the empty left seat and, as usual, finds himself the copilot. Dressed in cargo pants and a polo shirt, he is the typical handsome hunk.

"You know what?" he says, clicking on his four-point harness as Lucy goes through a quick but thorough preflight, starting with circuit breakers and switches, working her way down to the instruments and the throttle. "You're damn greedy," he says. "A helicopter hog."

"That's because it's my helicopter, big guy." She switches on the battery. "Twenty-six amps. Plenty of juice. Don't forget, I've got more hours than you—more certifications, too."

"Shut up," he says good-naturedly, always in a genial mood when the two of them fly. "Clear on the left."

"Clear on the right."

89

Flying is as close as he'll ever get to experiencing euphoria with her.

Lucy never finishes what she rarely starts. Rudy might have felt used after they drove away from the Radisson in Szczecin, were it not for his understanding of what happened. Near-death experiences or anything else that is terribly traumatic cause a simple reaction in most people. They crave the warmth of human flesh. Sex is a reassurance that one is alive. He wonders if this is why he constantly thinks about sex.

He's not in love with Lucy. He would never allow that to happen. The first time he saw her God knows how many years ago, he had no intention of being interested in her. She was climbing out of a monster Bell 412, having gone through the usual show-and-tell maneuvers that the FBI expects when an important personage, especially a politician, is touring the Academy. Rudy supposed, since Lucy was the only woman on the Hostage Rescue Team, it was politically correct for the Attorney

General or whoever he was to see a young, good-looking woman at the stick.

Rudy stared at her as she shut down the formidable twin-engine machine and climbed out, wearing a dark blue Battle Dress Uniform and soft black ankle-high boots. Rudy was surprised by her fiery beauty as he watched the way she walked with confidence and grace and not a trace of masculinity. He began entertaining the possibility that what he had heard about her wasn't true. Her body intrigued him as she moved. She seemed to ripple like an exotic animal, a tiger, he thought as she walked straight to the Attorney General, or whoever it was on that show-and-tell day, and politely shook his hand.

Lucy is athletic but definitely feminine and very pleasing to touch. Rudy has learned not to love her too much. He knows when to back away.

In minutes, the helicopter is up to full power, avionics and headsets on, the loud, fast beating of blades the music she and Rudy dance to and adore. He feels Lucy's spirits joyfully lift as the helicopter does.

"We're on the go," she says into her mike. "Hudson traffic, helicopter four-zero-seven Tango, Lima, Papa is southbound at thirty-fourth."

Hovering is what she likes most, and she can hold the chopper perfectly still, even in a stiff tailwind. Nosing around to the water, she pulls in power and takes off.

90

Scarpetta caught the earliest flight to Houston's George Bush Intercontinental Airport and, factoring in the hour time difference, landed at 10:15 a.m.

From there, the drive almost due north to Livingston was a tense hour and forty minutes. She had no interest in renting a car and finding her way to the prison. That was a wise decision. Although she hasn't counted, the route has taken numerous turns, the longest stretch of US-59 that rolls on forever. Scarpetta's thoughts are clipped, as if she is a new recruit taking orders.

She is in her most dispassionate mode, a persona she steps into when she testifies in court as defense attorneys poise themselves like carnivores, waiting for the first scent of her blood. Rarely is she wounded. Never fatally. Deep inside the refuge of her analytical mind, she has remained silent throughout the trip. She hasn't spoken to the driver, except to give her instructions. The driver is the sort who wants to be chatty, and Scarpetta told her as she was climbing into the black Lincoln at the beginning of the trip that she didn't want to talk. She had work to do.

"You got it," said the woman, who is dressed in a black livery suit that includes a cap and tie.

"You can take your cap off," Scarpetta told her.

"Why, thank you," the driver said with relief, taking it off immediately. "I can't tell you how much I hate this thing, but most of my passengers want me to look like a proper chauffeur."

"I'd rather you didn't," Scarpetta said.

The prison looms ahead, a modern fortress that looks like a monstrous freighter built of concrete with a hatchmark of windows running below the flat roof, where two workmen are busy talking and gesturing and looking around. Surrounding the expansive grass grounds are thick coils of razorwire that shine like fine sterling in the sun. Guards high up in their towers scan with binoculars.

"Schweeeew," the driver mutters. "I have to admit this makes me a little bit nervous."

"You'll be fine," Scarpetta assures her. "They'll show you where to park, and you'll stay in the car. I don't recommend you walk around at all."

"What if I have to use the ladies' room?" she worries, slowing at a guard booth that signals the beginning of maximum security and perhaps the most dreaded task Scarpetta has ever undertaken.

"Then I guess you'll have to ask someone," she absently replies, rolling her window down and handing a uniformed guard her driver's license and medical examiner's credentials, a bright brass shield and identification card inside a black wallet.

When she left her position in Richmond, she was as bad as Marino. She never turned in her badge. No one thought to ask for it. Or maybe no one dared. She may not literally be Chief anymore, but what Lucy said last night is right. No one can strip Scarpetta of who she is and how she performs in the work she still loves. Scarpetta knows how good she is, even if she would never say it.

"Who are you here to see?" the guard asks her, returning her license and credentials.

"Jean-Baptiste Chandonne." His name almost chokes her.

The guard is rather casual, considering his environment and responsibility. Based on his demeanor and age, he's probably been working in the prison system for a long time and scarcely notices the foreboding world he enters at the beginning of every shift. He steps back inside his booth and scans a list.

"Ma'am," he says, reemerging from his booth and pointing toward the glass front of the prison, "just drive up there and someone will tell you where to park. The PIO will meet you outside."

A Texas flag seems to wave Scarpetta on. The sky is blue glass, the temperature reminding her of autumn. Birds are having a conversation, nature going on, impervious to evil.

373

91

Life in Pod A does not change.

Condemned inmates come and go, and old names belong to silence. After days, or maybe weeks—Jean-Baptiste often loses track of time—the new ones who come in to await their deaths are the names associated with the cells formerly occupied by the old names of the others who awaited their deaths. Pod A, Cell 25 is Beast, who will be moved to a different holding cell in several hours. Pod A, Cell 30 is Jean-Baptiste. Pod A, Cell 31, directly to Jean-Baptiste's right, is Moth—called thus because the necrophiliac murderer who stirs after lights-out has trembling hands that flutter, and his skin is almost gray. He likes to sleep on the floor, and his prison-issue clothing is always covered with gray dust—like dust on the wings of a moth.

Jean-Baptiste shaves the tops of his hands, long swirls of hair drifting into the stainless-steel sink.

"All right, Hair Ball." Eyes peer through the tiny window in his door. "Your fifteen minutes are almost up. Two more minutes and I take the razor back."

"*Certainement.*" He lathers his other hand with cheap-smelling soap and resumes shaving, careful of his knuckles.

The tufts in his ears are tricky, but he manages.

"Time's up."

Jean-Baptiste carefully rinses the razor.

"You shaved." Moth speaks very quietly, so quietly that the other inmates rarely hear a word he says.

"*Oui, mon ami.* I look quite beautiful."

The crank key that looks like a crowbar bangs into a slot at the bottom of the door, and the drawer slides out. The officer backs up, out of reach of pale, hairless fingers depositing the blue plastic razor.

92

Moth sits and rolls a basketball against the wall precisely, so that it always rolls in a straight line back to him.

He is worthless, so feeble that his only pleasure in killing was having sex with dead flesh. Dead flesh has no energy, the blood no longer magnetic. Jean-Baptiste had a very effective method when he released his chosen ones to the ecstasy. A person with severe head injuries can live for a while, long enough for Jean-Baptiste to bite and suck living flesh and blood, thus recharging his magnetism.

"It is a lovely day, isn't it?" Moth's quiet comment drifts into Jean-Baptiste's cell, because he has the ears to hear the barely audible voice. "No clouds, but later there will be a few very high ones that will move south by late afternoon."

Moth has a radio and obsessively listens to the weather band.

"I see Miss Gittleman has a new car, a cute little silver BMW Roadster."

Through a slitted window in each cell, a death-row inmate has a view of the parking lot behind the prison, and for lack of anything else to look at from their second-floor solitary confinements, men stare out for the better part of the day. In a sense, this is an act of intimidation. Moth's mentioning Miss Gittleman's BMW is the best threat he can muster. Officers most likely will pass this on to other officers, who will pass on to Miss Gittleman, the young and very pretty assistant public information officer, that inmates appreciate her new car. No prison employee is eager for any details of their personal life to be known by offenders so vile that they deserve to die.

Jean-Baptiste is perhaps the only inmate who rarely looks out the slit that is supposed to be a window. After memorizing every vehicle, their colors, makes, models and even certain plate numbers and precisely what their drivers look like, he found no purpose in looking out at a blank blue or stormy sky. Getting up from the toilet without bothering to pull up his pants, he looks out his high window, Moth's comment having made him curious. He spots the BMW, then sits back down on the toilet, thinking.

He ponders the letter he sent the beautiful Scarpetta. He believes it has changed everything and fantasizes about her reading it and succumbing to his will.

Today, Beast will be allowed four hours to visit with clergy and family. He will leave for the short ride to Huntsville, to the Death House. At 6 p.m., he will die.

This also changes things.

A folded piece of paper quietly slips beneath the right corner of Jean-Baptiste's door. He rips off toilet paper and, again without bothering to pull up his pants, picks up the note and returns to the toilet.

Beast's cell is five down from Jean-Baptiste's, on the left, and he can always tell when a note slid from cell to cell to him is from

Beast. The folded paper takes on a certain texture of scraped gray, and the inside is smudged, the paper fiber of the creases weakened by repeated opening and folding, as each inmate along the way reads the note, a few of the men adding their own comments.

Jean-Baptiste crouches on his stainless-steel toilet, the long hair on his back matted with sweat that has turned his white shirt translucent. He is always hot when he is magnetized, and he is in a chronic state of magnetism as his electricity circulates through the metal of his confinement and races to the iron in his blood, and flows out again to complete another circuit, endlessly, endlessly, endlessly.

"Today," the semiliterate Beast wrote in pencil, "wont you be glad when they drive me away. You will miss me? May be not."

For once, Beast isn't insulting, although the kite reads like a taunt to other inmates, of this Jean-Baptiste is certain.

He writes back, "You don't have to miss me, *mon ami*."

Beast will know Jean-Baptiste's meaning, although he will know nothing more about what Jean-Baptiste will do to save Beast from his appointment with death. Footsteps ring on metal as officers walk by. He tears Beast's note into small pieces and stuffs them into his mouth.

93

She must have parked and been approached by the killer before she even took her keys out of the ignition.

Nic assumes the purse and wallet may have been tossed in the parking lot, and after two days, certainly someone would have picked them up. Unfortunately, finders-keepers appears to have prevailed. As much news coverage as Katherine Bruce's abduction is getting, whoever found her purse and wallet sure as hell knows that what he or she has is evidence. Some sniveling worm out there who lives according to situational ethics is not going to call the police now and basically admit that he or she intended to keep the purse or wallet or both until discovering they belonged to a murdered woman, assuming that Katherine has been murdered.

If she hasn't been yet, she will be soon.

Then it occurs to Nic with a jolt that if the purse and wallet were turned in, whoever had them would have called the mighty Baton Rouge task force, which, of course, would find some lame-brain reason for not releasing the information to the press, and certainly not to other brothers and sisters of the badge. Nic can't stop thinking about Wal-Mart and that she herself was at that very location within hours, perhaps, of when Katherine Bruce was abducted, driven away, probably to the same secret place the killer has taken all his victims.

Nic is haunted by the possibility, not a strong one, that Katherine Bruce might have been inside the Wal-Mart while Nic was there trolling, as she has done at all hours since returning from Knoxville.

Photographs of the pretty blonde victim constantly flash on the TV news and are in every newspaper Nic has picked up. She has no recollection of noticing anyone who looked even remotely similar to her while she was picking out a needlepoint pattern, when she doesn't know how to do needlepoint, and showing interest in gaudy lingerie she would never wear.

For some reason, the odd woman who fell down in the parking lot because of an injured knee drifts through Nic's mind every now and then. Something about that woman bothers her.

94

At high tide, small boats can enter creeks and bayous that are usually not possible to enter and almost never ventured into by rational people.

Darren Citron is known to rev up his old Bay Runner and skim the shallow water and just make it over the mudbar into the mouth of whatever waterway he intends to challenge on any given day. Right now, the tide's a little lower than he'd like, but he speeds full-throttle in Blind River and almost gets caught in the silt, which can be up to six feet deep. The muck can suck one's shoes off, and although Darren can usually manage to push his boat out, he doesn't like wading in water that's full of cotton-mouths.

A local boy, he is eighteen years old, perpetually tanned the hue of a burnt peanut, and he lives to fish and find new spots for hunting gators. Because of his latter preoccupation, Darren is not particularly admired. If he goes after big ones that can bring a good price for their hides, meat and heads, it requires a strong rope, a huge steel hook and, of course, bait. The higher the bait dangles over the water, the longer the gator has to be to reach it. The best bait is dogs. Darren gets them from shelters all over the area, his sweet demeanor fooling people. He does what he has to, rationalizing to himself that the animals will be put to sleep anyway. When he's gator hunting, he thinks about the gator, not the bait or how he got it. Gators bite at night, especially if Darren sits very still in his boat and plays a tape recording of dogs whining. He's skilled at disassociating from the bait, only thinking about the huge gator that's going to come out of the water, snap its jaws together and get caught on the hook. Then he moves in quickly and humanely shoots the reptile in the head with a .22 rifle.

He cruises through a waterway lined with lily pads and saw grass, dappled with shadows from cypress dressed in Spanish moss, their roots ropy. Gators go in and out of the water, especially if the female has laid eggs. Their long tails leave trails, and when Darren sees a particular spot with a lot of trails, he marks it on his mental map and comes back there after dark, if the weather and tides are right.

The water is carpeted in duck seed blooms, and a blue heron lifts off up ahead, unhappy about the intrusion of man and motor. Darren scans for trails. He is followed by iridescent dragonflies. Gator eyes remind him of tiny tunnels side by side, just above the surface of the water, before they catch him looking back. Around a bend, he spots a myriad of trails and a yellow nylon rope hanging from a tree. The bait on the huge steel hook is a human arm.

95

Today for the first time in more than five years, Benton speaks to Senator Frank Lord, both of them using pay phones.

It strikes Benton as almost comical, as he envisions the ever immaculately groomed and impeccably dressed Senator Lord driving from his Northern Virginia home, on his way to the Capitol, and pulling off at a gas station to use a pay phone. Benton orchestrated the conversation after receiving a very unexpected e-mail from the senator late last night.

Trouble, it read. *Tomorrow 7:15. Leave me a number.*

Benton e-mailed back the number of the pay phone he's using right now, having picked it out in advance last night. Always go for the simplest, most obvious plan, if possible. Certainly, it is beginning to seem that his meticulous and complicated ones are going awry in all directions.

He leans against a wall, watching his beat-up Cadillac, making sure no one goes near it or shows interest in him. Every alarm inside his head is hammering. Senator Lord is telling him about Scarpetta's letter from Chandonne, the one with the calligraphy.

"How did you find out about this?" Benton asks him.

"Jaime Berger called me last night. At home. Very concerned that Chandonne has set up a trap and Scarpetta's walking right into it. Berger wants my help, my intervention. People forget that I have my limitations. Well, my enemies don't forget it."

The senator wants to send legions of federal agents to Baton Rouge, but not even he can bend the law. The Baton Rouge Task Force has to invite the FBI into the investigation, and for all practical purposes to take it over. In these serial abductions—or murders, because that's what they are—there is an insurmountable jurisdictional problem with the feds storming in on their own. No federal laws have been broken.

"Damn incompetence," Senator Lord says. "Damn ignorant fools down there."

"It's close," Benton says into the phone. "The letter means the situation is very close to a possible conclusion. Not the way I wanted it. This is bad, very bad. I'm not worried about me."

"It can be handled?"

"I'm the only one who knows how. It will require exposure."

A long pause, then Senator Lord acquiesces. "Yes, I believe it will. But once that happens, there's no going back. We can't go through this again. Do you really . . . ?"

"I have to. The letter changes things dramatically, and you know how she is. He is luring her there."

"She's there now."

"Baton Rouge?" Benton is frightened.

"Texas. I mean Texas."

"Christ. Not good, either. No, no, no. The letter. This one's real. Texas is no longer safe for her."

For a moment he contemplates Scarpetta visiting Chandonne. Originally, he had tactical and personal reasons for wanting her to do this. But if he's honest with himself, he never really thought she would. He really didn't, despite his best efforts. Now she shouldn't be there. *Christ.*

"She's there even as we speak," Senator Lord reminds him.

"Frank, he's going to make a run for it."

"I don't see how. Not out of that place. No matter how clever he is. I'll alert them immediately."

"He's more than clever. The point is this: If he's luring her to Baton Rouge, then he must plan to be there. *I know him. I know her.* She'll head to Baton Rouge as soon as she leaves Texas. Unless he intercepts her first, in Texas, if he can work that fast. Hopefully he can't. But either way, she is in severe danger. Not just because of him, but his allies. They must be in Baton Rouge. His brother must be there. The killings now make sense. He's doing them. She's probably helping him. Since she hasn't been caught yet, my guess is he and Bev Kiffin are together, hiding."

"Isn't abducting women taking a tremendous risk for fugitives of their notoriety?"

"He's bored," Benton simply says.

96

Officers in the Polunsky Unit wear gray uniforms and black baseball caps.

Handcuffs dangle from the belts of the two officers walking Jean-Baptiste through a series of heavy doors slamming shut so loudly, they sound like large-caliber pistol fire inside a steel room. Every explosion is an empowerment for Jean-Baptiste as he walks freely, only his wrists shackled. All around him, tons of steel magnetize him into solar flares. With each step, the power grows stronger.

"Can't understand why anybody would want to visit you," one of the officers says to him. "This is a first, huh?"

His name is Phillip Wilson. He drives a red Mustang with the vanity tag KEYPR.

KEEPER. Jean-Baptiste figured that out the first day he was here.

He says nothing to the officers as he moves through another door in a wave of searing heat.

"Not even one visitor?" replies the second officer, Ron Abrams, white, slender, with thinning brown hair. "Pretty pitiful, aren't you, Monsieur Chandonne," he mockingly says.

The turnover rate among corrections officers is very high. Officer Abrams is new, and Jean-Baptiste senses that he wants to walk the infamous Wolfman out to the visitation area. New officers are always curious about Jean-Baptiste. Then they get used to him and then are disgusted. Moth says Officer Abrams drives a black Toyota SUV. Moth knows every car in the parking lot, just as he always knows the latest weather update.

The back of the tiny visitation booth is a heavy wire mesh painted white. Officer Wilson unlocks it and takes off Jean-Baptiste's cuffs and shuts him inside the booth, which has a chair, a shelf and a black phone attached to a metal cable.

"I'd like a Pepsi and the chocolate cupcakes, please," Jean-Baptiste says through the screen.

"You got money?"

"I have no money," Jean-Baptiste quietly replies.

"Okay. This time I do you a favor, since you've never had a visitor before and the lady coming in would be stupid to buy you anything, asshole." It is Officer Abrams who speaks so crudely.

Through the glass, Jean-Baptiste scans the sparkling-clean, spacious room, believing he doesn't need eyes to see the vending machines and everything in them, and the three visitors talking on phones to three other death-row inmates.

She is not here.

Jean-Baptiste's electrical current spikes with anger.

97

As often happens when a situation is urgent, the best efforts are foiled by mundaneness.

Senator Lord has never been the sort to hesitate in making phone calls himself. He has no egotistical insecurities and finds it is quicker to handle a matter than to explain it to someone else. The instant he hangs up at the pay phone, he returns to his car and drives north, talking on his hands-free to his chief counsel.

"Jeff, I need the number of the warden at Polunsky. Now."

Writing notes while driving in rush hour on I-95 is a special feat the senator was forced to learn years ago.

He enters a bad cell and can't hear his chief counsel.

Repeatedly calling him back, the senator gets no signal. When he does get through, he is greeted by voicemail, because Jeff is trying to call him back, too.

"Get off the phone!" the senator exclaims to no one who can hear him.

Twenty minutes later, a secretary is still trying to track down the warden.

Senator Lord senses—and this has happened before—that she isn't sure she believes the person on the other line is really Senator Frank Lord, one of the most powerful and visible politicians in the country. Usually, important people let less important people schedule appointments and make telephone calls.

Senator Lord concentrates on creeping traffic and angry drivers, and has been on hold for minutes. No one with intelligence or, better yet, a certainty of who she is talking to would dare to put him on hold. This is his reward for humility and taking care of himself efficiently, including picking up his own dry cleaning, stopping at the grocery store and even making his own restaurant reservations, despite recurring problems with maître d's writing nothing down, certain the call is a prank or someone trying to trick him into giving him the best table.

"I'm sorry." The secretary finally returns. "I can't seem to locate him. He's very busy this morning because there's an execution tonight. Can I take a message?"

"What is your name?"

"Jodi."

"No, Jodi, you can't take a message. This is an emergency."

"Well," she hesitates, "caller ID doesn't show you're calling from Washington. I can't just yank him out of an important meeting or whatever and then find out it's not really you."

"I don't have time for this. Find him. Or, for God's sake, does the man have an assistant?"

Again, he enters a bad cell and it takes fifteen minutes before he can get through to the secretary again. She has left her desk. Another young woman answers the phone and he loses her, too.

98

"I'm sick of this," Nic tells her father.

She drove to the Baton Rouge Police Department's old brick building and never got above the first-floor lobby. When she said she had possible evidence about the cases, a plainclothes detective eventually appeared and just stared at the quarters in the envelope. He looked at Polaroid photographs of them on the Wal-Mart parking lot and indifferently listened to Nic's rendition and theory while he continued to glance at his watch. She receipted the coins to him, and was certain when he returned to the so-called War Room, she became the joke of the day.

"We're all working the same cases, and those assholes won't talk to me. I'm sorry." Sometimes Nic forgets how much her father abhors swearing. "Maybe they know something that could help us with our cases in Zachary. But oh, no. I am welcome to hand over anything I know, but it doesn't work the same way."

"You look mighty tired, Nic," he says as they eat eggs scrambled with cheese and spicy sausage patties.

Buddy is off in make-believe land with his toys and the television.

"How 'bout some more grits?" her father asks.

"I can't. But you do make the best grits I've ever had."

"You always say that."

"It's always true."

"Be careful. Those boys in Baton Rouge don't like people like you. Especially women like you."

"They don't even know me."

"They don't need to know you to hate your guts. They want credit. Now, when I was coming along, credit meant you could buy your groceries at the nearby general store and pay later when you were able. No one went hungry. These days, credit means plain selfishness. Those good ol' boys in Baton Rouge want credit, credit, credit."

"Tell me about it." Nic butters another biscuit. "Every time you cook, I eat too much."

"People who want credit will lie, cheat and steal," her father reminds her.

"While women keep dying." Nic loses her appetite and sets the biscuit back on her plate. "Who's worse? The man doing it or these men who want credit and don't care about the victims or anything else?"

"Two wrongs never make a right, Nic," he says. "I'm glad you don't work down there. I'd be worried about your safety a lot more than I am now. And not because of this madman on the loose, but because of who your colleagues would be."

She looks around at the simple kitchen of her childhood. Nothing in the house has been upgraded or remodeled since her mother died. The stove is electric, white with four burners. The refrigerator is white; so are the countertops. Her mother had a

French country theme in mind, was going to find old furniture and blue-and-white curtains, maybe some interesting tiles for the walls. But she never got a chance. So the kitchen is white, just plain white. If any of the appliances quit for good, she's confident her father would refuse to get rid of them. He'd eat takeout food every night, if necessary. It tortures Nic that her father can't disengage from the past. Silent grieving and anger hold him hostage.

Nic pushes back her chair. She kisses the top of her father's head, and her eyes fill with tears.

"I love you, Papa. Take good care of Buddy. I promise one of these days I'll be a good mother."

"You're a good enough mother." He looks at her from his seat at the table as he idly picks at eggs. "It's not how much time but what that time's like."

Nic thinks of her mother. Her time was short, but every minute of it was good. That's the way it seems now.

"Now you're crying," her father says. "You going to tell me what on Earth is going on with you, Nic?"

"I don't know, I don't know. I'll be minding my own business and suddenly burst into tears. I think it's about Mama, like I told you. All that's going on down here has reminded me, or just opened some trapdoor in my mind. A door I didn't even know was there that's leading into a dark place I'm scared to death of, Papa. Please turn on the light for me. Please."

He slowly gets up from the table, knowing what she means. He sighs.

"Don't do this to yourself, Nic," he grimly says. "I already know what it did to me. I stopped my life. You know I did. When I came home that early evening and saw . . ." He clears his throat, fighting back tears. "I felt something move inside me, as if I pulled a muscle in my heart. Why would you want those images?"

"Because they're the truth. And maybe the images I have are worse because I can't see the real ones."

He nods and sighs again. "Go up in the attic. Under all those rugs piled in a corner, there's a small blue suitcase. Belonged to her. She got it with Green Stamps."

"I remember," Nic whispers, envisioning her mother carrying the blue suitcase out the door one day when she was headed to Nashville to visit her aunt after she'd had eye surgery.

"The lock code was never set because she said she'd never remember it. Zero-zero-zero, just like brand new." He clears his throat again, staring off. "What you want's in there. Some things I'm not supposed to have, but I was like you. Just had to know. And I taught the daughter of the police chief, so I got a few favors, I'm ashamed to admit it. Because I promised the chief I'd give her a better grade than she deserved and a recommendation for college that was just one big fat lie.

"My punishment is I got what I asked for," he continues. "Just don't bring that stuff down here. I don't ever want to see it again."

99

Assistant PIO Jayne Gittleman apologizes profusely for making Scarpetta wait.

For fifteen minutes, Scarpetta has stood outside the front door, right below the sign that reads *Allan B. Polunsky Unit,* the bright sun making her perspire. She feels dirty and disheveled from travel. Her patience is thin, despite her resolve to contain her emotions completely. More than anything right now, she wants to get this over with at last, at long last.

"The media's calling nonstop because we've got an execution tonight," Miss Gittleman explains.

She hands Scarpetta a visitor's tag, which she clamps to the lapel of the same suit she's worn on different planes since she left Florida. The pantsuit is black, and at least she ironed it inside her room at New York's Melrose Hotel last night after leaving her niece. Lucy does not know where Scarpetta is right now. If Scarpetta had mentioned it, Lucy would have tried to stop her or insisted on going with her. Taking a chance, Scarpetta headed west without an appointment, having no choice but to call the Polunsky Unit when she landed in Houston. Her confidence that Chandonne would see her was rewarded by the additional unpleasantry of learning she is on his visitors list. At least his sick joke proved useful. She is here. And perhaps the less time he has to think about her seeing him, the better.

Officers check Scarpetta's identification, and Miss Gittleman leads her through a series of loud steel doors, then through a garden with picnic tables under umbrellas, obviously meant for staff. She is cleared through five electronically locking doors, the walk far too short to suit her as she reaches the unnerving conclusion that she should not have come here. Chandonne is manipulating her, and she is going to regret this visit because it gives him what he wants and makes a fool of her.

Inside the visitors lobby, her shoes seem loud, and she is acutely aware of her appearance as she crosses the shiny tile floor. A strong believer in the psychology of dress and demeanor, her entrance is out of character and embarrassing. She would have preferred to be perfectly groomed in a power suit, probably pinstripe, and perhaps a white shirt with cufflinks. Possibly, she considers, power dressing wouldn't have sent the best message to this bastard who tried to kill her, but it would have made her feel less vulnerable to him.

Her knees weaken at the sight of Jean-Baptiste Chandonne sitting inside Booth 2. Clean-shaven, including his hands and head, he relaxes behind glass, drinking a Pepsi and eating a chocolate cupcake, pretending not to notice her.

She openly stares at him, refusing to play the game he has already begun, and it amazes her to see him shaven and dressed in white. He is ugly but almost looks normal without his long swirls of baby-fine hair that hung from him in a long, filthy fringe last time she saw him. He sips his Pepsi and licks his fingers as Scarpetta sits across from him and picks up the black phone.

His asymmetrical eyes drift, and he gives her his barracuda smile, his skin as pale as parchment. She notices his highly defined, muscular arms and that he has torn the sleeves off his white shirt, and then she sees that long, horrible hair. It peeks out from the armholes and the opening at his neck. Apparently, he has shaven only those areas of his body that are uncovered.

"How nice," she says coldly into the phone. "You cleaned up for me."

"But of course. It is lovely for you to come. I knew you would." His filmy eyes don't seem to focus when they briefly turn her way.

"Did you shave yourself?"

"Yes. Today. Just for you."

"Rather hard to do if you can't see," she remarks in a steady, strong voice.

"I don't need my eyes to see." He touches his tongue to a small, sharp tooth and reaches for his Pepsi. "What did you think about my letter?"

"What did you want me to think about it?"

"That I am an artist, of course."

"Did you learn your penmanship here in prison?"

"I have always been able to write in a beautiful hand. When my parents kept me locked in the basement as an innocent *petit* boy, I had endless hours to develop many talents."

"Who mailed the letter for you?" Scarpetta dominates with her questions.

"My dear dead lawyer." He clucks his tongue. "I honestly do not know why he committed suicide. But perhaps it is a good thing. He was worthless, you know. It runs in his bloodline."

Scarpetta bends down and takes a notepad and pen out of her

pocketbook. "You told me you have information for me. That's why I'm here. If you simply want to chat, I'm leaving right now. I have no interest in *visiting* with you."

"The other part of the bargain, Madame Scarpetta," he says as his crooked eyes float, "is my execution. Will you?"

"I have no problem with that."

He smiles and seems delighted.

"Tell me." He rests his chin on his hand. "What is it like?"

"Painless. An IV of sodium thiopental, which is the sedative. And pancuronium bromide, a muscle relaxant. Potassium chloride stops the heart." She clinically describes as he listens, enraptured. "Fairly inexpensive drugs, ironically and appropriately, considering their purpose. Death occurs in several minutes."

"And I will not suffer when you do this to me?"

"You will never suffer the way you've made others suffer. You'll instantly go to sleep."

"Then you promise you will be my doctor in the end?" He begins stroking the can of Pepsi, the hideous long nail on his right thumb caked with what looks like chocolate, probably from his cupcakes.

"I will do as you wish if you are willing to help the police. What is the information?"

He gives her names and locations, none of which mean anything to her. She fills twenty pages in her notepad, becoming increasingly suspicious that he is toying with her. The information is meaningless. Maybe.

At a pause, when he decides to take his time eating a cupcake, she says, "Where are your brother and Bev Kiffin?"

He wipes his hands and mouth on his shirt, sinewy muscles jumping with his every motion. Chandonne is strong and frighteningly fast. Repressing images is becoming increasingly difficult. She tries to shut off memories of that night in her house, when this very man who is separated from her only by glass tried to beat her to death. Then Jay Talley's face is there, when he fooled her, and later he came after her, too. That the fraternal twin brothers share a murderous obsession for her is incomprehensible. She doesn't quite believe it, and it surprises her that as she stares at Jean-Baptiste Chandonne, all she feels is a determination to forget past horrors. He is harmless in this place. In days, he will be dead.

She will not come back to administer the lethal injection. Lying to him doesn't bother her in the least.

He says nothing about Jay Talley and Bev Kiffin.

Instead, he tells her, "Rocco has a small château in Baton Rouge. It is quaint, in a restored neighborhood where many homosexuals live. Near downtown. I have stayed there many times."

"Have you ever heard of a Baton Rouge woman named Charlotte Dard?"

"Of course. Not beautiful enough for my brother."

"Did Rocco Caggiano murder her?"

"No." Chandonne sighs as if he is getting bored. "As I said, and you must listen to me more closely. She was not beautiful enough for my brother. The Red Stick." He subjects her to his hideous open-mouthed grin as his eyes continue to drift. "Did you know that everything you are is visible in your hands?"

Her hands are in her lap, holding the notepad and the pen. He talks about her hands as if he can see them, yet his eyes float as if he is blind.

Malingerer.

"In the hands of all the sons of men God places marks, that all the sons of men may know their own works. Every working of the mind leaves marks on the hand, forms the hand, which is the measure of intelligence and creativity."

She listens, wondering if he is on his way to an important point.

"In France, you find mostly artistic hands. Like mine." He holds up a shaved hand, his long, tapered fingers splayed. "And like yours, Madame Scarpetta. You have the elegant hands of an artist. And now you know why I do not touch the hands. *The Psychonomy of the Hand*, or *The Hand an Index of Mental Development*. Monsieur Richard Beamish. A very good book with many tracings of living hands, if you can find it, but alas, it was written in 1865 and not in your local library. There are two tracings that are you. The square hand, elegant but strong. And the artist's hand, elastic and flexible, again elegant. But more associated with an impulsive personality."

She does not comment.

"Impulsive. Here you are without notice. Suddenly here. A rather nervous sort. But sanguine."

He savors the word *sanguine*, which in medieval medicine meant the blood was the most dominant of the bodily humors. Sanguine people are supposed to be optimistic and cheerful. She is neither at the moment.

"You say you don't touch the hands. An explanation for why you didn't bite the hands of the women you slaughtered," she says blandly.

"The hands are the mind and the soul. I would not harm a manifestation of what I am releasing with my chosen ones. I only lick the hands."

Now he is moving in to disgust and degrade her, but she isn't finished with him yet.

"You didn't bite the bottoms of their feet, either," she reminds him.

He shrugs, fiddling with the can of Pepsi, which sounded empty the last time he set it down. "Feet are of no interest to me."

"Where are Jay Talley and Bev Kiffin?" she asks again.

"I am getting tired."

"Why would you protect your brother after the way he has treated you all of your life?"

"I am my brother," he weirdly says. "So your finding me makes it unnecessary for you to find him. Now, I am very tired."

Jean-Baptiste Chandonne begins rubbing his stomach and wincing as his eyes wander. "I think I am getting sick."

"You have nothing more to tell me? If not, I'm leaving."

"I am blind."

"You are a malingerer," Scarpetta replies.

"You took my physical eyesight, but not before I *saw* you." He touches his tongue to his pointed teeth. "Remember your lovely home with the shower in the garage? When you returned from a crime scene at the Richmond port, you went into that garage to change and disinfect, and you showered in there."

Anger and humiliation tighten her body. She had been examining a putrid, decomposing body inside a cargo container, and, yes, she went through her routine: taking off her protective coveralls and boots and tying them inside a heavy plastic bag that went in the trunk; then she drove home. Once inside her garage, which certainly was not a typical garage, she threw her scene clothes into an industrial-size stainless-steel sink. She stripped and stepped into the shower, because she will not track death into her house.

"The small windows in your garage door. Very much like the small window in my cell," he goes on. "I saw you."

Those unfocused eyes and that fishlike smile again.

His tongue is bleeding.

Scarpetta's hands are cold, her feet getting numb. The hair rises on her arms and the back of her neck.

"*Naked.*" He savors the word, sucking his tongue. "*I watched you undress. I saw you naked.* Such a joy, like a fine wine. You were Burgundy then, round and firm, complicated and to be drunk, not sipped. Now you are a Bordeaux, because when you speak, you are heavier, you see. Not physically, I don't think. I would have to see you naked to make that determination." He presses a hand against the glass, a hand that has battered human beings to splinters and mush. "A red wine, of course. You are always . . ."

"That's enough!" Scarpetta yells as her rage crashes out of its camouflage like a wild boar. "Shut up, you worthless piece of shit." She leans closer to the glass. "I'm not going to listen to your masturbatory talk. It doesn't *bother* me. *I don't care if you saw me naked.* Do you think it intimidates me to hear you babble on about your voyeurism and what you think of my body? Do you think I care if I blinded you when you were swinging that fucking hammer at me?

"You know what the best part is, Jean-Baptiste Chandonne? You're in here *because of me.* So who won? And, no, I won't be back here to put you to death. A stranger will do that. Just as you were a stranger to those you killed."

Jean-Baptiste suddenly turns back to the wire-mesh screen behind him.

"Who's there?" he whispers.

Scarpetta hangs up the black phone. She walks away.

"*Who's there!*" he screams.

100

Jean-Baptiste is quite fond of handcuffs.

The thick steel bracelets around his wrists are rings of magnetic strength. Power surges through him. He is calm now, even conversational, as Officers Abrams and Wilson escort him along corridors, stopping at every steel door and holding up their ID name tags and showing their faces through the glass windows. The officer on the other side releases the electronic lock, and the journey continues.

"She was very upsetting to me," he says in his soft voice. "I regret my outburst. She blinded me, you know, and will not say she is sorry."

"I don't know why she even came to see a dirtbag like you," Officer Abrams comments. "If anybody should be upset, it's her, after what you tried to do. I've read about it, know all about your worthless life."

Officer Abrams is making the big mistake of giving in to his emotions. He hates Jean-Baptiste. He would like to hurt Jean-Baptiste.

"I am quiet inside now," Jean-Baptiste says meekly. "But I feel sick."

The officers stop at another door, and Abrams shows his ID in the glass window. They pass through. Jean-Baptiste averts his face, staring down at the floor and looking away from each officer who grants them entrance deeper inside the prison.

"I eat paper," Jean-Baptiste confesses. "It is a nervousness of mine, and I have been eating a lot of paper today."

"You writing yourself letters?" Abrams snidely goes on. "No wonder you spend so much time on the toilet."

"This is very true," Jean-Baptiste agrees. "But this time it is worse. I feel weak, and my stomach hurts."

"It will pass, so to speak."

"Don't worry. If it doesn't, we'll get you to the infirmary." This time it is Officer Wilson who speaks. "They'll give you an enema. You'll probably like that."

Inside Pod A, the voices of inmates bounce off concrete and steel. The noise is maddening, and the only way Jean-Baptiste has been able to endure it all these months is to decide when he will hear and when he won't. If this isn't enough, he leaves, usually for France. But today he will begin his travel to Baton Rouge and be reunited with his brother. He is his brother. This point confuses him.

When he is with his brother, Jean-Baptiste experiences his brother's existence, which is apart from the existence of Jean-Baptiste.

When the two of them are separated, Jean-Baptiste is his brother, and their roles in their conquests unite in one delicious act. Jean-Baptiste picks up the beautiful woman, and she desires him, possibly desperately. They have sex. Then he releases her to the ecstasy, and when it is finished and she is free, Jean-Baptiste is slippery with her blood, his tongue thrilled by the taste of her salty sweetness and the metallic hint of the iron he needs. Later, his teeth sometimes ache, and he is prone to massaging his gums and washing himself obsessively.

Jean-Baptiste's cell comes into view, and he glances inside the control booth at the woman who sits there today. She is a difficulty, but not an impossible one. No one can watch all activities at all times, and as Jean-Baptiste walks slowly, very slowly, and holds his stomach, she barely glances at him. The early afternoon belongs to Beast. Now he has his visitors in a special holding cell on the other end of the pod, a much more civilized place to visit relatives and the clergy. Because visitors have been in and out for the past three or four hours, the woman in the console must pay special attention in the event Beast acts out. Why not? He has nothing to lose.

The door of the holding cell is made of bars, allowing the officers to note Beast's every move inside, ensuring he will not harm the sad, kind people who have come to see him. Beast looks at Jean-Baptiste through the bars, just as the woman in the booth unlocks Jean-Baptiste's door and Officers Abrams and Wilson remove Jean-Baptiste's handcuffs.

Beast screams and grabs at the bars of his holding cell, yelling and cursing and jumping up and down. All attention sharply turns in his direction, and Jean-Baptiste grabs Officers Wilson and Abrams by their thick leather belts and jerks so hard that he lifts them off their feet. Their shocked yells blend with the jarring, deafening noise in the pod as Jean-Baptiste slams them into a concrete wall to the left of the massive door, which he shuts just enough so it doesn't lock. He blinds them with his long, filthy thumbnail, and his magnetized hands crush their windpipes. As their faces turn a dusky blue, their flailing quickly stills. Jean-Baptiste killed them with virtually no blood-shed, just little trickles from their eyes and a cut on Officer Wilson's head.

Jean-Baptiste removes Officer Abrams's uniform and puts it on. He does this in seconds, it seems, pulling the black cap low over his face and slipping on the dead man's glasses. He walks out of the cell and then shuts the door, just one more loud metal clang as Beast struggles with officers far away and gets a faceful of pepper spray, which only makes him scream and resist more, this time sincerely.

One door after another, Jean-Baptiste passes through, holding up Officer Abrams's identification tag. So sure is he of success, he is completely at ease, even seems a little preoccupied, as officers click him through. Jean-Baptiste's feet are not on the ground, but in the air as he easily walks out of the prison, a free man, and digs Officer Abrams's car keys out of a pocket.

101

Inside the George Bush Intercontinental Airport, Scarpetta stands near a wall, out of traffic.

She sips black coffee, knowing it's the last thing she needs. Her appetite has abandoned her, and when she bought a hamburger less than an hour ago, she couldn't swallow the first bite. Caffeine makes her hands shake. A hit of Scotch would calm her down, but she won't dare, and the reprieve would only be temporary. Of all times, she needs to think clearly now, to somehow handle her stress without self-destructive assistance.

Please answer your phone, she silently begs.

Three rings and, "Yeah."

Marino is driving his loud truck.

"Thank God!" she exclaims, turning her back to passengers walking with purpose or running to their gates. "Where in God's name have you been? I've been trying to reach you for days. I'm so sorry about Rocco . . ."

For Marino's sake, she is.

"I don't want to talk about it," he replies, subdued and more unhappy than usual. "Where I've been is hell, if you want to know. Maybe broke my all-time record for drinking bourbon and beer and not answering the goddamn phone."

"Oh, no. Another fight with Trixie. I told you what I think of . . ."

"I don't want to talk about it," he says again. "No offense, Doc."

"I'm in Houston," she tells him.

"Oh, shit."

"I did it. I took notes. Maybe none of it is true. But he did say that Rocco has a place in some gay district near downtown. In Baton Rouge. Chances are good the house isn't in his name. But neighbors must know about him. Could be a lot of evidence in that house."

"On another subject, in case you ain't been listening to the news, a female arm turned up in one of the creeks down there," he informs her. "They're doing DNA. Might be the last lady, Katherine Bruce. If it is, he's getting frenzied. The location the arm was found in was right off Blind River, which runs into Lake Maurepas. This guy's got to be familiar with the bayous and so on around there.

"Word is, the creek where the arm was isn't easily accessible. You'd have to know where it is, and almost nobody goes there. He was using the arm as gator bait, on a hook suspended from a rope."

"Or he was displaying it for the shock effect."

"I don't think that's it," he says.

"Whatever the case, you're right, he's escalating."

"Probably looking for another one even as we speak," he says.

"I'm headed to Baton Rouge," Scarpetta says.

"Yeah, I figured you would." Marino's voice is barely audible over the thrumming of his V-8 engine. "All to help out with some stupid drug overdose that happened eight years ago."

"This isn't just about a drug overdose, Marino. And you know it."

"Whatever it's about, you ain't safe down there, which is why I'm heading that way. Been driving since midnight and have to stop every other minute for coffee, then I have to stop again every other minute for a john."

She reluctantly tells him about Rocco's connection to the Charlotte Dard case, that he represented a pharmacist, an alleged suspect.

It is as if Marino doesn't hear her.

"I still got another ten hours on the road. And I gotta sleep at some point. So I probably won't catch up with you until tomorrow," he says.

102

Jay hears about his mutant brother on the radio.

He isn't sure how he feels about it as he sweats inside the fishing shack, his head bleary, his beauty not quite what it was even a week ago. He faults Bev for this, for everything. The more often she goes to the mainland, the more often the beer supply is replenished. Jay used to go weeks, a month, without a beer. Of late, the refrigerator is never empty.

Resisting alcohol has always been a challenge for him, ever since he began tasting fine wines as a boy in France, wines that are for the gods, his father would say. As a free man with complete mastery of his life, Jay sipped, savored and enjoyed in moderation. Now he is held hostage by cheap beer. Since Bev's last shopping expedition, he has been drinking a case a day.

"I guess I'm gonna have to make another run," Bev says, her eyes fixed on his Adam's apple bobbing as he tilts a can straight up and drains it.

"Yeah, you do that." Beer trickles down his bare chest.

"Whatever you want."

"Fuck you. It's all about what you want." He steps closer to her, his face menacing. "I'm falling apart!" he yells at her as he crumples a beer can and hurls it across the room. "It's your fucking fault! How could anybody be holed up in here with a stupid cow like you and not have to drink his fucking brains out!"

He grabs another beer out of the refrigerator and pushes the door shut with his bare foot. Bev doesn't react. She resists the smile she feels inside. Nothing gives her more satisfaction than to see Jay out of control, confused and headed for hurting himself. At last she has found a way to get him back, and now that his monster brother is on the loose, Jay's going to get worse and do something, so she needs to keep up her guard. Her self-defense is to keep him drunk. She doesn't know why she didn't think of it a long time ago, but beer was scarce when she went to the mainland no more than once every four or six weeks.

Suddenly, his demands became once a month, twice a month, and each time she returned with cases of beer and was amazed by how much more he was drinking. Until lately, she had never seen him drunk. When he is drunk, he doesn't resist her advances, and she wipes him down with a wet towel as he sinks into unconsciousness. The next morning, he has no memory of what she did, of how she satisfied her own pleasure in creative ways, since he couldn't perform and wouldn't have, were he sober.

She watches him fumble with the radio, searching through static for the latest news updates, well on his way to being drunk again. As long as she's known him, he's had no body fat, his perfectly defined body a constant source of envy and humiliation for her. This will change quickly. It is inevitable. He'll get fat around his waist, and his pride will suffocate beneath puffiness and flab no matter how many push-ups and sit-ups and crunches he does.

Maybe his perfect face won't look so good, either. Wouldn't that be something if he got so ugly—as ugly as he thinks she is—that she didn't want him anymore.

What was that story in the Bible? Samson—the mighty, beautiful Samson—gave in to what's-her-name, and she cut off his magical hair, or something. He lost all his strength.

"You stupid bitch!" Jay calls out. "Why are you just standing here, staring? My brother's on his way here if he isn't already here. He'd figure out where I'd be. He always has."

"I hear twins think like that, are real tuned-in to each other." The word *twin* is a deliberate scorpion sting. "He won't hurt you. He won't hurt me. You forget I've met him before. Why, I think he likes me because I can get beyond his looks."

"He doesn't like anybody." Jay gives up on the radio and angrily turns it off. "You don't live in the real world. I've got to find him first before he does something stupid, sees some woman and does her, leaving his damn bite marks all over her and smashing her head."

"You ever watched him do it?" she casually asks.

"Go get the boat ready, Bev."

She can't remember the last time he said her name. It is rich, like melted butter.

Then he spoils the moment by adding, "It's your goddamn fault about the arm. Wouldn't have happened if you'd brought me some pups."

Since she returned from her errand-running on the mainland, all he's done is complain that she didn't bring gator bait, not the least bit grateful for what she did bring him.

She stares at the empty mattress by the wall.

"You got plenty of gator bait," she said the other day. "More than you know what to do with these days."

411

She convinced him that baiting a gator hook with human flesh would work just fine, maybe even better. Jay could have his fun with a reptile that was longer than he was tall. He'd watch it thrashing until he got bored, then shoot it in the head. Outlaw hunter that he is, he never keeps what he catches. He'd cut the nylon rope and watch the reptile slide into the water. Then he'd motor back to the shack.

This time it didn't work that way. All he vaguely remembers is baiting the hook and stringing it up over the thick branch of a cypress tree, and then hearing another boat not far away, someone else hunting gators or maybe gigging frogs. Jay got the hell out of there, the hook still baited and dangling from the yellow nylon line. He should have cut it down. He made a big mistake but won't admit it. She suspects there was no other hunter out there. Jay was hearing things and he didn't think straight. Had he, it would have entered his mind that when another hunter found the caught gator, the bait either would have been found hanging out of its jaws or discovered in its guts when the gator was field-dressed.

"Do what I say, damn it. Get the boat ready," he orders her. "So I can deal with him."

"And how do you think you'll do that?" Bev asks calmly, placated and pleased by the craziness in front of her.

"I already told you. He'll find me," Jay says, his head beginning to throb. "He can't live without me. He can't even die without me."

103

Late afternoon, Scarpetta sits fifteen rows back, her legs cramped.

On her left, a young boy, blond and cute, with braces on his teeth, despondently draws Yu-Gi-Oh! cards from a stack on his tray. On her right, an obese man, probably in his fifties, drinks screwdrivers next to the window. He is constantly pushing up wire-rimmed glasses, the oversized curved frames that remind Scarpetta of Elvis. The obese man noisily flips through the *Wall Street Journal* and periodically glances at Scarpetta, obviously hoping to engage her in conversation. She continues to ignore him.

The boy draws another Yu-Gi-Oh! card and places it faceup on the tray.

"Who's winning?" Scarpetta asks him with a smile.

"I don't have anybody to duel with," the boy replies without looking up.

He is probably ten and is dressed in jeans, a faded Spiderman shirt and tennis shoes. "You have to have at least forty cards to play," he adds.

"I'm afraid I'm disqualified, then."

He picks up a card, a colorful one with a menacing ax on it. "See," he says, "this one's my favorite. The Axe of Despair. It's a good weapon for a monster to have, worth a thousand points." He picks another card, this one called the Axe Raider. "A very strong monster with the ax," he explains.

She studies the cards and shakes her head. "Sorry. Too complicated for me."

"You want to learn how to play?"

"I couldn't possibly," she replies. "What's your name?"

"Albert." He draws more cards from the deck. "Not Al," he lets her know. "Everybody thinks they can call me Al. But it's Albert."

"Nice to meet you, Albert." She does not offer her name.

Scarpetta's seatmate next to the window shifts around to face her, his shoulder pressing against her upper arm. "You don't sound like you're from Louisiana," he says.

"I'm not," she replies, leaning away from him, her sinuses assaulted by the overpowering cologne he must have splashed on when he uprooted her to go to the restroom.

"Don't have to tell me that. One or two spoken words and I know." He sips his vodka and orange juice. "Let me guess. Not Texas, either. You don't exactly look Mexican." He grins.

She resumes reading a structural biology article in *Science* magazine and wonders when the man will get the not-so-subtle message to leave her alone.

Rarely is Scarpetta accessible to strangers. If she is, then usually within two minutes they ask where she's going and why and wander into the restricted airspace of her profession. Telling them she's a doctor doesn't stop the quizzing, nor does saying that she's a lawyer, and should she let on that she is both, the consequences are bad enough. But to go on and explain that she is a forensic pathologist will mean the ruination of her trip.

Next, JonBenet Ramsey, O. J. Simpson and other mysterious cases and miscarriages of justice bubble up, and Scarpetta is trapped, buckled in her seat at an altitude of some thirty thousand feet. Then there are those strangers who don't care if she works but would rather see her later for dinner, or preferably for a drink in a hotel bar that might lead to a hotel room. They, like the tipsy slob sitting to her right, would rather stare at her body than hear about her résumé.

"Looks like a mighty complicated article you're reading," he says. "I'm guessing you're some sort of schoolteacher."

She doesn't respond.

"You see, I'm good at this." He squints his eyes and snaps his thick fingers, pointing at her face. "A biology teacher. Kids are worthless these days." He lifts his drink from his tray and rattles the ice in the plastic cup. "I don't know how you stand being around them, to tell the truth," he goes on, apparently having decided she is a teacher. "Plus, they don't think twice about bringing a gun to school."

She feels his puffy eyes on her as she continues to read.

"You got children? I got three. Teenagers, all of them. Obviously, I got married when I was twelve." He laughs, and flecks of spittle spray through the air. "How 'bout I get your card from you—in case I need a little tutoring while both of us are in Baton Rouge? You changing planes or going there? I live in the downtown area, the name's Weldon Winn—with two n's. Good name for a politician, huh? Guess you can imagine the campaign slogans if I ever run for office."

"When are we landing?" Albert asks her.

She looks at her watch and forces a smile as the name Weldon Winn shocks her. "Not too much longer," she says to the boy.

"Yes, ma'am, I can just imagine signs all over Louisiana: *It's Win-Win with Winn*. Get it? And *Go with the Winner*. Maybe I'll be lucky and have an opponent named *Miracle*. So *Winn Needs No Miracle*. How 'bout that? And when *Mr. Miracle* slides hopelessly downhill in the polls, he'll be called *Miracle-Whipped*." He winks again.

"I suppose there's no chance you might run against a *she*," Scarpetta comments without looking up from her magazine, pretending she doesn't have a clue that Weldon Winn is the Middle District U.S. Attorney for Louisiana that Nic Robillard complained about.

"Hell. No woman would take me on."

"I see. So what kind of politician are you?" Scarpetta finally asks him.

"One in spirit only at the moment, pretty lady. I'm the U.S. Attorney for Baton Rouge."

He pauses to let the importance of his position sink in, finishing his screwdriver and craning his neck in search of a flight attendant. Spotting one, he holds up an arm and snaps his fingers at her.

It can't be chance that Weldon Winn just happens to be sitting next to her on a plane when she just happens to be on her way to assist in a suspicious death that, according to Dr. Lanier, just happens to have captured Weldon Winn's interest, after she just happens to have left Jean-Baptiste Chandonne.

She tries to figure out how Winn would have had time to intercept her in Houston. Maybe he was already there. She has no

416

doubt whatsoever that he knows who she is and why she's on this flight.

"Got a getaway in New Orleans, quite a cozy little palace in the French Quarter. Maybe you can visit while you're in the area. I'll be around for just a couple nights, got business with the governor and a few of the boys. I'd be more than happy to give you a personal tour of the capital, show you the bullethole in a pillar where Huey Long was shot."

Scarpetta knows all about the notorious Huey Long's assassination. When the case was reopened in the early nineties, the results of the new investigation were discussed at various forensic science academy meetings. She's had enough of the pompous Weldon Winn.

"For your own edification," she tells him, "the so-called bullethole in the marble pillar was not caused by a bullet intended for Huey Long or anyone else, but more likely from an imperfection in the stone or a chiseled facsimile of a bullethole to attract tourism. As a matter of fact," she adds, as Winn's eyes flatten and his smile freezes, "since the assassination, the Capitol was restored, and that particular pillar's marble panels were removed and never returned to their original location. I'm surprised you spend a lot of time at the state capital and don't know all this," she concludes.

"My aunt's supposed to pick me up and if I'm late, what if she isn't there?" Albert asks Scarpetta, as if the two of them are traveling together.

He has lost interest in his trading cards, which are neatly stacked next to a blue cell phone. "Do you know what time it is?" he says.

"Almost six," Scarpetta says. "If you're sleepy, take a little nap and I'll let you know when we're about to land."

"I'm not sleepy."

She recalls noticing him at the gate in Houston, playing with his cards. Because he was sitting next to other adults, she assumed he was accompanied and that his family or whoever he is traveling with were seated elsewhere on the plane. It never occurred to her that any parent or relative would allow a young child to travel alone, especially these days.

"Now isn't that something. Not too many people are experts on bulletholes," the U.S. Attorney comments as the flight attendant serves him another drink.

"No, I don't suppose too many people are." Scarpetta's attention is focused on the lost little boy next to her. "You aren't by yourself, are you?" she asks him. "And why aren't you in school?"

"It's spring break. Uncle Walt dropped me off, and a lady at the airport met me. I'm not tired. Sometimes I get to stay up really late, watching movies. We get a thousand channels." He pauses and shrugs. "Well, maybe not that many, but a lot. Do you have any pets? I used to have a dog named Nestlé because it was brown like chocolate chips."

"Let's see," Scarpetta says. "I don't have a dog the color of chocolate, but I have an English bulldog who's white and brown with very big lower teeth. His name is Billy. Do you know what an English bulldog is?"

"Like a pit bull?"

"Not anything like a pit bull."

Weldon Winn butts into the conversation. "Might I ask where you're staying while you're in town?"

"Nestlé used to miss me when I wasn't home," Albert wistfully says.

"I'm sure he did," Scarpetta replies. "I think Billy misses me, too. But my secretary takes good care of him."

"Nestlé was a girl."

"What happened to her?"

"I don't know."

"My, my, if you aren't a mysterious little lady," the U.S. Attorney says, staring at her.

Scarpetta turns to him, catching a cold glint in his eyes.

She leans close to him and whispers in his ear, "I've had enough of your bullshit."

104

The Learjet 35 belongs to Homeland Security, and Benton is the only passenger on it.

Landing at Louisiana Air in Baton Rouge, he hurries down the steps, carrying a soft-sided bag, not looking at all like the Benton his people once knew: facial hair, a black Super Bowl baseball cap and tinted glasses. His black suit is off the rack from Saks, where he blitzed through the men's department yesterday. Shoes are Prada, black, rubber soles. His belt is also Prada, and he wears a black T-shirt. None of the clothes, except the shoes and T-shirt, are a perfect fit. But he hasn't owned a suit in years, and it did cross his mind in the dressing room that he missed the soft new wools, cashmere and polished cotton of the past, when tailors made chalk marks on sleeves and cuffs that needed to be hemmed.

He wonders who Scarpetta gave his expensive clothes to after his alleged death. Knowing her as well as he does, aware of her great powers of denial, he suspects that either she didn't clean out his closets at all and had someone else do it, or she was assisted, possibly by Lucy, who would have had an easier time disposing of his personal effects since she knew he wasn't dead. Then again, it depends on how much of an actress Lucy felt she should or could be at the time. Pain crushes him as for an instant he feels Scarpetta's pain, imagines the unimaginable, her grief and how poorly she probably handled it.

Stop! A waste of time and mental energy to speculate. Idle thoughts. Focus.

As he walks briskly across the tarmac, he notices a Bell 407 helicopter, dark blue or black with pop-out floats, a wire strike, and bold, bright stripes. He notes the tail number: 407TLP.

The Last Precinct.

A flight from New York to Baton Rouge is about a thousand miles. Depending on the winds and fuel stops, she could have made it here in ten hours if she was unlucky with a headwind, and much less time than that with a tailwind. In either scenario, if she left early this morning, she should have gotten here by late afternoon. He contemplates what she's been doing since and wonders whether Marino is with her.

Benton's car is a dark red Jaguar, rented in New Orleans and delivered here to the parking lot, one of the privileges for those who fly private. At the front desk of the FBO, or fixed base operation, as small private airports with only a unicom are called, he speaks to a young lady. Behind her is a monitor showing the status of other incoming flights. There are few, his listed with the update that it has just landed. Lucy's helicopter isn't on the screen, indicating she arrived some time ago.

"I have a rental car that should be here." Benton knows it will be.

The senator will have made sure that all details have been handled.

The clerk looks through rental car folders. Benton catches the news and turns around to observe pilots watching CNN in a small corner lounge. On the screen is an old photograph of Jean-Baptiste Chandonne. Benton isn't surprised. Chandonne escaped early this afternoon after disguising himself as one of the two corrections officers he killed.

"God, talk about an ugly bastard," one of the pilots comments.

"You gotta be kidding me! No human being looks like that."

The photograph is a mug shot taken in Richmond, Virginia, where Chandonne was arrested three years ago. He was not clean-shaven at the time, and his face, even his forehead, was horrifically covered with baby-fine hair. Showing the old photograph is a shame. Chandonne could not have escaped from prison unless he is clean-shaven. When he is hairy, he is a conspicuous freak. For the public to see this old mug shot isn't helpful, especially if he wears caps or sunglasses, or employs other means of disguising his grotesquely deformed face.

The clerk is frozen behind the desk, staring with her mouth open at the TV across the room.

"If I saw him, I'd die of a heart attack!" she exclaims. "Is he for real, or is that weirdo hair fake and everything?"

Benton glances at his watch, the successful businessman in a hurry. His protective law-enforcement instincts, however, are impossible to suppress.

"He's real, I'm afraid," he tells the clerk. "I remember hearing about his murders a few years back. I guess we'd better be on the lookout with him on the loose."

"You can say that again!" She hands him the rental envelope. "I guess I need to run your charge card."

He pulls a platinum American Express card out of his wallet, which also holds two thousand dollars, mostly in hundred-dollar bills. More cash is tucked into various pockets. Not knowing how long he'll be here, he has come prepared. He initials the rental car form and signs it.

"Thank you, Mr. Andrews. Drive carefully," the clerk says with a bright smile that goes with the job. "And I hope you enjoy your stay in Baton Rouge."

105

Scarpetta's tension mounts as she and Albert watch baggage go by on the carousel inside Baton Rouge's main terminal.

The time is almost seven p.m., and she is beginning to entertain real worries that no one has come to meet him. He collects one suitcase and clings to Scarpetta's side as she reclaims her own bag.

"Looks like you found yourself a new friend." Weldon Winn is suddenly behind her.

"Come on," she says to Albert. They walk through automatic glass doors. "I'm sure your aunt will drive up any minute. She's probably having to circle because cars aren't allowed to park at the curb."

Armed soldiers in camouflage patrol inside the baggage area and outside on the sidewalk. Albert seems oblivious to the unsmiling military presence, to their fingers resting on the trigger guards of assault rifles. His face is bright red.

"You and me are going to talk, Dr. Scarpetta," U.S. Attorney

Winn finally says her name and dares to wrap an arm around her shoulder.

"I think it would be a very good idea for you to keep your hands off me," she quietly warns him.

He removes his arm. "And I think it might be a good idea for you to learn how things are done down here." He watches cars pull up to the curb. "We're going to meet, all right. Any information about ongoing investigations is important. And if someone's an informant . . ."

"I am no informant," she interrupts his outrageous intimation that if she doesn't fully cooperate with him, he'll subpoena her for deposition. "Who told you I was coming to Baton Rouge?"

Albert begins to cry.

"Let me let you in on a little secret, pretty lady. Nothing much happens around here that I don't know about."

"Mr. Winn," she says, "if you have a legitimate need to talk to me at some point, I'll be happy to do so. But in an appropriate venue—which a sidewalk outside an airport clearly isn't."

"And I'll certainly look forward to that." He holds up a hand and snaps his fingers, signaling his driver.

She slings her bag over her shoulder and takes Albert's hand. "Don't worry. It's all right," she tells him. "I'm sure your aunt's on her way. But if she's been delayed for some reason, I'm not going to leave you all by yourself, okay?"

"But I don't know you. I'm not supposed to go anywhere with strangers," he whines.

"We sat together on the plane, didn't we?" she replies as Weldon Winn's white stretch limousine pulls up to the curb. "So you know me a little bit, and I promise you're safe, perfectly safe."

Winn climbs into the backseat and shuts the door, disappearing behind dark tinted glass. Cars and taxis stop for pickups, trunks popping open. People hug loved ones. Albert's wide, runny eyes dart around furtively, his fears quickly broaching hysteria. Scarpetta senses Winn looking out at her as the limousine drives off, and her thoughts are scattered like marbles dashed to the floor. It is hard for her to sort through what she should do next, but she starts with dialing directory assistance on her cell phone and finds out in short order that there is no listing for a Weldon Winn or anyone with the last name of Winn in New Orleans, where he claims to have a place in the French Quarter. His number in Baton Rouge is unlisted.

"Why am I not surprised," she mutters, and all she can suppose is that someone told the U.S. Attorney she was arriving here in the early evening, and he flew to Houston and made sure he was on her connecting flight and seated next to her.

Added to that disturbing and enigmatic development is her responsibility for a child she doesn't know, whose family seems to have abandoned him.

"You have your aunt's phone number, don't you?" she says to Albert. "Come on, let's call her. And by the way," it occurs to her, "you haven't told me your last name."

"Dard," Albert says. "I have my own cell phone, but the battery's dead."

"I beg your pardon? What did you say your last name is?"

"Dard." He hunches a shoulder to wipe his face.

106

Albert Dard stares down at the dirty sidewalk, focusing on dried gum, gray and shaped like a small cookie.

"Why were you in Houston?" Scarpetta asks him.

"To change planes." He begins to sob.

"But where were you first, where did you leave from?"

"Miami," he replies, increasingly distraught. "I was with my uncle for spring break, and then my aunt said I had to come home right away."

"When did she say that?" Having given up on his aunt, Scarpetta takes Albert's hand, and they walk back inside the baggage area, headed for the Hertz rental car desk.

"This morning," he replies. "I think I did something bad. Uncle Walt walked into my bedroom and woke me up. He said I was going home. I was supposed to be with him another three days."

Scarpetta squats and looks him in the eyes, gently holding his shoulders. "Albert, where's your mother?"

He bites his bottom lip. "With the angels," he says. "My aunt says they're around us all the time. I've never seen even one."

"And your father?"

"Away. He's very important."

"Tell me your home phone number, and let's find out what's going on," she says. "Or maybe you have your aunt's cell number? And what is her name?"

Albert tells her his aunt's name and his home number. Scarpetta calls. After several rings, a woman answers.

"Is Mrs. Guidon in, please?" Scarpetta asks as Albert holds her hand tightly.

"May I ask who's calling?" The woman is polite, her accent French.

"I'm not someone she knows, but I'm with her nephew, Albert. At the airport. It appears there is no one to pick him up." She hands the phone to Albert. "Here," she says to him.

"Who is it?" he asks, oddly. After a pause, he says, "Because you're not here, that's why. I don't know her name." He scowls, his tone snippy.

Scarpetta does not volunteer her name to him. Albert lets go of her hand and balls up his fist. He begins smacking it against his thigh, punching himself.

The woman talks fast, her voice audible but unintelligible. She and Albert are speaking French, and Scarpetta stares at Albert with renewed bewilderment as he angrily ends the call and returns the cell phone to her.

"Where did you learn French?" she asks him.

"My mom," he gloomily says. "Aunt Eveline makes me talk it a lot." Tears fill his eyes again.

"I tell you what, let's get my rental car, and I'll take you home. You can show me where you live, can't you?"

He wipes his eyes and nods his head.

428

107

Baton Rouge is a skyline of black smokestacks of different heights, and a pearly smog hangs in a band across the dark horizon.

In the distance, the night is illuminated by the blazing lights of petrochemical plants.

Albert Dard's mood is improving as his new friend drives along River Road, not far from LSU's football stadium. Along a graceful bend in the Mississippi, he points to iron gates and old brick pillars up ahead.

"There," he says. "That's it."

Where he lives is an estate set back at least a quarter of a mile from the road, a massive slate roof and several chimneys rising above dense trees. Scarpetta stops the car, and Albert gets out to enter a code on a keypad, and the gates slowly open. They drive slowly to the classical-revival villa with its small, wavy glass windows and massive masonry front porch. Old live oak trees bend over the property as if to protect it. The only car visible is an old white Volvo parked in front on the cobblestone drive.

"Is your father home?" Scarpetta asks as her silver rental Lincoln bumps over pavers.

"No," Albert glumly replies as they park.

They get out and climb steep brick steps. Albert unlocks the door and deactivates the burglar alarm, and they enter a restored antebellum home with hand-carved molding, dark mahogany, painted panels and antique Oriental rugs that are threadbare and dreary. Wan light filters through windows flanked by heavy damask draperies held back with tasseled cords, and a staircase winds up to a second floor, where someone's quick footsteps sound against a wooden floor.

"That's my aunt," Albert says as a woman with bones like a bird's and unsmiling dark eyes descends the stairs, her hand gliding along the smooth, gleaming wooden banister.

"I am Mrs. Guidon." She walks with light, quick steps to the entrance hallway.

With her sensuous mouth and delicate nostrils, Mrs. Guidon would be pretty, were her face not hard and her dress so severe. A high collar is fastened with a gold brooch, and she wears a long black skirt and clumsy lace-up black shoes, and her black hair is tightly pinned back. She appears to be in her forties, but her age is hard to determine. Her skin is unlined and so pale it is almost translucent, as if she has never seen the sun.

"May I offer you a cup of tea?" Mrs. Guidon's smile is as chilly as the stale, still air.

"Yes!" Albert grabs Scarpetta's hand. "Please come have tea. And cookies, too. You're my new friend!"

"There will be no tea for you," Mrs. Guidon tells him. "Go up to your room right this minute. Take your suitcase with you. I will let you know when you can come down."

"Don't leave," Albert begs Scarpetta. "I hate you," he says to Mrs. Guidon.

She ignores him, obviously having heard this before. "Such a funny little boy who is very tired and cranky because it is very late. Now say good-bye. I'm afraid you won't see this nice lady again."

Scarpetta is kind to him as she says good-bye.

He trudges angrily up the stairs, looking back at her several times, his face painfully touching her heart. When she hears his footsteps on the wooden floor upstairs, she looks hard at her unpleasant and peculiar hostess.

"How cold you are to a little boy, Mrs. Guidon," she says. "What kind of people are you and his father, that you would hope a stranger would bring him home?"

"I am disappointed." Her imperious demeanor doesn't waver. "I thought a scientist of your renown would investigate before making assumptions."

108

Lucy and Marino connect by cell phone.

"Where's she staying?" she asks from her parked black Lincoln Navigator SUV.

She and Rudy figured out that the best way to be inconspicuous was to pull into the Radisson parking lot and sit with the engine and lights off.

"The coroner. I'm glad she ain't by herself in no hotel."

"None of us need to be in a hotel," Lucy says. "Damn, could you drive a louder truck?"

"If I had one."

"How does he check out? What's his name?"

"Sam Lanier. His background's clean as a whistle. When he called to check out the Doc, I got the impression he's an okay guy."

"Well, if he isn't, she'll be all right. Because he's about to have three other houseguests," Lucy says.

109

A fragile Wedgwood teacup lightly clinks against a saucer.

Mrs. Guidon and Scarpetta sit at a kitchen table made of a centuries-old butcher block that Scarpetta finds repulsive. She can't help but imagine how many chickens and other animals were slaughtered and chopped up on the worn, sloping wood with its hack marks, cracks and discoloration. It is an unpleasant by-product of her profession that she knows too much, and it is almost impossible to kill bacteria on porous materials such as wood.

"How many times must I demand to know why I'm here and how you managed to get me here?" Scarpetta's eyes are intense.

"I find it charming that Albert seems to have decided you are his friend," Mrs. Guidon remarks. "I try very hard to encourage him. He wants nothing to do with school sports or any other activities that might expose him to children his own age. He thinks he belongs right here at this table"——she taps the butcher block with her small, milky white knuckles—"talking to you and me as if he is our peer."

After years of dealing with people who refuse to answer questions or can't or are in denial, Scarpetta is skilled at catching truths as they subtly show themselves. "Why doesn't he associate with children his own age?" she inquires.

"Who knows? It is a mystery. He has always been odd, really, preferring to stay home and do homework, entertaining himself with those peculiar games children play these days. Cards with those awful creatures on them. Cards and computers, cards and more cards." Her gestures are dramatic, her French accent heavy, her English stilted and faltering. "He has been more this way as he gets older. Isolated and playing the card games. Often, he is home, stays in his room with the door shut and will not come out." Suddenly, she softens and seems caring.

Every detail Scarpetta observes is conflicting and disturbing, the kitchen an argument of anachronisms that seem a metaphor for this house and the people who live in it. Behind her is a cavernous fireplace, with formidable hand-forged andirons capable of bearing a load of wood large enough to heat up a room three times this size. A door leads outside, and next to it is a complicated alarm system keypad and an Aiphone with a video screen for the cameras that no doubt guard every entrance. Another keypad, this one much larger, indicates the old mansion is a smart house with multiple modems that allow the occupants to remotely control heating, cooling, lights, entertainment centers and gas fireplaces, and even turn appliances off and on. Yet the appliances and thermostats Scarpetta has seen so far have not been upgraded for what she estimates is at least thirty years.

A knife holder on the granite countertop is empty, and there are no knives in the porcelain sink, not a knife anywhere in sight. Yet hanging over the fireplace is a rack of nineteenth-century swords, and on the heavy chestnut mantel is a revolver with rubber grips, most likely a .38, in a black leather holster.

Mrs. Guidon follows Scarpetta's eyes, and for an instant, her face registers anger. She has made an oversight, a telling mistake. Leaving the revolver in plain view was not intentional. "I'm sure it hasn't escaped your notice that Mr. Dard is very security-conscious." She sighs, shrugging, as if taking her guest into her confidence and hinting that Mr. Dard is ridiculously cautious and paranoid. "Baton Rouge is high-crime. I'm sure you know that. Living in a house like this and having wealth causes concerns, although I'm not the type to be looking over my shoulder all the time."

Scarpetta hides how much she dislikes Mrs. Guidon and is infuriated about what Albert's life must be like. She wonders how far she can go to pry loose the secrets that haunt this very old estate.

"Albert seems very unhappy and misses his dog," she says. "Perhaps you should get him another one. Especially if he's lonely and has no friends."

"With him, I believe it is genetics. His mother—my sister— wasn't well." Mrs. Guidon pauses, then adds, "Of course, you know that."

"Why don't you tell me what I'm supposed to know? You seem to know so much about me."

"Now, you are perceptive," Mrs. Guidon replies with a touch of condescension. "But not as cautious as I would have guessed. Albert called me on your cell phone, remember? That was careless for someone of your reputation."

"What do you know of my reputation?"

"Caller ID came back to your name, and I am aware you haven't suddenly arrived in Baton Rouge for a little vacation. Charlotte's case is complicated. No one seems to have any idea what happened to her or why she went to a horrible motel frequented by truck drivers and the dregs of society. So Dr. Lanier has solicited your assistance, no? But I, at least, am relieved and grateful, and let's just say it was planned that you would sit next to Albert and drive him home, and here you are." She lifts her teacup. "All things happen for a reason, as you must know."

"How could you possibly have orchestrated all this?" Scarpetta pushes her, warns her, making it clear that she has had enough. "I don't suppose U.S. Attorney Weldon Winn is involved with your scheming, since he just happened to sit next to me, too."

"There is much you don't know. Mr. Winn is a close family friend."

"What family? Albert's father didn't show up at the airport. Albert doesn't seem to even know where he is. What did any of you suppose would happen to a young boy traveling alone?"

"He wasn't alone. He was with you. And now you are here. I wanted to meet you. Perfect."

"*Family friend?*" Scarpetta repeats. "Then why did Albert not know Weldon Winn, if he is such a good family friend?"

"Albert has never met him."

"That makes no sense."

"That's not for you to say."

"I'll say whatever I want, since you seem to have assigned Albert to me and were certain he would be safe with me—a perfect stranger—and that I would bring him home. How could you be sure I would take it upon myself to look after him or that I'm trustworthy?" Scarpetta pushes back her chair and gets up, and it scrapes loudly against heart-of-pine flooring. "He lost his mother, who the hell knows about the father, and he's lost his dog, and next he's abandoned and frightened. In my business, this is called child neglect, child abuse." Her anger flashes.

436

"I am Charlotte's sister." Mrs. Guidon gets up, too.

"All you've done is manipulate me. Or try to. I'm leaving now."

"Please let me show you around first," Mrs. Guidon says. "Particularly *le cave*."

"How could you possibly have a wine cellar in an area where the water table is so high that plantation houses have to be built on pillars?" Scarpetta asks.

"So you are not always observant. This house is on an elevation, built in 1793. The original owner found the perfect location for what he had in mind. He was a Frenchman, a wine connoisseur who often traveled back to France. Slaves constructed a wine cellar, like the ones he knew in France, and I doubt there is another one like it in this country." She walks to the door leading outside and opens it. "You simply must see it. Baton Rouge's best-kept secret."

Scarpetta stands where she is. "No."

Mrs. Guidon lowers her voice and is almost gentle when she explains, "You are wrong about Albert. I was circling the airport. I saw the two of you on the sidewalk. Had you left him, I would have picked him up, but based on what I know about you, you would not leave him. You are too caring, too decent. And you are wary about the evils in this world." She states this not with feeling but as fact.

"How could you have been circling the airport? I called you at home . . ."

"Programmed to roll over to my cell phone. I actually was looking at you when you called me." This amuses her. "I got to the house no more than fifteen minutes before you did, Dr. Scarpetta. I don't blame you for being angry and confused, but I wanted to talk to you when Jason wasn't here. Albert's father. Believe me, you are very fortunate that he isn't here." She hesitates, holding

437

the kitchen door open wide. "When he's around, there is no such thing as privacy. Please come." She motions to her.

Scarpetta looks at the keypads by the kitchen door. Outside, shadows fall in a black curtain from trees lush with new leaves. The woods are damp and earthy beneath a waning moon.

"I will let you out this way, then. The driveway is just to the side. But you must promise to come back and see the cave," she says.

"I'll go out the front." Scarpetta starts walking that way.

110

Benton drove around for a while, then checked into the Radisson under the assumed name of Tony Wilson.

· Inside his suite, he sits on the bed, his door secured with the dead-bolt lock and burglar chain. He requested a block on his telephone, not that he is expecting calls. The clerks at reception seemed to understand. He is a wealthy man from Los Angeles and wants privacy. The hotel is the finest one in Baton Rouge, its staff accustomed to accommodating a lot of people from all over who don't use the valets, preferring to come and go discreetly. They don't want to be bothered and rarely stay long.

Benton connects his laptop to the modem line in his room. He enters his code to release the lock of the new black briefcase he deliberately scuffed by scraping it against furniture and sliding it across the floor. He takes off his ankle holster and places his .357 magnum Smith & Wesson 340PD on the bed. It is double-action, loaded with five rounds of Speer Gold Dot 125-grain.

From the briefcase he removes two pistols: a pocket-friendly

.40-caliber Glock 27, capacity ten rounds, including one in the chamber. The ammunition is Hydra-Shok: 135-grain, center-post hollow-point with a notched jacket, velocity 1,190 feet per second, high-energy and with efficient stopping power, punches into the enemy and splays like a razor-sharp flower.

His second and most important pistol is the P 226 SL Sig Sauer nine-millimeter, capacity sixteen rounds, including one in the chamber. The ammunition is also Hydra-Shok: 124-grain, center-post hollow-point with notched jacket, velocity 1,120 feet per second, deep penetration and stopping power.

It is conceivable he can carry the three guns at once. He's done it before, the .357 Smith & Wesson in his ankle holster, the .40-caliber Glock in a shoulder holster, and the nine-millimeter Sig Sauer in the waistband at the small of his back.

Extra magazines for the pistols and extra cartridges for the .357 magnum go in a designer leather butt pack. Benton dresses in a loose-fitting London Fog jacket and baggy jeans that are slightly too long, a cap, tinted glasses and the rubber-soled Prada shoes. He could be a tourist. He could work in Baton Rouge and barely merit notice in this city of transients, where hundreds of professors, some of them eccentric, and thousands of oblivious students and preoccupied visiting scholars of all ages and nationalities abound. He could be straight. He could be gay. He could be both.

111

The next morning, muddy, sluggish water carries Scarpetta's eye to a riverboat casino, to the USS *Kidd* battleship and on to the distant Old Mississippi Bridge, then back to Dr. Sam Lanier.

In the few minutes she spent with him last night when she finally arrived at his door and he quickly escorted her to his guest house in back without walking her through the main house because he didn't want to awaken his wife, she decided she liked him. She worries that she shouldn't.

"In Charlotte Dard's case," she says, "how involved did you and your office get with the family in terms of trying to counsel or question them?"

"Not as much as I would have liked. I tried." The light in his eyes dims, and his mouth tightens. "I did talk to the sister, Mrs. Guidon. Briefly. She's an odd one. Anyway, orientation time. Let me show you where you are."

His abrupt change of subject strikes her as paranoid, as if he worries that someone might be listening. Swiveling around in his chair, he points west out the window.

"People are always jumping from the Old Mississippi Bridge. Can't tell you how many times I've fished bodies out of the river because some poor soul takes a leap—takes his time, too, while the police try to talk him down and people in their cars start yelling 'Go ahead and jump!' because he's slowing up traffic. Can you believe that?

"Now, down there straight ahead, I had a guy dressed in a shower curtain with an AK-47, tried to get on the USS *Kidd* to kill all the Russians. He got intercepted," he drolly adds. "Death and mental health are part of the same department, and we do all the pickups—commit about three thousand cases a year."

"And that works how, exactly?" Scarpetta inquires. "A family member requests an order of protective custody?"

"Almost always. But the police can request it. And if the coroner—in this case, me—believes the person is gravely disabled and acutely dangerous to himself or others and is unwilling or unable to seek medical attention, deputies are sent in."

"The coroner is elected. It helps if he's on good terms with the mayor, the police, the sheriff, LSU, Southern University, the district attorney, judges, the U.S. Attorney, not to mention influential members of the community." She pauses. "People in power can certainly influence the public on how to cast its votes. So the police recommend someone should be removed to a psychiatric hospital, and the local coroner agrees. In my world, that's called a conflict of interest."

"It's worse than that. The coroner also determines competency to stand trial."

"So you oversee the autopsy of a murder victim, determine cause and manner of death, then, if the alleged killer is caught, you decide if he's competent to stand trial."

"Do the DNA swab in the exam room. Then sits right here in my office, a cop on either side, attorney present. And I interview him. Or her."

"Dr. Lanier, you have the most bizarre coroner system I've ever heard of, and it doesn't sound to me as if you have any protection, should the powers that be decide they can't control you."

"Welcome to Louisiana. And if the powers that be try to tell me how to do my job, I tell them to kiss my ass."

"And your crime rate? I know it's bad."

"Worse than bad. Terrible," he replies. "By far, Baton Rouge has the highest rate of unsolved homicides in the entire country."

"Why?"

"Clearly, Baton Rouge is a very violent city. I'm not sure why."

"And the police?"

"Listen, I have a lot of respect for street cops. Most of them try very hard. But then you've got the people in charge who squash the good guys and encourage the assholes. Politics." His chair creaks as he leans back in it. "We've got a serial murderer running around down here. Have probably had more than one running around down here over the decades." He shrugs in a manner that is anything but easygoing or accepting. "Politics. How many times do I need to say the word?"

"Organized crime?"

"Fifth largest port in the country, the second largest petrochemical industry, and Louisiana produces some sixteen percent of the nation's oil. Come on." He gets up from his desk. "Lunch. Everybody's got to eat, and I have a feeling you haven't done much of that lately. You look pretty damn beat-up, and your suit's hanging a little loose around the waist."

Scarpetta can't begin to tell him how much she has grown to hate her black suit.

Three clerks glance up as Scarpetta and Dr. Lanier walk out of his office.

"You coming back?" an overweight woman with gray hair asks her boss, a cool steel edge to her voice.

Scarpetta is fairly sure this is the clerk Dr. Lanier has complained about.

"Who knows?" he responds in what Scarpetta would call the flat affect of an expert witness testifying in court.

She can tell he doesn't like her. Old, ugly specters hover between them. He seems relieved when the outer office door opens and a tall, good-looking man in navy range pants and a dark blue coroner's jacket walks in. His presence is a high energy that is several steps ahead of him, and the overweight clerk's eyes fasten on his face like dark, angry wasps.

Eric Murphy, the chief death investigator, welcomes Scarpetta to *Luysiana*. "Where are we going to lunch?" he asks.

"No matter what, you have to eat," Dr. Lanier says at the elevator. "I insist, and this is the place to do it. Like I said, I can't get rid of her."

He absently stabs the button for the parking garage.

"Hell, she's been working in this office longer than I have. Sort of an inherited sinkhole that gets passed on from one coroner to the next."

The elevator doors open inside a large parking garage. Car doors shut in muffled counterpoint as people head out to lunch, and Dr. Lanier points his key at what he calls his *unit*, a black Chevrolet Caprice with a blue light in the dash, a two-way radio, a police scanner and a special turbo-charged V-8 engine that is "required for all high-speed chases," he boasts, as Scarpetta helps herself to a backseat door and slides into the seat.

"You can't be sitting in back. It doesn't look right," Eric complains, holding open the front passenger door. "You're our guest, ma'am."

"Oh, please don't call me *ma'am*. I'm Kay. And my legs are shorter, which means I sit in the back."

"Call me anything you like," Eric cheerfully replies. "Everybody else does."

"From now on, I'm Sam. No more of this doctor shit."

"Don't be calling me doctor, either," Eric says. "For the good reason that I'm not one."

He gets inside the car, giving up on telling Scarpetta where to sit.

"Hell, the only time you were a doctor was when you were, what?" Dr. Lanier starts the engine. "Ten, maybe twelve years old, and molesting all the little girls in your neighborhood? Jesus God, I hate parking between concrete damn pillars."

"They have a way of moving in on you, don't they, Sam?" Eric turns around and winks at Scarpetta. "They grab at his vehicle on a regular basis. Look over there." He points at a concrete support gouged and streaked with black paint. "If you were working that crime scene, what would you conclude?" He peels cellophane off a pack of Dentyne chewing gum. "Let me give you a clue. That used to be the coroner's parking place, but not so long ago, the coroner—guess which one, and there's only one—complained it was way too narrow, and he'd be goddamned if he was parking there."

"Now, don't tell all my secrets." Dr. Lanier slowly creeps out of his spot. "Besides, it was my wife who did that bit of damage. She's a worse driver than I am, for the record."

"She's a death investigator, too." Eric turns around again. "Works for nothing, which is pretty much what the rest of us do."

"Shit." Dr. Lanier accelerates his high-speed-chase unit more than necessary inside a parking deck. "You get paid a hell of a lot more than you deserve."

"Can we talk now?" Scarpetta asks.

"I'm pretty sure we can. Maybe people get into my office, hell if I know. But nobody touches my car, or my Harley," Dr. Lanier replies.

In a firm, even voice, Scarpetta confronts him. "I happened to fly here with the Dards' young son sitting on one side of me and your U.S. Attorney, Weldon Winn, on the other. In fact, I ended up having to drive Albert Dard home. You want to tell me what that's about?"

"Scares the hell out of me."

"The boy just happens to be in Miami, is suddenly whisked to the airport yesterday morning and routed through Houston and just happens to be on my flight to Baton Rouge. Just as Winn happens to be on my flight. And by the way, you don't strike me as the sort who gets scared."

"Two things. One, you don't know me. Two, you don't know here."

"Where was Albert eight years ago when his mother died in that motel room?" Scarpetta asks. "Where was his father, and why is this mysterious father, quote, *gone all the time,* as the boy put it?"

"That I don't know. What I can tell you is I'm familiar with Albert. Last year, I had to examine the kid in the ER, was given a *heads-up,* in other words, especially in light of his wealthy family and the mysterious death of his mother. He was committed to a private psychiatric hospital in New Orleans."

"What on Earth for?" Scarpetta asks, adding, "A psychiatric history, and his family lets him travel alone?"

"But then he wasn't alone, according to what you've told me. His uncle put him in the hands of airline attendants, who also, no doubt, saw to it that he got to his proper gate in Houston. Then, best of all, you took care of him the rest of the time. He's not psychotic.

"The story is, three years ago last October, his aunt called nine-one-one and said her nephew—he was seven at the time, I believe—was bleeding badly and claimed to have been assaulted when he was out riding his bicycle. Story is, he was hysterical, scared out of his mind. Well, nobody assaulted that poor little kid, Kay. You said I could call you that. There was no evidence whatsoever of that. In fact, he's a cutter. Into self-mutilation. Apparently, that started up again with him not long before I examined him in the ER. Which was a pretty damn awful experience."

Scarpetta recalls the absence of knives in the Dard kitchen.

"You're absolutely certain his injuries were self-inflicted?" she asks.

"I try not to be absolutely certain of anything. I don't know of much that's an absolute certainty except death," Dr. Lanier replies. "But I found a lot of hesitation cuts. Just scratches, really. That's significant for someone getting started in this unfortunate pattern of self-destruction. His cuts were minor, all in places within reach but not readily visible to others. Stomach. Thighs. Buttocks."

"That would explain why I saw no scars when I was sitting next to him on the plane," Scarpetta remarks. "I would have noticed."

"What really disturbs me is the obvious," he says. "Somebody wants you here in Baton Rouge. Why?"

"You tell me. You tell me who leaked my travel plans, because it seems the most likely suspect is you—or whoever else in your office knew I was coming."

"I can see why you'd think that. No question about it. I knew enough to arrange the whole damn scenario, assuming I'm on friendly terms with Weldon Winn. And I'm not, can't stand the son of a bitch. He's dirtier than a landfill and got a lot of money. His explanation is he grew up with money. Well, guess what, he's from Myrtle Beach, South Carolina. His father managed a golf course, and his mother worked like a dog as a nurse's aid. The son of a bitch isn't from shit."

"How do you know all this?"

"Ask Eric."

The death investigator turns around and smiles. "I started out with the FBI. Now and then, I can find my way out of a paper bag and look for things."

"Point is, Weldon Winn is involved, deeply involved, with illegal activities," Dr. Lanier continues. "Now, how anyone will ever prove that, or even care, is another matter. What is a fact is that a number of people arrested here over the years have somehow managed to escape Project Exile, didn't get the automatic five years in federal prison added to their sentences for possession of a firearm while committing a crime. Our U.S. Attorney somehow overlooked those cases, as did the committee that's supposed to track them.

"One of the reasons I'm given so much grief in my lovely city is because I won't kowtow to the politicians. I'm up for reelection next year, and I've got a whole Noah's ark full of assholes who would love for me not to be coroner anymore. I'm not appreciated by any of the bad guys, don't socialize with them. I consider that a compliment."

Scarpetta says, "You and I talked on the phone. Your office arranged my rental car."

"A mistake. Damn stupid as hell of me. I should have done it myself, away from the office. My secretary is trustworthy. That certain clerk you just met may have overheard, snooped, I don't know."

They drive through a rather unremarkable area of Baton Rouge, at the edge of the university that dominates the town. Swamp Mama's on 3rd Street is a popular hangout for students. Dr. Lanier parks in a tow-away zone and tosses an *Officer of the Coroner*'s red metal plate on the dash, as if lunch has suddenly turned into a crime scene.

112

Marino turns into the Louisiana Air parking lot and stops cop-style, driver's window to driver's window, with Lucy's SUV.

"Good man. You got rid of the truck," Lucy commends him without saying hello. "Don't need a monster-garage truck with Virginia plates around here."

"Hey. I'm not stupid. Even if this is a piece of shit."

His rental truck is a six-cylinder Toyota. It doesn't even have mud flaps.

"Where'd you ditch it?" Lucy asks.

"The regular airport, long-term parking. Hope nobody breaks in to it. Everything I own's in there. Even if it ain't much."

"Let's go."

They park, but not near each other.

"Where's your boyfriend?" Marino asks as they walk toward the FBO.

"Prowling. Seeing if he can find Rocco's place in Spanish Town, the historic district where Rocco kept a place."

450

She stops briefly at the desk. "The Bell four-oh-seven," she says, not giving the tail number.

It isn't necessary. Her helicopter is the only one on the tarmac at the moment. The woman at the desk pushes a button that unlocks the door. A Gulf Stream is starting its engines, the roar painfully loud, and Lucy and Marino cover their ears, making sure they don't walk around the back of the plane and get blasted with exhaust, a good way to smell like jet fuel, which is sure to give one a headache when confined to a small cockpit. They hurry to the helipad, which is at the outer edge of the tarmac, far away from planes, because people ignorant of helicopters assume their rotor wash will kick up rocks and sand and scour the paint right off fixed-wing aircraft.

Marino is ignorant of helicopters and doesn't like them. He can barely force his massive body into the left seat, which doesn't adjust. He can't slide it back.

"Goddamn son of a bitch," is all he says, loosening his harness as far as it will go.

Lucy has already done her usual thorough preflight, checks breakers and switches and throttle one last time and turns on the battery. She waits for automatic checks to go through their routines and she goes through hers, flipping on the generator. Headset on, she eases the throttle up to 100 RPMs. This is a time when the GPS will be of no value, nor will any other navigational instruments. A flight chart isn't going to be of much use, either, so she spreads open a Baton Rouge map on her lap and runs her finger southeast, along Route 408, also known as Hooper Road.

"Where we're going is off the map," she says into her mike. "Lake Maurepas. We keep going in this direction, towards New Orleans, and hopefully don't end up at Lake Pontchartrain. We're

451

not going that far, but if we do, we've overflown Lake Maurepas, and Blind River and Dutch Bayou. I don't think that will happen."

"Fly fast," Marino says. "I hate helicopters, including yours."

"On the go," she announces and stabilizes into a hover, taking off into the wind.

113

Swamp Mama's is a bar that smells like beer, with old vinyl booths and a stained, unvarnished wooden floor.

While an LSU student waiter takes drink orders, Eric and Dr. Lanier disappear into the men's room.

"I tell you," Eric says as they push through the restroom's door. "I'd take her home with me any time. What about tonight?"

"She's not interested in you," Dr. Lanier says in a cadence that rises in pitch at the end of each sentence, causing his comments to sound like questions when they aren't. "Come on now."

"She's not married."

"Don't be messing with my consultants, especially this one. She'll eat you alive."

"Oh, please, God. Let her."

"Every time you get dumped by your latest girlfriend, you turn into a mental case."

They are conducting this conversation at the urinals, one of the

453

few places on the planet where they don't mind having their backs to the door.

"I'm trying to figure out how to describe her," Eric says. "Not pretty like your wife. Stronger-featured than that, and to me there's nothing sexier than a really great body in a suit or maybe a uniform."

"You're goofy as a shit-eating fly. Don't go buzzing around her geography, Eric."

"I like those little glasses she wears, too. I wonder if she's dating anybody. That suit doesn't hide what's important, you notice?"

"No, I didn't notice." Dr. Lanier vigorously scrubs his hands in the sink, as if he's about to perform a heart transplant. "I'm blind. Don't forget to wash up."

Eric laughs as he moves to the sink, blasts on the hot water and pumps globs of pink soap into his palms. "No kidding, what if I ask her out, Boss? What harm could there be in that?"

"Maybe you should try her niece. She's closer to your age. Very attractive and smart as hell. She might be too much of a handful for you. She's also with a guy. But they didn't sleep in the same room."

"When do I meet her? Maybe tonight? You cook? Maybe we can go to Boutin's?"

"What's the matter with you?"

"I ate oysters last night."

Dr. Lanier snatches paper towels out of a metal dispenser on the wall. He places a short stack of them on the edge of Eric's sink. Walking out of the men's room, he watches Scarpetta, noticing that every detail of her is unusual, even the way she reaches for her coffee, slowly, with deliberation, exuding confidence and power that has absolutely nothing to do with drinking coffee. She is scanning notes in a diary that has a black leather slipcover so she can refill it as often as needed. He suspects she is constantly refilling that diary. She's the sort who would record any detail or conversation that in her mind might prove important. Her meticulousness goes beyond her training. He slides in next to her.

"I recommend the gumbo," he says as his cell phone plays a thin, mechanical version of Beethoven's Fifth.

"Wish you'd set your ringer on something else," Eric comments.

"Lanier," he answers. He listens for a minute, frowning, his eyes fixing on Eric. "I'm leaving right now."

He gets up from the booth and tosses his napkin on the table.

"Come on," he says. "We got a bad one."

114

The terrain between the Baton Rouge airport and Lake Maurepas is a series of swamps, waterways and creeks that make Lucy nervous.

Even with pop-out floats, she would worry about a forced landing. How anyone would get to them is a valid question, and she doesn't want to imagine the reptiles that lurk in those dark waters, on mucky shores and in the shadows of moss-draped trees. In the baggage compartment, she always carries an emergency kit that includes handheld radios, water, protein bars and insect repellent.

Camouflaged in thick trees are duck blinds and an occasional fishing shack. She flies lower and slower but sees no signs of human occupation. In some areas, only a very small boat, perhaps an airboat, could work its way through narrow waterways that from the air look like veins reticulating through saw grass.

"See any gators down there?" she asks Marino.

"I ain't looking for gators. And there ain't nothing down there."

As creeks move into rivers and Lucy spots a faint blue line on the horizon, they begin to reach civilization. The day is balmy and partly cloudy, good weather for being on the water. A lot of boats are out, and fishermen and people on pleasure crafts stare up at the helicopter. Lucy is careful not to fly too low, avoiding any appearance of surveillance. She's just a pilot heading somewhere. Banking east, she starts looking for Blind River. She tells Marino to do the same.

"Why do you think they call it Blind River?" he says. "'Cause you can't see it, that's why."

The farther east they go, the more fishing camps they see, most of them well cared for, with boats docked in front. Lucy spots a canal, turns around and follows its convolutions south as it gets wider and turns into a river that empties into the lake. Numerous foreboding canals branch out from the river, and she circles, getting lower, finding not a single fishing shack.

"If Talley baited that hook with the arm," Lucy says, "then I have a feeling he's hiding out not too far from here."

"Well, if you're right and keep circling, he damn well is going to see us," Marino replies.

They head back, keeping up their scan, mostly concentrating on antennas and careful not to overfly petrochemical plants and find themselves intercepted. Lucy has spotted several bright orange Dauphine helicopters, the sort usually flown by the Coast Guard, which is now part of homeland security and constantly on alert for terrorists. Flying over a petrochemical plant is not a wise move these days. Flying into a thousand-foot antenna is worse. Lucy has pushed back the airspeed to ninety knots, in no hurry to return to the airport as she debates if now is the time to tell Marino the truth.

She won't be able to look at him while airborne and keeping

alert to avoid coming anywhere near obstacles. Her stomach tightens and her pulse speeds up.

"I don't know how to say this," she begins.

"You don't have to say nothing," he replies. "I already know."

"How?" She is baffled and scared.

"I'm a detective, remember? Chandonne sent two sealed letters, one to you, one to me, both of them inside NAJ envelopes. You never let me read yours. Said it was a lot of deranged crap. I could've pushed, but something told me not to. Then next thing, you've disappeared, you and Rudy, and a couple days later I find out Rocco's dead. All I ask is if Chandonne told you where to find him and gave you enough info to get Rocco pinned with a Red Notice."

"Yes. I didn't show you the letter. I was afraid you'd go to Poland yourself."

"And do what?"

"What do you think? If you found him inside that hotel room and finally confronted him, saw him up close for what he was, what would you have done?"

"Probably the same thing you and Rudy did," Marino says.

"I can tell you all the details."

"I don't want to know."

"Maybe you really couldn't have done it yourself, Marino. Thank God you didn't. He was your son," she tells him. "And in some very hidden part of your heart, you loved him."

"What hurts worse than him being dead is I never did," he says.

115

The first blood is three feet inside the front door, a single drop the size of a dime, perfectly round with a stellate margin reminiscent of a buzzsaw blade.

Ninety-degree angle, Scarpetta thinks. A drop of blood moving through the air assumes an almost perfect spherical shape that is maintained on impact if the blood falls straight down, at a ninety-degree angle.

"She was upright, or someone was," Scarpetta says.

She stands very still, her eyes moving from one drop to the next on the terracotta tile floor. At the edge of the rug in front of the couch is a bloody area that appears to have been smeared by a foot, as if the person who stepped on the blood-spotted tile slipped. Scarpetta moves in for a closer inspection, staring at the dry, dark red stain, then turning her head and meeting Dr. Lanier's eyes. He comes over, and she points out an almost indiscernible partial footwear impression of a heel with a small undulating tread pattern that reminds Scarpetta of a child's drawing of ocean waves.

Eric begins taking photographs.

From the couch, the signs of the struggle continue around a glass and wrought-iron coffee table that is askew, the rug rumpled beneath it, and just beyond, a head was slammed against the wall.

"Hair swipes." Scarpetta points out a bloody pattern feathering over the pale pink paint.

The front door opens and in walks a plainclothes cop, young, with dark, receding hair. He looks back and forth between Dr. Lanier and Eric, and fixes on Scarpetta.

"Who's she?" he asks.

"Let's start with who you are," Dr. Lanier says to him.

The cop seems threatening because he is frantic, his eyes darting back in the direction of an area of the house they can't see. "Detective Clark, with Zachary." He swats at a fly, the black hair on top of his fingers showing through translucent latex gloves stretched over his big hands. "I just got transferred into investigations last month," he adds. "So I don't know her." He nods again at Scarpetta, who hasn't moved from her spot by the wall.

"A visiting consultant," Dr. Lanier replies. "If you haven't heard of her, you will. Now tell me what happened here. Where's the body, and who's with it?"

"In a front bedroom—a guest room, it looks like. Robillard's in there, taking pictures and everything."

Scarpetta glances up at the mention of Nic Robillard's name.

"Good," she says.

"You know her?" Now Detective Clark seems very confused. He irritably swats at another fly. "Damn, I hate those things."

Scarpetta follows tiny spatters of blood on the wall and floor, some no bigger than a pinpoint, the tapered ends pointing in the direction of flight. The victim was down on the floor by the baseboard and managed to struggle back to her feet. Small, elongated drops on the wall are not the usual cast-off blood that Scarpetta is accustomed to seeing when a victim has been repeatedly beaten or stabbed and blood has flown off the weapon as it is swung through the air.

The point of origin is what appears to be a violent struggle in the living room, and Scarpetta envisions punching, grabbing, feet sliding and perhaps kicking and clawing, resulting in a bloody mess—but not thousands of drops of blood cast great distances from the swings of a weapon. Possibly, there was no weapon, Scarpetta ponders, at least not at this stage of the assault. Maybe early on, after the assailant came through the front door, the only weapon was a fist. Possibly, the assailant did not assume he would need a weapon, and then he lost control of the situation quickly.

Dr. Lanier glances toward the back of the house. "Eric, go on and make sure everything's secure. We'll be right in."

"What do you know about the victim?" Scarpetta asks Detective Clark. "What do you know about any of this?"

"Not much." He flips back several pages in a notepad. "Name's Rebecca Milton, thirty-six-year-old white female. All we really know at this time is she rents this house, and her boyfriend stopped by around twelve-thirty to take her to lunch. She doesn't answer the door, so he lets himself in and finds her."

"Door unlocked?" Dr. Lanier asks.

"Yes. He finds her body and calls the police."

"Then he identified her," Scarpetta says, getting up from her squatting position, her knees aching.

Clark hesitates.

"How good a look did he get?" Scarpetta doesn't trust visual identifications, and one should never assume that a victim found inside a residence is the person who lived there.

"Not sure," Clark replies. "My guess is he didn't stay in that bedroom long. You'll see when you get there. She's in bad shape, real bad shape. But Robillard seems to think the victim's Rebecca Milton, the lady who lives here."

Dr. Lanier frowns. "How the hell would Robillard know?"

"She lives two houses down."

"Who does?" Scarpetta asks, panning the living room like a camera.

"Robillard lives right over there." Detective Clark points toward the street. "Two houses down."

"Jesus God," Dr. Lanier says. "How weird is that? And she didn't hear anything, see anything?"

"It's the middle of the day. She was out on the street like the rest of us."

The house is that of a neat person with a reasonably good income and expensive tastes, Scarpetta notes. Oriental rugs are machine-made but handsome, and to the left of the front door is a cherry entertainment center with an elaborate sound system and large-screen television. Bright Cajun paintings hanging on the walls are joyous in their loud, primary colors and primitive depictions of fish, people, water and trees. Rebecca Milton, if she is the victim, loved art and life. In whimsical frames are photographs of a tan woman with shiny black hair, a bright smile and a slim body. In several other photographs she is in a boat or standing on a pier with another woman, also with dark hair, who looks enough like her to be her sister.

"We're sure she lived alone?" Scarpetta asks.

"It appears she was alone when she got attacked," Clark says, scanning pages in his notepad.

"But we don't know that for a fact."

He shrugs. "No ma'am. We don't know much of anything for a fact at the moment."

"I'm just wondering, because many of these pictures are of two women—two women who seem to have a close relationship. And a number of the photographs were taken inside this house or in what appears to be the front porch or perhaps in the backyard." She points out the hair swipes near the baseboard and interprets them. "Right here, she went down, or someone did, and whoever it was, the person was bleeding sufficiently for her hair to be bloody . . ."

"Yeah, well, she's got a big-time head injury. I mean, her face is smashed up bad," Clark offers.

Straight ahead is the dining room, with a centered antique walnut table and six matching chairs. The hutch is old, and behind its glass doors are dishes with gold around the rims. Beyond, through an open doorway, is the kitchen, and it does not appear that the killer or the victim moved in this direction, but off to the right of the living room, the pursuit continuing through a blue-carpeted hallway and ending in a bedroom that faces the front yard.

Blood is everywhere. It has dried a dark red, but some areas of the carpet are so soaked that the blood is still damp. Scarpetta pauses at the end of the hallway and examines blood droplets on the paneled wall. One drop is round, very light red inside and very dark around the rim. Surrounding it is a spray of other droplets, some almost too small to see.

"Do we know if she was stabbed?" Scarpetta turns around and asks Clark, who is hanging back at the beginning of the hallway, busy with a video camera.

Dr. Lanier has already walked inside the bedroom. He appears in the doorway and looks grimly at her. "She's been stabbed, all right," he replies in a hard voice. "About thirty or forty times."

"Along the wall here are sneeze or cough patterns of blood," Dr. Scarpetta tells him. "You can tell because the dark-rimmed drops here, here, and here"—she points them out—"indicate bubbles. Sometimes you see that when a person's bled into the airway or lungs. Or she may just have had blood in her mouth."

Scarpetta walks to the left edge of the bedroom door, where there is only a small amount of blood. Her eyes follow finger smears of whoever grabbed the door frame, and more drips on the carpet that continue through the doorway onto the hardwood floor. Her view of the body is blocked by Dr. Lanier, Eric and Nic Robillard. Scarpetta walks in and shuts the door behind her without touching any bloody surface, including the knob.

Nic sits on the back of her heels, a thirty-five-millimeter camera gripped in her gloved hands, her forearms resting on her knees.

If she's happy to see Scarpetta, she makes no sign of it. Sweat rolls down her neck, disappearing into the dark green Zachary Police Department polo shirt tucked in khaki cargo pants. Nic gets up and moves to one side so Scarpetta can approach the dead body.

"She's got really weird stab wounds," Nic comments. "The temperature of the room when I got here was seventy degrees."

Dr. Lanier inserts a long chemical thermometer under the body's arm. He leans close to the body, his eyes moving up and down it, taking his time. Scarpetta vaguely recognizes the woman as one she saw in some of the photographs scattered throughout the living room.

It isn't easy to tell. Her hair is matted with dried blood, her face swollen and deformed by contusions, cuts and smashed bones, the degree of tissue reaction to injuries consistent with her having survived for a while. Scarpetta touches an arm. The body is warm as in life. Rigor mortis hasn't begun, nor has livor mortis—or the settling of the blood due to gravity once circulation stops.

Dr. Lanier removes the thermometer, reads it and says, "Body temp's ninety-six."

"She's not been dead long at all," Scarpetta says. "Yet the condition of the blood in the living room, hallway and even some in here suggests the attack occurred hours ago."

"Probably the head injury is what got her, but it took a little while," Dr. Lanier says, gently palpating the back of the head. "Fractures. You get the back of your head smashed against a masonry plaster wall, and you're talking serious injuries."

Scarpetta isn't ready to comment on the cause of death, but she does agree that the victim suffered severe blunt-force trauma to her head. If the stab wounds cut or completely severed a major artery, such as the carotid, death would have occurred in minutes. This is unlikely—impossible, really—since it appears the woman survived for a while. Scarpetta sees no arterial spatter pattern. The woman may still have been barely alive when her boyfriend found her at 12:30 p.m. and was dead by the time the rescue squad arrived.

It is several minutes past 1:30 now.

The victim is dressed in pale blue satin pajamas, the bottoms intact, the top ripped open. Her belly, breasts, chest and neck are clustered with stab wounds that measure sixteen millimeters—or approximately three-quarters of an inch—with both ends blunt, one end slightly narrower than the other. Those injuries that are superficial indicate she wasn't stabbed with an ordinary knife. Almost in the center of those shallow wounds is an area of tissue bridging that indicates the weapon had some type of gap at the tip, or perhaps was a tool that had two stabbing surfaces, each of them a slightly different thickness and length.

"Now that's strange as hell," Dr. Lanier says, his head bent close to the body as he moves a magnifying lens over wounds. "Not any normal knife I've ever seen. How about you?" He looks at Scarpetta.

"No."

The wounds were made at various angles, some of them V- or Y-shaped due to twisting of the blade, which is common in stab injuries. Some wounds gape, others are button-hole-like slits, depending on whether the incisions are in line with the elastic fibers of the skin or cut across them.

Scarpetta's gloved fingers gently separate the margins of a wound. Again, she puzzles over the area of uncut skin stretching almost across the middle. She looks closely through a lens, trying to imagine what sort of weapon was used. Gently gathering the pajama top together, she lines up holes in the satin with wounds, trying to get some idea where the clothing was when the woman was stabbed. Three buttons are missing from the torn pajama top. Scarpetta spots them on the floor. Two buttons dangle by threads.

When she arranges the pajama top neatly over the chest, the way it would be were the victim standing, of course the holes don't line up with the stab wounds at all, and there are more holes in the satin than there are wounds. She counts thirty-eight holes and twenty-two wounds. Overkill, to say the least—overkill that is typical in lust murders, but also typical when the assailant and victim know each other.

"Anything?" Dr. Lanier asks her.

Scarpetta is still lining up holes and is getting somewhere. "It appears that her top was bunched up above her breasts when she was stabbed. See?" She moves up the top, which is so stained with blood, very little of the satin looks blue. "Some of the holes go through three layers of fabric. That's why there are more holes than wounds."

"So he shoved up her top before he stabbed her or while he was stabbing her? And then tore it open?"

"I'm not sure," Dr. Scarpetta replies. It's always so difficult to reconstruct, and a much more precise job will require uninterrupted hours under a good light in the morgue. "Let's turn her just a bit and check her back."

She and Dr. Lanier reach across the body and hold it by the left arm. They pull her over, but not all the way, and blood runs out of wounds. There are at least six stab wounds on her upper back and a long cut to the side of her neck.

"So she's running and he's stabbing. She's in front of him, at least at some point." It is Eric who deduces this as he and Nic return with several lamps and plug them in.

"Maybe," is all Scarpetta has to say about it.

"One smear on a wall in the hallway looks like she may have been pushed up or knocked up against it. About midway in the hallway. Maybe he shoved her against it and stabbed her in the back, and then she got away and ran in here," Nic proposes.

"Maybe," Scarpetta says again, and she and Dr. Lanier gently lower the body to the floor. "This much I can tell you: Her pajama top was in disarray when some of these stab wounds to her chest and belly were inflicted."

"The pushed-up top suggests a sexual motive," Eric says.

"This is a sexual murder with tremendous rage," Scarpetta replies. "Even if she wasn't raped."

"She might not have been." Dr. Lanier bends close to the body, collecting trace evidence with forceps. "Fibers," he comments.

"Could be from the pajamas. Despite what people think, rape isn't always involved. Some of these bastards can't do it, can't get it up. Or they'd rather masturbate."

Scarpetta asks Nic, "She was your neighbor. You're sure this is Rebecca and not the other woman in the photographs? The two women are very similar in appearance."

"It's Rebecca. The other woman is her sister."

"Lives with her?" Dr. Lanier asks.

"No. Rebecca lived alone."

"For now, that will be a pending identification until we can be sure with dental records or some other means," Dr. Lanier remarks as Eric takes photographs, using a six-inch plastic ruler as a scale, arranging it next to whatever he shoots.

"I'll get on it." Nic stares without blinking at the dead woman's battered, bloody face, the eyes dully staring out from swollen lids. "We weren't friends at all, never socialized, but I saw her on the street, doing yardwork, walking her dog . . ."

"What dog?" Scarpetta looks sharply at her.

"She has a yellow lab, a puppy, maybe eight months old. I'm not sure, but he's not fully grown and was a Christmas present. I think from her boyfriend."

"Tell Detective Clark to make sure the police go out and look for her dog," Dr. Lanier says. "And while you're at it, tell him to make sure they send everybody they've got to keep this place secure. We're going to be here a while."

Dr. Lanier hands Scarpetta a packet of cotton-tipped swabs, a small bottle of sterile water and a sterile tube. She unscrews the caps of both the bottle and the tube. Dipping a swab in the sterile water, she swabs the breasts for saliva, the cotton tips turning red with blood. Swabs of her vagina, rectum, of every orifice can wait until the body's at the morgue. She begins to collect trace evidence.

"I'm going outside," Nic says.

"Someone needs to set up more lights in here," Dr. Lanier's voice rises.

"Best I can do is bring in lamps, whatever else is around the house," Eric replies.

"That would help. Photograph them in situ before you move them, Eric, or some goddamn defense attorney will say the killer carried lamps into the bedroom . . ."

"A lot of hairs, dog hairs maybe, maybe from her dog . . ." Scarpetta is saying as she gently shakes forceps inside a transparent plastic evidence bag. "What? A yellow lab?"

Nic is gone.

"That's what she said. A yellow lab puppy," Dr. Lanier replies, the two of them alone with the body.

"The dog has to be found for a number of reasons, not the least is out of decency, to make sure the poor thing is all right," Scarpetta says. "But also for hair comparison. I can't be sure, but now I think I'm seeing quite a variety of animal hairs."

"So am I. Sticking to blood, mostly here." He points a blood-stained gloved finger at the woman's naked upper body. "Not on her hands or in her hair, though, which is where you might expect to find animal hairs if the origin of them is the floor, the carpet, here inside her residence."

Scarpetta is silent. She secures another hair in the forceps and shakes it loose inside a bag that must have at least twenty hairs in it now, the origin of all of them the dried blood on the belly.

Out on the street, someone has started whistling loudly. Voices are calling, "Here, Basil! Come, Basil!"

The front door opens and shuts repeatedly, the sounds of feet moving in the living room, the dining room, cops talking, and then a woman's voice, a woman crying and screaming.

"No! No! No! That can't be!"

"Ma'am, just show us in one of these pictures."

Scarpetta recognizes Detective Clark's voice. He is loud and trying not to sound upset, but the more the woman screams, the louder he gets.

"I'm sorry, but you can't go in there."

"She's my sister!"

"I'm really sorry."

"Oh, God, oh, God."

Then the voices are quiet, and conversation recedes into a background murmur. A few flies begin to stray into the house, drawn by the scent of death, the high-pitched droning straining Scarpetta's nerves.

"Tell them to stop opening the goddamn door!" She looks up from her kneeling position, sweat rolling down her face, her knees in terrible pain.

"Jesus. What's going on out there?" Dr. Lanier is angry, too.

"Heeerrrre, Basil! Come on, boy!"

Whistling.

"Yo! Basil! Where are you?"

The front door opens and shuts again.

"That's it!" Dr. Lanier gets to his feet.

He walks out of the bedroom, yanking off his bloody gloves. Scarpetta removes another animal hair, this one black, and places it inside an evidence bag. The hairs adhered to the body when the blood was wet. They are adhering to the belly, breasts and chest but not to the bottoms of the woman's bare feet, which are also smeared with dried blood, not from injuries, but from where she stepped.

Scarpetta's breath is hot and loud behind her surgical mask, sweat stinging her eyes as she waves off flies and goes over the woman's face with a lens, looking for more hairs, every crack in dried blood magnified and more horrible, every split and cut in the skin more ragged and gaping. Flecks of paint adhere to blood, possibly transferred from the living room wall. The variety of animal hairs recovered from the body supplies Scarpetta with an important piece of information.

"We found the dog." Nic is standing in the doorway.

Scarpetta is startled back to a different dimension, one that isn't a hideous, dry red landscape behind a magnifying glass.

"Basil, her dog."

"That's not where most of these hairs are from. I'm finding dozens, different kinds, different colors. Dog hairs, possibly. Much coarser than cat hairs. But I'm not positive."

Dr. Lanier walks back inside the room, brushing past Nic, snapping on fresh gloves.

"What I'm seeing here makes me think the hairs were transferred from the perpetrator—perhaps from his clothing—directly to her upper body. Maybe if he got on top of her."

She pulls the pajama bottoms down an inch, just far enough to expose the indentations left by their elastic waistband. She sits back on her heels and stares, then takes off her mask.

"Why would someone get on top of her and not take her pajama bottoms off?" Dr. Lanier puzzles. "Why would someone transfer all these dog or doglike hairs to her naked upper body and nowhere else? And why the hell would anybody have all these dog hairs all the hell over them to begin with?"

"We found Basil," Nic says again. "Hiding under a house across the street. Just cowering and shaking. He must have run off when the killer left, I guess. Who's going to take care of him, of Basil?"

"I expect the boyfriend will," Dr. Lanier replies. "If not, Eric loves dogs."

He tears open two packets containing sterile, plasticized homicide sheets. While Scarpetta spreads one on the floor, Dr. Lanier and Eric grip the body under the arms and behind the knees, lifting it, centering it on the sheet. They spread the second sheet on top of her, rolling up the edges, wrapping her like a mummy so no trace evidence will be added or lost.

116

Jay lifts a hand off the steering wheel to strike Bev, then changes his mind.

"You're stupid. You know that?" he says coldly. "What the hell did you think you were doing?"

"It didn't happen the way it was supposed to."

The radio inside his Cherokee continues with the six o'clock news as he drives toward Jack's Boat Landing.

". . . Dr. Sam Lanier, coroner of East Baton Rouge Parish, has not completed the autopsy yet, but sources close to the investigation have confirmed that the victim is thirty-six-year-old Rebecca Milton of Zachary. The cause of death isn't official, but sources say she was stabbed to death. Police do not believe the murder is related to the women reported missing from Baton Rouge over the past year . . ."

"Fools." Jay turns off the radio. "Just lucky for you if they aren't assuming that."

Four small dogs, mixed breeds, sleep in sunlight shining

through a back window of the SUV. Five cases of beer are stacked on the backseat. Bev worked hard today after dropping Jay off at the University Lake in the heart of LSU. He didn't say why he was going there or what he'd be doing all day, only to pick him up in the same spot where she dropped him off at half past five. Maybe he was looking for his escaped-convict brother. Maybe he was wandering around, enjoying being away from Bev and the fishing shack. He was probably trolling for pretty coeds. Bev imagines him having sex with one of them. Jealousy wakes up inside her. It smolders.

"You shouldn't have left me all day," she says to him.

"What were you thinking? You were going to abduct her in the middle of the day and take her back to the boat in broad daylight?"

"At first. Then I knew you wouldn't be happy."

He says nothing, his face hard as he drives, careful not to speed or commit any other traffic infraction that could get him pulled over.

"She didn't look like *her*. She had black hair. I don't know if she went to college."

Bev had been unable to resist the impulse. She had time on her hands, time enough to find that pretty lady she had fixed on at the Wal-Mart. Following her all night, she had learned that the lamb didn't live in the house in the Garden District but had a small place in Zachary. Her neighborhood was dark, and Bev started getting nervous that her lamb might get suspicious. Bev had turned off on a side street before getting a good fix on the address.

This morning, she cruised, looking for the green Ford Explorer, figuring just because it wasn't parked in the driveway didn't mean it wasn't in the garage. Obviously, she picked the wrong house. Once she was inside, she was committed.

What she never anticipated was that this particular lamb was going to fight like a wolf. The instant the black-haired woman answered the door, Bev reached inside her canvas bag and pulled out the gun and was shoved so hard it flew out of her hand. Bev rolled on the floor and slipped a buck tool out of the sheath on her belt. She managed to open what she thought was a blade, and the chase began. It seemed to go on and on for miles, with the woman running and yelling, and falling against a wall, which gave Bev the opportunity to grab her by her hair and slam her head against plaster, then kick her when she slid to the floor.

Damn if she didn't get back up and punch Bev in the shoulder, hard. It seems Bev was yelling, too, but she can't remember. There was a roaring in her head, like a freight train, and she stabbed and chased, blood flying in her face, on and on forever. It couldn't have lasted more than a minute or two. Bev pinned the woman to the bedroom floor and stabbed and stabbed, and now she isn't sure if any of it really happened.

Until she keeps hearing it on the radio. Until she remembers the buck knife's bloody bottle opener. She stabbed the woman with a bottle opener. *How could that have happened?*

She looks at Jay, passing by pawnshops and car dealers, and a Taco Bell that makes her want to stop.

Nachos with sour cream, cheese, chili and jalapeños.

Pizza places, auto shops and car dealers, and then the road narrows and is lined with mailboxes as they move along back to Jack's, then the bayou.

"Maybe we could stop and get us some peanut brittle," Bev says.

Jay won't speak to her.

"Well, have it your way. You and your fucking Baton Rouge.

Going back there because of your mangy brother. Well, wait 'til dark when it's easier."

"Shut up."

"What if he's not there?"

A stony silence.

"Well, if he is, he's probably in that damn creepy cellar, hiding, maybe getting the money stashed down there. We could use some more money, baby. All that beer I've been buying . . ."

"I told you to shut up!"

The colder he gets, the prouder she is of the red bruises and deep scratches on her arms, legs, chest and other parts of her body where she must have been injured during what she refers to as a *tussle.*

"They'll swab under her fingernails." Jay finally speaks to her. "They'll get your DNA."

"They don't have my DNA in any of their fancy databases," Bev replies. "No one ever took my DNA before you and me got the hell out of Dodge. I was just a nice lady running a campsite near Williamsburg, remember that?"

"Nice my ass."

Bev smiles. Her injuries are badges of courage and power. She didn't know she had it in her to fight like that. Why, one of these days, she might just go after Jay. Her bravado deflates. She could never overcome Jay. He could kill her with one punch to her temple. He's told her that. One punch and he'd fracture her skull, because women don't have very thick skulls. "Even stupid ones" like Bev, he says.

"What did you do to her? You know what I mean," he says. "You're blood-soaked down the front of your clothes. You get on top of her like a man?"

"No." It's none of his business.

"Then how did your clothes get bloody from the neck to your crotch, huh? You climb on top of some girl who's bleeding to death and jerk off?"

"It doesn't matter. They don't think it's related to the other ones," Bev says.

"What word did she say?"

"What do you mean, *what word*?" Bev's beginning to think he's getting loony.

"When she was begging. She must have begged for you to stop. What word did she say to describe it?"

"Describe what?"

"What it felt like to be so fucking afraid of pain and death! What word did she say!"

"I don't know." Bev tries hard to remember. "It seems like she said, *Why?*"

477

117

The room was cool and there were no odors.

Nic has read that line at least five times. Her mother might have been murdered just minutes before her husband—Nic's father—got home. Nic wonders if the killer heard her father's car and fled, or if it was just fate that the son of a bitch left when he did.

It is ten p.m. Nic, Rudy, Scarpetta, Marino and Lucy sit inside Dr. Lanier's guest house, drinking Community Coffee, the local favorite.

"Multiple abrasions and lacerations to the face," Scarpetta reviews the autopsy report.

She said right off that she did not intend to gloss over any detail in order to spare Nic's feelings. She would not be helping Nic if she did that.

"Abrasion and laceration of the forehead, periocular ecchymoses, fracture of the nasal bones, frontal teeth are loosened."

"So he beat her face up pretty good," Marino says, sipping his coffee, which is just the way he likes it, white with Cremora and heavily laced with sugar. "Any possibility this was someone she knew?" he asks Nic.

"She opened the door for him. She was found right near the door."

"Was she careful about keeping the doors locked?" Lucy looks at her intensely, leaning into the conversation.

Nic stares back at her. "Yes and no. At night, we locked up. But she knew Papa and I would be coming home soon, so she may not have had the door locked."

"That doesn't mean the person didn't ring the bell or knock," Rudy points out. "It doesn't mean your mom was afraid of whoever it was."

"No, it doesn't mean that," Nic says.

"Blunt-force trauma to the back of the head. Stellate laceration of vertex, three by four inches. Massive hematoma of vertex and back of the head. Fifty milliliters of liquid subscalpular blood . . ."

Marino and Lucy trade scene photographs back and forth. So far, Nic has not looked at them.

"Blood on the wall just left of the door," Marino observes. "Hair swipes. How long was your mother's hair?"

Nic swallows hard. "Shoulder length. She had blond hair, pretty much like mine."

"Something happened the minute he walked in. Blitz attack," Lucy says. "Not so different from what happened to Rebecca Milton. Not so different from what happens in any blitz attack, when a victim really enrages the perp."

"Would injuries like this be consistent with her head being slammed against the wall?" Rudy asks.

Nic is stoical. She reminds herself she is a cop.

Scarpetta meets Nic's eyes. "I know this is hard, Nic. We're trying to be honest. Maybe you won't have so many questions if we're honest."

"I'll always have questions, because we're never going to know who did this."

"Never say never," Marino replies.

"Right." Lucy nods.

"Comminuted non-depressed fracture of the biparietal and occipital bones, fractures of the orbital roofs, bilateral subdural hematomas, thirty mls free blood over each . . . okay, okay, okay . . ." Scarpetta turns a page. It is typed, not computer-printed. "She has stab wounds," she adds.

Nic shuts her eyes. "I hope she didn't feel any of this."

No one comments.

"I mean"—she looks at Scarpetta—"was she feeling all this?"

"She was feeling terror. Physically? It's hard to say what pain she felt. When injuries occur so quickly . . ."

Marino interrupts. "You know when you stick your hand in a drawer and cut yourself with a knife and don't feel it? I think it's like that unless it's slow. Slow like in torture."

Nic's heart seems to flutter, as if something is wrong with it.

"She wasn't tortured," Scarpetta says, looking at Nic. "Definitely not."

"What about the stabs?" Nic asks.

"Lacerations of fingers and palms. Defense injuries." She glances at Nic again. "Punctures of the right and left lung with two hundred mls of hemothorax on each side. I'm so sorry. I know this is hard."

"Would that have killed her? The lung injuries?"

"Eventually. But in combination with the head injuries, absolutely. She also had fractured fingernails on the right and left. Nonidentifiable material recovered from under the nails."

"Do you think it was saved?" Lucy asks. "DNA wasn't as advanced then as it is now."

"I wonder what the hell *nonidentifiable* is," Marino says.

"What kind of knife?" Nic asks.

"Short-bladed. But just how short-bladed, I can't tell."

"Maybe a pocketknife," Marino offers.

"Maybe," Scarpetta says.

"My mother didn't have a pocketknife. She didn't have any . . ." Nic starts to tear up, then regains control. "She wasn't into weapons, is what I'm saying."

"He might have had one," Lucy tells her kindly. "But my guess is, if the weapon was a pocketknife, he didn't think he needed a weapon. Might have just been something he carried around with him like a lot of guys do."

"Are the stab wounds different than the ones we saw today?" Nic asks Scarpetta.

"Absolutely," she says.

118

Nic begins to talk about her mother's antiques store.

She says her mother owned it but only worked there part-time to be available to her family. She says her mother was acquainted with Charlotte Dard.

Nic stares at her mug of coffee. "If I fire this thing up one more time in the microwave, you think I'll have caffeine D.T.s tomorrow?"

"Your mother and Charlotte Dard were friends?" Marino asks. "Shit. You don't mind my asking, why the hell haven't you mentioned this before?"

"This is the God's truth," Nic replies. "I never remembered it until just now. I guess I blocked out so much. I almost never think about my mother, or at least I didn't start to until these women began disappearing. Then today . . . that scene. What he did to Rebecca Milton. And now."

She gets up to reheat her coffee. The microwave runs loudly for a minute, the door opens, and she returns to the sofa, steam rising from coffee no longer fit to drink. It smells overcooked.

"Nic," Scarpetta says, "is your married name Robillard?"

She nods.

"What is your family name?"

"Mayeux. My mother's name is Annie Mayeux. That's why hardly anybody realizes I'm her daughter. With time, people forget anyway. Cops who remember her death never associate me with her. I never say anything." She sips her coffee, not seeming to mind the taste. "Her antiques shop specialized in stained-glass windows, doors, shutters, old salvage stuff, some of it really nice if you knew what you were looking for.

"And a lot of furniture was handmade out of cypress. Charlotte Dard was one of her customers, was remodeling her house and buying a lot of things from my mom's shop, and that's how the two of them got friendly. Not close." She pauses, searching her memory. "My mom talked about this rich woman with a sports car and how beautiful her house was going to be when it was all done.

"I guess Mrs. Dard's business helped out a lot. Papa never made much as a schoolteacher." Nic smiles sadly. "Mama did really well and was frugal. Most of what my father lives off now came from my mother, from how well she did with that shop."

"Mrs. Dard was a drug abuser," Scarpetta says. "She died from a drug overdose, an accident or a homicide. I suspect the latter. She supposedly was suffering blackouts not long before her death. Do you know anything about that?"

"Everybody around here does," Nic replies. "It certainly was the talk of Baton Rouge. She dropped dead in a motel room, the Paradise Acres Motel, sounds like the name of a cemetery. Off Chocktaw, a terrible part of town. Rumor was, she was having an affair and met up with the person there. I don't know anything more than what was in the news."

"What about her husband?" Lucy asks.

"Good question. I've never heard of anyone who's met him. How strange is that? Except he's some sort of aristocrat and travels all the time."

"Have you ever seen a picture of him?" Rudy asks.

Nic shakes her head.

"So he's not in the news."

"He's really private," Nic replies.

"What else?" Marino asks.

"Yeah, there's some kind of weird connection going on here, right?" Rudy looks at Scarpetta. "Some pharmacist came up as a suspect, and Rocco Caggiano was his lawyer."

Marino gets up for more coffee.

"Think," Lucy encourages Nic.

"Okay." She takes a deep breath. "Okay. Here's something. I think Charlotte Dard invited Mom to a cocktail party. I remember. Mom never went to cocktail parties. She didn't drink and was shy, felt out of place among uppity people. So this was a big deal that she was going. It was on the plantation, the Dard plantation. Mom went to drum up business for her shop. And out of respect for her best customer, Mrs. Dard."

"When was this?" Scarpetta asks.

Nic thinks. "Not long before my mother was killed."

"How long is not long?" Rudy asks.

"I don't know." Nic swallows hard again. "Days. Days, I think. She wore this dress, had to go out to buy it." She shuts her eyes again. A sob catches in her throat. "It was pink with white piping. It was still hanging on her closet door when she got killed, you know, hanging there to remind her it needed to go to the dry cleaner's."

"And your mother died less than two weeks before Charlotte Dard did," Scarpetta remarks.

"Kind of interesting," Marino points out, "that Mrs. Dard was so fucked up and having violent fits, and nobody worried about her throwing a fancy garden party?"

"I'm thinking that," Rudy says.

"You know what?" Marino adds. "I drove almost twenty hours to get here. Then Lucy made me airsick. I gotta go to bed. Otherwise, I'll be making deductions that will cause you to arrest Santa Claus for something."

"I didn't make you airsick," Lucy says. "Go to bed. You need your beauty sleep. I thought *you* were Santa Claus."

He gets up from the couch and leaves, heading to the main house.

"I'm not going to make it much longer, either." Scarpetta gets up from her chair.

"Time to go," Nic says.

"You don't have to." Scarpetta tries hard to help.

"Can I ask you just one last thing?" Nic says.

"Of course." She is so tired, her brain feels frozen.

"Why would he beat her to death?"

"Why did someone beat Rebecca Milton to death?"

"Things didn't go the way he planned."

"Would your mother have resisted him?" Lucy asks.

"She would have clawed his eyes out," Nic replies.

"Maybe that's your answer. Please forgive me. I can't be much use to you now. I'm too tired."

Scarpetta leaves the small living room and closes her bedroom door.

"How are you?" Lucy moves to the couch and looks at Nic. "This is tough, really tough. Too tough to describe. You're brave, Nic Robillard."

"Worse for my father. He gave up on life. Quit everything."

"Like what?" Rudy asks gently.

"Well, he loved to teach. And he loves the water, or used to. He and Mom. They had this little fishing camp where nobody would bother them. Out in the middle of nowhere, I mean nowhere. He's never been there since."

"Where?"

"Dutch Bayou."

Rudy and Lucy look at each other.

"Who knew about it?" Lucy asks.

"I guess whoever my mother chatted about it to. She was a talker, all right. Unlike my dad."

"Where's Dutch Bayou?" Lucy then asks.

"Near Lake Maurepas. Off Blind River."

"Could you find it now?"

Nic stares at her. "Why?"

"Just answer my question." She lightly touches Nic's arm.

She nods. Their eyes lock.

"Okay, then." Lucy doesn't stop looking at her. "Tomorrow. You ever been in a helicopter?"

Rudy gets up. "I gotta go. I'm beat."

He knows. In his own way, he accepts it. But he's not going to watch.

Lucy gives him her eyes, aware that he understands but in a way never will. "See you in the morning, Rudy."

He walks off, his feet light on the stairs.

"Don't be reckless," Lucy tells Nic. "You strike me as the type who would and probably has been."

"I've been engaging in my own sting operations," she confesses. "Dressing like potential victims. I look like a potential victim."

486

Lucy examines her closely, looking her over, making an assessment, as if she hasn't been making assessments all night.

"Yes, with your blond hair, body build, air of intelligence. But your demeanor isn't that of a victim. Your energy is strong. However, that could simply present more of a challenge to the killer. More exciting. A bigger coup."

"I've been wrongly motivated," Nic chastises herself. "Not that I don't want him caught. More than anything, I want him caught. But I admit I'm more aggressive, more bullheaded, maybe putting myself in danger, yes, because of a task force that doesn't want small-town girls like me in their club. Even though I'm probably the only one who's been trained at the best forensic academy in the U.S., trained by the best. Including your aunt."

"When you've been out there putting yourself in danger, did you observe anything?"

"The Wal-Mart where Katherine was abducted. I was there within hours of it happening. One thing still stands out, this lady who acted peculiar, fell down in the parking lot, said her knee went out from under her. Something bothered me. I backed off and wouldn't help her up. Something told me not to touch her. I thought her eyes were weird, scary. And she called me a lamb. I've been called a lot of things, but never a lamb. I think she was some homeless schizo."

"Describe what she looked like." Lucy tries to remain calm, tries not to make the evidence fit the case instead of the other way around.

Nic describes her. "You know, the funny thing about it is, she looked like this woman I saw a few minutes earlier inside the store. She was digging around in cheap lingerie, shoplifting."

Now Lucy is getting excited.

"It's never occurred to anyone that the killer might be a woman or at least have a woman who is an accomplice. Bev Kiffin," she says.

Nic gets up for more coffee, her hand shaking. She blames it on caffeine. "Who is Bev Kiffin?"

"On the FBI's Ten Most Wanted list."

"Oh my God." Nic sits back down, this time closer to Lucy. She wants to be close to her. She doesn't know why. But the near proximity of her is energizing and exciting.

"Promise me you won't go out there prowling again," Lucy tells her. "Consider yourself on my task force, okay? We do things together, all of us. My aunt, Rudy, Marino."

"I promise."

"You don't want to tangle with Bev Kiffin, who is probably bringing the abducted women to her partner, Jay Talley, number one on the FBI's Most Wanted list."

"They hiding out here?" Nic can't believe it. "Two people like that are hiding out here?"

"I can't think of a better place. You said your father has a fishing shack that he abandoned after your mother was murdered. Any possibility Charlotte Dard might have known about it, known where it was? Or is."

"Is. Papa never sold it. The place must be half-rotted by now. Mrs. Dard might have known, since my mother was so into salvage, the stuff she sold in her shop. She liked old weathered wood, would recommend using it for fireplace mantels, exposed beams, whatever. Especially, she liked the thick pilings the fishing shacks are built on. I don't know what she might have said to Mrs. Dard. But my mother was completely trusting. She thought everybody had their good qualities. The truth is, she talked too much."

"Can you show me where the fishing shack is, the one your father abandoned?"

"It's in Dutch Bayou, off the Blind River. I can show you."

"From the air?"

"I'm pretty sure," Nic says.

119

Benton leaves his Jaguar tucked in a church's back parking lot less than half a mile from the Dard plantation house.

Each time he hears a car or truck approaching from either direction, he crashes through underbrush and hides in thick woods across the road from the Mississippi River. In addition to not knowing who might come along, he is well aware that it would appear odd to see a man in a black suit, black T-shirt, black cap and black butt pack walking along the side of a narrow road in the rain. Someone might stop and ask if he's had car trouble. People would stare.

When he spots the gates that he drove past late last night, he leaves the pavement and enters the woods, this time penetrating deeper, until the mansion rises above trees, his scan constant. Looking where he steps, he does his best to avoid snapping fallen branches. Fortunately, the dead leaves are wet and silent. When he scouted the area last night, he didn't venture into the woods because it was too dark to see, and he didn't dare use a flashlight.

He did, however, climb over the gate, getting rust all over his jacket and jeans, one of many explanations for why he opted to wear his suit again.

He wondered how much the place had changed since he had been here last. In the dark, it was difficult to tell whether it had been kept in good repair, but his last act was to toss a rock near shrubbery around the front to see if the motion sensors lit up. They didn't. He tried again, and not a single light was triggered. If any of them are still in working order and he activates them this morning, they won't be conspicuous, even though the sun is blanketed in gray. The grounds used to have an elaborate camera system, but there was no way Benton would have been foolish enough to test cameras, to see if they would turn red and follow him as if they were alive.

The cars in the driveway are a new white Mercedes 500 AMC and an older-model white Volvo. The Mercedes was not here last night. He doesn't know who it belongs to and doesn't have time or means to run the Louisiana plate. The Volvo belongs to Eveline Guidon, or at least it did six years ago. Grateful for dark clothing, Benton freezes like a deer behind a thick, dripping tree when the front door of the mansion opens. He crouches low, completely out of view, about fifty feet to the left of the front steps.

U.S. Attorney Weldon Winn walks out, talking in his usual booming voice, more obese than when Benton last laid eyes on him. Expecting him to climb into his expensive car, Benton thinks fast. Weldon Winn's being here isn't according to plan but certainly is a bonus. It strongly hints that Jean-Baptiste Chandonne has sought or will seek asylum at his family's Baton Rouge stronghold, a plantation of incredible corruption that has escaped suspicion for decades because the people associated with it are either completely loyal or dead.

Benton, for example, is dead.

He watches Baton Rouge's despicable U.S. Attorney follow an old brick walkway to an old stone building with a dark Gothic door that leads down into the wine cellar, the centuries-old cave, almost half a mile of convoluted tunnels dug by slaves. Winn unlocks the door, steps inside and shuts it behind him. Benton moves swiftly in a crouch, soaking wet by now, ducking behind the cover of boxwoods, glancing repeatedly from the wine cellar to the house. His riskiest move is his next. He walks casually, upright, his back to the house.

Should anyone look out the window, the man in black may very well appear to be a Chandonne friend. The door is thick oak, and he barely makes out voices behind it.

120

Scarpetta can't release Albert Dard from her mind.

She imagines the scars on his little body and is well aware that self-mutilation is an addiction, and if he continues hurting himself, it seems likely that he will be committed to psychiatric hospitals again and again until he becomes as mentally ill as those patients whose diagnoses justify their being institutionalized.

Albert Dard doesn't need to be committed. He needs help. He needs for someone to at least attempt to find out why his anxiety increased so severely a year ago that he shut down, repressed his feelings and perhaps memories to such an extreme that now he needs self-inflicted pain to experience control, a brief release and an affirmation of his own existence. Scarpetta recalls the boy's almost dissociated state on the plane while he played with trading cards, violent ones relating to an ax. She envisions his extreme distress at the thought of no one meeting him, of an abandonment that she doubts is anything new.

With each passing moment, she becomes increasingly angry at

those who are supposed to take care of him and frightened for his safety.

Digging inside her pocketbook as she drinks coffee in Dr. Lanier's guest house, she finds the telephone number she wrote down when Albert waited for an aunt who did not intend to pick him up, but orchestrated events so that Scarpetta would take care of him. It no longer matters what manipulations or conspiracies were on Mrs. Guidon's mind. Perhaps it was all a lure to get Scarpetta to that house to see what she knows about Charlotte Dard's death. Perhaps Mrs. Guidon is now satisfied that Scarpetta knows nothing more about the death than has ever been known.

She dials the number and is startled when Albert answers the phone.

"It's the lady who sat next to you on the plane," she says.

"Hi!" he greets her, surprised and very pleased. "How come you're calling me? My aunt said you wouldn't."

"Where is she?"

"I don't know. She went outside."

"Did she leave the house in her car?"

"No."

"I've been thinking about you, Albert," Scarpetta says. "I'm still in town, but I'm leaving soon, and wondered if I could come by for a visit."

"Now?" The thought seems to make him happy. "You'd come see just me?"

"Would that be all right?"

He eagerly says it would.

121

Benton quietly, carefully opens the wine cellar door, his Sig Sauer drawn and cocked as he stands to one side of the narrow opening.

The conversation just beyond stops, and a male voice says, "You didn't shut it all the way."

Feet sound on steps, maybe five steps, and a hand, most likely Weldon Winn's, pushes the door to shut it, and Benton pushes back hard, the door opening wide and knocking Winn down the steps, where he lies, shocked and groaning, on the stone floor. Whoever he was talking to had seconds, no more, to flee down another set of steps. Benton can hear the person running fast, getting away, but there is nowhere for him—perhaps Jean-Baptiste—to go. The cave has an entrance and no exit.

"Get up," Benton says to Winn. "Slowly."

"I'm hurt." He looks up as Benton stands on the top step, shutting the door behind him, while he keeps the pistol pointed at Winn's chest.

"I don't give a goddamn if you're hurt. Get up."

Benton takes off his baseball cap and tosses it on top of Winn. Recognition is slow, then Winn's face blanches and his lips part as he lies twisted on the floor, tangled in his own raincoat, staring in horror.

"It can't be you," he says in awe. "It can't be!"

All the while this is going on, Benton listens for footsteps, for whoever escaped. He hears no one.

The small, windowless space has a cobweb-covered naked light-bulb overhead and a small, very old cypress table, covered with dark rings left by the countless bottles of wine that were tasted in here. Walls are damp stone, and attached to the one on the left of Benton are four iron rings in eyebolts. They are very old, but most of the rust is worn off. Nearby on the floor are coils of yellow nylon rope and an electrical receptacle.

"Get up," Benton says again. "Who else is down here? Who were you just talking to?"

The injured Weldon Winn moves with surprising agility as he suddenly rolls on the floor and pulls out a gun from under his coat.

Benton shoots him twice, once in the chest, once in the head, before Winn can even get his finger on the trigger. Gunshots are muffled by stone.

122

Marino's personal payload is enough to slow the helicopter by five knots.

Lucy isn't concerned. In this weather, she wouldn't push her machine up to maximum speed. There is no point in rushing to run into an antenna, and antennas are all over the place, rising out of swirling fog that makes the hairline obstacles and their strobes almost impossible to see in the distance. Lucy flies at five hundred feet, the conditions worse than they were when they took off in Baton Rouge twenty minutes ago.

"I don't like this," Marino's nervous voice sounds in Lucy's headset.

"You're not the one flying. Relax. Enjoy the flight. Can I get you anything, sir?"

"How 'bout a fucking parachute?"

Lucy smiles as both she and Rudy keep up their scan outside the cockpit.

"You mind if I let go of the controls for a minute?" she says to Rudy for Marino's benefit.

"You're shitting me!" Marino yells.

"Ouch." Lucy turns down the volume in her headset while Rudy takes the controls. "It's your ship." She repeats the standard line, ensuring that the other pilot knows for a fact that he's supposed to be flying at that precise moment.

Turning a small knob on her emergency watch, she changes the upper display to chronograph mode.

Nic has never been up in a helicopter, and she tells Marino to stop making matters worse.

"If we aren't safe with them," Nic says, "we aren't safe with anyone. Besides, you're more likely to get hit by a car than crash in this weather."

"That's a bunch of shit. There ain't no cars up here. And I'd appreciate it if you wouldn't use the crash word."

"Concentrate," Lucy tells everyone, and she's not smiling now as she glances at the GPS.

Yesterday, when she and Marino flew here and found the northwesternmost edge of the lake, she entered the coordinates into the GPS.

"We're exactly on track."

Descending to three hundred feet and slowing to eighty knots, she catches a glimpse of Lake Maurepas between rolling fog. The water is almost below them. Thank God. No fear of antennas over a lake or its creeks and bayous. She slows down more as Rudy leans forward, staring hard, trying to make out the shoreline.

"Nic?" Lucy asks. "You hearing me?"

"Yes," her voice comes back.

"Recognize anything down there?"

Lucy slows to sixty knots. If she reduces her airspeed more than that, she'll go ahead and hover, but she prefers not to do so out of ground effect with such poor visibility.

"Can you go back a little ways so we can find Blind River?" she asks. "Dutch Bayou branches off it right at the edge of the lake."

"Which direction?" Lucy slowly banks the helicopter around, not thrilled about returning to land at this altitude, grateful that yesterday she was fastidious about noting the locations of any obstacles.

Nic pauses, then her voice returns. "Well, if you follow the river toward the lake, Dutch Bayou would be at about three o'clock. To your right," she tells Lucy.

Swooping back around and getting on track, Lucy flies over water again.

"That's it," Nic says. "That's the river. See how it bends to the left. Well, we could see it better if we were higher."

"Forget it," Rudy says.

"I think . . . yes!" Nic is getting excited. "There it is, that very narrow creek. See it on your right. Dutch Bayou. My father's fishing shack isn't even a mile up it, on the left."

Nerves are suddenly on edge. Rudy pulls his pistol out of his shoulder holster. Lucy takes a deep breath, tenser and more apprehensive than she lets on, as she descends to a hundred feet, directly over a narrow bayou thick with cypress trees that appear ominous in the fog.

"At this altitude especially, they can already hear us," Lucy says calmly, focusing, thinking, trying not to react to what is quickly becoming a very dangerous situation.

Suddenly, a dilapidated gray shack materializes. Tied to a warped pier is a white boat that is completely incongruous with its surroundings.

Lucy swoops around the shack. "You sure, you sure?" She can't help it, her adrenaline is raising her voice.

"Yes! I recognize the roof! Papa used blue metal. I can still see some of the blue! And the same porch and screen door!"

Lucy drops to fifty feet, in a hover, and turns to the left, Rudy's window lined up with the boat.

"Shoot it!" Lucy yells at him.

Rudy slides open his window. He rapidly fires seventeen rounds into the bottom of the boat as the front door of the shack flies open and Bev Kiffin runs out with a shotgun. Lucy pushes the cyclic forward to push up her airspeed.

"Duck! But stay in your seats!"

Rudy has already slapped a new magazine into his gun. Although the seats in back are directly over the fuel cell, this isn't Lucy's concern. Jet-A is by no means as flammable as gasoline, and the most damage shotgun pellets might do is cause leaks. On the floor, there is less of the aircraft's skin to penetrate.

Rudy arms the floats.

The shotgun is pump-action with a magazine extender. Bev fires seven rounds, one right after another. Pellets shatter windows, smacking the composite skin, and hit the main rotor blade and engine cowling. If the burn can is penetrated, there's going to be a fire, and Lucy immediately cuts off the throttle and lowers the collective. Alarms go off in desperate warnings as she lowers the collective, presses the right pedal and turns into the wind, where there is no place to set down but an area of tall saw grass. Nitrogen explodes like another gunshot, and floats on the skids instantly inflate like rubber rafts. The helicopter lurches out of trim, and Lucy fights to stabilize it, realizing that at least one of the six floats has been penetrated by shotgun pellets.

The landing is hard enough to set off the ELT, or emergency

locator transmitter, and the helicopter rocks in dense grass and dark, muddy water, and lists hard to the right. Opening her door, Lucy looks down. Two of the three floats were penetrated and didn't inflate. Rudy shuts off the battery and the generator and everyone sits for a moment, stunned and listening to the abrupt silence outside as the helicopter lists to the right, sinking into the muck. Not more than three hundred feet away, they can see the boat taking on water, its bow rising as it sinks.

"At least she's not going anywhere," Rudy remarks as he and Lucy take off their headsets.

Lucy unscrews a large cap on her watch and pulls out the antenna, activating her ELT.

"Come on," she says. "We can't sit here."

"I can," Marino replies.

"Nic?" Lucy turns around. "You got any idea how deep the water is right here?"

"Not too deep, or there wouldn't be all this saw grass. It's the mud that's the problem. We could sink up to our knees."

"I'm not going anywhere," Marino says. "What for? The boat's sunk, so she ain't going anywhere, either. And I'm not getting snake-bit or eaten by a fucking alligator."

"Here's what we can do." Nic continues as if Marino isn't in the back with her. "The saw grass stretches all the way behind the shack, and I know the water's not that deep, because we used to put on high boots and collect mussels."

"I'm going," Lucy says, opening her door.

Inside the shack, dogs are barking loudly.

The problem for Lucy is that the fat float on her skid is going to make it impossible for her to lower herself gently, one foot at a time. She tightens the shoelaces on her ankle-high boots and hands Rudy her Glock and extra magazines.

Perched in the door frame like a skydiver, she says, "Here I go!"

She lands in the water feetfirst and is pleasantly surprised to find she sinks in just above her boots. If she steps quickly, she doesn't sink as much. Stepping closer, her face splattered with dirty water, she reaches out to take her weapon and wedges it into the back of her pants. She temporarily jams the extra magazines into a pocket.

Everybody takes turns holding on to guns and ammo as Rudy, then Nic, jumps out, exiting from the same side of the helicopter as Lucy did. Marino sits like an angry lump in the backseat.

"You gonna sit there until the chopper turns over on its side?" Rudy raises his voice. "Idiot! Get out!"

Marino slides across the seats and tosses Rudy his gun. He jumps, loses his balance and falls, his head hitting a float. When he manages to get to his feet, he is covered with mud and swearing.

"Shhhh," Lucy says. "Voices carry on the water. You all right?"

Marino wipes his hands on Rudy's shirt and angrily takes back his gun as both ELTs flash brightly on radar screens in airport towers and are picked up by any pilots who happen to be monitoring the emergency frequency.

They slog along, tensely keeping an eye out for snakes, hearing them rustle through the tall grass. When the four of them are within a hundred feet of the shack, pistols held high, barrels pointed up, the screen door whines open again and Bev dashes out on the pier with the shotgun, shrieking, screaming at them, insane and suicidal with desperation and rage.

Before she can even take aim, Rudy fires.

Crack-crack! Crack-crack! Crack-crack!

She hits the old wood planking and rolls into the water next to the half-sunken boat.

123

Albert Dard opens the imposing door, the front of his long-sleeve shirt spotted with blood.

"What happened?" Scarpetta exclaims as she steps inside.

She gets down and gently raises his shirt. In a tic-tac-toe pattern on his stomach are shallow cuts. Scarpetta lets out a long breath as she lowers his shirt and stands up.

"When did you do this?" She takes his hand.

"After she left and didn't come back. Then he left. The man on the plane. I don't like him!"

"Your aunt didn't come back?"

Scarpetta noted when she approached the house that a white Mercedes and Mrs. Guidon's old Volvo were parked in front.

"You have a place where I can do something about those cuts?"

He shakes his head. "I don't want to do anything."

"Well, I do. I'm a doctor. Come on."

"You are?" He seems dazzled, as if he's never imagined that women could be doctors.

503

He leads her up the stairs to a bathroom that, like the kitchen, hasn't been renovated in many years. Inside is an old-fashioned white tub, a white sink and a medicine cabinet, where she finds iodine but no Band-Aids.

"Let's get your shirt off." She helps him pull it over his head. "Can you be brave? I know you can. Cutting yourself hurts, doesn't it?"

She is dismayed by the multitude of scars covering his back and shoulders.

"I don't really feel it when I do it," he says, watching anxiously as she unscrews the cap from the iodine.

"I'm afraid you're going to feel this, Albert. A little sting." She lies the way all doctors do when some procedure is going to hurt like hell.

She works quickly while he bites his lip. He waves his hands to cool the burning while he tries not to cry.

"You *are* brave," she says, lowering the lid of the toilet and sitting on it. "You want to tell me why you started cutting yourself? Someone said it began several years ago."

He hangs his head.

"You can tell me." She takes both his hands. "We're friends, aren't we?"

He slowly nods.

"These people came," he whispers. "I heard cars. My aunt went outside, so I did too, only I hid. And they pulled this lady out of a car and she was trying to scream but they had her tied up." He points to his mouth, indicating a gag. "Then they pushed her into the cellar."

"The wine cellar?"

"Yes."

Scarpetta recalls Mrs. Guidon's insistence that she tour the wine cellar. Fear raises the hairs on the back of her neck. She is here. She doesn't know who else is here, except Albert, and someone could drive up at any moment.

"One of the people with the tied-up lady was a monster." Albert's voice rises almost to a squeal as his eyes widen in terror. "Like I've seen on TV, in scary movies, with these sharp teeth and long hair. I was so afraid he saw me behind the bush!"

Jean-Baptiste Chandonne.

"And then my doggie, Nestlé. She never came home again!" He begins to cry.

Scarpetta hears the front door open and close, then footsteps downstairs.

"Is there a phone up here?" Scarpetta whispers to Albert.

Terrified, he wipes away tears.

She repeats her question urgently.

He stares at her, paralyzed.

"Go lock yourself in your room!"

He touches the wounds on his stomach, then rubs them, causing them to bleed.

"Go! Don't make any noise."

He walks quickly, quietly down the hall and turns into a room.

For several minutes she waits, listening to footsteps until they stop. The footsteps sound like those of a man, relatively heavy, but not the sharp sound of hard leather against wood. He starts walking again, and Scarpetta's heart hammers as he seems to head toward the stairs. She hears him on the first step and walks out of the bathroom, because she does not want him—and she is certain he is Jean-Baptiste Chandonne—to find Albert.

At the top of the stairs she freezes, gripping the railing with all her might, looking down the staircase at him, the sight of him draining the blood from her head. She shuts her eyes and opens them again, thinking he will go away. Slowly, she takes one step at a time, holding on to the railing, staring. Midway, she sits down, staring.

Benton Wesley doesn't move as he too stares. His eyes glisten with tears that he quickly blinks away.

"Who are you?" Scarpetta's voice sounds miles away. "You aren't him."

"I am."

She begins to cry.

"Please come down. Or would you like me to come up and get you?" He doesn't want to touch her until she is ready. Until he is ready, too.

She gets up and slowly walks down the stairs. When she reaches him, she backs away, far away.

"So you're part of this, you bastard. You goddamn bastard." Her voice shakes so violently that she can barely speak. "So I guess you'd better shoot me, because now I know. What you've been doing all this time I thought you were dead. With them!" She looks at the stairs, as if someone is standing there. "You are one of them!"

"I'm anything but," he says.

Digging into a pocket of his suit jacket, he takes out a folded piece of white paper. He smooths it open. It is a National Academy of Justice envelope, just like the photocopy Marino showed her—the photocopy of the envelope containing the letters Chandonne wrote to Marino and her.

Benton drops the envelope to the floor where she can see it.

"No," she says.

"Please, let's talk."

"You told Lucy where Rocco was. You knew what she'd do!"

"You're safe."

"And you set me up to see *him*. I never wrote to him. It was *you* who wrote a letter supposedly from me, claiming I wanted to come see him and make a deal."

"Yes."

"Why? Why would you subject me to that? To make me stare at that man, that awful excuse for life?"

"You just called him a man. That's right. Jean-Baptiste Chandonne is a man, not a monster, not a myth. I wanted you to confront him before he died. I wanted you to take back your power."

"You had no right to control my life, to manipulate me that way!"

"Are you sorry you went?"

For an instant, she is speechless. Then she says, "You were wrong. He didn't die."

"I didn't anticipate his seeing you would give him cause to stay alive. I should have known. Psychopaths like him don't want to die. I suppose because he pled guilty in Texas, where he knew he would be death-eligible, I was fooled into thinking he really did want . . ."

"You were wrong," she accuses him again. "You've had too much damn time to play God. And I don't know what you've turned into, some, some . . ."

"I was wrong, yes. I miscalculated, yes. Became a machine, Kay."

He said her name. And it shakes her to her soul.

"There is no one here to hurt you now," he then says.

"Now?"

"Rocco is dead. Weldon Winn is dead. Jay Talley is dead."

"Jay?"

Benton flinches. "I'm sorry. If you still care."

"About Jay?" Confusion spins. She feels dizzy, about to faint. "Care about him? How could I? Do you know everything?"

"More than everything," he replies.

124

Inside the kitchen, they sit at the same butcher-block table where Scarpetta talked to Mrs. Guidon on a night Scarpetta scarcely remembers.

"I got in too deep," Benton is saying.

They are sitting across from each other.

"It was here, in this place of theirs, where a lot of the major players come to do their dirty business at the port and the Mississippi. Rocco. Weldon Winn. Talley. Even Jean-Baptiste."

"You've met him?"

"Many times," Benton says. "Here in this house. He found me amusing and much nicer to him than the others were. In and out, you name it. Guidon was the matron of the manor, you might say. As bad as the rest of them."

"Was?"

Benton hesitates. "I saw Winn go into the wine cellar. I didn't know the others were in there, thought maybe Jean-Baptiste was, hiding. It was her and Talley. I had no choice."

"You killed them."

"I had no choice," Benton repeats.

Scarpetta nods.

"Six years ago, another agent was working with me, Minor. Riley Minor. Supposedly from around here. He did something stupid, I'm not sure what. But they did their number on him." Benton nods in the direction of the wine cellar. "The torture chamber, where they make everybody talk. There are old iron rings in the walls from the slave days, and Talley was fond of heat guns and other means of deriving information. Quickly.

"When I saw them dragging Minor into the cellar, I knew the operation was over and I got the hell away."

"You didn't try to help him?"

"Impossible."

She is silent.

"If I hadn't *died*, I would have, Kay. If I hadn't *died*, I could never have been around you, Lucy, Marino. Ever. Because they would have killed you, too."

"You are a coward," she says, drained of emotion.

"I understand your hating me for all I made you suffer."

"You could have told me! So I wouldn't suffer!"

He looks at her for a long moment, remembers her face. It hasn't changed much. None of her has.

"What would you have done, Kay, had I told you my death had to be faked and I would never see you again?" he asks.

She doesn't have the answer she thought she might. The truth is, she wouldn't have allowed him to vanish, and he knows it. "I would have taken my chances." Grief closes her throat again. "For you, I would have."

"Then you understand. And if it's any consolation, I've suffered. Not a day has gone by when I didn't think of you."

She shuts her eyes and tries to steady her breathing.

"Then I couldn't take it anymore. Early on I became so miserable, so goddamn angry, and I began to figure a way. Like chess . . ."

"A game?"

"Not a game. I was very serious. One by one, to eliminate the major threats, knowing that once I came out, I could never go back, because if I failed, I would be recognized. Or simply killed during the process."

"I have never believed in vigilantism."

"I suppose you can talk to your friend Senator Lord about that. The Chandonnes heavily fund terrorism, Kay."

She gets up. "Too much, too much for one day. Too much." She glances up, suddenly remembering Albert. "Is that little mistreated boy really Charlotte Dard's son?"

"Yes."

"Please don't tell me you're his father."

"Jay Talley is. Was. Albert doesn't know that. He's always been given this mysterious line about a very prominent but busy father he's never met. A kid's fantasy. He still believes he has this omnipotent father somewhere. Talley had a brief affair with Charlotte. One night while I was here, there was a garden party and Charlotte invited an acquaintance, an antiques dealer . . ."

"I know," Scarpetta says. "At least that question will be answered."

"Talley saw her, spoke to her, went to her house. She resisted him, which is something he won't tolerate. He murdered her, and because Charlotte had seen the two of them together, and because Talley was tired of Charlotte, bored with her, he saw to it that she died. Met her, brought her pills."

"The poor little boy."

"Don't worry," Benton says.

"Where are Lucy and Marino? Where are Rudy and Nic?" Now she remembers them.

"Picked up by a Coast Guard helicopter about half an hour ago. After raiding Bev Kiffin and Jay Talley's hideout."

"How do you know?"

He gets up from the table. "I have my sources."

Senator Lord enters Scarpetta's mind again. The Coast Guard is now Homeland Security. Yes, Senator Lord would know.

Benton moves closer to her, looking into her eyes. "If you hate me forever, I'll understand. If you don't want to be with me I don't blame . . . well, you shouldn't. Jean-Baptiste is still out there. He will come after me. Somehow."

She says nothing, waiting for the hallucination to pass.

"Can I touch you?" Benton asks.

"It doesn't matter who else is out there. I've been through too much."

"Can I touch you, Kay?"

She lifts his hands and presses them against her face.